Hugo Victor Marie

Novels & Non-Fiction

Hugo Victor Marie

Novels & Non-Fiction

ISBN/EAN: 9783337815943

Printed in Europe, USA, Canada, Australia, Japan

Cover: Foto ©Andreas Hilbeck / pixelio.de

More available books at **www.hansebooks.com**

VICTOR MARIE HUGO
'93
PART FIRST.—AT SEA
BOOK FIRST.—THE WOODS OF LA SAUDRAIE.

During the last of May, 1793, one of the Parisian battalions led into Brittany by Santerre was scouring the terrible woods of La Saudraie in Astillé. The battalion had only three hundred men left, for it had been decimated by the cruel war. It was at the time when after Argonne, Jemmapes, and Valmy, there remained of the first battalion of Paris, originally numbering six hundred volunteers, twenty-seven men; of the second battalion, thirty-three men; and of the third, fifty-seven. It was a time of epic conflicts.

The battalions sent from Paris to La Vendeé numbered nine hundred and twelve men. Each battalion had three pieces of cannon. The troops had been quickly raised. On the twenty-fifth of April, Gohier being minister of justice, and Bouchotte minister of war, the section of the *Bon Conseil*, had proposed to send battalions of volunteers to La Vendée. Lubin, member of the commune, had made the report: the first of May, Santerre was ready to send out twelve thousand soldiers, thirty field-pieces and a battalion of gunners. These battalions organized hastily were so well organized, that they serve as models to-day: the companies of the line are made up on the principle governing them; the only change has been in the proportion between the number of soldiers and non-commissioned officers.

On the twenty-eighth of April the commune of Paris gave this order to Santerre's volunteers: "No mercy, no quarter." At the end of May, of the twelve thousand Parisian troops, two-thirds were dead.

The battalion engaged in the woods of La Saudraie was proceeding cautiously. They took their time. They looked to the right and to the left, in front of them and behind them at the same time. Kléber has said: "The soldier has an eye in his back." They had been marching for hours. What time could it be? What part of the day was it? It would have been difficult to say, for there is always a sort of twilight in such wild thickets, and it is never light in these woods.

The forest of La Saudraie was tragic. It was in these woods that the civil war began its crimes in the month of November, 1792. The ferocious cripple, Mousqueton, had come out of these gloomy depths; the number of murders committed there made one's hair stand on end. There was no place more frightful. The soldiers penetrated there cautiously. Everywhere was abundance of flowers; one was surrounded with a trembling wall of branches, from which hung the charming freshness of the foliage; sunbeams here and there made their way through the green shade; on the ground the gladiolus, the yellow swamp flag, the meadow narcissus, the gênotte, the herald of fine weather, and the spring crocus formed the embroidery and decoration of a thick carpet of vegetation, luxuriant in every kind of moss, from that resembling velvet, to that like stars. The soldiers advanced step by step in silence, noiselessly pushing aside the underbrush. The birds warbled above their bayonets.

La Saudraie was one of those thickets where formerly in times of peace they used to hold the Houicheba,—hunting birds at night; now they were hunting men there.

The wood was full of birch trees, beeches, and oaks; the ground flat; the moss and thick grass deadened the sound of the marching men; every path lost itself abruptly among the holly, wild sloe, ferns, hedges of rest-harrow, tall briers; it was impossible to see a man ten feet away.

Occasionally, a heron or a waterfowl passed through the branches, showing that there were swamps near by.

They marched on. They went at haphazard, full of anxiety, and fearing to find what they they sought. From time to time they came across traces of encampments, burnt places, trodden-down grass, sticks in the form of a cross, bloody branches. There soup had been made, there mass had been said, there wounds had been dressed. But those who had passed this way had disappeared. Where were they? Far away, perhaps. Perhaps close by, concealed, gun in hand. The woods seemed deserted. The battalion redoubled its precaution. Solitude and suspicion. There was nobody to be seen; the more reason for fearing somebody. They had to do with a forest of ill-repute. An ambuscade was probable.

Thirty grenadiers, detached as scouts and commanded by a sergeant, were marching in advance at a considerable distance from the main body of the troop. The vivandière of the battalion accompanied them. The vivandières join the vanguards from choice. They run a risk, but they expect to see something. Curiosity is one form of feminine bravery.

Suddenly the soldiers in this little squad experienced that thrill familiar to huntsmen, which indicates that they have reached their prey. They had heard something like a whisper in the midst of a thicket, and it seemed that some one had just seen a movement among the leaves. The soldiers made signs to each other.

In the sort of watch and search entrusted to scouts, the officers do not need to take part; whatever must be done is done of itself.

In less than a minute, the spot where the movement had been seen was surrounded; a circle of pointed muskets enclosed it, the obscure centre of the thicket was aimed at from all sides at once, and the soldiers with fingers on the trigger and eyes on the suspected place, only waited for the sergeant's command to riddle it with bullets. The vivandière, however, ventured to look through the brambles, and at the instant when the sergeant was about to cry: "Fire!" this woman cried: "Halt!"

And turning towards the soldiers: "Don't shoot, comrades!"

She rushed headlong into the thicket. They followed her. There was, indeed, some one there. In the densest part of the thicket, on the edge of one of those little round clearings made in the woods by the charcoal furnaces in burning roots of trees, in a sort of recess among the branches, a kind of leafy chamber, half open like an alcove, a woman was sitting ou the moss, with an infant at the breast, and in her lap the blond heads of two sleeping children. This was the ambuscade. "What are you doing here?" cried the vivandière.

The woman raised her head. The vivandière added fiercely,— "Are you mad to be here!"

And she continued,— "A little more and you would have been killed!"

And addressing the soldiers, she added,—

"It is a woman."

"By Jove, we see it is indeed!" said a grenadier.

The vivandière continued,—

"Come into the woods to be massacred! Did ever anybody imagine such stupidity as that?"

The woman stupefied, frightened, petrified, saw all about her as in a dream; these guns, these sabres, these bayonets, these fierce faces.

The two children woke up and began to cry.

"I'm hungry," said one.

"I'm afraid," said the other.

The little one went on nursing.

The vivandière spoke to it.

"You are quite right," she said.

The mother was dumb with fright.

The sergeant cried out to her,—

"Don't be afraid, we are the battalion of the *Bonnet-Rouge*."

The woman trembled from head to foot. She looked at the sergeant, whose rough face showed only his eyebrows, his moustache, and two coals which were his two eyes.

"Formerly the battalion of the *Croix-Rouge*, added the vivandière.

And the sergeant continued,—

"Who are you, madame?" The woman looked at him, terrified. She was thin, young, pale, and in rags; she wore the large hood of the Breton peasant, and the woollen cloak fastened at the neck with a string. She let her bare breast be seen with utter indifference. Her feet without stockings or shoes were bleeding.

"She is poor," said the sergeant.

And the vivandière in her soldierly and feminine voice, tenderly withal, resumed,—

"What is your name?"

The woman stammered almost indistinctly,—

"Michelle Fléchard."

Meanwhile the vivandière caressed the little head of the nursing child with her large hand.

"How old is this baby?" she asked.

The mother did not understand. The vivandière persisted.

"I asked you the age of the child."

"Ah!" said the mother, "eighteen months."

"It is too old," said the vivandière. "It ought not to nurse any longer. You must wean it. We will give it some soup."

The mother began to grow calmer. The two little ones which had awakened were more curious than frightened. They admired the plumes.

"Ah!" said the mother, "they are very hungry."

And she added: "I have no more milk."

"They shall have something to eat," cried the sergeant, "and you too. But that is not all. What are your political opinions?"

The woman looked at the sergeant, but gave no answer.

"Did you hear my question?"

She stammered: "I was placed in a convent when very young, but I am married, I am not a nun. The sisters taught me to speak French. The village was set on fire. We escaped in such haste that I did not have time to put on my shoes."

"I ask what are your political opinions?"

"I don't know."

The sergeant continued,—

"There are spies about. If caught, spies are shot. You see. Speak. You are not a gypsy. What is your country?"

She still looked at him, evidently without understanding.

The sergeant asked once more: "What is your country? "

"I do not know," she said.

"What, you don't know your own country."

"Ah! my country, yes, indeed."

"Well, what is your country?"

The woman answered: " It is the farm of Siscoignard, in the parish of Azé."

It was the sergeant's turn to be amazed. He remained lost in thought for a moment, then replied,—

"What did you say?"

"Siscoignard."

"But that is not a country."

"It is my country."

And, after a moment of reflection, the woman added,—"I understand, sir. You are from France. I am from Brittany."

"Well?"

"It is not the same country."

"But it is the same fatherland!" exclaimed the sergeant.

The woman merely replied,—

"I am from Siscoignard!"
"Have it Siscoignard, then," replied the sergeant.
"Does your family belong there?"
"Yes."
"What do they do?"
"They are all dead. I have no relatives now."
The sergeant, who was clever with his tongue, continued to question her.
"People have parents, you devil, or have had them! Who are you? Speak!"
The woman heard in amazement this *ou on en a eu*, which sounded more like the cry of a wild-beast than human speech.
The vivandière felt the need of coming to her aid. She renewed her caresses to the nursing child, and patted the cheeks of the other two.
"What do you call the baby? " she asked; "I see it is a girl,"
The mother answered: "Georgette."
"And the oldest? he is a man, the scamp."
"René-Jean."
"And the younger one? He is a man, too, and a chubby-faced fellow besides."
"Gros-Alain," said the mother.
"They are pretty little things," said the vivandière; you seem to be somebody."
Meanwhile, the sergeant persisted in talking.
"Tell me, madame. Have you a house?"
"I had one."
"Where was it?"
"At Azé."
"Why are you not in your house?"
"Because it is burned."
"Who burned it?"
"I don't know. There was a battle."
"Where did you come from?"
"From there."
"Where are you going?"
"I don't know."
"Come to the point. Who are you?"
"I don't know."
"You don't know who you are?"
"We are people who have escaped."
"To what party do you belong?"
"I don't know."
"Do you belong to the Blues? Do you belong to the Whites? Whom are you with?"
"I am with my children."
Here was a pause. The vivandière said,—
"I never had any children. I didn't have time."
The sergeant began again,—
"But your parents. Come, madame, tell us about your parents. My name is Radoub; I am a sergeant, I belong in rue du Gherche-Midi; my father and mother belonged there, too. I can tell you about my parents. Tell us about yours. Tell us who your parents were."
"They were the Fléchards."
"Yes; the Fléchards are the Fléchards, as the Radoubs are the Radoubs. But people have some occupation. What was the occupation of your parents? What did they do? What did they make? What did they *fledge* these *Fledghards* of yours?"
"They were farmers. My father was infirm and unable to work, because he had been cudgelled by the seigneur, his seigneur, our seigneur, which was a kindness, for my father had poached a rabbit, and the penalty for this offence was death; but the seigneur had mercy and said; 'Give him only a hundred blows,' and my father was made a cripple."
"Go on."
"My grandfather was a Huguenot. The priest had him sent to the galleys. I was very young."
"Go on."
"My husband's father was a salt smuggler. The king had him hanged."
"And your husband, what does he do?"
"At the present time he is fighting."
"For whom?"
"For the king."
"For whom else?"
"Why, for his seigneur?"
"For whom else?"
"Why, for the priest."
"The accursed names of brutes!" exclaimed a grenadier.
The woman shook with fear.

"You see, madame, we are Parisians," said the vivandière kindly.

The woman clasped her hands and cried: "Oh, my Lord Jesus!"

"No superstitions," resumed the sergeant.

The vivandière sat down beside the woman and drew to her the oldest of the children, who made no resistance. Children feel confidence just as they feel afraid, without knowing why. They have a monitor within.

"My poor good woman, you have some pretty brats, at any rate. I can guess their ages. The largest is four years old, his brother three. Indeed that nursing kid is a famous greedy-gut. You see, madame, you have nothing to fear. You shall join the battalion. You can do as I do. I call myself Houzarde; it is a nickname. But I prefer to be called Houzarde rather than Mamzelle Bicorneau, like my mother. I am the vivandière or canteen-woman, as the one is called who serves out the drink when any one is shot or killed. The devil and his train! Our feet are nearly the same size, I will give you some of my shoes. I was in Paris the tenth of August. I gave Westermann a drink. He was walking. I saw Louis XVI., Louis Capet they call him, guillotined. He didn't like it. Why, just listen. They say that the thirteenth of January he was having chestnuts cooked, and laughing with his family! When they forced him to lie down on the *bascule*, as they call it, he had on neither coat nor shoe; he wore only his shirt, a quilted vest, gray cloth breeches, and gray silk stockings. I saw that myself. The carriage he was brought in was painted green. You see, come with us, we have good boys in the battalion; you shall be vivandière number two; I will teach you the profession. Oh! it is very simple! You have your can and your little bell, you go about in the tumult, in the midst of the firing of the platoons, among the cannon shots, in the uproar, shouting: "Who wants a drink, children?" It is no more difficult than that. I give everybody a drink. Yes, indeed. The Whites as well as the Blues; although I am a Blue, and a good Blue too. But I give everybody a drink. The wounded are thirsty. People die without regard for opinions. When people are dying you ought to press their hands. How silly it is to fight! Come with us. If I am killed you will be my successor. You see, that is the way I seem; but I am a good woman and a brave man. Don't have any fear."

When the vivandière had stopped speaking, the woman murmured: " Our neighbor's name was Marie-Jean, and our servant's Maria-Claude."

In the meantime the Sergeant Kadoub was reprimanding the grenadier,—

"Hold your tongue. You have frightened the woman. You mustn't swear before ladies."

"All the same, as far as an honest man can understand it, it is a genuine massacre," replied the grenadier. "The idea of these Chinese peasants having their father-in-law crippled by the seigneur, their grandfather sent to the galleys by the priest, and their father hung by the king, and then insist on fighting. In the name of common sense! And they thrust themselves into a revolt and let themselves be crushed for the seigneur the priest and the king!"

"Silence in the ranks," cried the sergeant.

"We'll be silent, sergeant," continued the grenadier, "but that won't prevent its being a pity for a pretty woman like that to run the risk of having her neck broken for the handsome eyes of a priest."

"Grenadier," said the sergeant, "we are not in the Club des Piques at Paris. None of your eloquence."

And he turned towards the woman.

"And your husband, madame? What is he doing? What has he become?"

"He hasn't become anything, because he has been killed."

"Where?"

"In the hedge."

"When?"

"Three days ago."

"Who killed him?"

"I don't know."

"What, you don't know who killed your husband?"

"No."

"Was it a Blue? Was it a White?"

"It was a bullet."

"And three days ago?"

"Yes."

"From which direction?"

"From Ernée. My husband fell. There!"

"And since your husband is dead, what are you going to do?"

"I am carrying away my children."

"Where are you carrying them?"

"Straight ahead."

"Where do you sleep?"

"On the ground."

"What do you get to eat?"

"Nothing."

The sergeant made up the military face of touching his nose with his moustache.

"Nothing."

"That is to say wild plums, mulberries in the brambles, if there are any left from last year, myrtle seeds, fern shoots."

"Yes. As much as to say nothing."

The oldest of the children, seeming to understand, said: "I'm hungry."

The sergeant took a piece of soldier's bread out of his pocket and handed it to the mother. The mother broke the bread in two pieces, and gave them to the children. The little ones eagerly devoured it.

"She hasn't kept any for herself," muttered the sergeant.

"It is because she isn't hungry," said a soldier.

"It's because she is their mother," said the sergeant. The children interrupted them.

"I want a drink," said one.

"I want a drink," repeated the other.

"Is there no brook in these devilish woods?" said the sergeant.

The vivandière took the copper cup hanging from her belt beside her bell, turned the spigot of the keg which hung from her shoulder by a strap, let a few drops run into the cup, and held it to the children's lips.

The first drank and made up a face.

The second one drank and spit it out.

"Why, it's good," said the vivandière.

"Is it Coupe-Figure?" asked the sergeant.

"Yes, and of the best. But they are peasants."

And she wiped the cup.

The sergeant continued,—

"And you are making your escape in this way?"

"I am obliged to."

"Across the country in a bee line."

"I ran with all my might, and then I walked, and then I fell down."

"Poor creature!" said the vivandière.

"People are fighting everywhere," stammered the woman. "I am surrounded on all sides with gunshot. I don't know what it all means. They have killed my husband. I only understand that."

The sergeant thumped the ground with the butt of his musket, and exclaimed,—

"In the name of a jackass, what a beastly war this is!"

The woman continued: "Last night we slept in an *émousse*."

"All four of you?"

"All four of us."

"Slept?"

"Slept."

"Then," said the sergeant, "you slept standing."

And he turned to the soldiers.

"Comrades, a great, old, hollow trunk of a tree, that a man would have to squeeze himself into as if 'twere a knife-case, these shy creatures call that an *émousse*. What do you think about it? They are not obliged to be Parisians."

"Slept in the trunk of a hollow tree!" said the vivandière; "and with three children!"

"And when the little ones bawled," the sergeant went on to say, "it must have been funny enough for those who were passing and saw nothing at all, to hear a tree crying: 'Papa! Mamma!'"

"Fortunately, it is summer-time," sighed the woman.

She looked on the ground, resigned, with an expression in her eyes of that astonishment which comes from sudden misfortune.

The soldiers quietly formed a circle around the pitiful group.

A widow, three orphans, flight, desertion, solitude, mutterings of war all around the horizon, hunger, thirst, no food but grass, no roof but the heavens.

The sergeant approached the woman and looked at the nursing child. The little one left the breast, turned her head gently, looked with her beautiful blue eyes at the frightful hairy face, rough and tawny, which bent over her, and began to smile.

The sergeant straightened himself up, and a great tear was seen to roll down his cheek and rest on the end of his moustache like a pearl.

He raised his voice,—

"After all this, it is my opinion that the battalion ought to become a father. Is it agreed? Let us adopt these three children."

"Long live the Republic!" cried the grenadiers.

"Done," said the sergeant.

And he extended his hands above the heads of mother and children.

"Behold," he said, "the children of the battalion of *Bonnet-Rouge*."

The vivandière leaped for joy.

"Three heads in one bonnet!" she cried.

Then she burst into sobs, embraced the poor widow effusively, and said to her,—

"The baby already looks like a general!"

"Long live the Republic!" repeated the soldiers.

And the sergeant said to the mother,—

"Come, *citoyenne*."

BOOK SECOND.— THE CORVETTE "CLAYMORE."

CHAPTER I.

ENGLAND AND FRANCE.

In the spring of 1793, at the time when France, attacked on all her frontiers at once, was touchingly diverted by the fall of the Girondists, this is what took place in the Channel Islands.

One evening, the first of June, in Jersey, in the little lonely bay of Bonne-nuit, about an hour before sunset, during one of those fogs convenient for escape, because they are dangerous for navigation, a corvette was preparing to set sail. The crew of this vessel was French, but it belonged to the English fleet stationed on the lookout at the eastern point of the island. The Prince of la Tour-d'Auvergne, who belonged to the house of Bouillon, commanded the English Fleet, and it was by his orders, and for an urgent and special service, that the corvette had been detached.

This corvette, enrolled at Trinity House as the "Claymore," was to all appearances a merchant ship, but in reality was a sloop of war. She had the clumsy, peaceful aspect of a merchantman; this was a mere blind, however. She had been built for a double purpose, deception and strength: to deceive, if possible; to fight, if necessary. For the service that she had to perform this night, her cargo between decks had been replaced by thirty carronades of heavy calibre. Either because a storm was in prospect, or to give an innocent appearance to the vessel, these thirty carronades were shut in, that is securely fastened within by triple chains, and the mouths pushed up against the closed port-holes; there was nothing to be seen from the outside; the port-holes were concealed; the lids closed; it was as if the corvette wore a mask. These carronades had wheels with bronze spokes, an ancient model, called "*modèle radié.*"

Corvettes usually have no cannons except on the upper deck; this one, constructed for surprise and stratagem, had no guns on the upper deck and as we have just seen, had been built in such a way as to be able to carry a battery between decks.

The "Claymore" was of a heavy, dumpy build, and yet she was a good sailor. Her hull was one of the most solid in all the English navy, and in battle she was almost equal to a frigate, although her mizzen-mast was small, with merely a brigantine rig. Her rudder, of rare scientific shape, had a uniquely curved frame, which had cost fifty pounds sterling in the dockyards of Southampton.

The crew, all French, was composed of emigrant officers and deserted sailors. They were picked men, not one of them was not a good seaman, good soldier, and good royalist. They had a threefold fanaticism: the ship, the sword, and the king.

Half a battalion of marines, which could be disembarked in case of necessity, was scattered among the crew.

The captain of the corvette "Claymore" was a chevalier of Saint-Louis, the Count de Boisberthelot, one of the best officers of the old Royal Navy; the second officer was the chevalier de la Vieuville, who had commanded the company of the French guards, in which Hoche was the sergeant, and her pilot was Philip Gacquoil, the most intelggent sailor in Jersey.

It was evident that this vessel had some extraordinary service before her. Indeed, a man had just gone on board, who had every appearance of starting on an adventure. He was a tall old man, straight and sturdy, with a stern face, whose age it would have been difficult to tell exactly, because he seemed at once old and young; one of those men, full of years and strength, with white locks on his brow and fire in his eye; forty years in point of vigor, and eighty in point of authority.

At the moment he set foot on the corvette, his seacloak flew open, and it could be seen that underneath this cloak he was dressed in the wide breeches called '*bragoubras*, top boots, and a vest of goat-skin, showing the upper side of the leather embroidered with silk, and the under side with the hair in its rough, natural state, the complete costume of the Breton peasant.

These old-fashioned Breton vests served a double purpose, being worn for festivals as well as work days, and were reversible, showing as was desirable either the hairy or the embroidered side; goat-skin all the week, gala dress on Sunday.

As if to add a studied and exact truthfulness to the peasant costume worn by the old man, it was threadbare at the elbows and knees, and appeared to have been in use a long time, and his cloak, made of coarse material, resembled that of a fisherman. This old man had on the round hat of the day, with high crown and broad brim, which when turned down gives it a rustic appearance, and when caught up with a cord and cockade has a military air. He wore this hat after the peasant fashion with the rim flattened out, without cord or cockade.

Lord Balcarras, governor of the island, and the Prince of la Tour-d'Auvergne, had accompanied him in person and installed him on board the vessel. Gélambre, the secret agent of the princes, and formerly one of the bodyguard of the Count d'Artois, had himself seen to the arrangement of his cabin, extending his care and attention, although himself an excellent gentleman, so far as to carry the old man's valise. On leaving him to go ashore again, M. de Gélambre had made a profound bow to this peasant; Lord Balcarras had said to him: "Good luck, general," and the Prince of la Tour-d'Auvergne had said: "*Au revoir*, cousin."

"The peasant" was the name by which the crew began at once to designate their passenger, in the short conversations seamen have together; but without knowing more about him, they understood that this peasant was no more a peasant than the man-of-war was a merchant man.

There was little wind. The "Claymore" left Bonnenuit, passed in front of Boulay Bay, and was for some time in sight, running along the shore, then she became dim in the increasing darkness, and was lost to view.

An hour later, Gélambre, having returned home to Saint-Hélier, despatched by the Southampton express to the Count d'Artois, at the Duke of York's headquarters, the following four lines,—

"Monseigneur, she has just sailed. Success certain. In a week the whole coast will be on fire from Granville to Saint-Malo."

Four days before, Prieur, the representative of Marne, on a mission to the army on the coast of Cherbourg, and for the time being residing at Granville, had received a message in the same handwriting as the preceding despatch, reading thus,—

"Citizen representative, June 1st, at flood-tide the sloop of war, "Claymore," with masked battery, will set sail, to carry to the coast of France a man whose description is as follows: tall, old, white hair, peasant's dress, aristocratic hands. I will send you more details tomorrow. He will land on the second, in the morning. Send word to the cruisers, capture the corvette, have the man guillotined."

CHAPTER II.

A NIGHT ON SHIPBOARD, AND CONCERNING THE PASSENGER.

The corvette, instead of going to the south and steering towards Saint-Catherine's, bore to the north, then turned to the west and ran resolutely into the arm of the sea between Sark and Jersey, called the passage de la Déroute. There was at that time no lighthouse on any point along these two coasts.

The sun had set, the night was dark, more so than usual in summer; there was a moon, but heavy clouds more like autumn than summer covered the sky like a ceiling, and to judge from all appearances the moon would not be visible till she touched the horizon just before setting. Clouds hung low over the sea, and covered it with fog.

All this darkness was favorable.

The intention of the pilot, Gacquoil, was to leave Jersey on the left and Guernsey on the right, and by a bold course between the Hanois and the Douvres to make for a bay somewhere on the shore of Saint-Malo, not so short a route as by the Minquiers, but safer, because the French cruisers had standing orders to keep especial watch between Saint-Hélier and Granville.

If the wind were favorable, if nothing unexpected occurred, and by setting all sails, Gacquoil hoped to reach the French coast by daybreak.

All was going well; the corvette had just passed Gros-Nez; about nine o'clock it began to grow sulky, as the sailors say, and there was some wind and sea; but the wind was favorable, and the sea strong without being violent. However, occasionally a heavy sea swept over the bow of the vessel.

The "peasant" when Lord Balcarras had called "general," and to whom the Prince of la Tour d' Auvergne had said, "Cousin" had sea-legs, had walked the deck with calm unconcern. He did not seem to notice that the vessel was very much tossed about. Now and then he drew out of his pocket a cake of chocolate, broke off a piece and ate it; although his hair was white, he had all his teeth.

He spoke to no one, except occasionally a few words in a low tone to the captain, who listened with deference, and seemed to consider this passenger more the commander than himself.

The "Claymore," skilfully piloted, sailed, unnoticed in the fog, by the long northern cliff of Jersey, hugging the shore on account of the dangerous reef Pierres-de-Leeq, in the middle of the straits between Jersey and Sark. Gacquoil, standing at the helm signalling la Grève de Leeq, Gros-Nez, and Plimont in turn, guided the vessel through these chains of reefs, groping his way, as it were, but still with the certainty of a man who is at home and knows his way on the ocean. The corvette had no light forward, for fear of betraying its passage in these guarded waters. They congratulated themselves on having the fog. They reached the Grande-Etape; the fog was so thick that the outline of the tall pinnacle could hardly be discerned. Ten o'clock sounded from the tower of Saint-Ouen, a sign that the wind was still abaft. All continued to go well; the sea grew more tempestuous as they drew near to la Corbière.

A little after ten, the Count de Boisberthelot, and the Chevalier de la Vieuville accompanied the man in peasant's garb to his cabin, which was the captain's stateroom. Just as he was about to enter it, lowering his voice, he said to them,—

"You know, gentlemen, the important secret. Be silent till the moment the explosion occurs. You two are the only ones here who know my name."

"We will carry it to the grave," replied Boisberthelot. "As for me," replied the old man, "if I were to die, I would not utter it."

And he entered his cabin.

CHAPTER III.

NOBLE AND PLEBEIAN IN ALLIANCE.

The commander and the second officer went up on deck again and began to talk together, walking side by side. They were evidently speaking about their passenger, and this is very nearly the conversation that the wind scattered in the darkness.

Boisberthelot muttered low in la Vieuville's ear,—

"We shall see if he is a leader."

La Vieuville replied: "At any rate, he is a prince."

"Almost."

"A nobleman in France, but a prince in Brittany."

"Like the la Trémoilles, and like the Rohans."

"To whom he is related."

Boisberthelot continued: "In France and in the king's coaches, he is a marquis, as I am a count and as you are a chevalier."

"The coaches are far off!" exclaimed la Vieuville. "We are more likely to ride in a tumbril."

A silence ensued.

Boisberthelot went on,—

"For want of a French prince, they take a Breton prince."

"For want of a thrush—no, for want of an eagle—they take a crow."

"I should prefer a vulture," said Boisberthelot.

And la Vieuville replied: "Of course! a beak and talons."

"We shall see."

"Yes," replied la Vieuville, "it is time there was a leader. I am of Tinténiac's opinion: 'A leader and powder!' Wait, commander, I know nearly all the leaders, possible and impossible; those of to-day, of yesterday, and to-morrow; but not one is the figure-head needed. In this devilish la Vendée, a general is needed who is at the same time an attorney; he must annoy the enemy, dispute the mills, the thickets, the ditches, the pebbles with them, have serious quarrels with them, take advantage of everything, be constantly on the watch, make examples of them; he must neither sleep nor show pity. At the present time, there are heroes in this army of peasants, but there are no captains. D'Elbée is nobody; Lescure is ill, Bonchamps is tender-hearted, he is good, he is stupid; La Rochejacquelin is a splendid sub-lieutenant; Silz is an officer for the open field, unequal to a war of expedients; Cathelineau is an innocent wagoner; Stofflet is a tricky gamekeeper; Bérard is silly; Boulainvilliers is absurd; Charette is horrible; and I will say nothing at all of Gaston the barber. For, by thunder! what is the good of a revolution, and what difference is there between the republicans and ourselves, if we are to let noblemen be commanded by wig-makers?"

"This beastly revolution has taken hold of us, as well."

"An itch that France has caught!"

"Itch of the Third Estate," replied Boisberthelot.

"England alone can save us from it."

"She will do it without doubt, captain."

"At any rate, it is hideous."

"Certainly, louts everywhere! The monarchy which has Stofflet for general-in-chief, M. de Maulevrier's gamekeeper, has nothing to envy the republic, with Pache, son of the Duke de Castries's porter, for minister. What counterparts in this war of la Vendée! On one side Santerre, the brewer; on the other, Gaston, the hairdresser!"

"My dear la Vieuville, I make an exception of this Gaston. He hasn't acted badly in his command at Guémenée. He shot three hundred Blues very prettily, after making them dig their own graves."

"Very good; but I could have done just as well myself."

"Indeed, without doubt. And so could I."

"The great deeds of war," continued la Vieuville, "require nobility in those who accomplish them. These are matters for chevaliers, not for wig-makers."

"Still in this Third Estate," replied Boisberthelot, "there are estimable men. Take, for example, the clockmaker Joly. He was a sergeant in the Flanders regiment; he becomes a Vendéan chief; he commands a company on the coast; he has a son, who is a republican, and while the father serves with the Whites, the son serves with the Blues. They meet. Battle. The father takes his son prisoner, and blows his brains out."

"That is good," said la Vieuville.

"A royalist Brutus," replied Boisberthelot.

"That doesn't prevent it from being intolerable to be commanded by a Coquereau, a Jean-Jean, a Moulins, a Focart, a Bouju, a Chouppes!"

"My dear chevalier, the indignation is the same on both sides. We are full of *bourgeois*; they are full of nobles. Do you suppose that the *sans-culottes* are content to be commanded by the Count de Canclaux, the Viscount de Miraud, the Viscount de Beauharnais, the Count de Valence, the Marquis de Custine, and the Duke de Biron!"

"What slop!"

"And the Duke de Chartres!"

"Son of Egalité. Ah, when will he be king, that fellow? Never!"

"He is on his way to the throne. His crimes assist him."

"And his vices hinder him," said Boisberthelot.

Again there was a silence, and Boisberthelot went on to say,—

"He wished, however, for a reconciliation. He came to see the king. I was there at Versailles, when they spat on his back."

"From the grand staircase?"

"Yes."

"They did well."

"We called him, Bourbon le Bourbeaux."

"He is bald, he has pimples, he is a regicide. Bah!"

And la Vieuville added: "I was with him at Ouessant."

"On the 'Saint-Esprit'?"

"Yes."

"If he had obeyed the signal that Admiral d'Orvilliers gave him to keep to the windward, he would have hindered the English from passing."

"Certainly."

"Is it true that he hid himself in the hold?"

"No, but we must say so, all the same."

And la Vieuville burst out laughing.

Boisberthelot continued: "There are some fools yet. Take this Boulainvilliers, of whom you were speaking, M. Vieuville; I knew him, I have seen him near to. At first the peasants were armed with pikes; if he didn't get it into his head to make pikemen of them! He wanted to teach them the exercise *de la pique-en-biais et de la pique-trainante-le-fer-devant!* He dreamed of transforming these savages into soldiers of the line. He pretended to teach them how to mass battalions, and to form battalions into hollow squares. He jabbered to them in the old military language; for chief of a squad, he said '*cap d'escade*,' a term applied to corporals under Louis XVI. He was determined to form a regiment with all these poachers; he had regular companies, the sergeants of which formed a circle every evening, receiving the countersign from the colonel's sergeant; he repeated it to the sergeant of the lieutenants, and he repeated it to his neighbor, who passed it to the one nearest, and so on from ear to ear, till the last. He cashiered an officer for not rising with head uncovered to receive the word of command from the mouth of the sergeant. You can judge how that succeeded. This booby couldn't understand that peasants like to be led in peasant-fashion, and that you can't make drilled soldiers out of backwoodsmen. Yes, I know that Boulainvilliers."

They walked on a few steps, each busied with his own thoughts.

Then the conversation continued,—

"By the way, is it true that Dampierre has been killed?"

"Yes, commander."

"Before Condé?"

"In the camp of Pamaro; by a cannon-ball."

Boisberthelot sighed.

"The Count de Dampierres. Another one of us, who was on their side!"

"A pleasant journey to him!" said la Vieuville.

"And the ladies, where are they?"

"At Trieste."

"Still?"

"Still."

And la Vieuville exclaimed: "Oh, this republic! What havoc to so little purpose! To think that this revolution has come about from the deficit of a few millions!"

"Look out for insignificant beginnings."

"Everything is going wrong," replied la Vieuville.

"Yes, la Rouarie is dead; du Dresnay, an idiot. What melancholy leaders all these bishops are: this Coucy, bishop of la Rochelle; this Beaupoil Saint-Aulaire, bishop of Poitiers; this Mercy, bishop of Luçon, Mme. de l'Eschasserie's lover—"

"Her name is Servanteau, you know, commander: l'Eschasserie is the name of her estate."

"And that false bishop of Agra, who is the curate of I don't know what!"

"Of Dol. His name is Guillot de Folleville. He is brave, however, and he fights."

"Priests when we want soldiers! Bishops, who are no bishops! Generals who are no generals!"

La Vieuville interrupted Boisberthelot.

"Commander, have you the *Moniteur* in your cabin?"

"Yes."

"What are they playing in Paris, now?"

"'Adèle,' 'Paulin' and the 'Cavern.'"

"I should like to see that."

"You will see it. We shall be in Paris in a month."

Boisberthelot thought a moment and added,—

"At the latest. Mr. Windham has told Lord Hood so."

"Then, commander, everything is not going so badly?"

"Gracious! All would go well, if only the war in Brittany were well conducted."

La Vieuville shook his head.

"Commander," he asked, "shall we land the marines?"

"Yes, if the coast is for us; no, if it be hostile. Sometimes war has to break open the doors, sometimes she slips through. Civil war should always have a false key in her pocket. Everything possible will be done. The most important thing is the chief."

And Boisberthelot added thoughtfully,—

"La Vieuville, what would you think of the Chevalier de Dieuzie?"

"The young man?"

"Yes."

"For a commander?"

"Yes."

"That he, again, is an officer for the open field, and for pitched battles. The thicket only knows the peasant."

"Then resign yourself to General Stoffiet and to General Cathelineau."

La Vieuville considered a moment and said,—

"We need a prince—a prince of France—a prince of the blood—a real prince."

"Why? He who names a prince——"

"Names a coward. I know it, commander. But it is for the effect on the great, stupid eyes of the louts."

"My dear chevalier, princes would not come."

"We can dispense with them."

Boisberthelot made that mechanical movement of rubbing the forehead with the hand, as if expecting to bring out an idea.

He continued: "At last, let us consider the present general."

"He is a great nobleman."

"Do you believe that he will answer?"

"If he is strong!" said la Vieuville.

"That is to say, cruel," said Boisberthelot.

The count and the chevalier looked at each other.

"Monsieur du Boisberthelot, you have spoken the word. Cruel. Yes that is what we need. This is a merciless war. It is the time for bloodthirsty men. Regicides have cut off Louis XVI.'s head; we will tear the four limbs from the regicides. Yes, the general necessary is General Inexorable. In Anjou and upper Poitou the chiefs play the magnanimous; they flounder in generosity, nothing succeeds. In the Marais and in the Retz country, the chiefs are terrible, everything moves on. It is because Charette is cruel that he holds out against Parrein. Hyena against hyena."

Boisberthelot had no time to reply to la Vieuville. La Vieuville was suddenly cut short by a cry of despair, and at the same time a noise was heard wholly unlike any other sound. This cry and these sounds came from within the vessel.

The captain and lieutenant rushed towards the gun-deck, but could not get down. All the gunners were pouring up in dismay. Something terrible had just happened.

CHAPTER IV.

TORMENTUM BELLI.

One of the carronades of the battery, a twenty-four pounder, had broken loose.

This is the most dangerous accident that can possibly take place on shipboard. Nothing more terrible can happen to a sloop of war in open sea and under full sail.

A cannon that breaks its moorings suddenly becomes some strange, supernatural beast. It is a machine transformed into a monster. That short mass on wheels moves like a billiard-ball, rolls with the rolling of the ship, plunges with the pitching, goes, comes, stops, seems to meditate, starts on its course again, shoots like an arrow, from one end of the vessel to the other, whirls around, slips away, dodges, rears, bangs, crashes, kills, exterminates. It is a battering ram capriciously assaulting a wall. Add to this, the fact that the ram is of metal, the wall of wood.

It is matter set free; one might say, this eternal slave was avenging itself; it seems as if the total depravity concealed in what we call inanimate things had escaped, and burst forth all of a sudden; it appears to lose patience, and to take a strange mysterious revenge; nothing more relentless than this wrath of the inanimate. This enraged lump leaps like a panther, it has the clumsiness of an elephant, the nimbleness of a mouse, the obstinacy of an axe, the uncertainty of the billows, the zigzag of the lightning, the deafness of the grave. It weighs ten thousand pounds, and it rebounds like a child's ball. It spins and then abruptly darts off at right angles.

And what is to be done? How put an end to it? A tempest ceases, a cyclone passes over, a wind dies down, a broken mast can be replaced, a leak can be stopped, a fire extinguished, but what will become of this enormous brute of bronze? How can it be captured? You can reason with a bull-dog, astonish a bull, fascinate a boa, frightened a tiger, tame a lion; but you have no resource against this monster, a loose cannon. You cannot kill it, it is dead; and at the same time it lives. It lives with a sinister life which comes to it from the infinite. The deck beneath it gives it full swing. It is moved by the ship, which is moved by the sea, which is moved by the wind. This destroyer is a toy. The ship, the waves, the winds, all play with it, hence its frightful animation. What is to be done with this apparatus? How fetter this stupendous engine of destruction? How anticipate its comings and goings, its returns, its stops, its shocks? Any one of its blows on the side of the ship may stave it in. How foretell its frightful meanderings? It is dealing with a projectile, which alters its mind, which seems to have ideas, and changes its direction every instant. How check the course of what must be avoided? The horrible cannon struggles, advances, backs, strikes right, strikes left, retreats, passes by, disconcerts expectation, grinds up obstacles, crushes men like flies. All the terror of the situation is in the fluctuations of the flooring. How fight an inclined plane subject to caprices? The ship has, so to speak, in its belly, an imprisoned thunderstorm, striving to escape; something like a thunderbolt rumbling above an earthquake.

In an instant the whole crew was on foot. It was the fault of the gun captain, who had neglected to fasten the screw-nut of the mooring-chain, and had insecurely clogged the four wheels of the gun carriage; this gave play to the sole and the framework, separated the two platforms, and finally the breeching. The tackle had given way, so that the cannon was no longer firm on its carriage. The stationary breeching, which prevents recoil, was not in use at this time. A heavy sea struck the port, the carronade insecurely fastened, had recoiled and broken its chain, and began its terrible course over the deck.

To form an idea of this strange sliding, let one image a drop of water running over glass.

At the moment when the fastenings gave way, the gunners were in the battery. Some in groups, others scattered about, busied with the customary work among sailors getting ready for a signal for action. The carronade, hurled forward by the pitching of the vessel, made a gap in this crowd of men and crushed four at the first blow; then sliding back and shot out again as the ship rolled, it cut in two a fifth unfortunate, and knocked a piece of the battery against the larboard side with such force as to unship it. This caused the cry of distress just heard. All the men rushed to the companion-way. The gun deck was vacated in a twinkling.

The enormous gun was left alone. It was given up to itself. It was its own master, and master of the ship. It could do what it pleased. This whole crew, accustomed to laugh in time of battle, now trembled. To describe the terror is impossible.

Captain Boisberthelot and Lieutenant la Vieuville, although both dauntless men, stopped at the head of the companion-way and dumb, pale, and hesitating, looked down on the deck below. Some one elbowed past and went down.

It was their passenger, the peasant, the man of whom they had just been speaking a moment before.

Reaching the foot of the companion-way, he stopped.

CHAPTER V.

VIS ET VIR.

The cannon was rushing back and forth on the deck. One might have supposed it to be the living chariot of the Apocalypse. The marine lantern swinging overhead added a dizzy shifting of light and shade to the picture. The form of the cannon disappeared in the violence of its course, and it looked now black in the light, now mysteriously white in the darkness.

It went on in its destructive work. It had already shattered four other guns and made two gaps in the side of the ship, fortunately above the water-line, but where the water would come in, in case of heavy weather. It rushed frantically against the framework; the strong timbers withstood the shock; the curved shape of the wood gave them great power of resistance; but they creaked beneath the blows of this huge club, beating on all sides at once, with a strange sort of ubiquity. The percussions of a grain of shot shaken in a bottle are not swifter or more senseless. The four wheels passed back and forth over the dead men, cutting them, carving them, slashing them, till the five corpses were a score of stumps rolling across the deck; the heads of the dead men seemed to cry out; streams of blood curled over the deck with the rolling of the vessel; the planks, damaged in several places, began to gape open. The whole ship was filled with the horrid noise and confusion.

The captain promptly recovered his presence of mind and ordered everything that could check and impede the cannon's mad course to be thrown through the hatchway down on the gun deck—mattresses, hammocks, spare sails, rolls of cordage, bags belonging to the crew, and bales of counterfeit assignats, of which the corvette carried a large quantity—a characteristic piece of English villany regarded as legitimate warfare.

But what could these rags do? As nobody dared to go below to dispose of them properly, they were reduced to lint in a few minutes.

There was just sea enough to make the accident as bad as possible. A tempest would have been desirable, for it might have upset the cannon, and with its four wheels once in the air there would be some hope of getting it under control. Meanwhile, the havoc increased.

There were splits and fractures in the masts, which are set into the framework of the keel and rise above the decks of ships like great, round pillars. The convulsive blows of the cannon had cracked the mizzen-mast, and had cut into the main-mast.

The battery was being ruined. Ten pieces out of thirty were disabled; the breaches in the side of the vessel were increasing, and the corvette was beginning to leak.

The old passenger, having gone down to the gun deck, stood like a man of stone at the foot of the steps. He cast a stern glance over this scene of devastation. He did not move. It seemed impossible to take a step forward. Every movement of the loose carronade threatened the ship's destruction, A few moments more and shipwreck would be inevitable.

They must perish or put a speedy end to the disaster; some course must be decided on; but what? What an opponent was this carronade! Something must be done to stop this terrible madness—to capture this lightning—to overthrow this thunderbolt.

Boisberthelot said to La Vieuville,—

"Do you believe in God, chevalier?"

La Vieuville replied: "Yes—no. Sometimes."

"During a tempest."

"Yes, and in moments like this."

"God alone can save us from this," said Boisberthelot.

Everybody was silent, letting the carronade continue its horrible din.

Outside, the waves beating against the ship responded with their blows to the shocks of the cannon. It was like two hammers alternating.

Suddenly, in the midst of this inaccessible ring, where the escaped cannon was leaping, a man was seen to appear, with an iron bar in his hand. He was the author of the castastrophe, the captain of the gun, guilty of criminal carelessness, and the cause of the accident, the master of the carronade. Having done the mischief, he was anxious to repair it. He had seized the iron bar in one hand, a tiller-rope with a slip-noose in the other, and jumped down the hatchway to the gun deck.

Then began an awful sight; a Titanic scene; the contest between gun and gunner; the battle of matter and intelligence, the duel between man and the inanimate.

The man stationed himself in a corner, and with bar and rope in his two hands, he leaned against one of the riders, braced himself on his legs, which seemed two steel posts, and livid, calm, tragic, as if rooted to the deck, he waited.

He waited for the cannon to pass by him.

The gunner knew his gun, and it seemed to him as it the gun ought to know him. He had lived long with it. How many times he had thrust his hand into its mouth! It was his own familiar monster. He began to speak to it as if it were his dog.

"Come!" he said. Perhaps he loved it.

He seemed to wish it to come to him.

But to come to him was to come upon him. And then he would be lost. How could he avoid being crushed? That was the question. All looked on in terror.

Not a breast breathed freely, unless perhaps that of the old man, who was alone in the battery with the two contestants, a stern witness.

He might be crushed himself by the cannon. He did not stir.

Beneath them the sea blindly directed the contest.

At the moment when the gunner, accepting this frightful hand-to-hand conflict, challenged the cannon, some chance rocking of the sea caused the carronade to remain for an instant motionless and as if stupefied. "Come, now!" said the man. It seemed to listen.

Suddenly it leaped towards him. The man dodged the blow.

The battle began. Battle unprecedented. Frailty struggling against the invulnerable. The gladiator of flesh attacking the beast of brass. On one side, brute, force; on the other, a human soul.

All this was taking place in semi-darkness. It was like the shadowy vision of a miracle.

A soul—strange to say, one would have thought the cannon also had a soul; but a soul full of hatred and rage. This sightless thing seemed to have eyes. The monster appeared to lie in wait for the man. One would have at least believed that there was craft in this mass. It also chose its time. It was a strange, gigantic insect of metal, having or seeming to have the will of a demon. For a moment this colossal locust would beat against the low ceiling overhead, then it would come down on its four wheels like a tiger on its four paws, and begin to run at the man. He, supple, nimble, expert, writhed away like an adder from all these lightning movements. He avoided a collision, but the blows which he parried fell against the vessel, and continued their work of destruction.

An end of broken chain was left hanging to the carronade. This chain had in some strange way become twisted about the screw of the cascabel. One end of the chain was fastened to the gun-carriage. The other, left loose, whirled desperately about the cannon, making all its blows more dangerous.

The screw held it in a firm grip, adding a thong to a battering-ram, making a terrible whirlwind around the cannon, an iron lash in a brazen hand. This chain complicated the contest.

However, the man went on fighting. Occasionally, it was the man who attacked the cannon; he would creep along the side of the vessel, bar and rope in hand; and the cannon, as if it understood, and as though suspecting some snare, would flee away. The man, bent on victory, pursued it.

Such things cannot long continue. The cannon seemed to say to itself, all of a sudden, "Come, now! Make an end of it!" and it stopped. One felt that the crisis was at hand. The cannon, as if in suspense, seemed to have, or really had—for to all it was a living being—a ferocious malice prepense. It made a sudden, quick dash at the gunner. The gunner sprang out of the way, let it pass by, and cried out to it with a laugh, "Try it again!" The cannon, as if enraged, smashed a carronade on the port side; then, again seized by the invisible sling which controlled it, it was hurled to the starboard side at the man, who made his escape. Three carronades gave way under the blows of the cannon; then, as if blind and not knowing what more to do, it turned its back on the man, rolled from stern to bow, injured the stern and made a breach in the planking of the prow. The man took refuge at the foot of the steps, not far from the old man who was looking on. The gunner held his iron bar in rest. The cannon seemed to notice it, and without taking the trouble to turn around, slid back on the man, swift as the blow of an axe. The man, driven against the side of the ship, was lost. The whole crew cried out with horror.

But the old passenger, till this moment motionless, darted forth more quickly than any of this wildly swift rapidity. He seized a package of counterfeit assignats, and, at the risk of being crushed, succeeded in throwing it between the wheels of the carronade. This decisive and perilous movement could not have been made with more exactness and precision by a man trained in all the exercises described in Durosel's "Manual of Gun Practice at Sea."

The package had the effect of a clog. A pebble may stop a log, the branch of a tree turn aside an avalanche. The carronade stumbled. The gunner, taking advantage of this critical opportunity, plunged his iron bar between the spokes of one of the hind wheels. The cannon stopped. It leaned forward. The man using the bar as a lever, held it in equilibrium. The heavy mass was overthrown, with the crash of a falling bell, and the man, rushing with all his might, dripping with perspiration, passed the slip-noose around the bronze neck of the subdued monster.

It was ended. The man had conquered. The ant had control over the mastodon; the pigmy had taken the thunderbolt prisoner.

The mariners and sailors clapped their hands.

The whole crew rushed forward with cables and chains, and in an instant the cannon was secured.

The gunner saluted the passenger.

"Sir," he said, "you have saved my life."

The old man had resumed his impassive attitude, and made no reply.

CHAPTER VI.

THE TWO SCALES OF THE BALANCE.

The man had conquered, but the cannon might be said to have conquered as well. Immediate shipwreck had been avoided, but the corvette was not saved. The damage to the vessel seemed beyond repair. There were five breaches in her sides, one, very large, in the bow; twenty of the thirty carronades lay useless in their frames. The one which had just been captured and chained again was disabled; the screw of the cascabel was sprung, and consequently levelling the gun made impossible. The battery was reduced to nine pieces. The ship was leaking. It was necessary to repair the damages at once, and to work the pumps.

The gun deck, now that one could look over it, was frightful to behold. The inside of an infuriated elephant's cage would not be more completely demolished.

However great might be the necessity of escaping observation, the necessity of immediate safety was still more imperative to the corvette. They had been obliged to light up the deck with lanterns hung here and there on the sides.

However, all the while this tragic play was going on, the crew were absorbed by a question of life and death, and they were wholly ignorant of what was taking place outside the vessel. The fog had grown thicker; the weather had changed; the wind had worked its pleasure with the ship; they were out of their course, with Jersey and Guernsey close at hand, farther to the south than they ought to have been, and in the midst of a heavy sea. Great billows kissed the gaping wounds of the vessel—kisses full of danger. The rocking of the sea threatened destruction. The breeze had become a gale. A squall, a tempest, perhaps, was brewing. It was impossible to see four waves ahead.

While the crew were hastily repairing the damages to the gun-deck, stopping the leaks, and putting in place the guns which had been uninjured in the disaster, the old passenger had gone on deck again.

He stood with his back against the main-mast.

He had not noticed a proceeding which had taken place on the vessel. The Chevalier de la Vieuville had drawn up the marines in line on both sides of the main-mast, and at the sound of the boatswain's whistle the sailors formed in line, standing on the yards.

The Count de Boisberthelot approached the passenger.

Behind the captain walked a man, haggard, out of breath, his dress disordered, but still with a look of satisfaction on his face.

It was the gunner who had just shown himself so skilful in subduing monsters, and who had gained the mastery over the cannon.

The count gave the military salute to the old man in peasant's dress, and said to him,—

"General, there is the man."

The gunner remained standing, with downcast eyes, in military attitude.

The Count de Boisberthelot continued,—

"General, in consideration of what this man has done, do you not think there is something due him from his commander?"

"I think so," said the old man.

"Please give your orders," replied Boisberthelot.

"It is for you to give them, you are the captain."

"But you are the general," replied Boisberthelot.

The old man looked at the gunner.

"Come forward," he said. The gunner approached.

The old man turned towards the Count de Boisberthelot, took off the cross of Saint-Louis from the captain's coat and fastened it on the gunner's jacket.

"Hurrah!" cried the sailors.

The mariners presented arms.

And the old passenger pointing to the dazzled gunner, added,—

"Now, have this man shot."

Dismay succeeded the cheering.

Then in the midst of the death-like stillness, the old man raised his voice and said,—

"Carelessness has compromised this vessel. At this very hour, it is perhaps lost. To be at sea is to be in front of the enemy. A ship making a voyage is an array waging war. The tempest is concealed, but it is at hand. The whole sea is an ambuscade. Death is the penalty of any misdemeanor committed in the face of the enemy. No fault is reparable. Courage should be rewarded, and negligence punished."

These words fell one after another, slowly, solemnly, in a sort of inexorable metre, like the blows of an axe upon an oak. And the man, looking at the soldiers, added,— "Let it be done."

The man on whose jacket hung the sinning cross of Saint-Louis, bowed his head. At a signal from Count de Boisberthelot, two sailors went below and came back bringing the hammock-shroud; the chaplain, who since they sailed had been at prayer in the officers' quarters, accompanied the two sailors; a sergeant detached twelve marines from the line and arranged them in two files, six by six; the gunner, without uttering a word, placed himself between the two files. The chaplain, crucifix in hand, advanced and stood beside him. "March," said the sergeant.—The platoon marched with slow steps to the bow of the vessel. The two sailors carrying the shroud, followed. A gloomy silence fell over the vessel. A hurricane howled in the distance. A few moments later, a light flashed, a report sounded through the darkness, then all was still, and the sound of a body falling into the sea was heard. The old passenger, still leaning against the mainmast, had crossed his arms, and was buried in thought. Boisberthelot pointed to him with the forefinger of his left hand, and said to la Vieuville in a low voice,—"La Vendée has a head."

CHAPTER VII.

A VOYAGE IS A LOTTERY.

But what was to become of the corvette?

The clouds which all night long had mingled with the waves, at last shut down over the water till the horizon had entirely disappeared, and the sea was, as it were, wrapped in a mantle. Nothing but fog. Always a perilous situation, even for a ship in seaworthy condition.

In addition to the fog there was a heavy swell.

The time had been profitably employed; the corvette had been lightened by throwing overboard everything that could be cleared away of the wreck made by the carronade—the disabled guns, the broken gun carriages, timbers twisted off or unnailed, pieces of broken wood and iron; the port-holes had been opened, and the corpses and human remains wrapped in tarpaulins, slid on planks into the sea.

The sea was beginning to be too rough for safety. Not that a tempest was exactly impending; on the contrary, the hurricane howling behind the horizon seemed to be decreasing in force, and the squall moving to the north; but the waves were still very high, indicating shallow water, and crippled as the vessel was, she had little power of resistance to the shocks of the great waves, and they might be death to her.

Gacquoil was at the helm, thoughtful.

Sea captains are wont to put the best face on the matter, in misfortune.

La Vieuville who was naturally gay in times of disaster, addressed Gacquoil,—

"Well, pilot," he said, "the hurricane missed us. Its attempt to sneeze came to naught. We shall get out of it. We shall have wind, that is all." Gacquoil replied seriously,—

"A heavy wind makes a heavy sea."

Neither gay nor sad, such is the sailor. His reply had a meaning of alarm in it. For a leaking ship to be in a heavy sea is to fill rapidly. Gacquoil had emphasized this prophecy with a slight frown. Perhaps la Vieuville had spoken these almost jovial and trifling words a little too soon after the disaster of the gun and the gunner. There are things which bode ill luck when at sea. The ocean is secret; one, never knows what she will do. It is necessary to be on the watch.

La Vieuville felt the need of becoming serious.

"Where are we, pilot?" he asked.

The pilot replied,—

"We are in the hands of God."

A pilot is a master; it is always best to let him have his own way, and often to have his own say.

Besides, this sort of man speaks but little. La Vieuville walked away.

La Vieuville had asked the pilot a question, the horizon gave the answer.

The sea suddenly burst into sight.

The fog which hung over the waves lifted, all the dark upheaving of the billows was spread out in a mysterious twilight as far as one's eyes could reach, and this is what was seen,—

The sky seemed to have a lid of clouds over it; but the clouds no longer touched the sea; in the east appeared a whiteness, which was the dawn of day; in the west, another fading whiteness, which was the setting of the moon. These two bright places opposite each other, made two narrow bands of pale light along the horizon, between the dark sea and the cloudy sky.

Against these two bright strips were outlined black figures, straight and motionless. To the west, three high rocks, standing like Celtic cromlechs, stood out against the moonlit sky.

To the east, against the pale morning sky, rose eight sail ranged in order, and at regular distances, in a threatening line.

The three rocks were a reef; the eight sail, a squadron.

Behind the corvette was the Minquiers, a rock of ill repute; before her, the French fleet. In the west, destruction; in the east carnage; she was between a shipwreck and a battle.

For facing the reef, the corvette had a broken hull, disjointed rigging, shattered masts; for facing battle, she had a battery of which twenty-one guns out of thirty were disabled, and the best of her gunners were dead.

The dawn was very faint, and there was still a little night before them. This darkness might even last for some time, being caused principally by high, heavy, dense clouds, having the appearance of a solid arch.

The wind which had at last carried away the low fog was driving the vessel on the Minquiers.

In her excessively weak and disabled condition, she scarcely obeyed the helm, she rolled rather than sailed, and buffeted by the waves gave herself up to their mercy.

The tragic reef of the Minquiers was more rugged then than at the present time. Several of the towers of this citadel of destruction have been worn away by the incessant undermining of the sea; the shape of the reefs is constantly changing; waves are not called *lames* without reason; each tide is a saw-tooth. At this time, to touch on the Minquiers, was to perish.

As for the cruisers, they were the squadron from Cancale, afterwards made famous under the command of that Captain Duchesne whom Léquinio called "Father Duchêne."

The situation was critical. The corvette had unconsciously, while the cannon was loose, deviated from her course and sailed more towards Granville than towards Saint-Malo. Even if she had been manageable and able to carry sail, the Minquiers would have barred her return to Jersey, and the cruisers barred her from reaching France.

However, there was no tempest, but as the pilot had said, there was a heavy sea. The sea tumbling beneath a rough wind, and over the rocky bottom, was wild.

The sea never tells at once what it means to do. There is everything in this abyss, even chicanery. One might almost say that the sea had designs; it advances and retreats, it proposes and retracts, it prepares a squall and then gives up its plan, it promises destruction and does not keep its word, it threatens the North, and strikes the South. All night the corvette "Claymore" had been in the fog, and feared a storm; the sea had just broken its promise, and in a cruel fashion; it had given warning of a tempest and brought out a reef. It was still shipwreck in another form.

To destruction on the rocks was added extermination in battle. One enemy supplemented the other.

La Vieuville cried out with a bold laugh,—

"Shipwreck on one hand, battle on the other. Both sides have thrown double fives."

CHAPTER VIII.

9—380.

The corvette was now nothing but a wreck.

In the pale, scattered light, in the blackness of the clouds, in the confused shifting of the horizon, in the mysterious wrinkling of the waves, there was a sepulchral solemnity. Except the hostile whistling of the wind, everything was silent. The catastrophe was rising majestically from the depths. It seemed more like an apparition than an attack. Nothing moved on the rocks, nothing stirred on the ships. It was a strange, colossal silence. Were they dealing with reality? It was like a dream passing over the sea. In legends there are such visions: the corvette was, in a certain sense, between a demon reef and a phantom fleet.

The Count de Boisberthelot gave orders in an undertone to La Vieuville, who went down to the gun-deck; then the captain seized his spyglass and came and stood at the stern near the pilot.

Gacquoil was bending all his efforts to keep the vessel out of the trough of the sea; for, if it were struck on the side by the wind and the waves, it would inevitably capsize.

"Pilot," said the captain, "where are we?"

"Off the Minquiers."

"On which side?"

"The worst."

"What bottom?"

"Small rocks."

"Can we bring the broadside to bear on them?"

"One can always die," said the pilot.

The captain directed his glance toward the west and examined the Minquiers; then he turned it toward the east and scrutinized the sails in sight.

The pilot continued, as if talking to himself,—

"It is the Minquiers. It serves as a resting-place for the laughing sea-mew and the great black-mantled gull, on their way from Holland."

In the meantime, the captain had counted the ships.

There really were eight vessels correctly disposed and raising their warlike profiles above the water. In the centre stood the lofty hull of a three-decker.

The captain questioned the pilot,—

"Do you know these ships?"

"Certainly!" replied Gacquoil.

"What are they?"

"It is the squadron."

"Of France?"

"Of the devil."

There was silence. The captain continued,—

"Are all the cruisers there?"

"Not all."

In fact, the second of April, Valazé had announced to the Convention that ten frigates and six ships of the line were cruising in the channel. The captain recollected this.

"In all," he said, "the squadron has sixteen vessels. There are only eight here."

"The rest," said Gacquoil, "are spying along the coast farther down."

The captain, still looking through the glass, murmured: "A three-decker, two first-class frigates, and five of the second class."

"But I too made them out," grumbled Gacquoil.

"Good vessels," said the captain. "I have had some command of them myself."

"For my part," said Gacquoil, "I have seen them close to. I don't mistake one for another. I have their description in my head."

The captain handed his spyglass to the pilot.

"Pilot, can you make out the three-decker distinctly?"

"Yes, commander, it is the 'Côte d'Or.'"

"They have re-named her," said the captain. "She used to be the 'Etats de Bourgogne.' A new ship. Hundred and twenty-eight guns."

He took a note-book and pencil out of his pocket, and wrote in the former the number one hundred and twenty-eight.

He went on to say: "Pilot, what is the first sail to port?"

"It is the 'Experimenté.'"

"First-class frigate; fifty-two guns. She was fitted out at Brest two months ago."

The captain put the number fifty-two down in his note-book.

"Pilot," he continued, "what is the second sail to port?"

"The 'Dryade.'"

"First-class frigate; forty eighteen-pounders. She has been in India. She has a fine naval record."

And he wrote down forty under the number fifty-two; then, raising his head, he said,—

"Now to starboard."

"Commander, these are all second-class frigates. There are five of them."

"What is the first, starting from the three-decker?"

"The 'Résolue.'"

"Thirty-two eighteen-pounders. And the second?"

"The 'Richemont.'"

"Same strength. Next?"

"The 'Athée.'"

"Queer name to go to sea with. Next?"

"The 'Calypso.'"

"What next?"

"The 'Preneuse.'"

"Five frigates of thirty-two guns each."

The captain wrote one hundred and sixty under the first numbers.

"Pilot," he said, "you recognize them well."

"You," replied Gacquoil, "know them well, captain. To recognize is one thing, to know is better."

The captain was looking intently at his note-book, and was adding up the numbers to himself.

"Hundred and twenty-eight, fifty-two, forty, hundred and sixty."

Just at this moment, la Vieuville came up on deck.

"Chevalier," the captain cried out to him, "we are in the face of three hundred and eighty cannon."

"So be it," said la Vieuville.

"You have just been inspecting, la Vieuville; just how many guns have we fit for use?"

"Nine."

"So be it," said Boisberthelot in his turn.

He took the spyglass from the pilot's hands and studied the horizon.

The eight still, black ships seemed motionless, but they were growing larger.

They were approaching imperceptibly.

La Vieuville gave the military salute.

"Commander," he said, "here is my report. I distrusted this corvette 'Claymore.' It is always annoying to embark suddenly on a vessel which does not know you, or that does not love you. English ship—traitor to the French—that slut of a carronade proved it. I have made the inspection. Anchors good. They are not of half-finished iron, but of forged bars soldered with the trip-hammer. The flukes are solid. Cables excellent, easy to pay out, of the regular length, hundred and twenty fathoms. Ammunition in abundance. Six gunners dead. A hundred and seventy-one rounds apiece."

"Because there are only nine guns left," murmured the captain.

Boisberthelot pointed his spyglass towards the horizon. The squadron was still slowly approaching.

There is one advantage about the carronades, three men are enough to work them, but they have one inconvenience, they do not carry as far nor aim as accurately as cannon. So it was necessary to let the squadron come within range of the carronades.

The captain gave his orders in an undertone. Silence reigned on the vessel. No signal to make ready for battle was given, but the order was executed all the same. The corvette was as unfit to fight against men as it was to battle with the waves. Every possible expedient was employed with this remnant of a war vessel. All the hawsers and spare cables were collected together at the gangway, near the tiller ropes, to use for strengthening the masts in case of necessity. The cockpit was prepared for the wounded. According to the naval custom of that day, the deck was barricaded, which was a safeguard against bullets but not against cannon balls. The ball-gauges were brought, although it was a little late to test their calibres; but so many accidents had not been foreseen. Each sailor received a cartridge-box, and placed a pair of pistols and a dirk in his belt. The hammocks were stowed away, the artillery pointed, the musketry prepared, the axes and grappling-irons put in their places, the stores of cartridges and bullets made ready, and the powder-magazine opened. Each man took his post. All this without a word spoken, and as if in a death chamber. It was swift and melancholy.

Then the corvette showed her broadside. She had six anchors, like a frigate. They cast all six of them; the cock-bill at the bow, the hedge anchor at the stern, the flood anchor toward the open sea, the ebb anchor toward the rocks, the bower anchor to starboard, and the sheet anchor to port.

The nine carronades remaining in good condition were put into form, all nine of them on one side,—the side toward the enemy.

The squadron had no less silently completed their preparations. The eight vessels now formed a semicircle, of which the "Minquiers" made the chord. The "Claymore," enclosed in this semicircle, and pinioned by its own anchor besides, was backed by the reef; that is to say, by shipwreck.

It was like a pack of hounds around a wild boar, making no sound, but showing their teeth.

It seemed as if one side were waiting for the other.

The gunners of the "Claymore" were stationed by their guns.

Boisberthelot said to la Vieuville,—

"I think it would be well to open fire,"

"A flirt's notion," said la Vieuville.

CHAPTER IX.

SOME ONE ESCAPES.

The passenger had not left the deck, he was watching everything, unmoved.

Boisberthelot approached him. "Sir," he said, "the preparations are completed. Here we are cramped into our tomb, but we shall not yield. We are prisoners of the squadron or of the reef. To surrender to the enemy or founder on the rocks, we have no other alternative. Only one resource remains, death. To fight is better than shipwreck. I would rather be shot than drowned; if I must die, I prefer fire to water. But to die is our fate, not yours. You are the man chosen by the princes, you have a great mission, to direct the war in La Vendée. Without you, the monarchy may be lost; you must live then. It is our duty to remain here, yours to get away. Go, general,— leave the ship. I will give you a man and a boat. It is not impossible to reach the shore by a roundabout way. It is not yet day, the waves are high, the sea is dark, you will escape. There are times when to flee is to conquer."

With his stern head, the old man made a solemn sign of acquiescence.

The Count de Boisberthelot raised his voice,

"Soldiers and sailors," he cried.

All movement ceased, and from every part of the vessel faces were turned toward the captain.

He continued,—

"The man who is among us represents the king. He has been entrusted to our care, we must preserve him. He is necessary to the throne of France; for want of a prince he will be, at least so we hope, the chief of la Vendée. He is a great general. He was to reach France with us, he must reach it without us. To save his life is to save all."

"Aye, aye, aye!" cried all the voices of the crew.

The captain continued,—

"He too, will incur serious dangers. To reach the shore is no easy matter. It ought to be a large boat to brave the high sea, but it must be a small one to escape the cruisers. It is important to land at some point which will be safe, and rather in the vicinity of Fougères than of Coutances. It needs a plucky sailor, a good swimmer, and a good oarsman; one who belongs to this country and knows the channel. It is still dark enough for the boat to get away from the vessel without being discovered. And then we shall have smoke which will help to conceal her. Her small size will take her through shallow water. Where the panther is caught, the weasel escapes. There is no help for us; there is for him. The oars will carry the boat away; the hostile ships will not see it; and besides, we will divert their attention meanwhile. Is it agreed?"

"Aye, aye, sir!" cried the crew.

"There is not a minute to lose," continued the captain, "Is there a man willing to go?"

A sailor stepped out of the ranks in the darkness and said: "I am."

CHAPTER X.

DOES HE ESCAPE?

A few moments later, one of those little boats called a "gig," especially designed for the captain's use, left the ship. In this boat there were two men, the old passenger in the stern, and the sailor who had volunteered to go, in the bow. The night was still very dark. The sailor, conforming to the captain's design, rowed vigorously in the direction of the Minquiers. No other way of escape was possible. Some provisions had been thrown in the bottom of the boat, a bag of biscuit, a smoked beefs tongue, and a cask of water.

"As soon as the boat touched the water, la Vieuville, scoffer even in the face of destruction, leaned over the stern of the corvette and sneered out this farewell to the boat: "She is a good one for escape, and a fine one for drowning."

"Sir," said the pilot, "jest no more."

The boat quickly rowed off, and was almost immediately a good distance away from the corvette. Wind and waves seconded the oarsman, and the little craft was rapidly making her escape, rocking in the twilight, and concealed in the great furrows of the waves.

A strange, gloomy suspense hung over the sea.

Suddenly, in this vast, tumultuous ocean silence, rose a voice, which, increased by the speaking-trumpet, as by the brazen mask of ancient tragedy, seemed almost superhuman.

It was Captain Boisberthelot who was speaking,—

"Mariners of the king," he cried, "nail the white flag to the main-mast. We are going to see our last sunrise."

And a cannon shot left the corvette.

"Long live the king!" shouted the crew.

Then from the edge of the horizon was heard another cry, immense, distant, confused, but yet distinct,—

"Long live the Republic!"

And a noise like that of three hundred thunderbolts burst over the depths of the ocean.

The battle was beginning.

The sea was covered with fire and smoke.

Clouds of spray made by the shots falling into the water burst from the waves on every side.

The "Claymore" began to shower flame on the eight ships. At the same time, the whole squadron, grouped in a crescent around the "Claymore," opened fire from all its batteries. The horizon was all ablaze. It was like a volcano rising out of the sea. The wind twisted round and round the vast crimson of battle, in the midst of which the ships appeared and disappeared like spectres. In the foreground, the corvette stood out against this red background like a black skeleton.

From the top of the main-mast the white banner with its design of fleur-de-lis could be made out.

The two men in the boat were silent.

The triangular-shaped shoals of the Minquiers, a kind of submarine Trinacrium, are larger than the whole island of Jersey; the sea covers them; their culminating point is a plateau, rising above the highest tides, and separated from this toward the northeast are six mighty rocks ranged in a straight line, giving the effect of a great wall crumbling away here and there. The sound between the plateau and the six rocks is only navigable to craft drawing very little water.

Beyond this sound is the open sea.

The sailor who had taken charge of the boat, entered the sound. In this way he put the Minquiers between the battle and the boat. He pulled skilfully through the narrow channel, avoiding the reef to port as well as to starboard; the rocks now concealed the battle. The glare on the horizon, and the furious din of the cannonading began to decrease as the distance became greater; but from the continuance of the reports it was evident that the corvette was still holding her own, and that she intended to exhaust her hundred and seventy-one broadsides to the very last. Soon the boat entered safe water, beyond the reef, beyond the battle, beyond the reach of bullets.

Gradually, the appearance of the sea became less gloomy, shimmering patches abruptly drowned in darkness increased in size, the foam burst into jets of light, pale gleams floated over the tops of the waves. Day dawned.

The boat was out of the reach of the enemy; but the most difficult task was yet to be accomplished. The boat was saved from the cannon shots, but not from shipwreck. It was in a high sea, a mere shell, without deck, without sail, without compass, with nothing to rely on but oars, in the face of the ocean and the storm, an atom at the mercy of monsters.

Then in this boundlessness, in this solitude, lifting a face made pallid by the dawn, the man in the bow of the boat fixed his gaze on the man in the stern and said to him,—

"I am the brother of the one you ordered shot."

BOOK THIRD.— HALMALO.

CHAPTER I.

THE PERSUASIVE POWER OF HUMAN SPEECH.

The old man slowly raised his head. The sailor who had just spoken to him was about thirty years old. His face was sea-tanned, his eyes were strange; they had the shrewd glance of the sailor and the open frankness of the peasant. He held the oars firmly in his two hands. He looked gentle. In his belt he had a dirk, two pistols, and a rosary. "Who are you?" said the old man.

"I have just told you."
"What do you want of me?"
The man laid down his oars, folded his arms, and replied,—
"To kill you."
"As you like," said the old man.
The other raised his voice.
"Prepare."
"For what?"
"To die."
"Why?" asked the old man.
There was a silence. The sailor seemed confused for a moment by the question. He replied,—
"I say that I mean to kill you."
"And I ask why?"
The sailor's eyes flashed,—
"Because you have killed my brother."
The old man replied calmly,—
"I began by saving his life."
"That is true. You saved him first and then killed him."
"It was not I who killed him."
"Who did kill him, then?"
"His own fault."
The sailor stared with open mouth at the old man; then his eyebrows contracted again into a savage frown.
"What is your name?" asked the old man.
"My name is Halmalo, but I can kill you without your knowing my name."
At this moment the sun rose. A sunbeam struck the sailor full in the eyes and vividly lighted up his wild face. The old man regarded

him attentively.

The cannonading which still continued, now began to be interrupted and agonizingly irregular. A dense smoke sank down over the horizon. The boat, no longer guided by the oarsman, was drifting to leeward.

The sailor drew one of the pistols out of his belt with his right hand and took his rosary in his left.
The old man rose and drew himself up to his full height.
"Do you believe in God?" he asked.
"Our Father who art in Heaven," replied the sailor, making the sign of the cross.
"Have you a mother?"
"Yes."
He made the sign of the cross a second time. Then he continued,—
"I have said it. I give you one minute, monseigneur." And he cocked his pistol.
"Why do you call me monseigneur?"
"Because you are a seigneur. That is evident."
"Have you a seigneur, yourself?"
"Yes, and a great one. Can one live without a seigneur?"
"Where is he?"
"I don't know. He has left the country. He is the Marquis de Lantenac, Viscount de Fontenay, prince in Brittany; he is the seigneur of

the Sept-Forêts (seven forests). I have never seen him, but that doesn't prevent his being my master."
"And if you were to see him, would you obey him?"
"Certainly. I should be a pagan if I didn't obey him! One owes obedience first to God; then to the king, who stands in the place of God; and then to the seigneur, who represents the king. But that is not the question; you have killed my brother, and I must kill you."

The old man replied,—
"In the first place, I killed your brother. I did right."
The sailor tightened his grasp on the pistol.
"Now then."
"Go on," said the old man.
And calmly added, "Where is the priest?"
The sailor looked at him. "The priest?"
"Yes, the priest. I gave your brother a priest, you owe me a priest."

"I have none," said the sailor.

And he added: "Do they have priests in mid-ocean?"

The convulsive reports of the battle were growing more and more distant.

"Those who are dying over yonder have theirs," said the old man.

"It is true," muttered the sailor. "They have the chaplain."

The old man continued: "You will be the means of losing my soul, which is a serious matter."

The sailor bowed his head in thought.

"And in losing my soul," the old man went on to say, "you lose your own. Listen. I pity you. You may do what you wish. As for me, I did my duty just now; first, in saving your brother's life, and then in taking it from him; and I am doing my duty at this moment in trying to save your soul. Consider. It concerns you. Do you hear the cannon shots at this instant? There are men dying over there; there are desperate souls in mortal agony; there are husbands there who will nevermore see their wives; there are fathers who will nevermore see their children; brothers who, like yourself, will never see their brothers again. And whose fault is it? It is the fault of your own brother. You believe in God, do you not? Well, you know that God is suffering at this very moment; God suffers in His Christian son, the king of France, who is a child like the child Jesus, and who is imprisoned in the fortress of the Temple; God suffers in His church in Brittany; God suffers in His insulted cathedrals, in His desecrated Gospels, in His violated houses of prayer; God suffers in His assassinated priests. What did we come to do, we ourselves, in this vessel which is perishing at this very moment? We came to God's assistance. If your brother had been a good servant, if he had faithfully performed the duty of a wise and useful man, the accident would not have happened to the carronade, the corvette would not have been disabled; she would not have gone out of her course; she would not have fallen into the hands of this fleet of destruction, and we should be landing on the shores of France now, of all us, brave warriors and seamen as we are, sword in hand, waving the white banner, numerous, content, joyful, and we should be aiding the brave peasants of La Vendée in saving France, in saving the king, in doing God's work. That is what we came to do, that is what we should be doing, that is what I, the only one left, set out to do. But you are against it. In this contest of the godless against the priest, in this strife of regicides against the king, in this conflict of Satan against God, you are for Satan. Your brother was the first auxiliary of the devil, you are the second. He began, you are finishing it. You are for the regicides against the throne, you are for the godless against the church. You take God's last resource away from Him. Because I shall not be there,—I who represent the king,—hamlets will go on burning, families weeping, priests bleeding, Brittany suffering, the king will remain in prison, and Jesus Christ in distress. And who will have done all this? You. Go on; it is your affair. I counted on you to bring about the contrary. I am deceived. Ah, yes,—it is true,—you are right,—I have killed your brother. Your brother was courageous, I rewarded him; he was guilty, I punished him. He failed in his duty; I have not failed in mine. What I have done, I would do again. And I swear it, by the great Saint Ann d'Auray, who sees us now, that, under similar circumstances to those in which I had your brother shot, I would shoot my own son. Now you are the master. Yes. I pity you. You have lied to your captain. You, a Christian, are faithless; you, a Breton, are without honor; I have been entrusted to your loyalty, and accepted by your treason; you give me dead to those to whom you promised me alive. Do you know whom you destroy here? It is yourself. You take my life from the king, and you give your eternity to the devil. Go on; commit your crime; it is well. You sell your part in Paradise cheaply. Because of you, the devil will conquer; because of you, the churches will fall; because of you, the pagans will continue to melt bells into cannon; they will shoot men with that which saved their souls. While I am speaking, the bell which rang for your baptism may be killing your mother. Go on; aid the devil. Don't stop. Yes, I condemned your brother; but know this, that I am an instrument of God. Ah! you judge the means God chooses! Are you going to take it on yourself to judge the thunderbolt which is in heaven? Wretched man, it will judge you. Take care what you do. Do you even know whether I am in a state of grace? No. Go on all the same. Do what you will. You are free to cast me into hell, and to cast yourself in with me. The damnation of us both is in your hands. The one responsible before God will be yourself. We are alone, face to face in the abyss. Go on,—make an end of it,—finish. I am old, and you are young; I am without arms, and you are armed; kill me."

While the old man, standing all the while, uttered these words in a voice above the noise of the sea, the undulations of the billows made him appear now in shadow, now in the light; the sailor had grown livid; great drops of sweat fell from his brow; he trembled like a leaf; occasionally, he kissed his beads; when the old man had ended, he threw down his pistol and fell on his knees.

"Forgive me, monseigneur! Pardon me," he cried. "You speak like the good God. I am wrong. My brother did wrong. I will do everything to atone for his crime. Dispose of me. Order, and I will obey."

"I forgive you," said the old man.

CHAPTER II.

A PEASANT'S MEMORY IS WORTH A CAPTAIN'S KNOWLEDGE

The provisions in the boat were not useful.

The two fugitives, obliged to take a very circuitous route, were thirty-six hours in reaching the shore. They passed a night on the sea; but the night was fine, with too much moon, however, for people who were trying to escape.

They were obliged first to keep away from France, and to reach the open sea towards Jersey.

They heard the final cannonade of the battered corvette, like the final roar of a lion killed by hunters in the woods. Then silence fell over the sea.

This corvette, the "Claymore," died in the same way as the "Vengeur," but glory has ignored it. He who fights against his country is never a hero.

Halmalo was a marvellous mariner. He worked miracles of skill and intelligence; this improvised journey amid the reefs, the billows, and the enemy's watch, was a masterpiece. The wind had decreased and the sea become smoother.

Halmalo avoided the Caux des Minquiers, passed the "Chausée-aux-Boeufs," and, in order to rest a few hours, took shelter in the little creek situated to the north at low tide, and then rowing back to the south found a way to pass between Granville and the Chausey islands, without being detected either from the lookout at Chausey or at Granville. He entered the bay of Saint-Michael, a bold venture on account of the vicinity of Cancale, an anchorage for the cruisers.

On the evening of the second day, about an hour before sunset, he left Mount Saint-Michael behind him, and started to land on a beach which is always deserted, because its shifting sands are unsafe.

Fortunately, the tide was high.

Halmalo pushed the boat as far up as he could, tried the sand, found it firm, ran aground, and jumped ashore.

The old man stepped over the side of the boat after him, and examined the horizon.

"Monseigneur," said Halmalo, "we are at the mouth of the Couesnon. There is Beauvoir to starboard, and Huisnes to port. The bell tower in front of us is Ardevon."

The old man bent down over the boat, took a biscuit out of it and put it in his pocket, and said to Halmalo,—

"Take the rest."

Halmalo put what remained of the meat, with the rest of the biscuits, in a bag, and threw it over his shoulder. Having done this, he said,—

"Monseigneur, shall I lead the way or follow you."

"Neither."

Halmalo looked in amazement at the old man.

The old man continued: "Halmalo, we are going to separate. It will not do for us to be together. There must be a thousand or only one."

He paused and drew out of one of his pockets a bow of green silk, very like a cockade, in the centre of which was embroidered a fleur-de-lis, in gold. He continued,—

"Can you read?"

"No."

"Very good. A man who can read is a nuisance. Have you a good memory?"

"Yes."

"Good. Listen, Halmalo. You must go to the right, and I will go to the left. I shall go in the direction of Fougères, and you must go towards Bazouges. Keep your bag, which gives you the appearance of a peasant. Conceal your weapons. Cut a stick for yourself in the hedges. Creep through the rye, which is high. Crawl behind the fences. Climb over the hedges, and go across the fields. Keep at a distance from those you meet. Avoid the roads and bridges. Do not enter Pontorson. Ah! you will have to cross the Couesnon. How will you do that?"

"Swim across?"

"Good. And then there is a ford. Do you know where it is?"

"Between Ancey and Vieux-Viel."

"Good. You really belong to the country."

"But night is coming on. Where will monseigneur sleep?"

"I will take care of myself. But where will you sleep?"

"There are hollow-trees. Before I was a sailor, I was a peasant."

"Throw away your sailor cap; it will betray you. You will easily find a *carapousse* somewhere."

"Oh, a tarpaulin.—I can find that anywhere. The first fisherman I see will sell me his."

"Good. Now, listen. You know the woods."

"Everywhere."

"All over the country?"

"From Noirmoutier to Laval."

"Do you know their names too?"

"I know the woods, I know their names, I know all about them."

"You will not forget anything?"

"Nothing."

"Good. Now, pay attention. How many leagues can you walk a day?"

"Ten, fifteen, eighteen, twenty, if necessary."

"It will be necessary. Don't lose a word of what I am going to tell you. You must go to the woods of Saint-Aubin."

"Near Lamballe?"

"Yes. On the edge of the ravine between Saint-Rieul, and Plédélica there is a great chestnut-tree. You must stop there. You will see nobody."

"Which does not prove that nobody will be there, I know."

"You must make the call. Do you know how to make the call?"

Halmalo puffed out his cheeks, turned toward the sea, and the "to-who," of an owl was heard.

It seemed to come from the depths of night; it was a perfect imitation and uncanny.

"Good," said the old man. "You have it."

He handed the green silk bow to Halmalo.

"Here is my badge of command. Take it. It is important that nobody should know my name at present. But this bow will be enough. The fleur-de-lis was embroidered by Madame Royale, in the Temple prison."

Halmalo put one knee on the ground. He received the embroidered bow with trembling, and touched it to his lips; then, stopping, as if afraid to kiss it,—

"May I?" he asked.

"Yes, since you kiss your crucifix."

Halmalo kissed the fleur-de-lis.

"Get up," said the old man.

Halmalo rose and placed the knot in his breast. The old man continued: "Listen carefully to this. This is the order: 'Rise in revolt. No quarter.' Then on the edge of the woods of Saint-Aubin give the call. You must give it three times. The third time you will see a man come out of the ground."

"From a hole under the trees, I know."

"This man is Planchenault, also called Cœur-de-Roi. Show him this knot. He will understand. Then go, whatever way you can, to the woods of Astillé; you will find there a knock-kneed man surnamed Mousqueton, and who shows pity to nobody. You will tell him that I love him, and that he is to stir up his parishes. You will then go to the woods of Couesbon, which is one league from Ploërmel. Make the call of the owl; a man will come, out of a hole; it will be M. Thuault, seneschal of Ploërmel, who has belonged to what is called the Constitution Assembly, but on the good side. Tell him to arm the castle of Couesbon, belonging to the Marquis de Guer, a refugee. Ravines, groves, uneven ground, good place. M. Thuault is an upright man, and a man of sense. Then go to Saint-Guen-les-Toits, and speak to Jean Chouan, who is, in my eyes the real chief. Then go to the woods of Ville-Anglose, where you will see Guitter, called Saint-Martin. Tell him to have an eye or a certain Courmesnil, son-in-law of old Goupil de Préfeln, and who leads the Jacobins of Argentan. Remember all this well. I write nothing because nothing must be written. La Rouarie wrote out a list, but that lost everything. Then go to the woods of Rougefeu, where Miélette is, who leaps ravines, balancing himself on a long pole."

"That is called a leaping-pole."

"Do you know how to use it?"

"Should I be a Breton, and should I be a peasant, if I didn't? The leaping-pole is our friend. It makes our arms large and our legs long."

"That is to say, it makes the enemy small and the distance short. A good machine."

"Once with my *ferte* I held out against three excise men armed with sabres."

"When was that?"

"Ten years ago."

"Under the king?"

"Indeed it was."

"Did you fight under the king then?"

"Indeed I did."

"Against whom?"

"Faith, I don't know. I was a salt smuggler."

"Good."

"They called that fighting against the gabelles. Are the gabelles the same thing as the king?"

"Yes, no. But it isn't necessary for you to understand that."

"I beg pardon of monseigneur, for having asked monseigneur a question."

"Let us go on. Do you know la Tourgue?"

"Do I know la Tourgue! I come from there."

"How is that?"

"Because I am from Parigné."

"To be sure, la Tourgue adjoins Parigné."

"Do I know la Tourgue! The big round castle which belongs to my seigneur's family. There is a great iron door separating the new building from the old; it couldn't be burst open with a cannon. In the new building is the famous book about Saint Bartholomew, that people come to see out of curiosity. There are frogs in the grass. I played with the frogs there when I was a little boy. And the underground passage! I know. There is, perhaps, no other person but myself who knows it."

"What underground passage? I don't know what you mean."

"It was made for other days, for the times when la Tourgue was besieged. The people inside could escape by passing through a tunnel under the ground which comes out in the forest."

"To be sure there is a subterranean passage of this kind from the castle of "la Jupellière," and one from the castle of la Hunaudaye, and from the tower of Champéon; but there is nothing of the kind at la Tourgue."

"Yes, there is, monseigneur. I don't know the passages which monseigneur mentions. I know the one at la Tourgue, because I belong to that country. And besides, there is nobody but myself who knows this way. It is never spoken of. It has been forbidden, because this passage served Monsieur de Rohan, in times of war. My father knew the secret, and he showed it to me. I know the secret of entering it, and the secret of getting out. If I am in the forest I can go into the tower, and if I am in the tower I can go into the forest, without being seen. And when the enemy enters, there is nobody there. That is what la Tourgue is. Ah! I know it." The old man remained silent for a moment.

"You are evidently mistaken; if there were such a secret there, I should know it."

"Monseigneur, I am sure of it. There is a turning stone there."

"Oh, yes! You peasants believe in turning stones, in singing stones, in stones which go to drink in the night from a neighboring brook. All sheer nonsense."

"But as I have made it turn, the stone—"

"As others have heard them sing, comrade. La Tourgue is a strong, secure fortress, easy to defend; but he who counted on getting out through an underground passage would be a simpleton."

"But, monseigneur,—"

The old man shrugged his shoulders.

"We have no time to lose. Let us talk business."

This peremptory tone put an end to Halmalo's persistence.

The old man continued,—

"Let us go on. Listen. From Rougefeu, go to the woods of Montchevrier, where Bénédicité is,—the chief of the Twelve. He is another good man. He says his *benedicite* while he is having people shot. In war, no sentimentality. From Montchevrier go to—"

He stopped short.

"I am forgetting the money."

He took from his pocket a purse and a pocketbook and placed them in Halmalo's hands.

"In this pocketbook there are thirty thousand francs in assignats, something like three livres, ten sous: to be sure the assignats are counterfeit, but the genuine ones are worth no more; and in this purse,—pay attention,—there are one hundred louis d'or. I give you all that I have. I do not need anything here. Besides, it is better that no money should be found on my person. To go back again. From Montchevrier go to Antrain, where you will see Monsieur de Frotté. From Antrain go to la Jupellière, where you will see Monsieur de Rochecotte; from la Jupellière to Noirieux, where you will see the Abbé Baudonin. Can you remember all that?"

"As well as my *Pater*."

"You will see Monsieur Dubois-Guy at Saint Brice-en-Cogle, M. de Turpin at Morannes, which is a fortified town, and the Prince de Talmont at Château Gonthier."

"Will a prince speak to me?"

"If I speak to you."

Halmalo took off his cap.

"Everybody will receive you well when they see Madame Royale's fleur-de-lis. Do not forget that you will have to go to places where there are *montagnards* and *patards*. You must disguise yourself. That is easy enough. These republicans are so stupid, that with a blue blouse, a three-cornered hat and a tricolored cockade, you can go anywhere. There are no longer regiments, there are no longer uniforms, the companies are not numbered; everybody wears whatever rag he pleases. Go to Saint-Mhervé. There you will see Gaulier, called Grand-Pierre. Go to the district of Parmé, where the men blacken their faces. They put gravel and a double charge of powder in their guns in order to make more noise. They do well; but tell them above all to kill, to kill, to kill. Go to the camp of La Vache Noire, which is on a height, in the midst of the wood of La Charnie, then to the camp of L'Avoine, then to the camp of Vert, then to the camp of the Fourmis. Go to the Grand-Bordage, also called the Haut-du-Pré, which is inhabited by a widow whose daughter Treton, called the Englishman, married. The Grand-Bordage is in the parish of Quelaines. You must go to Epineux-le-Chevreuil, Sillé-le-Guillaume, Parannes, and all the men in every wood. You will find friends, and you must send them to the border of the upper and the lower Maine; see Jean Treton in the parish of Vaisges, Sans-Regret at Bignon, Chambord at Bonchamps, the Corbin brothers at Maisoncelles, and Petit-Sans-Peur at Saint-Jean-sur-Erve. He is the same as Bourdoiseau. Having done all this, and given the word of command 'Revolt! No quarter!' you must rejoin the grand army, the royal, catholic army, wherever it may be. You will see MM. d'Elbée, de Lescure, de la Rochejaquelein, all the chiefs who are still alive. Show them my badge of command. They will know what it means. You are only a sailor, but Cathelineau is only a carter. Tell them this from me: 'It is time to unite the two wars, the great and the small.' The great one makes more noise, the small one does more work. La Vendée is good, La Chouannerie is worse, and in civil war the worse is the better. The success of a war is measured by the amount of harm that it does."

He stopped speaking.

"Halmalo, I am telling you all this. You do not understand the words, but you understand the meaning. You won my confidence by the way you managed the boat; you do not know geometry, but you work marvels of skill on the water: he who can steer a boat, can pilot an insurrection; from the way you managed the intricacies of the sea, I am sure that you will be successful in carrying out all my commissions. To return. Tell all this to the chiefs, as near as you can, in your own words, but it will be all right,—

"'I prefer war in the forest to war in the open field; I do not intend to draw up a hundred thousand peasants in line before the shot of the Blues, and Monsieur Carnot's artillery; before the end of a month, I want five hundred thousand slaughterers in ambush in the woods. The republican army is my game. Poaching is waging war. I am the strategist of the thickets.' Well, there is another word that you will not understand; never mind, you will take in this: No quarter! and ambuscades everywhere! I want a guerilla warfare in Vendée. Add that the English are on our side. Let us place the republic between two fires. Europe will help us. Let us put an end to the Revolution. Kings will war against it with kingdoms, let us war against it with parishes. Say that. Do you understand?"

"Yes. We must have fire and blood everywhere."

"That's it."

"No quarter."

"Not for anybody. That's it."

"I am to go everywhere."

"And be on your guard. For in this country it is an easy matter to put a man to death."

"Death doesn't concern me. He who takes his first step may be wearing his last shoes."

"You are a brave man."

"And if I am asked the name of monseigneur?"

"It must not be known yet. Say that you do not know it and that will be the truth."

"Where shall I see monseigneur again?"

"Where I shall be."

"How shall I know it?"

"Because everybody will know it. Before the end of a week, I shall be talked about. I shall make examples; I shall avenge the king and religion, and you will know that it is I of whom they are talking."

"I understand."

"Forget nothing."

"Have no fear."

"Start now. God be with you. Go."

"I will do all that you have told me. I will go. I will speak the word. I will obey. I will command."

"Very well."

"And if I succeed—"

"I will make you chevalier de Saint-Louis."

"Like my brother; and if do not succeed, you will have me shot?"

"Like your brother."

"Agreed, monseigneur."

The old man bowed his head and seemed lost in deep reverie. When he raised his eyes, he was alone. Halmalo was only a black speck on the horizon.

The sun had just set. The gulls and the hooded seamews were flocking in from the sea outside.

That sort of restlessness just before night was felt in the air; the tree-frogs croaked, the kingfishers flew up whistling from the pools of water, the gulls, the rooks, the carabins, made their evening commotion; the birds on the shore called to each other; but not a human sound. It was a profound solitude. Not a sail in the bay, not a peasant on the land. As far as the eye could reach, a desert expanse. The great sand-thistles rustled. The white sky of twilight cast a broad pale gleam over the beach. The ponds in the distance, scattered over the dark plain, looked like sheets of pewter spread out on the ground. The wind blew from the sea.

BOOK FOURTH.— TELLMARCH.

CHAPTER I.

THE TOP OF THE DUNE.

The old man waited till Halmalo had disappeared from sight, then he wrapped his cloak about him and set forth. He walked slowly, thoughtfully. He went toward Huisnes, while Halmalo had gone toward Beauvoir.

Behind him, an enormous black triangle, with a cathedral for tiara, and a fortress for breastplate, with its two great towers to the east, one round, the other square, which help the mountain to bear the weight of church and village, rose Mount Saint-Michael, which is to the ocean what Cheops is to the desert.

The quicksands in the bay of Saint-Michael's change their sand-dunes imperceptibly. At that time between Huisnes and Ardevon there was a very high dune, which has now entirely disappeared. This dune, levelled by an equinoctial storm, was exceptional in being ancient, and bearing on its summit a memorial stone erected in the twelfth century in commemoration of a council held at Avranches against the assassins of Saint Thomas of Canterbury. From the top of this dune, the whole country could be seen, and one could get his bearings.

The old man went toward this dune and ascended it. When he had reached the top, he stopped by the monument, sat down on one of the four posts which marked the corners, and began to examine the sort of map lying at his feet. He seemed to be trying to find a route in a country once familiar to him. In this vast landscape, indistinct in the twilight, there was nothing clear but the horizon, a black line on the white sky.

He could see the roofs of eleven towns and villages; he could make out several leagues away, the steeples along the coast, which are very high, in order to serve as landmarks to people at sea.

After a few moments, the old man seemed to have found in the dim twilight what he was looking for: his eyes fastened on an enclosure of trees, walls, and roofs, which could just be seen half-way between the plain and the wood; this was a farm; he nodded his head with satisfaction as though saying to himself: "There it is," and he began to trace with his finger in the air a way through the hedges and fields. Now and then he examined a rather indistinct and shapeless object, moving above the principal roof of the farm, and he seemed to ask: "What is it?" It was colorless and confused because of the gloom; it was not a weathercock, because it fluttered, and there was no reason why it should be a flag.

He was weary; he was willing to rest on this spot where he was sitting, and he gave himself up to that sort of vague forgetfulness, which the first moment of repose brings to a tired man. There is an hour of the day which might be called noiseless, it is the quiet twilight hour. It was that hour now. He was enjoying it; he was looking about; he was listening; to what? tranquillity. Even the cruel have their sad moments. Suddenly this tranquillity was not disturbed, but made more intense, by passing voices; they were the voices of women and children. There are sometimes such unexpected chimes of joy in the darkness. The group from which the voices came could not be seen on account of the thickets, but it was walking along at the foot of the dune, going toward the plain and the forest. These voices came up clear and fresh to the old man lost in thought; they were so near that he caught all they said.

A woman's voice said,—

"We must hurry along, Flécharde. Is this the way?"

"No, it is this way."

And the dialogue continued between the two voices, one loud, the other timid.

"What do you call this farm where we are living now?"

"L'Herbe-en-Pail."

"Are we far from it?"

"About a quarter of an hour."

"Let us hurry, so as to get our soup."

"We really are late."

"We must run. But your babies are tired. We are only two women, we can't carry three brats. And then, Flécharde, you are already carrying one. A regular lump of lead. You have weaned the greedy little thing, but you are always carrying her. A bad habit; oblige me by making her walk. Well! so much the worse, our soup will be cold!"

"Oh, what good shoes you have given me! I should think they were made for me."

"They are better than going barefooted."

"Hurry up now, René-Jean."

"He is the one who has kept us back. He has to speak to every little peasant girl he meets. That is because he is a man."

"To be sure, he is going on five years."

"Tell me, René-Jean, why did you speak to that little girl in the village?"

A child's voice,—that of a boy, replied,—

"Because I know her."

The woman added,—

"What, you know her?"

"Yes," replied the boy, " ever since she played with me this morning."

"Oh, how big he is!" exclaimed the woman, "we have only been in the country three days, he is no larger than my thumb, and he has a sweetheart already."

The voices grew fainter. All sound died away.

CHAPTER II.

AURES HABET ET NON AUDIET.

The old man remained still. He was not thinking, hardly even dreaming. All about him was peace, drowsiness, confidence, solitude. It was still daylight on the dune, but almost night on the plain, and entirely so in the woods. The moon was rising in the east. A few stars pierced the pale blue of the zenith. This man, though full of tremendous cares, had plunged himself into the unspeakable tenderness of the infinite. He felt arising in him that obscure dawn of hope, if the word hope can be applied to the expectations of civil war. For the moment, it seemed to him that in escaping from the sea which had been so inexorable to him, and in touching land, all danger had vanished. No one knew his name, he was alone, lost to the enemy, without a trace left behind him, for the surface of the sea betrays nothing, concealed, ignored, not even suspected. He felt a strange, supreme composure. A little more and he would have been asleep.

It was the profound silence over the earth and in the heavens which had for this man, who had been a prey to tumult within and without, such a strange charm in this serene hour.

Nothing was heard except the wind blowing from the sea, but the wind is a continuous bass, which almost ceases to be a sound, it is so habitual.

Suddenly, he started to his feet.

His attention had just been abruptly awakened; he looked about the horizon. Something gave his eye a peculiar fixed expression.

He was looking at the steeple of Cormeray, directly in front of him beyond the plain. Indeed, something extraordinary was taking place in this steeple.

The outline of this steeple was clearly defined; the tower could be seen, surmounted by the spire, and between the tower and the spire, the belfry, square, without screen, and open on all four sides, according to the style of Breton bell towers.

But this belfry appeared alternately open and closed at regular intervals; its lofty window showed all white, then all black; the sky could be seen through, then it was seen no longer; it would be light, then eclipsed, and the opening and shutting followed each other a second apart, with the regularity of a hammer on an anvil.

This steeple in Cormeray was about two leagues away in front of the old man; just about as far to his right on the horizon, he saw the steeple of Baguer-Pican; the belfry of this steeple was opening and shutting in the same way as that in Cormeray.

He looked to his left at the steeple of Tanis; the belfry of the tower at Tanis was opening and shutting just the same as that at Baguer-Pican.

He looked at all the steeples on the horizon, one after another, to the left, the steeples of Courtils, of Précey, of Crollon, and of Croix-Avranchin; to the right, the steeples of Raz-sur-Couesnon, Mordrey, and the Pas; in front of him, the steeple of Pontorson. The belfries of all the steeples were alternately black and white.

What did it all mean?

It signified that all the bells were ringing.

To appear and disappear in this way they must be pulled furiously.

What was it then? evidently the tocsin.

They were sounding the alarm, sounding it frantically, sounding it everywhere, in all the belfries, in every parish, in every village, and not a sound reached his ears.

This was owing to the distance, which prevented the sounds from reaching so far, and because of the sea breeze blowing from the opposite direction, which carried all land noises far away from him.

All these bells madly calling from every side, and at the same time, silence; nothing could be more weird.

The old man looked and listened.

He did not hear the tocsin, but he saw it.

To see the tocsin—a strange sensation.

With whom are these bells angry?

Against whom is this tocsin sounding?

CHAPTER III.

THE ADVANTAGE OF LARGE LETTERS.

Certainly they were after somebody.

Who?

This man of steel shuddered.

He could not be the one. No one could have found out his coming; it was impossible for the acting representatives to have been informed already; he had hardly landed. The corvette had evidently foundered without a man escaping. And even in the corvette no one knew his name except Boisberthelot and La Vieuville.

The bells continued their wild play. He watched them and counted them mechanically, and his thoughts, driven from one conjecture to another, fluctuated between complete security and terrible uncertainty. However, after all, this tocsin could be explained in many ways, and he finally assured himself, by repeating, "Surely, nobody knows of my arrival, and nobody knows my name."

For some moments there had been a slight sound above and behind him. This sound was like the rustling of a leaf on a wind-shaken tree. At first, he paid no heed to it; then, as the sound continued, one might say insisted, he at last turned around. It was a leaf to be sure, but a leaf of paper. The wind was trying to detach a large placard pasted to the monument above his head. This placard had been put up only a short time before, for it was still damp, and yielded to the wind, which had begun to play with it and to unfasten it. The old man had climbed up the dune from the opposite side, and had not seen this placard when he reached the top.

He mounted the post on which he had been sitting, and placed his hand on the corner of the placard which was flapping in the wind; the sky was cloudless the twilights are long in June; the foot of the dune was dark, but the top was light; a part of the placard was printed in large letters, and there was still enough daylight to read them He read this,—

"The French Republic, one and indivisible.

"We, Prieur de la Marne, active representative of the people near the army of tlic coast of Cherbourg, order: The former Marquis de Lantenac, viscount de Fontenay, the so-called prince of Brittany, secretly landed on the coast of Granville, is declared an outlaw. A price is put on his head. The sum of sixty thousand livres will be paid to him who will deliver him up, dead or alive. This sum will not be paid in assignats, but in gold. A battalion of the army of the coast of Cherbourg will be sent immediately in pursuit of the former Marquis de Lantenac. The parishes are ordered to lend every assistance. Given at the town hall of Granville, this second day of June, 1793. Signed

"Prieur de la Marne."

Underneath this name there was another signature in much smaller characters, which was not legible, because there was so little daylight left.

The old man pulled down his hat over his eyes, drew his cloak closely up under his chin, and went quickly down the dune. It was evidently unsafe to remain longer on this prominent summit.

He had possibly stayed there too long already; the top of the dune was the only point in the whole landscape which still remained visible.

When he reached the foot of the dune and was in darkness, he walked more slowly.

He started to go, as he had planned, towards the farm, probably having good reasons for thinking he would be safe in this direction.

Everything was deserted. It was an hour when there were no passers-by. He stopped behind a thicket, took off his cloak, turned the hairy side of his vest out, fastened his ragged cloak around his neck again by the cord, and started on his way.

It was bright moonlight.

He came to a place where two roads met and where there stood an old stone cross. On the pedestal of the cross, he noticed a white square, probably a placard like the one he had just read. He went nearer to it.

"Where are you going?" said a voice.

He turned around.

A man was there in the thicket, tall like himself, old like himself, like him with white hair, and with garments more ragged. Almost his double. This man was leaning on a long stick.

The man said again,—

"I ask where you are going?"

"In the first place, where am I?" he said, with an almost haughty calmness.

The man replied,—

"You are in the seigneurie of Tanis. I am its beggar, you are its seigneur."

"I?"

"Yes, you, sir, the Marquis de Lantenac."

CHAPTER IV.

THE CAIMAND.

The Marquis de Lantenac,—henceforth we will call him by his name,—replied gravely,—
"You are right. Deliver me up."
The man continued,—
"We are both at home here: you in the castle, I in the thicket."
"Make an end of it. Do your work. Give me up," said the marquis.
The man continued,—
"You were going to the farm of Herbe-en-Pail, were you not? "
"Yes."
"Don't go there."
"Why?"
"Because the Blues are there."
"How long since?"
"For three days."
"Did the inhabitants of the farm and the hamlet make any resistance?"
"No, they opened all the doors."
"Ah!" said the marquis.
The man pointed to the roof of the farmhouse, which could be seen some distance away, above the trees.
"Do you see the roof, monsieur le marquis?"
"Yes."
"Do you see what is above it?"
"Floating?"
"Yes."
"It is a flag."
"The Tricolor," said the man.
This was the object which had already attracted the marquis's attention when he was on the top of the dune.
"Are they not sounding the tocsin?" asked the marquis.
"Yes."
"Why?"
"Evidently on your account."
"But it can't be heard."
"The wind prevents it."
The man continued, "Have you seen your placard?"
"Yes."
"They are searching for you;" and glancing towards the farm, he added, "There is a half battalion there."
"Of repubicans?"
"Parisians."
"Well," said the marquis, "let us go on."
And he took a step in the direction of the farm.
The man seized him by the arm.
"Don't go there."
"And where would you have me go?"
"Home with me."
The marquis looked at the beggar.
"Listen, marquis, my home is not fine, but it is safe. A hut lower than a cave. For a floor, a bed of seaweed, for ceiling, a roof of branches and grass. Come. You would be shot at the farm. With me you will go to sleep. You must be tired; and to-morrow morning the Blues will march away, and you can go wherever you please."
The marquis. scrutinized the man.
"On which side are you?" asked the marquis. "Are you a republican? Are you a royalist?"
"I am poor."
"Neither royalist, nor republican?" "I think not."
"Are you for or against the king?"
"I have no time for that."
"What do you think of what is going on?"
"I have nothing to live on."
"Why do you come to my assistance?"
"I saw that you were an outlaw. What is the law? So one can be out of it. I don't understand. As for me, am I in the law? am I out of the law? I know nothing about it. To die of hunger, is that to be in the law?"
"How long have you been dying of hunger?"
"All my life."

"And you wish to save me?"
"Yes."
"Why?"
"Because I said, 'There is another poorer than I. I have the right to breathe, he has not.'"
"It is true. And you would save me?"
"Surely. We are brothers, monseigneur. I ask for bread, you ask for life. We are both beggars."
"But do you know that a price has been put on my head?"
"Yes."
"How did you know?"
"I read the placard."
"You know how to read?"
"Yes, and to write, too. Why should I be a brute?"
"Then, since you know how to read, and since you have read the placard, you know that the man who betrays me will win sixty thousand francs."
"I know it."
"Not in assignats."
"Yes, I know, in gold."
"Do you know that sixty thousand francs is a fortune? "
"Yes."
"And that the one who will deliver me up will make his fortune?"
"Well, what next?"
"His fortune!"
"That is just what I thought. When I saw you, I said to myself, 'Only think of it, the one who betrays this very man, will win sixty thousand francs and make his fortune! Let us hasten to conceal him.'"

The marquis followed the poor man. They entered a thicket. Here was the beggar's den. It was a sort of room that a grand old oak had let this man have in its heart. It was hollowed out under its roots, and covered with its branches. It was dark, low, concealed, out of sight. There was room for two people in it.

"I foresaw that I was going to have a guest," said the beggar.

This sort of underground dwelling, more common than one would suppose in Brittany, is called in the language of the peasants, "*carnichot.*" This name also applies to hiding-places made inside of thick walls.

It was furnished with several pots, a pallet of straw or seaweed, washed and dried, with a thick covering of kersey; some tallow dips, with a tinder-box, and hollow twigs of furze for matches.

They bent down, crept along a little way, entered the room, cut up into odd compartments by the great tree-roots, and sat down on a heap of seaweed, which formed the bed. The space between two roots, where they entered, and which served as a doorway, let in some light. Night had come, but the eye adjusts itself to darkness, and there is always a trace of light to be found in darkness. A reflection of moonlight threw a mysterious pallor over the entrance. In a corner there was a jug of water, a loaf of buckwheat bread, and some chestnuts.

"Let us have some supper," said the poor man.

They shared the chestnuts; the marquis added his piece of biscuit: they bit the same loaf of buckwheat, and drank from the jug one after the other.

They talked together.

The marquis began to question the man.

"So, whether anything happens or not, it is all the same to you?"

"Very nearly. You are seigneurs, you people. These are your affairs."

"But what happens "

"Happens beyond our reach."

The beggar added, "And then there are other things happening still farther away from us, the sun rising, the moon waxing and waning; it is with such things that I am concerned."

He took a alp from the jug, and said,—

"What good, fresh water!" Then he added, "How do you like this water, monseigneur?"

"What is your name?" said the marquis.

"My name is Tellmarch, and they call me the *caimand.*"

"I know. *Caimand* is one of your provincial words."

"Which means beggar. They have named me besides, the old man." He continued: "For forty years I have been called the old man."

"Forty years! Why, you are young."

"I never was young. You are always young, monsieur le marquis. You have the legs of twenty, you climb up the great dune; as for me I can hardly walk at all; a quarter of a league tires me out. Still, we are of the same age; but the rich have an advantage over us, for they eat every day. Eating preserves one."

After a silence, the beggar continued: "Poverty and riches—it is a troublesome problem. That is the cause of calamities. At least, so it seems to me. The poor want to be rich, the rich do not want to be poor. I believe that is at the bottom of it. I don't mix myself up with it. Events are events. I am neither for the debtor nor for the creditor. I know that there is a debt and that it is being paid. That is all. I should have liked it better if they had not killed the king, but it would be difficult for me to tell why. In reply to that they tell me: But once they used to hang men to trees for nothing at all. I myself have seen a man with a wife and seven children hanged for shooting one of the king's deer. There are two sides to be considered."

He was silent again, then added,—

"You understand. I don't know exactly, people come and go, and things happen, but as for me, I am up among the stars."

Tellmarch stopped again to think, then continued,—

"I am a little of a bone-setter, a little of a doctor. I am familiar with herbs, and have some experience with plants; the peasants see me in a brown study and that makes me pass for a sorcerer. Because I dream, they think I know."

"You belong to this country?" asked the marquis.

"I have never been out of it."

"Do you know me?"

"Certainly. The last time I saw you was when you passed through here, two years ago. You went from here to England. Just now I noticed a man on the top of the dune. A tall man. Tall men are rare; Brittany is a country of small men. I looked carefully. I had read the placard. I said wait! And when you came down, it was moonlight and I recognized you."

"But I do not know you."

"You have seen me, but you never looked at me."

And Tellmarch, the *caimand*, added,—

"I used to see you. A beggar does not look with the same eyes as the passers-by."

"Have I ever met you before?"

"Often, for I am your own beggar. I was the poor man at the foot of the road to your castle. You used to give me alms, sometimes; but the giver pays no attention, the receiver watches and observes. A beggar is a spy. But as for me, though often sad, I try not to be a malicious spy. I held out my hand, you saw the hand only, and you dropped in it the alms which I needed in the morning to keep me from dying of hunger at night. I have sometimes been twenty-four hours without eating. Sometimes, a sou saved my life. I owe life to you. I give it back to you."

"'Tis true, you are saving me."

"Yes, I am saving you, monseigneur."

And Tellmarch's voice grew serious.

"On one condition."

"What is that?"

"That you do not come here to work evil."

"I come here to do good," said the marquis.

"Let us go to sleep," said the beggar.

They lay down side by side on the bed of seaweed. The beggar fell asleep immediately. The marquis, although very tired, remained absorbed in thought for a time, then he looked at the poor man in the darkness, and lay down again. Lying on this pallet was like lying on the ground; he took advantage of it to put his ear to the earth and listen. There was a dull humming underground; sound is known to be propagated under the earth; he heard the noise of the bells.

The tocsin was still sounding.

The marquis fell asleep.

CHAPTER V.

SIGNED "GAUVAIN."

When he awoke it was day.

The beggar was up, not in the hut, for there was not room to stand upright there, but outside near the entrance. He was leaning on his stick. The sun shone on his face.

"Monseigneur," said Tellmarch, "it has just struck four from the belfry of Tanis. I heard the four strokes. So the wind has changed, it is blowing off shore: I hear no other sound, so the tocsin has ceased. Everything is quiet at the farm and in the hamlet of Herbe-en-Pail. The Blues are either asleep, or have gone. The worst of the danger is over; it would be wise for us to separate. It is my time for going away."

He indicated a point on the horizon.

"I am going that way."

He pointed in the opposite direction.

"You must go this way."

The beggar saluted the marquis solemnly.

Pointing to what was left of the supper he added: "Carry the chestnuts with you, if you are hungry."

A moment later, he had disappeared among the trees.

The marquis rose and went in the direction Tellmarch had pointed out to him.

It was the charming morning hour called in the old Norman peasant tongue, the "piperette du jour,"—the song sparrow of the day. The finches and hedge sparrows were chirping. The marquis followed the path by which they had come the night before. He left the thicket and was again at the parting of the roads marked by the stone cross. The placard was still there, white and almost gay in the light of the rising sun. He remembered that there was something at the bottom of the placard which he could not read the evening before because the letters were so small, and there was so little light. He went up to the pedestal of the cross. The placard ended, just under the signature, "Preur de la Marne" with these two lines in small characters: "The identity of the former Marquis de Lantenac verified, he will be immediately executed. Signed: Chief of battalion, commanding the reconnoitring column, Gauvain."

"Gauvain!" said the Marquis.

He stopped in deep amazement, his eyes fastened on the placard.

"Gauvain!" he repeated.

He started off, turned back, looked at the cross, retraced his steps and read the placard once more.

Then he walked slowly away. If any one had been near him, they would have heard him murmur in an undertone: "Gauvain!"

At the foot of the cross road where he was stealing along, the roofs of the farm, which lay behind him to his left, could not be seen. He was skirting a steep height, all covered with furze in bloom, of the species called long-thorn. The summit of this height was one of those points of land called in the country a *hure* or head. At the foot of the height the view was abruptly lost in the trees. The foliage was, as it were, soaked in light. All nature rejoices deeply in the morning. Suddenly, the landscape became terrible. It was like an ambuscade bursting forth. A strange deluge of wild cries and gunshots fell over the fields and woods full of sunlight, and in the direction of the farm a great smoke pierced by bright flames arose, as if the hamlet and the farm were nothing but a bundle of straw burning. It was sudden and fearful, an abrupt change from peace to madness, a burst of hell in the clear dawn, a horror with, out warning. They were fighting near Herbe-en-Pail. The marquis stopped. There is no one, who, under similiar circumstances would not have felt that curiosity is stronger than danger; one must know, if he has to die in consequence. He climbed up the height, at the foot of which passed the hollow path. From there he might be seen, but he could see. In a few moments he was on the "hure." He looked about him. To be sure there was firing and a fire. The noise could be heard, the fire could be seen. The farm was the centre of some strange calamity. What was it? Was the farm of Herbe-en-Pail attacked? And by whom? Was it a battle? Was it not rather a military execution? The Blues, as they had been ordered by a revolutionary decree, very often punished refactory farms and villages by setting them on fire; to make an example of them they burned every farm and every hamlet which had not felled the trees prescribed by law, and which had not opened passages through the thickets for the republican cavalry. This had been notably carried out, and very recently, in the parish of Bourgon, near Ernée. Was Herbe-en-Pail in the same condition? It was evident that none of the strategic openings ordered by the decree had been made in the thickets and hedges of Tanis and Herbe-en-Pail. Was this the punishment? Had the advance guard now occupying the farm received orders? Was not this advance-guard a part of one of those investigating columns called *colonnes infernales*, or columns of hell. The height on the summit of which the marquis had taken up his place of observation, was surrounded on every side by a very wild, dense thicket. This thicket, called the grove of Herbe-en-Pail, but which had the proportions of a wood, extended as far as the farm, and hid in its depths, like all Breton thickets, a network of ravines, paths, and byways, labyrinths where the republican armies would lose themselves. The execution, if it were an execution, must have been cruel, for it was short. Like all brutal things it was soon over. The atrocity of civil warfare admits of such cruelties. While the marquis, multiplying his conjectures, hesitating to go down, hesitating to remain, was listening and watching, this din of extermination ceased, or rather was dispersed. The marquis was aware of something in the thicket like the scattering of an infuriated and joyous troop. There was a frightful swarming under the trees. They were rushing from the farm into the woods. Drums were beating. No more firing was heard. It was now like a battue; they seemed to be hunting about, pursuing, tracking; it was evident that they were in search of some one: the noise was widespread and deep; it was a medley of words of anger and of triumph, a clamorous uproar; nothing could be distinguished; suddenly, as a feature stands out against smoke, something became articulate and certain in this tumult. It was a name,—a name repeated by a thousand voices, and the marquis heard clearly this cry,— "Lantenac! Lantenac! the Marquis de Lantenac!" He was the one for whom they were searching.

CHAPTER VI.

THE SUDDEN CHANGES OF CIVIL WAR.

Suddenly all around him, and on every side at once, the thicket was filled with guns, bayonets, and swords, a tricolored flag arose in the shade, the cry of "Lantenac!" burst on his ear, and at his feet through the brambles and branches passionate faces appeared. The marquis was alone, standing on a summit which could be seen from every point of the wood. He could hardly see those who were crying his name, but all could see him. If there were a thousand guns in the woods, he was a target for them. He could distinguish nothing in the thicket but eager eyes fixed on him.

He took off his hat, turned up the rim, broke a long, dry thorn from a furze-bush, drew a white cockade from his pocket, fastened the brim and the cockade back to the crown of the hat with the thorn, and putting the hat on his head again, so that the raised rim showed his forehead and his cockade, he said in a loud voice, speaking to the whole forest at once,—

"I am the man you are seeking. I am the Marquis de Lantenac, Viscount de Fontenay, Prince of Brittany, Lieutenant-general of the armies of the king. Make an end of it. Aim! Fire!"

And opening his goat-skin vest, he exposed his bare breast.

He dropped his eyes, looking for the pointed guns, and saw himself surrounded with men on their knees.

A great cry arose: "Long live Lantenac! Long live monseigneur! Long live the general!"

At the same time, hats were thrown in the air, swords flourished joyfully, and throughout the whole thicket sticks were seen rising with brown woollen caps whirling on the end of them.

It was a Vendean band, which surrounded him. This band fell on their knees when they saw him.

A legend runs that in the old Thuringian forests there used to be strange beings, a race of giants, more or less than men, who were considered by the Romans as horrible beasts, and by the Germans as divine incarnations, and who, according to the occasion, ran the risk of being exterminated or worshipped.

The marquis felt something the same as one of these beings must have done, when, expecting to be treated as a monster, he was straightway worshipped as a god.

All these eyes, full of a terrible fire, were fixed on the marquis with a sort of savage love.

This tumultuous crowd was armed with guns, swords, scythes, poles, sticks; all had large felt hats, or brown caps, with white cockades, a profusion of rosaries and amulets, wide breeches open at the knee, sheepskin jackets, leather gaiters, bare legs, long hair, and while some looked fierce, all had a frank expression in their faces.

A young, handsome-looking man made his way through the kneeling soldiers, and with long strides went up towards the marquis. Like the peasants, this man wore a felt hat with turned-up rim and a white cockade, and a sheepskin jacket, but his hands were white and his linen fine, and he wore outside his vest a scarf of white silk, from which hung a sword with a gold hilt.

When he reached the hure, he threw down his hat, unfastened his scarf, knelt on one knee, presented scarf and sword to the marquis, and said,—

"We were searching for you, and we have found you. Here is the sword of command. These men are now yours. I was their commander, I am promoted to a higher rank, I am your soldier. Accept our homage, monseigneur. Give your orders, general."

Then he made a sign, and the men bearing the tricolored flag, came out of the woods. They climbed up to where the marquis stood, and laid down the flag at his feet. It was the flag he had just caught a glimpse of through the trees.

"General," said the young man who had presented him with the sword and scarf, "this is the flag we have just taken from the Blues, who were at the farm of Herbe-en-Pail. Monseigneur, my name is Gavard. I belong to the Marquis de la Rouarie."

"Very good," said the marquis.

And, calm and serious, he put on the scarf. Then he drew the sword, and waving it above his head, he said,—

"Stand, and long live the king!"

All rose to their feet. And through the depths of the wood sounded a wild, triumphant shout: "Long live the king! Long live our marquis! Long live Lantenac!"

The marquis turned towards Gavard.

"How many are you?"

"Seven thousand."

As they were going down from the height, and while the peasants tore away the underbrush before the steps of the Marquis de Lantenac, Gavard continued,—

"Monseigneur, nothing could be more simple. Everything is explained by a word. The people were only waiting for a spark. The notice posted up by the republicans, in making known your presence, has roused the country to insurrection for the king. Besides, we had been secretly informed by the Mayor of Granville, who is one of our men, and the same who saved the Abbé Ollivier. Last night they sounded the tocsin."

"For whom?"

"For you."

"Ah!" said the marquis.

"And here we are," added Gavard.

"And there are seven thousand of you?"

"To-day. To-morrow there will be fifteen thousand. It is the contingent of the country. When Monsieur Henri de la Rochejaquelin set out to join the Catholic army, they sounded the tocsin, and in one night six parishes, Isernay, Corqueux, Echaubroignes, Aubiers, Saint-Aubin, and Nueil, raised ten thousand men for him. They had no ammunition, but they found sixty pounds of blasting-powder at a quarry-master's, and Monsieur de la Rochejaquelin set out with that. We were quite sure that you would be somewhere in this forest, and we were searching for you."

"And you attacked the Blues at the farm of Herbe-en-Pail?"

The wind had prevented their hearing the toscin. They suspected nothing; the people of the hamlet, who are a set of louts, had received them well. This morning we invested the farm, the Blues were asleep, and by a turn of the hand the thing was done. I have a horse. Will you condescend to accept it, general?"

"Yes."

A peasant led forward a white horse in military harness. The marquis, without making use of the assistance Gavard offered him, mounted the horse.

"Hurrah!" cried the peasants, for English cries are very much employed on the Breton coast, which has constant intercourse with the Channel Islands.

Gavard gave the military salute, and asked,—

"Where will your headquarters be, monseigneur?"

"At first in the forest of Fougrèes."

"That is one of your seven forests, marquis."

"We must have a priest."

"We have one."

"Who?"

"The vicar of La Chapelle-Erbrée."

"I know him. He has made the voyage to Jersey."

A priest stepped out of the ranks and said,—

"Three times."

The marquis turned his head.

"Good-morning, vicar. You are going to have some business."

"So much the better, marquis."

"You will have many to confess. Those who wish it. We force nobody."

"Monsieur le Marquis," said the priest, Gaston, at Guéménée forced the republicans to confession."

"He is a wig-maker," said the marquis; "but death should be free."

Gavard, who had gone to give some orders, returned,—

"General, I await your command."

"At first the rendezvous will be in the forest of Fougères. Let the men disperse and go there."

"The order is given."

"Didn't you tell me that the people of Herbe-en-Pail had received the Blues well?"

"Yes, general."

"Did you burn the farm?"

"Yes."

"Did you burn the hamlet?"

"No."

"Burn it."

"The Blues tried to defend themselves, but they were a hundred and fifty, and we were seven thousand."

"Who are these Blues?"

"Santerre's Blues."

"Who ordered the drums to beat while the king's head was being cut off. So it is a Parisian battalion?"

"A half battalion."

"What is it called?"

"General, 'Battalion of Bonnet-Rouge' is on their flag."

"Wild beasts."

"What is to be done with the wounded?"

"Put an end to them."

"What is to be done with the prisoners?

"Shoot them."

"There are about eighty."

"Shoot them all."

"There are two women."

"Shoot them also."

"There are three children."

"Bring them here. We will see what can be done with them."

And the marquis started off on his horse.

CHAPTER VII.

NO MERCY: THE WATCHWORD OF THE COMMUNE. NO QUARTER: THE WATCHWORD OF THE PRINCES.

While this was taking place near Tanis, the beggar was travelling toward Crollon. He penetrated the ravines, under vast hollow bowers, inattentive to everything, attentive to nothing, as he had said himself, dreaming rather than thinking, for thoughts have an aim, but dreams have none, wandering, roving, stopping, eating here and there a bunch of wild sorrel, drinking from the springs, occasionally raising his head to catch distant sounds, then returning to the dazzling fascination of nature, sunning his rags, perhaps hearing the noise of men but listening to the songs of the birds.

He was old and slow; he could not go far; as he had said to the Marquis de Lantenac, a quarter of a league wearied him; he took a short cut toward la Croix-Avranchin, and it was evening when he returned.

A little way beyond Macey, the path that he followed led over a sort of culminating point free from trees, from which one could see a long distance, and follow the whole horizon from the west to the sea.

His attention was attracted by smoke.

Nothing is more gentle than smoke, nothing more frightful. There is the smoke of peace, and the smoke of villany. Smoke, the density and color of smoke, it makes all the difference between peace and war, between brotherhood and hatred, between hospitality and the grave, between life and death. Smoke rising through the trees may signify the most charming thing in the world, the hearth; or the most terrible, a conflagration; and all the happiness, as well as all the unhappiness of man, is sometimes centred in the very thing scattered to the wind.

The smoke that Tellmarch saw was alarming.

It was black, with now and then a sudden gleam of redness, as if the coals from which it came were irregular and had begun to die out, and it rose above Herbe-en-Pail.

Tellmarch hastened towards this smoke. He was very weary, but he was anxious to know what it was. He reached the top of a hill adjoining the hamlet and the farm.

Neither hamlet nor farm was there.

A heap of ruins was burning, and this was Herbe-en-Pail.

It is a more impressive sight to see a hut burn than a palace. A hut on fire is lamentable. Devastation falling on misery, a vulture attacking an earthworm, there is a strange contrariety about it that oppresses the heart.

According to the Bible story, the sight of a conflagration changes a human being to a statue; Tellmarch was for a moment such a statue. The spectacle under his eyes made him immovable. This destruction was going on in silence. Not a cry arose; not a human sigh mingled with the smoke; this furnace was struggling to devour this village, and succeeding, without a sound save the snapping of the timbers and the crackling of the thatch. Occasionally, the smoke cleared away, the roofs fallen in, displayed the yawning rooms, the brazier showed its rubies, scarlet rags and poor old crimson colored furniture appeared in these vermilion interiors, and Tellmarch was dazed with the viciousness of the disaster.

Some trees belonging to a chestnut-grove next the houses had taken fire and were blazing up.

He listened, trying to catch the sound of a voice, an appeal, a cry; nothing stirred except the flames; all was silent except the fire. Had all of them fled?

Where was that group of people living and working at Herbe-en-Pali? What had become of this little people?

Tellmarch came down from the hill.

A funereal enigma confronted him. He approached it slowly and with a steady gaze. He advanced toward this ruin with the slowness of a shadow; he felt like a phantom in this tomb.

He reached what had been the door of the farmhouse; and he looked into the court, which now was without walls and was confounded with the hamlet grouped around it.

What he had seen before was nothing. He had only seen the terrible as yet,—the horrible appeared to him now.

In the middle of the court, there was a black heap, vaguely outlined on one side by flames, on the other by the moon; this heap was a pile of men; these men were dead.

All around this heap there was a great pool, smoking a little; the fire was reflected in this pool; but it had no need of fire to make it red; it was blood.

Tellmarch approached it. He began to examine, one after another, these prostrate bodies; all were corpses.

The moon was shining; the fire too.

These corpses were soldiers. All were barefooted; their shoes had been taken off; their weapons had been taken away, too; they still had on their uniforms, which were blue. Here and there, in the heap of limbs and heads, could be seen hats full of holes with tricolored cockades. They were republicans. They were the Parisians who, the day before, were there all alive, keeping garrison in the farm of Herbe-en-Pail. These men had been executed; this was proved by the symmetrical position of the bodies: they had been struck down on the spot, and with care. They were all dead. Not a death-rattle sounded from the heap.

Tellmarch passed the corpses in review without omitting a single one; all were riddled with bullets.

Those who had shot them, probably in haste to go elsewhere, had not taken time to bury them.

As he was going away, his eyes fell on a low wall in the courtyard, and he saw four feet protruding from behind the corner of this wall.

These feet had shoes on; they were smaller than the others; Tellmarch went towards them. They were the feet of women.

Two women were lying side by side behind the wall; they also had been shot.

Tellmarch bent over them. One of these women wore a sort of uniform; beside her was a cask, broken and empty; she was a vivandière. She had four bullets in her head. She was dead.

Tellmarch examined the other. She was a peasant woman. She was pallid and her mouth was open. Her eyes were closed. There was no wound on her head. Her clothing, which her wearisome wandering had doubtless torn to rags, had come open in her fall, and exposed her half-naked body. Tellmarch pushed them open still more, and saw a round wound made by a bullet in her shoulder; her collar-bone was broken. He looked at her livid breasts.

"A nursing mother," he murmured.

He touched her. She was not cold.

She had no other injury than the broken collar-bone and the wound on her shoulder.

He placed his hand on her heart and felt a feeble fluttering. She was not dead.

Tellmarch rose to his feet and cried in a terrible voice:—

"Is there nobody here?" "It is you, the caimand!" replied a voice, so low that he could hardly hear it.

And at the same time a head appeared from a hole in the ruins.

Then another face appeared in another place.

They were two peasants, who were hiding; the only ones who had survived.

The familiar voice of the caimand had reassured them, and brought them out of the nook where they were crouching.

They came up to Tellmarch still all of a tremble.

Tellmarch could have screamed, but he was unable to speak: such are deep emotions.

He pointed to the woman stretched out at his feet.

"Is she still alive?" said one of the peasants.

Tellmarch nodded assent.

"Is the other woman alive?" asked the other peasant.

Tellmarch shook his head.

The peasant who appeared first added,—

"All the others are dead, are they not? I saw it all. I was in my cellar. How one thanks God in times like these for not having a family! My house was burned. Lord Jesus! they have killed them all. This woman had children. Three children, all little things! The children cried: "Mother!" The mother cried: "My children!" They killed the mother and carried away the children. I saw it all, my God! my God! my God! Those who massacred them all have gone. They were satisfied. They took away the little ones and killed the mother. But she is not dead, is she; she is not dead? Tell me, caimand, do you believe you can save her? Do you want us to help you carry her to your carnichot?"

Tellmarch nodded assent.

The woods touched the farm. They quickly fashioned a litter out of leaves and brakes. They placed the woman, still motionless, on the litter and started to go through the thicket, the two peasants carrying the litter, one at her head, the other at her feet, while Tellmarch held the woman's arm, and felt her pulse.

As they went along, the two peasants talked, and, over the bleeding woman, whose pale face was lighted up by the moon, they gave utterance to exclamations of dismay.

"All killed!"

"Everything burned!"

"Ah, Lord God! Is this the way it is going to be now?"

"It was that tall old man who wanted it done."

"Yes, he gave the orders."

"I did not see him when they were shooting. Was he there?"

"No, he had gone. But it is all the same: it was all done by his order."

"Then he was the one who did it all."

"He said: 'Kill! Burn! No quarter!'"

"He is a marquis."

"Yes, for he is our marquis."

"What do they call him?"

"He is Monsieur de Lantenac."

Tellmarch raised his eyes towards heaven first, and muttered between his teeth,—

"If I had known it!"

PART SECOND— IN PARIS.

BOOK FIRST.—CIMOURDAIN.

CHAPTER I.

THE STREETS OF PARIS AT THIS PERIOD.

The people lived in public, they ate from tables spread in front of their doors, the women sat on church steps making lint and singing the Marseillaise; Parc Monceaux and the Luxembourg gardens were parade grounds; there were smiths' shops in full blast at every crossing; they made guns under the eyes of the passers-by, who applauded them; this was the word in everybody's mouth: "Patience, we are in the midst of revolution." The people smiled heroically. They went to the play as they did in Athens during the Peloponnesian War; there were notices posted at the corners of the streets: "The Siege of Thionville." "The Mother of a Family Rescued from the Flames."

"The Club of Sans Souci."
"The Oldest of the Popes Joan."
"The Philosopher-Soldiers."
"The Art of Loving in the Village."

The Germans were at the gates; it was rumored that the king of Prussia had engaged boxes at the opera. Everything was frightful and nobody was frightened. The mysterious law against the suspected, Merlin de Donai's crime, made the guillotine threaten the heads of all. A denounced lawyer, named Seran, sat by his window, in dressing-gown and slippers and played the flute while waiting to be arrested.

Nobody seemed to have time enough. Everybody was in haste. Not a hat without a cockade. The women said: The red cap is becoming to us. Paris seemed to be full of removals. The bric-à-brac shops were encumbered with crowns, mitres, sceptres of gilded wood and decorated with fleurs-de-lis, the relics of royal houses: the destruction of the monarchy was in progress. In old-clothes shops there were copes and rochets to be had for the asking. At the Porcherons' and at Ramponneau's, men decked out in surplices and stoles, mounted on asses, caparisoned with chasubles, had wine from the public-house poured into a cathedral ciboria. In Rue Saint-Jacques, barefooted street-pavers stopped a pedler's cart with boots and shoes to sell, clubbed together, and bought fifteen pairs of shoes to send to the Convention for our soldiers.

Busts of Franklin, Rousseau, Brutus, and it must be added, of Marat, were everywhere; underneath one of these busts of Marat, in Rue Cloche-Perce, was hung up under glass, in a black wooden frame, a speech against Malouet, with testimony in support of it and these two lines on the margin:

"These details were given me by Sylvian Bailly's mistress, a good patriot who was kindly disposed toward me. Signed: Marat."

In the Place du Palais-Royal, the inscription on the fountain: *Quantos effundit in usus!* was covered over with two great pictures painted in distemper, one representing Cahier de Gerville denouncing the rallying cry of the "Chiffonistes" of Arles to the National Assembly the other, Louis XVI., brought back from Varennes in his royal coach, and under this coach a plank fastened by ropes, on each end of which was a grenadier with fixed bayonet.

Few large shops were open; haberdashers' and toy shops on wheels were dragged about by women, and were lighted with candles, the tallow dripping over the goods; stalls in the open air were kept by ex-nuns in blonde wigs; one stocking-mender, darning stockings in a stall, was a countess; another seamstress was a marchioness: Madame de Boufflers lived in a garret from which she could see her own mansion. Street criers went about, offering newspapers. Those who wore cravats hiding their chins were called "écrouelleux,"— scrofulous. Strolling singers swarmed. The crowd hooted Pitou, the royalist song-writer, formerly so popular, because he had been imprisoned twenty-two times, and was brought before the revolutionary tribunal for having slapped his hindquarters in pronouncing the word *civisme;* seeing that his head was in danger, he exclaimed: "But it is the opposite of my head, which is guilty!" this made the judges laugh, and saved him. This same Pitou made fun of the fashion for Greek and Latin names; his favorite song was about a cobbler named "Cujus," and whose wife he called " Cujusdam."

They made revolutionary songs and dances; they no longer said gentleman and lady, but citizen and citizeness. They danced in ruined cloisters, with church lamps on the altar, with two sticks crossed and bearing four candles under the arched roof, and tombs beneath their feet.

They wore blue tyrant jackets. They had "liberty cap" shirt pins made of red, white, and blue stones. Rue Richelieu was called the Street of the Law; the Faubourg Saint-Antoine, was called the Faubourg of Glory; there was a statue of Nature in the Place de la Bastille.

Certain well-known characters were pointed out: Chatelet, Didier, Nicolas, and Garnier-Delaunay, who stood guard at Duplay the carpenter's door; Voullaut, who never missed a guillotine day, and followed the wagons carrying the condemned, and who called it, "going to the red mass"; Montflabert, a revolutionary juror, and a marquis, who called himself "Dix-Août" (tenth of August.)

People watched the pupils of the Military School as they passed by; they were termed by the decree of the Convention "aspirants to the School of Mars," and by the people, "Robespierre's pages."

The people read the proclamations of Fréron, denouncing those suspected of the crime of "negotiantism." Young swells collected at the door of the mayoralty, to scoff at civil marriages, placing themselves in the way of the bride and bridegroom and saying: "married civilly." At the Invalides the statues of saints and kings had on Phrygian caps. They played cards on the curbstones at the crossings; playing-cards, too, were in a state of revolution; kings were replaced by genii; queens, by the Goddess of Liberty; knaves, by Equality personified; and aces, by characters representing Law.

They tilled the public gardens; they ploughed up the gardens of the Tuileries. With all this, especially among the conquered parties, was mingled a strange, haughty weariness of life; a man wrote to Fouquier-Tinville,—

"Have the kindness to release me from life. Here is my address." Champcenetz was arrested for having cried out in full sight of the Palais-Royal: "When will the revolution of Turkey be? I want to see the republic *à la Porte.*"

Newspapers were everywhere. Wig-makers curled women's wigs in public, while the master read the *Moniteur* aloud; others, surrounded by a crowd, made comments, with vehement gesticulations, on the journal *Entendons-nous*, belonging to Dubois-Crancé, or the *Trompéte du Père Belle-rose*. Sometimes, barbers were also pork-butchers; and hams and chitterlings might be seen hanging beside a dummy with golden hair; Merchants sold wines of the *emigrés* on the public streets; one merchant proclaimed wines of fifty-two sorts; others sold second-hand harp-shaped clocks, and *duchesse* sofas; one wig-maker had this for a sign: "I shave the clergy, comb the hair of the nobility, accommodate the Third Estate."

"People went to have their fortunes told by Martin, number 173 Rue d'Anjou, formerly Rue Dauphine. There was lack of bread, there was lack of coal, there was lack of soap; numbers of milch cows might be seen passing along as they came from the provinces. At la Vallée, lamb sold for fifteen francs a pound. An order of the Commune assigned a pound of meat to each person every ten days. The people formed in line in front of the shops; one of these lines has become famous; it reached from the door of a grocer's shop in Rue du Petit-Carreau to the middle of Rue Montorgueil. Forming the line, was called "holding the cord" on account of a long rope which those in file held in their hands one behind another. The women were brave and sweet in their misery. They spent whole nights awaiting their turn to enter the bakers' shops. Expedients were used with success during the revolution; this universal distress was alleviated by two perilous means, the assignat and the maximum; the assignat was the lever, the maximum the fulcrum. This empiricism was the saving of France. The enemy, both in Coblentz and in London, gambled in assignats.

Girls went about selling lavender water, garters, and braids of hair, and dabbling in stocks. On the Perron, in Rue Vivienne, there were stockbrokers with dirty shoes, greasy hair, and fur capes trimmed with fox tails, and *magoiets* from Rue de Valois, in polished boots, toothpicks in their mouths, shaggy hats on their heads, to whom the girls spoke familiarly. The people went in pursuit of them as they did of the thieves, whom the royalists called "active citizens." Beyond this, there was very little theft. Cruel destitution, stoical integrity. The barefooted and the starving, with eyes solemnly cast down, passed by the windows of the jewelry shops in the Palais Egalité. While the Section Antoine was searching the house of Beaumarchais, a woman picked a flower in the garden; the people boxed her ears. Wood cost four hundred francs in silver, a cord; people could be seen in the streets sawing up their beds for wood; in winter-time, the fountains were frozen; two pails of water cost twenty sous; everybody turned water-carrier. A Louis d'or was worth three thousand, nine hundred and fifty francs. A ride in a hackney-coach cost six hundred francs. After using a hackney-coach for a day this conversation was overheard:—

"Coachman, how much do I owe you?"

"Six thousand francs."

A greengrocer woman made twenty thousand francs a day. A beggar said: "For the sake of charity, assist me! I need two hundred and thirty livres to pay for my shoes."

At the entrance to the bridges might be seen colossal figures sculptured and painted by David, which Mercier insulted by calling them: "Enormous wooden puppets." These enormous figures represented Federalism and Coalition overthrown. No faltering among this people. The gloomy joy of having made an end of thrones. Volunteers abounded, exposing their breasts. Each street had its battalion. The flags of the districts came and went, each with its own device. On the flag of the district of the Capucins was this inscription: "Nobody shall shave us." On another: "No more nobility except, in the heart." On every wall there were placards large, small, white, yellow, green, red, printed, and written, with this exclamation: "Long live the Republic!" The little children lisped: "*Ça ira!*"

These little children were to be the great future.

Later on, the tragic city was succeeded by the cynical city; the streets of had two very distinct aspects during the revolution, before and after the ninth Thermidor: the Paris of Saint-Just gave place to the Paris of Tallien; and, these are the continual antitheses of God; immediately after Sinai, la Courtille appeared.

An outburst of public madness now appeared. It was a repetition of what had been seen eighty years before. The people left Louis XIV. as they left Robespierre, with a great need for breath; hence the Regency which opens the century and the Directory with which it closes. Two saturnalia after two reigns of terror. France fled from the puritan cloister as from the monarchical cloister, with the joyfulness of an escaped nation.

After the ninth Thermidor, Paris was gay, insanely gay. An unhealthy joy burst forth. The frenzy of dying was succeeded by the frenzy of living, and grandeur outdid itself. They had a Trimalcion, called "*Grimod de la Regnière;*" they had the "*Almanach des Gourmands.*" They dined to the sound of trumpets in the entresols of the Palais Royal, with orchestras of women beating the drum and sounding the trumpet.

The "rigodooner" reigned, bow in hand; they took supper "in oriental fashion" at Méot's house, surrounded with perfumes. The artist Boze, painted his daughters, charming, innocent girls of sixteen years, "en guillotines," that is to say in low-necked dresses with red underwaists.

The boisterous dances in the ruined churches were followed by the balls of Ruggieri, of Luquet Wenzel, of Mauduit, of la Montansier; serious women making lint, were followed by sultanas, savages, nymphs; barefooted soldiers covered with blood, mud, and dust, were followed by barefooted women decorated with diamonds; dishonesty appeared simultaneously with immodesty; it had its purveyors in the upper classes, and associations of thieves in the lower classes; a swarm of pickpockets filled Paris, and everybody was obliged to keep watch over his "luc," that was his pocketbook; it was one of the pastimes to go to the Place-du-Palais-de-Justice to see the women thieves on the stool; they were obliged to fasten their petticoats securely.

As people came from the theatres, street-boys offered cabs, saying "citizen and citizeness there is room for two; they no longer cried "The old Franciscan" and the "Friend of the People," but in their places "Punch's Letter" and "The Rogues' Petition;" the Marquis de Sade presided over the Section des Piques, in Place Vendôme.

The reaction was jocund and ferocious; the "Dragons of Liberty" of '92 came to life again under the name of "Chevaliers of the Dagger." At the same time, there appeared in the booths the type, Jocrisse. They had "The Wonder," and besides these marvellous women the "Inconceivables," they swore by the "*paole victimé*" and the "*paole verte;*" they retrograded from Mirabeau to Bobêche.

Thus Paris sways to and fro; it is the enormous pendulum of civilization; it touches alternately one pole and then the other, Thermopylæ and Gomorrha. After '93, the, Revolution passed through a singular occultation, the century seemed to forget to finish what it had begun, some strange orgy was interposed, took the foreground, pushed the frightful apocalypse in to the background, veiled the inordinate vision, and burst into a laugh after the fright; tragedy disappeared in parody, and on the edge of the horizon, carnival smoke mysteriously effaced Medusa.

But in '93, where we now are, the streets of Paris still had all the grandiose and wild appearance of the beginning. They had their orators; there was Varlet, who went about in a booth on wheels, from the top of which he harangued to the passers-by; they had their heroes, one of which was called "the captain of the iron-tipped sticks." They had their favorites—Guffroy, author of the pamphlet "Rougiff." Some of these popular favorites were mischievous; others were healthful. One among them all was honest and fatal; he was Cimourdain.

CHAPTER II.

CIMOURDAIN.

Cimourdain was a pure-minded but gloomy man. He had "the absolute" within him. He had been a priest, which is a solemn thing. Man may have, like the sky, a dark and impenetrable serenity; that something should have caused night to fall in his soul is all that is required. Priesthood had been the cause of night within Cimourdain. Once a priest, always a priest.

Whatever causes night in our souls may leave stars. Cimourdain was full of virtues and truth, but they shine out of a dark background.

His history was quickly told. He had been a village priest and a tutor in a great family; then a little inheritance fell to him, and he became free.

He was, above all, an obstinate man. He made use of meditation as one does of pincers, he believed that he had no right to leave an idea till he had thought it out to the end; he thought desperately. He knew all the languages of Europe and others somewhat; this man studied ceaselessly, which helped him to keep his chastity, but there is nothing more dangerous than such repression.

As a priest he had, though pride, chance, or loftiness of soul, kept his vows; but he had not been able to keep his belief. Science had destroyed his faith; dogma had vanished in him. Then examining himself, he had felt as though he were mutilated, and being unable to change himself as a priest, he tried to make himself over as a man, but in an austere fashion; he had been deprived of a family, he adopted his country; he had been refused a wife, he espoused humanity. Such vast repletion is at bottom emptiness.

His parents, peasants, in making a priest, of him, had wished to remove him from the people; he had come back to the people.

And he had returned with passionate fondness. He regarded their suffering with a fierce tenderness. First a priest, then philosopher, and lastly, athlete. Louis XV. was still alive when Cimourdain began to feel dimly that he was a republican. Of what republic? The republic of Plato, perhaps, and perhaps also of the republic of Draco.

It was forbidden him to love, he began to hate. He hated lies, monarchy, theocracy, his priestly robes; he hated the present, and he called aloud to the future; he foresaw it, he anticipated it, he imagined it frightful and magnificent; he knew, that for the liberation of this lamentable human misery, something like an avenger, who would be at the same time a liberator, was needed. He worshipped the catastrophe from afar.

In 1789, this catastrophe came, and found him ready. Cimourdain threw himself into this vast plan of human renovation, logically, that means for a mind of his stamp inexorably; logic is pitiless. He had lived during the great years of the Revolution, and had been thrilled by all its commotions: in '89 the fall of the Bastille, the end of torture for the people; in '90, the nineteenth of June, the end of feudalism; in '91 Varennes, the end of royalty; in '92 the coming of the Republic. He had seen the sunrise of the Revolution; he was not a man to be afraid of this giantess; far from that, this growth on every side had given him new life; and although almost an old man,— he was fifty years old, and a priest ages sooner than other men,—he began to grow too. From year to year, he had watched events as they increased in size, and he had grown like them. At first, he had feared that the Revolution would miscarry, he watched it, it was in the right, he insisted that it would succeed; and in proportion to its frightfulness his confidence increased. He wished that this Minerva, crowned with the stars of the future, might be also a Pallas, with Medusa's head for a buckler. He wished that her divine eye might be able in time of need to cast an infernal glare at the demons and pay them back terror for terror.

Thus he had come to '93.

"Ninety-three" was the war of Europe against France, and of France against Paris. And what was the Revolution? It was the victory of France over Europe, and of Paris over France. Hence the immensity of that terrible moment?, '93, greater than all the rest of the century.

Nothing could be more tragic than Europe attacking France and France attacking Paris. A drama with epic proportions.

"Ninety-three" was a year of intensity. The storm was raging then in all its fury and all its grandeur. Cimourdain felt at ease in it. This life of bewilderment, savage and splendid, suited his spread of wings. This man, like the sea-eagle, possessed a deep, internal composure, together with a taste for external danger. Certain winged creatures, ferocious and calm, are made to struggle against mighty winds. Souls of the tempest, like these, exist.

He was capable of exceptional pity, which he reserved alone for the wretched. To the kind of suffering which causes horror, he was ready to devote his life. Nothing was loathsome to him. In this consisted his characteristic kindness. He was hideously and divinely helpful. He sought for ulcers that he might kiss them. Fine actions, ugly in appearance, are the most difficult to perform; these he preferred. One day, at the Hôtel-Dieu, a man was dying, choked by a tumor in his throat, a horrible, fetid abscess, possibly contagious, and which had to be emptied at once. Cimourdain was there. He applied his mouth to the tumor, sucked it, spitting out as his mouth filled, emptied the abscess, and saved the man's life. As he was still wearing the priest's robes at this time, some one said,—

"If you should do that for the king, you would be made a bishop."

"I would not do it for the king!" replied Cimourdain.

This action and this reply made him popular in the dismal quarters of Paris.

So much so that he could do what he pleased with those who suffered, those who wept, and those who threatened. At the time of the indignation against the monopolists,—an indignation so prolific in error,—it was Cimourdain who, without a word, prevented the plundering of a vessel laden with soap at the Saint-Nicholas quay, and scattered the infuriated mob who were stopping the carriages at the barrier of Saint-Lazare.

It was he who, ten days after the tenth of August, led the people to overthrow the statues of the kings. In their fall, they killed; in Place Vendôme, a woman, Reine Violet, was crushed by Louis XIV., around whose neck she had put a rope that she was pulling. This statue of Louis XIV. had been standing a hundred years; it was erected the twelfth of August, 1692; it was pulled down the twelfth of August, 1792. In the Place de la Concorde, a man named Guinguerlot, was beaten to death on the pedestal of Louis XV. for having called the demolishers rascals. The statue was broken to pieces. Later, they made it into sous. One arm alone escaped; it was Louis

XV.'s right arm that he extended with the gesture of a Roman emperor. It was at Cimourdain's request that the people sent a deputation to carry this arm to Latude, the man who had been buried thirty-seven years in the Bastille. When Latude, with the iron collar about his neck, and chains about his loins, lay rotting alive in the bottom of this prison, by order of the king whose statue dominated Paris, who could have told him that this prison would fall? that this statue would fall? that he would escape from the tomb, and that the monarchy would enter in? that he, the prisoner, would be master of this bronze hand which had signed his warrant? and that nothing would be left of this king of mud but this brazen arm?

Cimourdain was one of those men who have a voice within them, and who listen to it. Such men seem absent-minded; they are not; they are all attention.

Cimourdain knew everything and nothing. He knew everything about science, and nothing at all about life. Hence his inflexibility. His eyes were bandaged like Homer's Themis. He had the blind certainty of the arrow, which sees only the mark and flies to it. In a revolution, nothing is more terrible than a straight line. Cimourdain went straight ahead, as sure as fate.

Cimourdain believed that, in social geneses, the extreme point is the solid earth; an error peculiar to minds which replace reason with logic. He went beyond the Convention; he went beyond the Commune; he belonged to the Evêché.

This convention, called the Evêché because it holds its meetings in a hall of the old Episcopal palace, was rather a complication of men than an assembly. There, as at the Commune, were seen silent and significant spectators who, as Garat said, had as many pistols about them as pockets. The Evêché was a strange mixture,—a mixture both cosmopolitan and Parisian, which is not a contradiction, for Paris is the place where the heart of nations beats. There was the great plebeian incandescence. Compared to the Evêché, the Convention was cold, and the Commune lukewarm. The Evêché was one of those revolutionary formations, like volcanic formations. The Evêché was made up of everything: ignorance, stupidity, integrity, heroism, anger, and the police. Brunswick had agents in it. There were men in it worthy of Sparta, and men worthy of the galleys. Most of them were mad but honest. La Gironde, through the mouth of Isnard, temporary president of the Convention, had uttered this monstrous prediction,—

"Be on your guard, Parisians. There will not be left one stone on another of your city, and people will one day search for the place where Paris stood."

This speech created the Evêché. There were men, and, as we have just said, men of all nations, who had felt the need of gathering close about Paris. Cimourdain joined this group.

This group reacted against reaction. It was born of that public need of violence, which is the terrible and mysterious side of revolutions. Strong in this force, the Evêché began its work immediately. In the commotion of Paris, the Commune made use of the cannon, the Evêché sounded the tocsin.

Cimourdain believed, in his implacable ingenuousness, that everything is right in the service of truth; this fitted him for ruling the extreme parties. Rascals felt that he was honest, and were satisfied. Crimes are flattered to be presided over by a virtue. It both restrains them and pleases them. Palloy, the architect, who planned the destruction of the Bastille and sold the stones to his own profit, and who, when appointed to whitewash Louis XVI.'s dungeon, in his zeal covered the wall with bars, chains and iron collars; Gonchon, the suspected orator of the faubourg Saint-Antoine, whose receipts were afterwards found; Fournier, the American, who, on the seventeenth of July, fired a pistol at Lafayette, which it was said Lafayette had paid for; Henriot, who came out of Bicêtre, and had been valet, mountebank, thief and spy before he was a general, and levelled his guns at the convention; La Reynie, formerly grand vicar of Chartres, who had replaced his breviary with *Père Duchesne;* all these men respected Cimourdain, and at times, all that was necessary to keep the worst of them from flinching, was to let them feel this terrible, convincing frankness before them in judgment.

In this way, Saint-Just terrified Schneider.

At the same time, the majority of the Evêché, composed largely of poor, violent men, who were good, believed in Cimourdain and followed him. He had as vicar, or aide-de-camp, as one pleases, another republican priest, Danjou, whom the people loved because he was so tall, and they had christened him the Abbé Six-Pieds, or Six-Feet. Cimourdain had led that intrepid chief, called Général la Pique, wherever he pleased, and also that bold Truchon, called the Grand-Nicholas, who tried to save Madame de Lamballe's life, by giving her his arm, and making her jump over the corpses; which would have been successful had it not been for the barber Carlot's cruel jestings.

The Commune watched the Convention, the Evêché watched the Commune; Cimourdain, a just mind, and loathing intrigue, had broken many a mysterious thread in the hands of Pache, whom Beurnonville called the "man in black." Cimourdain, at the Evêché, was on an equality with everybody. He was consulted by Dobsent and Momoro. He spoke Spanish to Gusman, Italian to Pio, English to Arthur, Flemish to Pereyra, German to the Austrian Proly, bastard son of a prince. He created an understanding between these discordant elements. Hence his situation was obscure but strong. Hébert feared him.

Cimourdain had, at this time, and among these tragic groups, the power of the fates. He was a spotless man who thought himself infallible. Nobody had ever seen him shed a tear. Unapproachable, icy virtue. He was the frightfully just man.

There was no half way for a priest in revolution. A priest could only give himself up to this prodigious and atrocious chance, from the lowest or the highest motives; he must be infamous or sublime. Cimourdain was sublime, but sublime in isolation, in inaccessibility, in inhospitable gloom; sublime when surrounded by precipices. The lofty mountains have such forbidding virginity.

Cimourdain had the appearance of an ordinary man, dressed in common clothes, poor in aspect. When young, he had been tonsured; when old, he was bald. The little hair he had was gray. His forehead was broad, and on this forehead there was a sign for a close observer. Cimourdain had an abrupt, impassioned, and solemn way of speaking; his voice, stern, his tone peremptory; his mouth sad and bitter; his eye clear and penetrating, and over all his face there was a strange look of scorn.

Such was Cimourdain.

No one to-day knows his name. History has more than one such terrible Unknown.

CHAPTER III.

A HEEL NOT DIPPED IN THE STYX.

Was such a man really a man? Could the servant of the human race have any affection? Had he not too much soul to have any heart? This world-wide embrace, which took in all and everything, could it reserve itself for any one person? Could Cimourdain love? Let us answer, Yes.

When he was young, and a tutor in an almost princely mansion, he had one pupil, the son and heir of the family, and he loved him. It is so easy to love a child. What can one not forgive a child? One can pardon him for being a seigneur, a prince, a king. The innocence of his tender years makes one forget the crimes of his race; the feebleness of the creature makes one forget the exaggeration of rank. He is so small that one pardons him for being great. The slave pardons him for being the master. The old negro worships the little white boy.

Cimourdain had conceived a passion for his pupil. Childhood is so ineffable that one can pour out all one's affection on it. All the power of loving in Cimourdain had, so to speak, fallen on this child; the sweet, innocent being had become a sort of prey to this heart condemned to solitude. He loved him with all the tenderness at once of father, brother, friend and creator. He was his son, the son not of his flesh, but of his spirit. He was not his father, and this was not his work; but he was the master, and this was his masterpiece. Of this little lord he had made a man. Who knows? a great man, perhaps. For such are dreams. Unknown to the family,—does one need permission to create an intelligence, a will, an integrity?—he had communicated to the young viscount, his pupil, all the progress that he had in himself, he had inoculated him with the dreadful virus of his virtue; he had infused into his veins his convictions, his conscience, his ideals; into this aristocratic brain he had poured the soul of the people.

The mind suckles, intelligence is a breast. There is an analogy between the nurse giving her milk, and the teacher giving his thought. Sometimes the teacher is more the father than the father himself, just as the nurse is more the mother than the mother herself.

This deep spiritual paternity bound Cimourdain closely to his pupil. The mere sight of this child touched him.

Let us add this: it was easy to replace the father, for the child had no father; he was an orphan; his father was dead, his mother was dead; he had no one to watch over him but a blind grandmother, and a great uncle who was away. The grandmother died; the great uncle, the head of the family, a soldier and possessed of great estates, appointed to offices at court, avoided the old family castle, lived at Versailles, went to the army, and left the orphan alone in the solitary towers. So the tutor was master in every sense of the word.

Let us add this, besides; Cimourdain had seen the child who had been his pupil, born. The orphan child when very small had had a serious illness; Cimourdain, at this time of danger, had watched over him day and night; the physician attends the patient, the nurse saves his life, and Cimourdain had saved the child. His pupil owed to him not only his education, his instruction, his knowledge, but he owed to him his recovery, and health; his pupil not only owed to him his thoughts, but he owed to him his life. We adore those who owe everything to us. Cimourdain adored this child.

The natural separation of their lives came about. When his education was completed, Cimourdain was obliged to leave the child, grown to a young man. With what cold and unconscionable cruelty those separations are made! How calmly families dismiss the teacher who has left his thought in a child, a nurse who leaves in it her love. Cimourdain, paid and sent away, left high life, and went back to the lower ranks of society; the partition between the great and the lowly was closed again: the young lord, an officer of birth and instantly made captain, set out for a garrison somewhere; the humble tutor already in the bottom of his heart an unsubmissive priest, hastened to go down again to that dark ground-floor of the church, called the lower clergy, and Cimourdain lost sight of his pupil.

The revolution had come; the memory of this being, of whom he had made a man, continued to smoulder in him, hidden but not extinguished by the immensity of public matters.

To model a statue and give it life is a noble work; to model an intelligence and give it truth, is still nobler. Cimourdain was the Pygmalion of a soul.

A mind can have a child.

This pupil, this child, this orphan, was the only being on earth that he loved.

But, even in such an affection, was such a man vulnerable?

We shall see.

BOOK SECOND.—THE PUBLIC HOUSE OF THE RUE DU PAON.

CHAPTER I.

MINOS, ÆACUS, AND RHADAMANTHUS.

In Rue du Paon there was a public house, called a café. This café had a back room, which is now historical. It was there that men, so powerful and so closely watched that they hesitated to speak to one another in public, occasionally met almost secretly. It was there, on the twenty-third of October, 1792, that the famous kiss was exchanged between la Montague and la Gironde. Although he does not admit it in his "Mémoires," it was there that Garat came for information that gloomy night, when he stopped his carriage on the Pont-Royal, to listen to the tocsin, after he had put Clavière in a place of safety in Rue de Beaune.

On the twenty-eighth of June, 1793, three men were gathered around a table in this back room. Their chairs did not touch; they were seated on different sides of the table, leaving the fourth vacant. It was about eight o'clock in the evening; it was still light in the street, but dark in the back room, and a hanging lamp, then a luxury, lighted the table.

The first of these three men was pale, young, solemn, with thin lips, and a cold face. He had a nervous twitching in his cheek, which must have hindered him from smiling. He was powdered and gloved, there was not a wrinkle in his light blue coat, well brushed and buttoned up. He wore nankeen breeches, white stockings, a high cravat a plaited shirt frill, shoes with silver buckles.

The two other men were one, a sort of giant, the other a sort of dwarf. The tall man was carelessly dressed in a loose coat of scarlet cloth, his neck bare in a necktie unfastened and falling below his shirt frill, his vest open for lack of buttons; he wore top-boots; his hair was in disorder, though it showed traces of having been dressed, and there was horse-hair in his wig. His face was pitted with smallpox, he had an angry frown between his eyelids, a kindly pucker in the corners of his mouth, thick lips, large teeth, a porter's hand, flashing eyes. The small man was yellow, and looked deformed when he was seated; he carried his head thrown back, his eyes were bloodshot, there were livid spots on his face; he wore a handkerchief tied over his smooth, greasy hair; he had no forehead, and a terrible, enormous mouth. He wore long pantaloons, slippers, a waistcoat which seemed to have been white satin once, and over this waistcoat, a loose jacket, in the folds of which a hard straight line betrayed a dagger.

The first of these men was called Robespierre; the second, Danton; the third, Marat.

They were alone in this room. In front of Danton stood a glass and a wine-bottle covered with dust, suggesting Luther's beer-glass; in front of Marat, a cup of coffee; in front of Robespierre, papers.

Near the papers was seen one of those heavy leaden inkstands, round and ridged, which will be remembered by those who were schoolboys in the beginning of this century. A pen was thrown down beside the inkstand. On the papers was placed a large copper seal bearing the words, "Palloy fecit," and which formed an exact miniature model of the Bastille.

A map of France was spread out in the centre of the table.

Outside the door was stationed Marat's watch-dog, that Laurent Basse, porter at number 18 Rue des Cordeliers, who, the thirteenth of July, or about two weeks after this twenty-eighth of June, was to strike the head of a woman named Charlotte Corday, with a chair; she was at this time in Caen, dreaming vague dreams. Laurent Basse was the printer's devil of the *Ami du Peuple*. This evening he had been brought by his master to the café in Rue du Paon, and ordered to keep the room closed where Marat, Danton, and Robespierre were, and not to let anybody enter unless it were some one from the Committee, of Public Safety, from the Commune, or the Évêché.

Robespierre did not wish to close the door against Saint-Just, Danton did not wish to close it against Pache, Marat did not wish to close it against Gusman.

The conference had already lasted a long time. Its subject was the pile of papers on the table which Robespierre had been reading. The voices began to grow higher. Something like anger was brewing between these three men. Outside, loud words were occasionally heard from within. At this period the custom of public tribunals seemed to have created the right to listen. It was the time when Fabricius Pâris, the copying clerk looked through the key-hole to see what the Committee of Public Safety was doing. Which, by the way, was not in vain, for it was Pâris who warned Danton the night of the thirtieth of March, 1794. Laurent Basse had put his ear to the door of the back room where Danton, Marat, and Robespierre were. Laurent Basse served Marat, but he belonged to the Évêché.

CHAPTER II.

MAGNA TESTANTUR VOCE PER UMBRAS.

Danton had just arisen, quickly pushing back his chair.

"Listen," he cried. "There is only one urgency, the Republic in danger, I know but one thing, that is to deliver France from the enemy. For that all means are good. All! All! All! When I am dealing with every danger, I have recourse to every expedient, and when I fear everything, I risk everything. My thought is a lioness. No half-way measures, no prudery in revolution. Nemesis is not a prude. Let us be frightful and useful. Does the elephant look where he puts his foot? Let us crush the enemy."

Robespierre replied gently,— "I am willing," and he added, "The question is to know where the enemy is."

"It is outside, and I have driven it there," said Danton.

"It is within, and I am watching it," said Robespierre.

"And I will drive it out again," replied Danton.

"You cannot drive away an internal enemy."

"What can be done then?"

"It must be exterminated."

"I give my consent," said Danton in his turn, and he continued: "I tell you it is outside, Robespierre."

"Danton, I tell you it is within."

"Robespierre, it is on the frontier."

"Danton, it is in Vendée."

"Calm yourselves," said a third voice "it is every where; and you are lost."

It was Marat who spoke.

Robespierre looked at Marat and replied calmly,—

"Truce to generalities. I am exact. Here are the facts."

"Pedant!" grumbled Marat.

Robespierre placed his hand on the pile of papers before him, and continued,—

"I have just read you the despatches from Prieur de la Marne. I have just communicated to you the information given by this Gélainbre. Danton, listen, foreign war is nothing, civil war is everything. Foreign war is a scratch on the elbow; civil war is an ulcer which eats your vitals. This is the result of all that I have just read to you: La Vendée until now scattered among several chiefs, is on the point of concentrating herself. She is henceforth going to have a single captain,—"

"A central brigand," murmured Danton.

"He is" continued Robespierre, "the man landed near Ponterson the second of June. You have seen what he is. Notice that this landing coincides with the arrest of the acting representatives, Prieur de la Côte d'Or and Rom me at Bayeux, by the traitorous district of Calvados, the second of June, the same day."

"And their removal to the castle of Caen," said Danton.

Robespierre went on:—

"I will continue the summing up of the despatches. The forest war is organizing on a vast scale. At the same time, a descent from the English is in preparation; Vendéans and English; that is, Britain with Brittany. The Hurons of Finisterre speak the same language as the Topinambous of Cornwall. I have laid before your eyes an intercepted letter from Puisaye, in which it says that 'twenty thousand redcoats distributed among the insurgents will raise a hundred thousand.' When the peasant insurrection is completed, the English will make their descent. This is the plan, follow it on the map."

Robespierre placed his finger on the map and continued,—

"The English have the choice of landing from Cancale to Paimpol. Craig would prefer the bay of Saint-Brieuc; Cornwallis, the bay of Saint-Cast. That is mere detail. The left bank of the Loire is guarded by the Rebel Vendéan army, and for twenty-eight leagues of open country between Ancenis and Pontorson, forty Norman parishes have promised their aid. The invasion will be made at three points, Plérin, Iffiniac, and Pléneuf; from Plérin they will go to Saint-Brieuc, and from Pléneuf to Lamballe; the second day, they will reach Dinan, where there are nine hundred English prisoners, and at the same time they will occupy Saint Jouan and Saint-Méen, and will leave cavalry there; the third day, two columns will go, one toward Jouan-sur-Bédée, the other to Dinan-sur-Becherel, which is a natural fortress, and where they will set up two batteries; the fourth day, they will be at Rennes. Rennes is the key of Brittany. Whoever has Rennes has all. If Rennes is taken, Châteauneuf and Saint-Malo will fall. There are a million cartridges and fifty field-pieces at Rennes."

"Which they would sweep away," murmured Danton.

Robespierre continued,—

"I will finish. From Rennes, three columns will attack—one, Fougères; one, Vitré; the other, Redon. As the bridges are cut away, the enemy will provide themselves with pontoons and madriers,—you have seen this fact, stated precisely,—and they will have guides for the points where the cavalry can ford. From Fougères they will radiate to Avranches; from Redon, to Ancenis; and 115 from Vitré to Laval. Nantes will surrender, Brest will surrender. Redon opens the way the entire length of the Vilaine, Fougères gives them the road to Normandy, Vitré gives them the road to Paris. In two weeks they will have an array of brigands, with three hundred thousand men, and all Brittany will belong to the King of France."

" That is to say, to the King of England," said Danton.

"No, to the King of France."

And Robespierre added, —

" The King of France is worse. A foreigner can be driven out in fifteen days, but it takes eighteen hundred years to root out a monarchy."

Danton, who had sat down again, put his elbows on the table and rested his head in his hands, deep in thought.

"You see the danger," said Robespierre, "Vitré gives the road to Paris for the English."

Danton raised his head and brought his two great clenched hands down on the map, as though it were an anvil. "Robespierre, didn't Verdun open the way to Paris for the Prussians?"

"Well?"

"Well, we will drive out the English as we drove out the Prussians."

And Danton rose from his seat again.

Robespierre laid his cold hand on Danton's feverish fingers. "Danton, Champagne was not for the Prussians, and Brittany is for the English. To recapture Verdun was foreign war; to recapture Vitré is civil war."

And Robespierre muttered in a cold, deep voice, —

"A serious difference."

He added, —

"Sit down again, Danton, and look at the map instead of pounding it with your fist."

But Danton clung to his own opinion.

"That is carrying it too far!" he exclaimed, "to look for the catastrophe in the west, when it is coming in the east. Robespierre, I agree with you that England is rising on the ocean; but Spain is rising from the Pyrénées; but Italy is rising from the Alps, and Germany is rising across the Rhine. And the great Russian Bear is at the bottom of it. Robespierre, the danger is in a circle, and we are within it. Coalition without, treason within. In the South, Servant has left the door of France ajar for the king of Spain. In the North, Dumouriez is passing over to the enemy. Moreover, he has always threatened Holland less than Paris. Nerwinde wipes out Jemmapes and Valmy. The philosopher, Radaut SaintEtienne, a traitor, like the Protestant that he is, corresponds with the courtier Montesquieu. The army is reduced. There is not a battalion now with more than four hundred men; the brave regiment of Deux Ponts is reduced to a hundred and fifty men; the camp of Pamars has surrendered; there are no more than five hundred bags of flour left at Givet; we are falling back on Landau; Wurmser pressed Kléber; Mayence is yielding bravely; Condé, cowardly; Valenciennes, also. But this does not prevent Chancel, who is defending Valenciennes, and old Féraud, who is defending Condé from being two heroes, as well as Meunier, who was defending Mayence. But all the others are traitors: Dharville, at Aix-la-Chapelle; Mouton, at Brussels; Valence, at Bréda; Meuilly, at Limbourg; Miranda, at Maestricht; Stengel, a traitor; Lanou, a traitor; Ligonnier, a traitor; Menou, a traitor; Dillon, a traitor; —hideous corn of Dumouriez. We ought to make examples of them. Custine's countermarches look suspicious to me; I suspect Custine of preferring the lucrative prize of Frankfort to the useful prize of Coblentz. Frankfort can pay four millions of war tribute. Grant it. What is that compared to crushing that nest of refugees? Treason, I call it. Meunier died the thirteenth of June; Kléber is alone. Meantime, Brunswick is increasing and advancing. He sets up the German flag in all the French places that he takes. The Margrave of Brandenburg is the arbiter of Europe; he pockets our provinces, he will appropriate Belgium, you will see; one would say that we were working for Berlin. If that goes on, and if we do not see to it, the French Revolution will have been made for the benefit of Potsdam; its sole result will have been the enlargement of Frederick II.'s little state, and we shall have killed the King of France for the King of Prussia."

And Danton burst into a frightful laugh.

Danton's laugh made Marat smile.

"You each have your hobby; yours, Danton, is Prussia; yours, Robespierre, la Vendée. Now I will give my views. You do not see the real danger; it is here,—the cafés and the gaming-houses. The café of Choiseul is Jacobin, the café Patin is royalist; the café Rendez-Vous attacks the National Guard, the café of Porte-Saint-Martin defends it; the café of the Regence is against Brissot, the café Corezza is for it; the café Procope swears by Diderot, the café of the Théâtre-Français swears by Voltaire; at the Rotonde they tear up the assignats; the cafés Saint-Marçéau are in a rage; the café Manouri is debating the question of flour; at the café Foy there is gluttony and uproar; at the Perron, there is the buzzing of the hornet-drones of finance. This is the serious matter."

Danton laughed no longer. Marat continued to smile. The smile of a dwarf, worse than a giant's laugh.

"Are you jesting, Marat?" growled Danton.

Marat gave that convulsive movement of his hip, which was famous. His smile died away.

"Ah, I recognize you. Citizen Danton. It was you who called me that fellow Marat, before the whole convention. Listen. I pardon you. We are passing through a period of folly. Ah, am I jesting? Indeed, what sort of a man am I? I denounced Chazot, I denounced Pétion, I denounced Kersaint, I denounced Moreton, I denounced Dufriche-Valazé, I denounced Ligonnier, I denounced Menou, I denounced Banneville, I denounced Gensonné, I denounced Biron, I denounced Lidon and Chambon; was I wrong? I scent treason in the traitor, and I find it worth while to denounce the criminal before the crime. I am in the habit of saying the day before, what the rest of you say the day after. I am the man who proposed a complete plan of criminal legislation to the assembly. What have I done just now? I have asked that the sections be instructed, in order to discipline them for revolution; I have broken the seals of thirty-two strong boxes; I have reclaimed the diamonds placed in Roland's hands; I have proved that the Brissotins gave blank warrants to the Committee of General Safety; I have noted the omissions in Lindet's report on the crimes of Capet; I voted the execution of the tyrant within twenty-four hours; I defended the battalions, Mauconseil and Republican; I prevented the reading of the letter from Narbonne and from Malouet; I have made a motion in favor of the wounded soldiers; I caused the suppression of the Committee of Six; in the affair of Mons, I foresaw the treason of Dumouriez; I have asked that a hundred thousand relatives of the refugees be taken as hostages for the commissioners surrendered to the enemy; I proposed that all representatives who should cross the barriers be declared traitors; I unmasked the Rolandine faction in the troubles at Marseilles; I insisted that a price should be put on the head of the son of Egalite; I defended Bouchotte; I called for the nominal appeal that Isnard might be driven from the chair; I caused it to be declared that the Parisians were worthy of their country;—that is why I am treated like a dancing-jack by Louvet. Finisterre demanded my expulsion, the city of London hopes to have me exiled, the city of Amiens wishes to have me muzzled, Coburg wants to have me arrested, and Lecointe-Puiraveau proposes to the convention to declare me mad. Ah! Citizen Danton, why did you bring me to your secret meeting, if it was not to have my advice? Did I ask you for permission to come? Far from it. I have no taste for interviews with contra-revolutionists such as Robespierre and yourself. Moreover, I ought to have expected it, you have not understood me; you no more than Robespierre, Robespierre no more than you. So there is no statesman here? you must be taught to spell politics; you must dot your *i*'s. What I have said to you, means this: you are both mistaken. The danger is neither in London, as Robespierre believes; nor in Berlin, as Danton believes; it is in Paris. It is in the absence of unity, in the right that each one has to draw his own conclusions; to commence with you two, in minds grovelling in the dust, in the anarchy of wills——"

"Anarchy!" interrupted Danton, "who has caused that if not you?"

Marat did not stop.

"Robespierre, Danton, the danger is in this heap of cafés, in this heap of gaming-houses, in this heap of clubs: club of the Noirs; club of the Fédérés; club of the Dames; club of the Impartiaux, which dates from Clermont-Tonnerre, and was the monarchical club of 1790; a social circle conceived by the priest, Claude Fauché; club of the Bonnets de Laine, founded by the gazetteer Prudhomme, et cætera; without counting your club of the Jacobins, Robespierre; and your club of the Cordeliers, Danton. The danger is in the famine which caused the bag-porter Blin to hang the baker of the market Palu, Francois Denis, to the lantern of the Hotel de Ville, and in the justice which hung the bag-porter Blin for having hung the baker Denis. The danger is in the paper money, which is depreciating. An assignat of a hundred francs fell on the ground in Rue du Temple, and a passer-by, a man of the people, said: " It is not worth the trouble of picking it up. " The stockjobbers and the monopolists, there lies the danger! To hang the black flag from the Hotel de Ville, a fine step! You arrest the Baron of Trenck, that is not enough. I would have the neck of that old prison intriguer wrung. Do you think you have escaped from the difficulty because the president of the Convention placed a civic crown on the head of Labertèche who received forty-one sabre cuts at Jemmapes, and whose eulogist Chenier became? Comedies and jugglery. Ah! you do not look at Paris! Ah! you look for the danger from afar, when it is near at hand. What good does your police do, Robespierre? For you have your spies: Payan, in the Commune; Coffinhal, in the Revolutionary Tribunal; David, in the Committee of General Safety; Couthon, in the Committee of Public Welfare. You see that I am informed. Well, know this: the danger is above your heads, the danger is under your feet; conspiracy, conspiracy, conspiracy; the people in the streets read the papers together, and shake their heads at one another; six thousand men, without tickets of civism—returned refugees, Muscadins, and Mathevons,—are concealed in cellars and attics, and in the wooden galleries of the Palais-Royal; people form a line in the baker's shop; good women wring their hands on the doorsteps, saying: "When shall we have peace?" It is of no use for you to shut yourselves up in the hall of the Executive Counsel to be by yourselves, for all that you say is known; and to prove it, Robespierre, here are the words you said last evening to Saint- Just: " Barbaroux is beginning to have a big belly, which will hinder him in his flight." Yes, the danger is everywhere, and, above all, at the centre. In Paris the ex -nobles plot, the patriots go barefooted, the aristocrats, arrested the ninth of March, are already released. The splendid horses, which ought to be put to the cannons on the frontier, spatter us in the streets; bread is worth three francs, twelve sous for four pounds, the theatres play immoral pieces, and Robespierre will have Danton guillotined."

"Ugh!" said Danton.

Robespierre examined the map attentively.

"What we need," cried Marat, abruptly, "is a dictator. Robespierre, you know that I want a dictator."

Robespierre raised his head.

"I know, Marat, either you or me."

"I or you," said Marat.

Danton muttered, between his teeth,—

"The dictatorship, try it!"

Marat saw Danton's frown.

"Wait," he added. "One last effort. Let us come to some agreement. The situation is worth the trouble. Haven't we already come to an agreement about the thirty-first of May? The question as a whole is more serious than Girondism, which is a question of detail. There is truth in what you say; but the truth, the whole truth, the real truth, is what I say. In the South, Federalism; in the West, Royalism; in Paris, the duel of the Convention and the Commune; on the frontiers, the retreat of Custine, and the treason of Dumouriez. What does it all amount to? Dismemberment. What do we need? Union. Our safety lies in that; but we must make haste. Paris must take the management of the Revolution. If we lose an hour, the Vendéans may be at Orleans, and the Prussians in Paris to-morrow. I grant you this, Danton; I yield that to you, Robespierre. So be it. Well, the conclusion is the dictatorship. Let us take the dictatorship, and let us three represent the Revolution. We are the three heads of Cerberus. Of these three heads, one speaks, that is you, Robespierre: the other roars, that is you, Danton——"

"The other bites," said Danton; "that is you, Marat."

"All three bite," said Robespierre.

There was a silence. Then the conversation, full of portentous repartees, began again.

"Listen, Marat; before marrying, we must become acquainted. How did you know what I said yesterday to Saint-Just?"

"That concerns me, Robespierre."

"Marat!"

"It is my duty to enlighten myself, and it is my business to keep myself informed."

"Marat!"

"I love knowledge."

"Marat!"

"Robespierre, I know what you said to Saint-Just, as I know what Danton said to Lacroix, as I know what happens on the Quai des Théatins, in the mansion of Labriffe, a den where the nymphs of emigration repair; as I know what takes place in the house of the Thilles, near Gonesse, belonging to Valmerange, former administrator of the posts, where Maury and Cazalès used to go, where Sieyès and Vergniaud have gone since, and where now a certain one goes once a week."

As he said "A certain one," Marat looked at Danton.

Danton exclaimed,—

"If I had two atoms of power, this would be terrible."

Marat continued,—

"I know what you said, Robespierre, as I know what happened in the tower of the Temple, when they fattened Louis XVI. there so well, that in the month of September alone, the wolf, the she- wolf, and the cubs ate eighty-six baskets of peaches. At the same time, the people were starving. I know this as I know that Roland was hidden in a house looking out on a back court in Rue de la Harpe; as I know that six hundred pikes of the fourteenth of July were made by Faure, the Duke of Orléans's locksmith; as I know what was done at the house of Saint-Hilaire, Sillery's mistress; on days when there was to be a ball, old Sillery himself rubbed chalk on the floors of the yellow drawing-room in Rue Neuve-des-Mathurin; Buzot and Kersaint dined there. Saladin dined there the twenty-seventh, and with whom, Robespierre? With your friend, Lasource."

"Words, words," murmured Robespierre. "Lasource is not my friend."

And he added thoughtfully,—

"Meanwhile, there are eighteen manufactories of false assignats in London."

Marat continued in a calm voice, but with a slight trembling, which was alarming,—

"You are the *Faction des Importants*. Yes, I know it all, in spite of what Saint-Just calls "State silence.""

Marat emphasized these words, looked at Robespierre and went on to say,—

"I know what is said at your table when Lebas invites David to eat the cooking of his betrothed, Elizabeth Duplay, your future sister-in-law, Robespierre. I am the enormous eye of the people, and from the depths of my cellar, I look on. Yes, I see; yes, I hear; yes, I know. Little things content you. You admire yourself. Robespierre courts the admiration of his Madame de Chalabre, the daughter of the Marquis de Chalabre, who played whist with Louis XV. the evening of Damiens' execution. Yes, people carry their heads high. Saint-Just lives in a cravat. Legendre is proper, new overcoat and white vest, and a shirt frill to make one forget his apron. Robespierre imagines that history will care to know that he had on an olive frock coat at the Constituante, and a sky-blue coat at the Convention. He has his portrait all over the walls of his room——"

Robespierre interrupted him in a voice even more calm than Marat's.

"And you, Marat, you have yours in all the sewers."

They continued in a conversational tone, the slowness of which emphasized their replies and repartees, and added a strange irony to the threats.

"Robespierre, you have termed those who desire the overthrow of thrones, the 'Don Quixotes of the human race.'"

"And you, Marat, after the fourth of August, in number 559 of your *Ami du Peuple*,—Ah, I have kept the number, it will be useful, —you have asked to have the nobles receive their titles back again. You said: 'A duke is always a duke.'"

"Robespierre, in the meeting of the seventh of December, you defended the Roland woman against Viard."

"Just as my brother defended you, Marat, when you were attacked at the Jacobins. What does that prove? Nothing."

"Robespierre, we know the cabinet of the Tuileries, where you said to Garat: 'I am weary of the Revolution.'"

"Marat, it was here in this public-house, that you embraced Barbaroux, the twenty-ninth of October."

"Robespierre, you said to Buzot: 'What is the Republic?'"

"Marat, it was in this public-house that you invited three men from Marseilles to breakfast with you."

"Robespierre, you have a strong marketman, armed with a cudgel, to escort you."

"And you, Marat, the day before the tenth of August, you asked Buzot to help you escape to Marseilles, disguised as a jockey."

"In September when the courts were in session, you hid yourself, Robespierre."

"And you, Marat, you displayed yourself."

"Robespierre, you flung the red cap on the ground."

"Yes, when a traitor hung it up. What adorns Dumouriez, defiles Robespierre."

"Robespierre, you refused to veil Louis XVI.'s head, while the soldiers were passing by."

"I did better than to veil his head, I cut it off."

Danton interfered, but as oil interferes in fire.

"Robespierre, Marat, calm yourselves."

Marat did not like to be named second. He turned round.

"Why does Danton meddle in this?" he said.

"Why do I meddle? For this reason. To prevent fratricide; to prevent a quarrel between two men who serve the people; because there is enough foreign war, because there is enough civil war, and because there will be too much domestic war; because it was I who brought about the Revolution, and I do not want it spoiled. That is why I am meddling."

Marat replied without raising his voice,—

"You had better meddle with making your accounts."

"My accounts!" exclaimed Danton. "Go ask for them in the defiles of Argonne, in Champagne delivered, in conquered Belgium, in the armies where I have already four times exposed my breast to bullets! Go ask for them in the Place de la Révolution, on the scaffold of the twenty-first of January, on the throne abolished, on the guillotine, that widow——"

Marat interrupted Danton.

"The guillotine is a virgin; men lie with her, but she does not become fruitful."

"What do you know about it, Danton? I would make her pregnant!"

"We shall see," said Marat.

And he smiled.

Danton saw this smile.

"Marat," he exclaimed, "you are a sneak, I am a man for open air and daylight. I hate the life of a reptile. It would not suit me to be a wood-louse. You live in a cellar; I live in the street. You have nothing to say to anybody; any passer-by can see me and speak to me."

"Pretty boy, will you come up where I live?" muttered Marat.

And ceasing to smile, he assumed a peremptory tone.

"Danton, give account of the thirty-three thousand crowns, ready money, that Montmorin paid to you in the name of the king, under pretext of indemnifying you in your capacity of attorney at the Châtelet."

"I was concerned with the fourteenth of July," said Danton, haughtily.

"And the Garde-Meuble? and the crown diamonds?"

"I was concerned with the sixth of October."

"And the plunder committed by your *alter ego*, Lacroix, in Belgium?"

"I was concerned with the twentieth of June."

"And the loans made à la Montansier?"

"I impelled the people to the return from Varennes."

"And the opera house, built with money furnished by you?"

"I armed the sections of Paris."

"And the hundred thousand francs, the secret funds of the Minister of Justice?"

"I caused the tenth of August."

"And the two millions for the Assembly's secret expenses, of which you took a fourth?"

"I stopped the marching enemy and prevented the allied kings from passing."

"Prostitute!" said Marat.

Danton rose.

"Yes," he cried, "I am a harlot, I have sold my body, but I have saved the world."

Robespierre began to bite his nails. He could neither laugh nor smile. Laughing, Danton's lightning, and smiling, Marat's sting, were left out of him.

Danton replied,—

"I am like the ocean; I have my ebb and flow; at low tide my shallow places appear, at high tide my billows are seen."

"Your froth," said Marat.

"My tempest," said Danton.

Marat had arisen at the same time as Danton. He too burst forth. The adder suddenly became a dragon.

"Ah!" he cried, "ah, Robespierre! ah, Danton! You are now willing to listen to me! Well, I tell you, you are lost. Your policy results in the impossibility to go any farther; there is no exit for you; and you have managed to close all the doors before you, except that of the grave."

"That is our greatness," said Danton.

And he shrugged his shoulders.

Marat continued,—

"Danton, take care. Vergniaud, too, has a large mouth, thick lips, and an angry frown; Vergniaud, too, is pock-marked like Mirabeau and like you; that did not prevent the thirty-first of May. Ah! you shrug your shoulders. Sometimes shrugging the shoulders shakes off one's head. Danton, I tell you, your harsh voice, your loose necktie, your Hessian boots, your little suppers, your big pockets, all look to Louisette."

Louisette was the pet name Marat gave to the guillotine.

He continued,—

"And as for you, Robespierre, you are a Modérée, but that will not do you any good. Go, powder yourself, dress your hair, play the coxcomb, wear fine linen, prink, and be curled and painted, but you will go to Place-de-Grève, all the same; read Brunswick's declaration; still you will be treated like the regicide Damiens, and you will look as fine as a new pin while waiting to be quartered alive."

"Echo of Coblentz," said Robespierre between his teeth.

"Robespierre, I am not an echo of anything, I am the outcry of all. Ah! you are young. How old are you, Danton? Thirty-four years. How old are you, Robespierre? Thirty-three. Well, as for me, I have always been alive; I am suffering humanity, I am six thousand years old."

"That is true," replied Danton. "for six thousand years, Cain has been preserved in hatred like a toad in a stone. The rock is broken, and Cain leaps forth among men, and that is Marat."

"Danton!" exclaimed Marat, and a livid light appeared in his eyes.

"Well, what?" said Danton.

Thus these three terrible men went on talking. A quarrel of thunderbolts.

CHAPTER III.

THE THRILL OF HIDDEN CHORDS.

There was a lull in the conversation; for a moment these Titans each became lost in thought. Lions are disturbed by hydras. Robespierre had grown very pale, and Danton very red. Both trembled. The light died out of Marat's eye; a calmness, an imperious calmness came over the face of this man, the terror of the terrible."

Danton felt that he was conquered, but was unwilling to admit it. He resumed,—

"Marat talks very loud about dictatorship and unity, but he has only one power, that of dissolution."

Robespierre compressed his thin lips, and added,—

"I am of the opinion of Anacharsis Cloots; I say neither Roland nor Marat."

"And for my part," replied Marat, "I say, neither Danton nor Robespierre."

He looked steadily at both and added,—

"Let me give you some advice, Danton. You are in love, you think of marrying again, don't meddle any more with politics, be wise!"

And stepping back towards the door to go out, he gave them this ominous farewell.

"Adieu, gentlemen."

Danton and Robespierre shuddered.

At the same time, a voice rose from the other end of the room, saying,—

"You are wrong, Marat."

All turned round. During Marat's outburst, some one had come in by the rear door, without their notice.

"It is you, Citizen Cimourdain," said Marat. "Good evening."

It was Cimourdain, indeed.

"I say that you are wrong, Marat," he repeated.

Marat turned green, which was his way of growing pale.

Cimourdain added,—

"You are useful, but Robespierre and Danton are necessary. Why do you threaten them? Union, union, citizen! the people want to be united."

This coming in had the effect of cold water, and like the arrival of a stranger in midst of a family quarrel, it calmed at least the surface, if not the depths.

Cimourdain stepped towards the table.

Danton and Robespierre knew him. They had often noticed in the public tribunes of the Convention, this powerful but obscure man whom the people saluted. Robespierre, always inclined to formality, asked,—

"Citizen, how did you get in?"

"He belongs to the Evêché," replied Marat, in a voice with a strange touch of submission in it.

Marat defied the Convention, led the Commune, and feared the Evêché.

This is a law.

Mirabeau felt Robespierre moving at an unknown depth, Robespierre felt Marat moving, Marat felt Hébert moving, Hébert felt Babeuf moving. As long as the strata under-ground are quiet, the political man may walk along, but under the most revolutionary there is a subsoil, and the bravest stop in alarm when they feel beneath their feet the movement that they have caused above their heads.

To know how to distinguish the agitation arising from covetousness, from the agitation arising from principles, to fight the one and aid the other, in this lies the genius and the power of great revolutionary leaders.

Danton saw that Marat was yielding.

"Oh! Citizen Cimourdain is welcome," he said.

And he held out his hand to Cimourdain. Then he said,—

"Parbleu, let us explain the situation to Citizen Cimourdain. He comes at just the right moment. I represent the Mountain, Robespierre represents the Committee of Public Welfare, Marat represents the Commune, Cimourdain represents the Evêché. He shall be our umpire."

"So be it," said Cimourdain, solemnly and simply. "What is the question?"

"About la Vendée," replied Robespierre.

"La Vendée!" said Cimourdain.

And he added,—

"There lies the great danger. If the Revolution comes to naught, it will come to naught through la Vendée. One Vendée is more to be feared than ten Germanys. For France to live, Vendée must be killed."

These few words won Robespierre.

Robespierre, however, put this question,—

"Were you not formerly a priest?"

His priestly air did not escape Robespierre. He recognized by his exterior what was in the man.

Cimourdain replied: "Yes, citizen."

"What of that?" exclaimed Danton. "When priests are good, they are worth more than other men. In times of revolution, priests are melted up into men, as bells into money and cannons. Danjou is a priest, Daunou is a priest, Thomas Lindet is bishop of Evreux. Robespierre, you sit at the Convention side by side with Massieu, Bishop of Beauvais. The grand-vicar Vaugeois belonged to the Committee of Insurrection of the tenth of August. Chabot is a Capuchin. It was Dom Gerle who invented the oath of the tennis court; it was the Abbé Audran who caused the National Assembly to be declared superior to the king; it was the Abbé Goutte who asked the

Legislature to have the dais taken away from Louis XVI.'s arm-chair; it was the Abbé Grégoire who provoked the abolition of royalty."

"Supported by the player, Collot-d'Herbois," sneered Marat. "The two together did the work; the priest overthrew the throne, the comedian threw down the king."

"Let us return to la Vendée," said Robespierre.

"Well," asked Cimourdain, "what is the matter there? What is this Vendée doing?"

Robespierre replied,—

"She has a chief. She is going to be tremendous."

"Who is this chief, Citizen Robespierre?"

"He is a former Marquis de Lautenac, who calls himself Prince of Brittany."

Cimourdain started.

"I know him," he said. "I have been a priest at his house."

He thought for a moment, and then added,—

"He was fond of women before he became a warrior."

"Like Biron, who was a Lauzun," said Danton.

And Cimourdain added thoughtfully—

"Yes, he was formerly a man of pleasure. He must be terrible."

"Frightful," said Robespierre. "He burns villages, puts an end to the wounded, massacres the prisoners, shoots the women."

"The women?"

"Yes, among others he had a mother of three children shot. Nobody knows what became of the children. Besides he is a captain. He understands warfare."

"To be sure," replied Cimourdain. "He was in the war with Hanover, and the soldiers said: 'Richelieu uppermost, Lantenac at the bottom.' Lantenac was the real general. Talk about him to your colleague, Dussaulx."

Robespierre remained thoughtful for a moment, then the conversation continued between him and Cimourdain.

"Well, Citizen Cimourdain, this man is in Vendée."

"How long has he been there?"

"Three weeks."

"He must be outlawed."

"That has been done."

"A price must be set on his head."

"It has been done."

"A large sum of money must be offered to the one who captures him."

"It has been done."

"Not in assignats."

"It has been done."

"In gold."

"It has been done."

"And he must be guillotined."

"It will be done."

"By whom?"

"By you."

"By me?"

"Yes, you will be commissioned by the Committee of Public Welfare with full power."

"I accept," said Cimourdain.

Robespierre was swift in his selections, a characteristic of a statesman. He took from the pile before him a sheet of white paper, with this printed heading: French Republic, one and indivisible. Committee of Public Welfare.

Cimourdain continued,—

"Yes, I accept. Terror against terror, Lantenac is cruel. I shall be cruel. War to the death against this man. I will deliver the Republic from him, so it please God."

He stopped, then added,—

"I am a priest; all the same, I believe in God."

"God has gone out of fashion."

"I believe in God," said Cimourdain, unmoved.

With a nod of the head, Robespierre gloomily assented,

Cimourdain continued,—

"To whom shall I be sent as a delegate?"

"The commandant of the reconnoitring column sent against Lantenac. Only, I warn you, he is a noble."

Danton exclaimed,—

"There is another thing that I care very little about.

A noble? Well, what of it? It is the same with nobles as with priests. If they are good, they are excellent. Nobility is a prejudice, but one must not have it more in one sense than in another, not more for than against it. Robespierre, isn't Saint-Just a noble? Florelle de Saint-Just. Parbleu! Anacharsis Cloots is a baron. Our friend, Charles Hesse, who never misses a meeting of the Cordeliers, is a prince, and brother of the reigning landgrave of Hesse-Rothenburg. Montaut, Marat's intimate friend, is Marquis de Montaut. In the Revolutionary tribunal, there is a member who is a priest, Vilate, and a member who is a noble, Leroy, Marquis de Montflabert. Both are trustworthy."

"And you forget," added Robespierre, "the head of the Revolutionary jury,—"

"Antonelle?"

"Who is the Marquis Antonelle," said Robespierre.

Danton added,—

"Dampierre was a nobleman, who has just given his life before Condé, for the Republic; and Beaurepaire, who blew his brains out rather than open the gates of Verdun to the Prussians, was a nobleman."

"Which does not alter the fact," growled Marat, "that the day Condorcet exclaimed, 'The Gracchi were noblemen!' Danton cried out to him: 'All noblemen are traitors, beginning with Mirabeau, and ending with yourself!'"

Cimourdain's solemn voice now rose.

"Citizen Danton, Citizen Robespierre, perhaps you are right in your confidence, but the people are distrustful, and they are not wrong in their distrust. When a priest is charged to look after a nobleman, the responsibility is increased twofold, and the priest must be inflexible."

"Certainly," said Robespierre.

Cimourdain added: "And inexorable."

Robespierre continued,—

"Well said, Citizen Cimourdain. You will have to deal with a young man. You will have the advantage over him, being twice his age. You will have to direct him, but you must manage him. It seems that he has military talents; all accounts are agreed on that point. He belongs to a corps of the army of the Rhine, which has been detached to go to Vendée. He has reached the frontier, where he is showing admirable intelligence and bravery. He is leading the reconnoitring column in a superior manner. For two weeks, he has held the old Marquis de Lantenac in check. He restrains him and drives him before him. He will end by driving him back to the sea, and overthrowing him there. Lantenac has the art of an old general, and he has the audacity of a young captain. This young man already has enemies, and some are envious of him. The Adjutant-General, Léchelle, is jealous of him."

"This Léchelle," interrupted Danton, "wants to be general in chief! he has nothing to recommend him, but a pun: a ladder is needed to mount upon a wagon. Nevertheless, Charette is beating him."

"And he doesn't want any one but himself to beat Lantenac," continued Robespierre. "The misfortune of the Vendéan war lies in such rivalries as these. Heroes badly commanded, that is what our soldiers are. A mere captain of hussars, Chérin, enters Saumur with a trumpet playing, 'Ca ira'; he takes Saumur, and might have gone on and taken Cholet, but he had no orders, and stopped. All the commands of la Vendée ought to be changed. The body-guards are scattered, the forces dispersed; a scattered army is a paralyzed army; it is a rock ground to powder. In the camp at Paramé there are nothing but tents. Between Tréguier and Dinan there are a hundred little useless posts which might be made into a division to cover the whole coast. Léchelle, supported by Parrein, is leaving the northern coast unguarded, under pretext of protecting the southern coast, and in this way opening France to the English. To raise half a million peasants, and a descent from England on France, is Lantenac's design. The young commander of the reconnoitring column is pushing on this Lantenac at the point of the sword, and defeating him without Léchelle's permission; but Léchelle is his general; so Léchelle complains of him. Opinions concerning this young man are divided. Léchelle wants to have him shot. Prieur de la Marne wants to make him adjutant-general."

"This young man," said Cimourdain, "has great qualities, so it seems to me."

"But he has one fault."

It was Marat who interrupted.

"What is it?" asked Cimourdain.

"Clemency," said Marat.

And Marat added,—

"He is decided in battle and soft-hearted afterwards. That makes him indulgent, that makes him pardon; he merciful, protect the religieuses and nuns, save the wives and the daughters of the aristocracy, release prisoners, set priests at liberty."

"A serious fault," murmured Cimourdain.

"A crime," said Marat.

"Sometimes," said Danton.

"Often," said Robespierre.

"Almost always," added Marat.

"When dealing with the enemies of one's own country, always," said Cimourdain.

Marat turned toward Cimourdain.

"And what would you do with a Republican general who gave a Royalist general his liberty?"

"I should be of Léchelle's opinion, I should have him shot."

"Or guillotined," said Marat.

"Either," said Cimourdain.

Danton began to laugh.

"I should like one as well as the other."

"You are sure to have one or the other," growled Marat.

And his eyes, leaving Danton, turned to Cimourdain.

"So, Citizen Cimourdain, if a Republican general flinches, you would have his head cut off?"

"Within twenty-four hours."

"Well," replied Marat, "I am of Robespierre's opinion; we must send Citzen Cimourdain as a delegate of the Committee of Public Welfare to the commandant of the reconnoitring column of the coast army. What is the name of this commandant?"

Robespierre replied,—

"He is a *ci-devant*, a noble."

And he began to turn over the papers.

"Let us send the priest to guard the noble," said Danton,

"I distrust a priest alone; I distrust a noble alone; when they are together, I am not afraid of them; one will watch over the other, and they will do."

The expression of indignation peculiar to Cimourdain's eyebrows deepened; but finding the observation just at bottom, he began to speak in his harsh voice, without looking toward Danton.

"If the Republican commandant who is entrusted to my care makes a false step, the penalty will be death."

Robespierre, with his eyes still on the papers, said,—

"Here is the name. Citizen Cimourdain, the commandant over whom you will have full power is a former viscount; his name is Gauvain."

Cimourdain grew pale.

"Gauvain!" he exclaimed.

Marat noticed Cimourdain's pale face.

"The Viscount Gauvain!" repeated Cimourdain.

"Yes," said Robespierre.

"Well?" said Marat, fixing his eye on Cimourdain.

There was a pause. Then Marat said,—

"Citzen Cimourdain, on the conditions named by yourself, do you accept the mission of delegate to the commandant, Gauvain? Is it agreed?"

"Agreed," said Cimourdain.

He grew paler and paler.

Robespierre took the pen near him, wrote in his slow and formal handwriting four lines on the sheet of paper with the heading, "Committee of Public Welfare," signed it, and passed the sheet and the pen to Danton; Danton signed it; and then Marat, who did not take his eyes from Cimourdain's pale face, signed it after Danton."

Robespierre took the sheet of paper again, dated it, and gave it to Cimourdain, who read,—

"Year II. of the Republic.

"Full power is granted to Citizen Cimourdain, delegated commissioner from the Committee of Public Welfare to Citizen Gauvain, commandant of the reconnoitring column of the coast army.

Robespierre.—Danton.—Marat."

And below these signatures,—

"Twenty-eighth of June, 1793."

The Revolutionary Calendar, called the Civil Calendar, was not in existence legally at this period, and was not adopted by the Convention, according to the proposition of Romme, till the fifth of October, 1793.

Marat watched Cimourdain while he read the paper.

Marat said in an undertone, as if speaking to himself:

"All that will have to be specified by a decree of the Convention, or by a special resolution of the Committee of Public Welfare. There is something yet to be done."

"Citizen Cimourdain," asked Robespierre, "where do you live?"

"Court of Commerce."

"Wait; so do I," said Danton; "you are my neighbor."

Robespierre added,—

"There is not a moment to be lost. To-morrow, you will receive your commission in due form, signed by all the members of the Committee of Public Welfare. This is a confirmation of the commission which will accredit you especially with the active representatives Phillieaux, Prieur de la Marne, Lecointre, Alquier, and others. We know who you are. Your powers are unlimited. You can make Gauvain general or send him to the scaffold. You will have your commission to-morrow at three o'clock. When will you start?"

"At four o'clock," said Cimourdain.

And they separated.

On his way home, Marat informed Simonne Evrard that he should go to the Convention the following day.

BOOK THIRD.—THE CONVENTION.

CHAPTER I.

THE CONVENTION.

We are approaching the mountain top.
Here is the Convention.
The attention must be fixed on this summit.
Never did anything higher appear on man's horizon.
There is Mt. Himalaya, and there is the Convention.
The Convention is perhaps the culminating point in history.

During the lifetime of the Convention, for it lived as an assembly, people did not realize its significance. Its grandeur was exactly what escaped the contemporaries; they were too much frightened to be dazzled. There is a sacred horror about everything grand. It is easy to admire mediocrity and hills; but whatever is too lofty, a genius as well as a mountain, an assembly as well as a masterpiece, seen too near, is appalling. Every summit seems an exaggeration. Climbing wearies. The steepnesses take away one's breath; we slip on the slopes, we are hurt by the sharp points which are its beauty; the foaming torrents betray the precipices, clouds hide the mountain tops; mounting is full of terror, as well as a fall. Hence, there is more dismay than admiration. People have a strange feeling of aversion to anything grand. They see abysses, they do not see sublimity; they see the monster, they do not see the prodigy. Thus the Convention was judged at first. The Convention was measured by the shortsighted, when it was made to be contemplated by eagles.

To-day it is in perspective, and it stands out against the deep sky in a serene and tragic distance—the immense profile of the Revolution.

II.

The fourteenth of July gave it birth.
The tenth of August thundered it forth.
The twenty-first of September founded it.

The twenty-first of September, the equinox, the equilibrium, Libra. The balance. In accordance with Romme's suggestion, "It was under this sign of Equality and Justice that the Republic was proclaimed. A constellation announced its coming.

The Convention is the first avatar of the people. With the Convention, the great new page is turned, and the future of to-day begins.

Every idea must have a visible covering; every principle must have a dwelling-place; a church is God within four walls; every dogma must have a temple. When the Convention came into existence, there was a first problem to be solved; where to locate the Convention.

First, the Ménage was taken, then the Tuileries. A frame-work was raised, with scenery, a great camaieu, painted by David, seats systematically arranged, a square tribune, parallel pilasters, with socles like blocks, and long rectilinear stems, rectangular alveoles, where the multitude crowded, and which were called public tribunes; a Roman velarium, Greek draperies, and within these right angles and these straight lines the Convention was established; in this geometrical space the tempest was confined. On the tribune, the red cap was painted in gray. The Royalists began by laughing at this gray red cap, this artificial hall, this monument of pasteboard, this sanctuary of papier-maché, this pantheon of mud and spittle. How quickly all that was to disappear! The columns were of barrel staves, the arches of batten, the bas-reliefs of mastic, the entablatures were of deal boards; the statues were made of plaster, the marbles were paint, the walls were linen; and out of this temporary structure, France has made an everlasting institution.

When the Convention held its sessions in the hall of the Ménage, the walls were completed, covered with notices which had flooded Paris at the time of the return from Varennes. One read thus: "The king returns; whoever cheers him will be beaten, whoever insults him will be hanged." Another, thus: "Peace. Hats on the head. He is going to pass before his judges." Another, thus: "The king has aimed at the nation. He has hung fire; it is the nation's turn to shoot now." Another: "Law! Law!" It was within these walls that the Convention judged Louis XVI.

At the Tuilleries, where the Convention began to sit on the tenth of May, 1793, and which was called the National Palace, the place of assembly occupied the entire space between the Pavilion de l'Horloge, called Pavilion of Unity, and the Pavilion Marsan, called Pavilion of Liberty. The Pavilion de Flore was called the Pavilion of Equality. The assembly hall was reached by the grand staircase of Jean Bullant. Under the second story occupied by the assembly, the entire ground floor of the palace was a sort of long guardroom, filled with bundles and camp beds of the armed troops which watched over the Convention. The assembly had a guard of honor, called the "grenadiers of the Convention."

A tricolored ribbon separated the castle, where the assembly was held, from the garden where the people came and went.

III.

Let us finish describing the hall where the sessions were held. Everything about that terrible place is full of interest.

What struck one's notice on entering was a lofty statue of Liberty, standing between two large windows.

Forty-two metres long, ten metres wide, eleven metres high, these were the dimensions of what had once been the theatre of the king, and which was to be the theatre of the Revolution. The elegant, magnificent hall built by Vigarani for the courtiers disappeared beneath the rough timber-work which in '93 supported the weight of the people. This framework on which the public tribunes were erected, had for its only point of support, a single post, a detail worthy of note. This post was in one single piece, and was ten metres in length. Few caryatides have accomplished as much as this post; for years it held up the weight of the Revolution. It bore cheering, enthusiasm, insults, noise, tumult, the immense chaos of anger, riot. It never gave way. After the Convention, it saw the Conseil des Anciens. The eighteenth Brumaire relieved it.

Percier then replaced the wooden pillar with columns of marble, which were less durable.

The ideal of architecture is sometimes strange; the architect of the Rue de Rivoli had the trajectory of a cannon-ball for his ideal, the architect of Carlsruhe had a fan for his ideal; a gigantic bureau drawer seems to have been the ideal of the architect who planned the hall where the Convention first sat the tenth of May, 1793; it was long, high, and flat. On one of the long sides of the parallelogram was a wide semicircle; this was the amphitheatre, with seats for the representatives, but without tables or desk; Garan-Coulon, who wrote much, wrote on his knee; opposite the seats was the tribune; in front of the tribune, a bust of Lepelletier-Saint-Fargeau; behind the tribune, the president's arm-chair.

The head of the bust came a little above the edge of the tribune, which caused its removal later on.

The amphitheatre was composed of nineteen semi-circular benches, rising one behind another; portions of the benches, prolonged the amphitheatre into the two corners.

Below, in the horseshoe at the foot of the tribune, stood the ushers.

On one side of the tribune, in a black wooden frame, was fastened to the wall a placard nine feet high, bearing on two pages, separated by a sort of sceptre, the declaration of the rights of man; on the other side was an empty space which was filled later by a similar frame containing the constitution of the year II., the two pages of which were separated by a sword. Above the tribune, above the head of the orator, from a deep box divided into two compartments, filled with people, fluttered three great tricolored flags resting almost horizontally on an altar bearing this word, "LAW." Behind this altar rose, like the sentinel of free speech, an enormous Roman fasces, as tall as a column. Colossal statues straight against the wall, faced the representatives. The president had Lycurgus on his right and Solon on his left, above the Mountain was Plato.

The pedestals of these statues were simple dies, placed on a long, projecting cornice extending all around the hall and separating the people from the assembly. The spectators leaned their elbows on this cornice.

The black wooden frame containing the rights of man, reached to the cornice and cut into the design of the entablature, breaking the straight line; this caused Chabot to complain, "It is ugly," he said to Vadier.

The heads of the statues were crowned alternately with wreaths of oak and laurel.

A green drapery, painted with similar crowns in a darker shade of green, fell in deep, straight folds from the cornice of the periphery, and entirely covered the wall of the lower part of the hall occupied by the assembly. Above this drapery, the wall was white and cold. In this wall, as if hollowed out with a punch, with neither moulding nor foliage were two rows of public tribunes, square at the base and round at the top; according to the rule, for Vitruvius was not dethroned; the archivaults were superimposed on the architraves. There were ten tribunes on each of the long sides of the hall, and at each of the two ends two huge boxes; in all, twenty-four. Into these the multitudes flocked.

The spectators in the lower row of tribunes overflowed on all the gunnels, and formed in groups on all the reliefs of the architecture. A long iron car, securely fastened breast high, served as a railing for the upper tribunes and protected the spectators from the crowding of the throngs coming up the staircase. Once, however, a man was pushed over into the assembly; he fell a little on Massieu, bishop of Beauvais, and so was not killed, and said: "Well! so a bishop is really good for something!"

The hall of the Convention could hold two thousand people: on days of insurrection, three thousand.

The convention had two sessions, one in the daytime, one in the evening.

The back of the president's chair was round, decorated with gilt nails. His table rested on four winged monsters with a single foot, that seemed to have come out of the Apocalypse to be present at the Revolution. They looked as if they had been taken out of Ezekiel's chariot to draw Samson's tumbrel.

On the president's table there was a great bell, almost as large as a church bell, a large copper inkstand, and a folio volume bound in parchment, which contained the official reports.

Decapitated heads, borne on the end of a pike, dripped blood on this table.

The tribune was reached by means of nine steps. These steps were high, steep, and difficult to mount; Gensonné stumbled one day as he was ascending them. "They are scaffold stairs!" he said. "Serve your apprenticeship," exclaimed Carrier.

In the corners of the hall, where the wall semed too bare, the architect had placed fasces for ornamentation, with the axe outside.

On the right and on the left of the tribune, there were pedestals bearing two candelabra twelve feet high, each with four pairs of lamps. Each public box had similar candelabra. On the pedestals of these candelabra there were carved circles, which the people called "guillotine collars."

The seats of the Assembly rose almost to the cornice of the tribunes; the representatives and the people could converse together.

The exits of the tribunes opened into a labyrinth of corridors, usually filled with a furious din.

The convention crowded the palace and overflowed into the neighboring mansions. Hôtel de Longueville and Hôtel de Coigny. Hôtel de Coigny was where the royal furniture was removed after the tenth of August, if a letter of Lord Bradford's can be believed. It took two months to dismantle the Tuileries.

The commitee had their quarters in the vicinity of the hall; the Committees of Legislature, Agriculture, and Commerce were in the Pavilion Egalité; those of the Marine, Colonies, Finance, Assignats and Public Welfare in the Pavilion Liberté. The committee of War was in the Pavilion Unité.

The Committee of General Safety communicated directly with the Committee of Public Welfare by means of a dark passage lighted day and night by a reflector, where the spies of every party came and went. People never spoke there.

The bar of the Convention was several times removed. Usually, it was at the president's right hand.

At the ends of the hall, the vertical partitions which closed the concentric semicircles of the aniphitentre, left between them and the wall two narrow, deep lobbies from which opened two dark square doors. These were means of entrance and exit.

The representatives entered the hall directly by a door opening from the Terrace des Feuillants.

This hall, dimly lighted in the daytime by small windows, poorly lighted in the evening with ghastly lamps, had a strange nocturnal gloom about it. This dim illumination, together with the evening shades, made the sessions by lamplight dismal. The people could not see each other; from one end of the hall to the other, from right to left, groups of indistinct faces insulted each other. People met without recognizing one another. One day as Laignelot was hurrying to the tribune he ran against some one in the inclined passage.

"Beg pardon, Robespierre," he said. "Whom do you take me for?" replied a harsh voice. "Beg pardon, Marat," said Laignelot.

Two of the lower tribunes, to the right and left of the president were reserved, for strange to say, there were privileged spectators at the Convention. These were the only tribunes having any drapery. In the centre of the architrave this drapery was caught up by two gold tassels. The tribunes for the people were bare.

The effect of all this was intense, savage, regular. Savage correctness; this is a suggestion of the whole Revolution. The hall of the Convention offers the most complete specimen of what artists have since called "architecture Messidor"; it was massive and slender. The builders of that period took symmetry for beauty. The last word of the Renaissance had been spoken under Louis XV., and a reaction followed. The noble in art had been carried to insipidity, and purity to monotony. There is such a thing as prudery in architecture. After the dazzling orgies in form and color of the eighteenth century, art was put on a diet, and allowed nothing but the straight line. This sort of progress ended in ugliness. Art reduced to a skeleton, was the result. This was the advantage of this kind of wisdom and abstinence; the style was so sober that it became lean.

Setting aside all political feeling, and looking at it from an architectural point of view, there was something about this hall that made one shiver. One recalled confusedly, the former theatre, the garlanded boxes, its blue and crimson ceiling, its facetted chandeliers, its girandoles, with diamond reflections, its dove-colored hangings, its profusion of cupids and nymphs on the curtains and draperies, the whole royal and erotic idyl painted, carved and gilded, which had filled this stern place with its smile, and one saw all about him these hard right angles, cold and sharp as steel; it was something like Boucher guillotined by David.

IV.

Whoever saw the Assembly never gave a second thought to the hall. Whoever saw the drama gave no thought to the theatre. Nothing was more deformed, nor more sublime. A pile of heroes, a herd of cowards. Wild beasts on a mountain, reptiles in a marsh. There swarmed, jostled, challenged, threatened, fought and lived, all those combatants who are to-day but phantoms.

A gathering of Titans.

On the right, the Gironde,—a legion of thinkers; on the left the mountain,—a group of athletes. On one side, Buissot, who received the keys of the Bastille; Barbaroux, whom the Marseilles troops obeyed; Kervélégan, who had the battalion of Brest garrisoned in the Faubourg Saint Marceau, under his hand; Gersonné, who established the supremacy of representatives over generals; the fatal Gaudet, to whom the queen showed the sleeping dauphin one night at the Tuileries, Gaudet kissed the child's forehead and caused the father to lose his head; Salles, the fanciful denouncer of the intimacies between the Mountain and Austria; Sillery, the humpback of the Right, as Couthon was the cripple of the Left. Lause-Duperret, who when called a "rascal" by a journalist, invited him to dine with him, saying: "I know that rascal means simply a man who does not think as we do"; Rabaut-Saint-Etienne, who commenced his Almanac of 1790 with these words: "The revolution is ended"; Quinette, one of those who overthrew Louis XVI.; the Jansenist Camus, who framed the evil constitution of the clergy, believed in the miracles of the deacon Pâris, and knelt down every night before a Christ seven feet high, nailed against the wall of his room; Fauchet, a priest who, with Camille Desmoulins, caused the fourteenth of July; Isnarn, who committed the crime of saying "Paris will be destroyed," at the same moment that Brunswick said: "Paris will be burned"; Jacob Dupont, the first one to exclaim "I am an Atheist," and to whom Robespierre replied: "Atheism is aristocratic"; Lanjuinais, a stern, wise, and brave Breton; Ducos, the Euryalus of Boyer-Fonfréde; Rebecqui, the pylades of Barbaroux, Rebecqui gave in his resignation because Robespierre had not been guillotined; Richaud, who fought the permanency of the Sections; Lasource, who uttered this murderous apophthegm: "Woe to thankful nations!" and who afterwards at the foot of the scaffold, was to contradict himself by hurling this proud speech at those of the Mountain: "We die because the people are asleep, and you will die because the people will awaken"; Biroteau, who had the abolition of inviolability decreed, and was thus unconsciously the forger of the chopping-knife, and erected the scaffold for himself; Charles Villatte, who shielded his conscience behind this protestation: "I do not wish to vote under the knife"; Louvet, the author of *Faublas*, who was to end as a bookseller in the Palais Royal with Lodoïska behind the counter; Mercier, the author of the "Tableau de Paris," who exclaimed: "Every king felt for the nape of his neck the twenty-first of January"; Marec, whose anxiety was the faction of ancient boundaries; the journalist Carra, who said to the executioner at the foot of the scaffold: "It annoys me to die. I should have liked to see what follows"; Vigée, who had the title of grenadier in the second battalion of Mayence-et-Loire, who, when threatened by the public tribunes, cried out: "I ask that at the first murmur of the public tribunes, we withdraw and march to Versailles, sword in hand!" Buzot, destined to die of hunger; Valazé, victim of his own dagger; Condorcet, who was to die at Bourg-la-Reine, changed to Bourg-Egalité, denounced by the Horace he carried in his pocket; Pétion, whose fate was to be worshipped by the multitude in 1792, and devoured by the wolves in 1794; twenty others beside, Pontécoulant. Marboz, Lidon, Saint-Martin, Dussaulx, the translator of "Juvenal," who took part in the campaign of Hanover; Boileau, Bertrand, Lesterp-Beauvais, Lesage, Gomaire, Gardien, Mainvielle, Duplantier, Lacaze, Antiboul, and at their head a Barnave called Vergniaud.

On the other side, Antoine-Louise-Léon Florelle de Saint-Just, pale, with a low forehead, regular profile, mysterious eye, exceedingly melancholy, twenty-three years of age; Merlin de Thionville, whom the Germans called Feuer-Teufel, "fire devil"; Merlin de Douai, the guilty author of the "Law of the Suspected"; Soubrany, whom the people of Paris, on the first Prairial asked to have for a general; the former priest Lebon, holding a sword in his hand which had once scattered holy water; Billaud-Varennes, who foresaw the magistracy of the future, no judges but arbiters; Fabre d'Eglantine who made a charming discovery, the Republican calendar, just as Rouget de Lisle had a sublime inspiration, the Marseillaise, and neither were guilty of a second offence; the attorney of the Commune, who said: "A dead king is not a man less"; Grougon, who entered Tripstadt, Newstadt, and Spire, and saw the Prussian army flee; Lacroix, a lawyer turned general, made chevalier de Saint-Louis six days before the tenth of August; Fréron Thersite, son of Fréron-Zoile; Ruth the inexorable investigator of the iron press, destined for a great Republican suicide:—he was to kill himself the day the Republic died; Fouché, with the soul of a demon, and the face of a corpse; Camboulas, the friend of Father Duchesne, who said to Guillotin: "You belong to the club of the Feuillants, but your daughter belongs to the club of the Jacobins"; Jagot, who gave this savage reply to those complaining about the nakedness of the prisoner: " A prison is a garment of stone"; "Javogues, the terrible spoiler of the tombs of Saint-Denis; Osselin, the proscriber, who hid in his house Madame Charry, one of the proscribed; Bentabolle, who, when he presided, made signs to the tribunes to cheer or to hoot; the journalist Robert, the husband of Mademoiselle Kéralio, who wrote:

"Neither Robespierre nor Marat come to my house; Robespierre may come whenever he wishes; Marat never"; Garan-Coulon, who had proudly demanded, when Spain interposed in the trial of Louis XVI., that the Assembly should not condescend to read a letter from a king in behalf of a king; Grégoire at first a worthy bishop of the Primitive Church, but who afterwards under the Empire obliterated the Republican Grégoire with Count Grégoire; Amar, who said,—

"The whole earth condemns Louis XVI. To whom then shall we appeal for judgment? To the planets?"

Rouyer, who was opposed to having the cannon fired from the Pont-Neuf the twenty-first of January, saying,—

"A king's head will not make any more noise in falling than the head of any other man;" Chénier, André's brother; Vadier, one of those who laid a pistol on the tribune; Tanis, who said to Momoro,—

"I want Marat and Robespierre to embrace each other at my table in my house."

"Where do you live?"

"At Charenton."

"I should have been surprised if it were anywhere else," said Momoro. Legendre, who was the butcher of the French Revolution, as Pride was the butcher of the Revolution of England.

"Come, let me knock you down!" he exclaimed to Lanjuinais. And Lanjuinais replied.—

"First let it be decreed that I am an ox." Collot d'Herbois, that melancholy comedian, wearing over his face the ancient mask with two mouths which said yes and no, approving with one what it blamed with the other, branding Carrier at Nantes and defying Châlier at Lyons, sending Robespierre to the scaffold, and Marat to the Pantheon; Génissieux who demanded the penalty of death for those who wore the medallion, "*Louis XVI. martyrisé*; Léonard Bourdon, the schoolmaster, who offered his house to the old man of Mont Jura; Topsent, the sailor; Goupilleau, the lawyer; Laurent Lecointre, a merchant; Duhem, a physician; Sergent, the sculptor; David, the painter; Joseph Egalité, a prince.

Besides these, Lecointe Puiraveau, who asked to have Marat decreed to be "in a state of lunacy;" Robert Lindet, the disquieting creator of that devil-fish, whose head was the Committee of General Safety, and which covered France with twenty-one thousand arms called the Revolutionary Committees; Lebœuf, about whom Girey-Dupré, in his "Christmas of False Patriots" wrote this verse,—

"Lebœuf saw Legendre and bellowed."

Thomas Paine, an American, and merciful; Anacharsis Cloots, a German baron, a millionaire, atheist, Hébertist, candid; the upright Lebas, friend of the Duplays; Rovère, one of those rare men who are wicked for wickedness' sake, because art for art's sake exists more than people are aware of; Charlier who wished to have the aristocrats formally addressed; Tallien, an elegist and cruel, who will cause the ninth Thermidor from love; Cambacérès, an attorney who will be prince; Carrier, an attorney who will be a tiger; Laplanche, who exclaimed one day: "I demand priority for the alarm-gun;" Thuriot, who wanted to have the jury of the Revolutionary Tribunal vote by acclamation; Bourdon de l'Oise, who challenged Chambon, denounced Paine, and was denounced by Hébert; Fayau who proposed "to send an incendiary army" to la Vendée; Tavaux, who came near being a mediator between la Gironde and the Mountain; Venier, who asked to have the Girondist Chiefs and the chiefs of the Mountain serve as common soldiers; Rewbell, who shut himself up in Mayence; Bourbotte, who had his horse killed under him, at the taking of Saumur; Guimberteau, who directed the army of the coast of Cherbourg; Jard-Panvilliers, who directed the army of the coast of Rochelle; Lecarpentier, who directed the squadron of Cancale; Roberjot, for whom the ambush of Rastad was waiting; Prieur de la Marne, who in camp wore his old counter-epaulet of major; Levasseurde la Sarthe, who with a word decided Surrent, commandant of the battalion of Saint-Amand, to commit suicide; Reverchon, Maure, Bernard de Saintes, Charles Richard, Lequinio, and at the head of this group a Mirabeau called Danton.

Outside these two camps, and respected by both, rose a single man, Robespierre.

V.

Below crouched Terror, which can be noble, and Fear which is base. Beneath passion, beneath heroism, beneath devotion, beneath rage, was the melancholy crowd of the anonymous. The dregs of the Assembly were called la Plaine. It contained everything drifting; men who doubted, who hesitated, who recoiled, who procrastinated, those who were spies, each fearing somebody. The Mountain was the elite; la Plaine was the common crowd. La Plaine was summed up and condensed in Sieyés.

Sieyés was a deep man who had grown shallow. He had stopped at the Third-Estate and had never been able to rise to the height of the people. Certain minds are so constituted that they never pass beyond mediocrity. Sieyés called Robespierre a tiger, and he called Sieyés a mole. This metaphysician had arrived not at wisdom, but at prudence. He was the courtier, not the servitor of the Revolution. He took a shovel and went to work with the people in the Champ-de-Mars, harnessed to the same wagon with Alexandre de Beauharnais. He advised energy, but never made use of it. He said to the Girondists: "Put the cannon on your side." There are thinkers who are fighters, such as Condorcet with Vergniaud, or Camille Desmoulins with Danton. There are thinkers who are anxious to live; such were with Sieyés.

The most generous vats have their dregs. Below even the Plaine there was the Marais. Hideous stagnation disclosing the transparencies of egotism. There the fearful trembled in dumb expectation. The infamous without shame; latent anger; revolt under servitude. They were cynically frightened; they had all the courage of cowardice; they preferred la Gironde and chose the Mountain; the final result depended on them; they poured out on the successful side; they delivered Louis XVI. to Vergniaud, Vergniaud to Danton, Danton to Robespierre, Robespierre to Tallien. They pilloried Marat while he was alive, and deified Marat after he was dead. They upheld everything till the day when they overthrew everything. Their instinct was to give a decisive push to everything that tottered. In their eyes, as they had been brought into service on condition that there should be solidity, to waver was to betray them. They were numbers, they were force, they were fear. Hence the daring of baseness.

They were the cause of May 31st, the eleventh Germinal, the ninth Thermidor; tragedies knotted by giants and untied by dwarfs.
VI.

With these men full of passion, were mingled men full of dreams. The Utopia was there in all its forms; in its warlike form, which admitted the scaffold, and in its innocent form which abolished capital punishment; a spectre when facing thrones, an angel when facing the people. Opposed to the fighting minds were the brooding minds. The first had war in their heads; the others, peace; one brain, Carnot, gave birth to fourteen armies; another brain, Jean Derby, meditated an universal democratic confederation. In the midst of this furious eloquence, among these voices howling and raging, there were fecund silences. Lakanal was silent, and thought out public national education; Lanthenas was silent, and created the primary schools; Revellière-Lepaux was silent, and dreamed of elevating philosophy to the dignity of religion. Others busied themselves with questions of detail, less pretentious and more practical. Guyton-Morveaux studied the salubrity of hospitals; Maire, the abolition of actual servitude; Jean-Bon-Saint-André, the suppression of arrest and imprisonment for debt; Romme, the proposition of Chappe; Duboë, the ordering of the archives; Coren-Fustier, the creation of the cabinet of Anatomy and the Museum of Natural History; Guyomard, river navigation and the damming of the Escaut.

Art had its monomaniacs; January 21st, while the head of the monarchy was falling in the place de la Revolution, Bézard, representative from l'Oise, went to see a picture by Rubens, found in a garret in Rue Saint-Lazare. Artists, orators, prophets, great men like Danton, petty men like Cloots, gladiators and philosophers, all were striving for the same end,—progress. Nothing disconcerted them. The grandeur of the Convention lay in finding out how much reality there was in what men called impossible. At one extreme, Robespierre had his eye fixed on Law; at the other extreme, Condorcet had his eye fixed on Duty.

Condorcet was a dreamer and a clear-sighted man; Robespierre was a man of executive ability; and sometimes in the final crises of worn-out societies, execution means extermination. Revolutions have two slopes, ascent and descent, and bear, terraced on these slopes, all the seasons from ice to flowers. Each zone of these slopes produces men suited to its climate, from those who live in the sun to those who live in lightning.

VII.

People showed each other the corner of the passage on the left where Robespierre whispered in the ear of Garat, Clavière's friend, this terrible epigram: "Clavière has conspired wherever he has respired." In this same nook, convenient for asides and whispered anger, Fabre and d'Eglantine had quarrelled with Romme, and reproached him for disfiguring his calendar by changing Fervidor to Thermidor.

People pointed out the corner where the seven representatives of the Haute-Garonne sat, elbow to elbow; the first called to pronounce their verdict on Louis XVI., they replied one after another: Mailhe, "death"; Delmas, "death"; Projean, "death"; Calés, "death"; Ayral, "death"; Julien, "death"; Dasaby, "death."

An eternal reverberation which has filled all history, and which, since human justice exists, has always given the echo of the grave to the wall of the tribunal. People pointed out, among this riotous crowd of faces, all those men who had been the cause of the hubbub of tragic votes:—Paganel, who said,—

"Death. A king is of no use until he is dead." Millaud, who said,—

"If death did not exist to-day, it would be necessary to invent it." The old Raffron du Trouillet, who said,—

"Death, come quickly!" Goupilleau, who exclaimed,—

"The scaffold immediately. Slowness aggravates death." Sieyés, who exclaimed with funereal conciseness,—

"Death." Thuriot, who rejected the appeal to the people proposed by Buzot,—

"What! primary assemblies! what! forty-four thousand tribunals! Trial without end. The head of Louis XVI. would have time to turn white before it would fall." Augustin-Bon Robespierre, who exclaimed after his brother,—

"I know nothing of a humanity which slaughters nations, and pardons despots; to ask a reprieve is to substitute an appeal to tyrants for the appeal to the people. Foussedoire, Bernardin de Saint-Pierre's substitute, who said,—

"I have a horror of shedding human blood, but the blood of a king is not the blood of a man. Death." Jean-Bon-Saint-André, who said,—

"No free people, unless the tyrant dies." Lavicomterie, who proclaimed this formula,—

"While the tyrant breathes, liberty suffocates. Death." Chateauneuf-Randon, who cried,—

"The death of Louis the Last." Guyardin, who gave utterance to this wish,—

"Let the 'Barrière-Renversée' be executed (the Barrière-Renversée, or overthrown barrier, was the Barrière du Trône). Tellier, who said,—

"Let a cannon of the size of Louis XVL's head be forged, to use against the enemy."

And the indulgents: Gentil, who said,—

"I vote for imprisonment. To make a Charles I. is to make a Cromwell." Bancal, who said,—

"Exile. I want to see the first king of the universe condemned to learn a trade in order to earn his living." Albouys, who said,—

"Banishment. Let this living spectre go to wander about thrones." Zangiacomi, who said,—

"Let us keep Capet alive for a scarecrow." Chaillon, who said,—

"Let him live, I would not put to death one whom Rome would canonize."

While these sentences were falling from these stern lips, and one after another became historical, in the tribunes, women wearing low-necked dresses and jewels, holding the list, counted the voices and pricked each vote with a pin.

Wherever tragedy enters in, horror and pity remain.

To see the Convention during any period of its reign was to see the judgment of the last Capet over again; the legend of January 21st seemed mingled with all its proceedings; the dreadful assembly was full of those fatal breaths, which had blown over the old torch of monarchy lighted for eighteen centuries, and had put it out; the decisive trial for all kings in one king was like the crises in the great war on the Past; at whatever session of the Convention one was present, the shadow cast by the scaffold of Louis XVI. seemed to brood over it; the spectators related to each other the resignation of Kersaint, the resignation of Roland, how Duchâtel, the deputy of the Deux-Sèvres, being ill, was brought on his bed, and, while dying, voted for the king's life, which caused Marat to laugh; people looked around for the representative, forgotten by history to-day, who, after that session of thirty-seven hours, dropped on his bench overcome with weariness and sleep, and, awakened by the usher when it was his turn to vote, opened his eyes, said "Death!" and fell asleep again.

At the time Louis XVI. was condemned to die, Robespierre had eighteen months longer to live; Danton, fifteen months; Vergniaud, nine months; Marat, five months and three weeks; Lepelletier-Saint-Fargeau, one day. Short and terrible breath from human mouths!

VIII.

The people had one window opening on the Convention, the public tribunes, and when this was insufficient they opened the door, and the street entered the Assembly.

These invasions of the multitude into the senate are one of the most extraordinary sights of history. These irruptions were usually cordial. The street-crossing fraternized with the curule-chair. But it was a terrible cordiality which the people showed one day when in three hours they took the cannon and forty thousand guns, from the Invalides.

Each instant the session was interrupted by a march of men; deputations, petitions, homages, offerings were received at the bar. The pike of honor from the Faubourg-Saint-Antoine entered, borne by women. The English offered twenty thousand shoes to our barefooted soldiers.

"Citizen Arnoux," said the *Moniteur*, "priest of Aubignan, commandant of the battalion de la Drôme, asks to march to the frontiers, and to have his parish preserved for him."

Delegates came from the sections, bringing on hand-barrows, dishes, patens, chalices, monstrances, piles of gold, silver, and silver-gilt, as offerings to the country from this multitude in rags, and asked as a recompense permission to dance the carmagnole, or Revolutionary dance, before the Convention. Chenard, Narbonne, and Vallière came singing verses in honor of the Mountain.

The Section of Mont-Blanc brought the bust of Lepelletier, and a woman placed a red cap on the head of the president, who kissed it; "the citizenesses of the Section du Mail" threw flowers to "the legislators"; "pupils of the country" came, to the sound of music, to thank the Convention for having "prepared the prosperity of the age"; the women from the Section of the Gardes-Françaises offered roses; the women from the Section of the Champs-Elysées offered a wreath of oak leaves; the women from the Section of the Temple came to the bar to take the oath "to marry none but true Republicans"; the Section of Molière presented a medal of Franklin, which was decreed to be suspended from the crown of the statue of Liberty; the Enfants-Trouvés, declared "children of the Republic" filed in, dressed in the national uniform; the young girls from the Section of Ninety-two came in long, white dresses, and the following day the *Moniteur* contained this line: "The president received a bouquet from the hands of a young beauty."

The orators saluted the crowds; sometimes they flattered them, they said: "You are infallible, you are irreproachable, you are sublime"; the people have a childish side, they like these sugarplums. Sometimes the disturbance went through the Assembly, entering in a rage and going out peacefully, as the Rhône passes through Lake Leman, looking like mud when it enters, and deep blue when it leaves it.

Sometimes it was less pacific, and Henriot had gridirons for heating the cannon balls brought to the door of the Tuileries.

IX.

At the same time the Assembly freed itself from the revolution; it produced civilization. A furnace, but a forge. In this vat where terror boiled, progress fermented. Out of this chaos of shadow and this stormy flight of clouds, shone immense rays of light parallel to the eternal laws. Rays which have remained on the horizon and forever visible in the sky of the people, and which are justice, toleration, goodness, reason, truth, love.

The Convention promulgated this great axiom: "The liberty of one citizen ends where the liberty of another citizen begins," which comprises in two lines the entire law of human society. It declared indigence sacred; it declared infirmity sacred, in the blind and the deaf-mutes who became wards of the State; maternity sacred, in the girl-mother, whom it consoled and relieved; childhood sacred, in the orphan that it caused to be adopted by the country; innocence sacred, in the acquittal of the accused, whom it indemnified. It branded the slave trade; it abolished slavery. It proclaimed civic joint responsibility. It decreed gratuitous instruction. It organized national education: by the normal school in Paris, by the central school in the principal towns, and primary schools in the Commune. It created conservatories and museums. It decreed unity of the Code, unity of weights and measures, unity of calculation by the decimal system. It established the finances of France, and caused public credit to follow the long monarchical bankruptcy. It brought the telegraph into use, gave endowed hospitals for the aged, clean hospitals to the sick, the Polytechnic school to instruction, the Bureau of Longitudes to science, the institute to the human mind.

It was cosmopolitan as well as national. Of the eleven thousand two hundred and ten decrees passed by the Convention, one third have a political aim, two thirds have a humanitarian aim. It declared morals to be the universal foundation of society, and conscience the universal foundation of law. And all this—slavery abolished, brotherhood proclaimed, humanity protected, human conscience rectified, the law of work transformed to a privilege, and from being onerous made helpful, national wealth strengthened, childhood brightened and assisted, letters and science propagated, light shed on every summit, help for all the wretched, encouragement of all principals,—all this the Convention brought about, having in its vitals that hydra, la Vendée, and on its shoulders that pile of tigers, the kings.

X.

Tremendous stage! All types; human, inhuman, and superhuman were there. Epic gathering of antagonism; Guillotine avoiding David, Bagire insulting Chabot, Gaudet jeering at Saint-Just, Vergniaud scorning Danton, Louvet attacking Robespierre, Buzot denouncing Egalité, Chambon branding Pache,—all execrating Marat.

And how many other names ought to be recorded still! Armonville, called Bonnet-Rouge, because he would only sit in a Phrygian cap, a friend of Robespierre, and wishing "after Louis XVI. to have Robespierre guillotined" from a love of equilibrium; Massieu, a colleague and double of that good Lamourette, a bishop made to leave his name to a kiss; Lehardy du Morbihan stigmatizing the priests of Brittany; Barère, the man of majorities, who presided when Louis XVI. appeared at the bar, and who was to Paméla what Louvet was to Lodoïska; the orator Daunou, who said, "Let us gain time;" Dubois Crancé, in whose ear Marat stooped to whisper; the Marquis de Chateauneuf; Laclos, Hérault de Séchelles, who drew back before Henriot, exclaiming, "Gunners, to your guns!" Julien who compared the Mountain to Thermopylæ; Gamon, who wished to have one of the public tribunes reserved solely for women; Laloy, who bestowed the honors of the session on bishop Gobel, who came to the Convention to lay down the mitre and to don the red cap; Lecomte, who exclaimed, "So the honors are for any who will lay down his priestly robes!" Féraud, whose head Boissy-d'Anglas saluted, leaving it an open question to history, whether Boissy-d'Anglas saluted the head, that is to say the victim, or the pike, that is to say the assassins; the two brothers Duprat, one a Montagnard, the other, a Girondist, who hated each other, as did the two brothers Chénier.

At this tribune were spoken those giddy words which sometimes, though unknown to him who has uttered them, produce the prophetic accent of revolutions, and in consequence of which material facts seem abruptly to assume a strange discontent and passion, as if they had taken offence at the things they had just heard; passing events seem incensed at what is spoken; catastrophes arise full of wrath, and as if exasperated by the words of men. So a voice in the mountain is enough to let loose an avalanche. A word too much may be followed by a caving in. If the word had not been spoken, it would not have happened. It seems sometimes as if events were irascible.

It was in this way, by the chance word of an orator misunderstood, that Madame Elizabeth's head was made to fall. At the Convention, intemperance of language was allowable. Threats flew and crossed each other in a discussion like firebrands in a conflagration.

Pétion. Robespierre come to the point.

Robespierre. The point is yourself, Pétion. I will come to it, and you will see it.

A Voice. Death to Marat.

Marat. The day Marat dies there will be no more Paris, and the day Paris perishes, there will be no more Republic.

Billaud-Varennes rises and says: "We are willing."—Barère interrupts him: "You speak like a king." Another day Phillipeaux said: "A member has drawn his sword on me."

Audouin. President, call the assassin to order.

The President. Attention.

Audouin. President, I call you to order myself.

The people laughed rudely.

Lecointre. The priest of Chant-de-Bout complains of Fauchet, his bishop, who forbids him to marry.

A Voice. I don't see why Fauchet, who has his mistresses, wishes to prevent others from having wives.

Another Voice. Priest take a wife!

The tribunes joined in the conversation. They addressed the Assembly familiarly. One day Representative Ruamps went up into the tribune. One of his hips was much larger than the other. One of the spectators cried out to him: "Turn that to the right side, for you have a cheek like David." Such were the liberties that people took with the Convention. Once, however, in the tumult of April 11th, 1793, the president caused a disorderly spectator in the tribune to be arrested.

One day the session had old Buonarotti for a witness. Robespierre takes the floor and speaks two hours, looking at Danton, sometimes straight in the eye, which was serious, sometimes askance, which was worse. He thundered to the end, however. He ended in an explosion of indignation, full of ominous words: "We know the intriguers, we know the corrupters and the corrupted, we know the traitors; they are in this assembly. They hear us, we see them and our eyes do not leave their faces. Let them look above their heads, and they will see the sword of the law; let them look into their consciences and they will see their infamy. Let them be on their guard." And when Robespierre had ended, Danton with his face turned to the ceiling, his eyes half-closed, one arm over the back of his seat, throws himself back and is heard to hum,—

"Cadet Roussel fait des discours

Qui ne sont pas longs quand ils sont courts."

The imprecations called for retorts.—Conspirator!—Assassin!—Villain!—Factionist!—Moderate!—They denounced each other to the bust of Brutus which was there. Apostrophes, insults, challenges. Angry looks from one side to the other, threatening fists, pistols half shown, daggers half drawn. Tremendous blazing of the tribune. Some talked as if they were leaning against the guillotine. Heads wagged, ominous and terrible. Montagnards, Giroudins, Feuillants, Modérantistes, Terroristes, Jacobins, Cordeliers, eighteen regicide priests.

All these men! A mass of smoke driven in every direction.

XI.

Minds, a prey to the wind.

But this wind a miraculous wind.

To be a member of the Convention was to be a billow of the ocean. And this was true of the greatest. The impelling force came from above. In the Convention there was a will power belonging to all and belonging to none. This will power was an idea, indomitable and boundless, which blew from the height of heaven into the darkness below. We call this the Revolution. When this idea passed, it overcame one and lifted up another; it carried away some on the top of the wave, and shipwrecked others. This idea knew where it was going, and drove the gulf before it. To impute the Revolution to men is to impute the tide to the billows.

Revolution is an action of the Unknown. Call it good action or bad, according as you aspire to the future or the past, but leave it to whatever has caused it. It seems the common work of great events and great individuals combined, but it is in reality the resultant of events. Events spend, men pay. Events dictate, men sign. July 14 is signed Caraille Desmoulins, August 10 is signed Danton, September 2 is signed Marat, September 21 is signed Grégoire, January 21 is signed Robespierre; but Desmoulins, Danton, Marat, Grégoire, and Robespierre are mere clerks. The immense and awful author of these great pages has a name, God; and a mark, Fate. Robespierre believed in God. Of course!

Revolution is one form of the inherent phenomenon which presses us on every side, and which we call necessity.

Before this mysterious complication of benefits and suffering arises the "Why?" of history.

"Because." This, the reply of one who knows nothing, is also the reply of one who knows everything.

In the presence of these climacteric catastrophes which destroy and give life to civilization, one hesitates to judge the details. To blame or praise men on account of the result, is almost like praising or blaming figures on account of the sum total. Whatever is to happen, happens; whatever is to blow, blows. The eternal serenity does not suffer from these north winds. Above Revolutions, Truth and Justice reign, as the starry heavens above the tempest.

XII.

Such was this boundless Convention; an intrenched camp of the human race attacked by all the powers of darkness at once, the night fires of a besieged army of ideas, the immense bivouac of minds on the edge of a precipice. Nothing in history can be compared to this gathering, both senate and populace, conclave and street crossing, areopagus and public square, tribunal and the accused.

The Convention always yielded to the wind; but the wind came from the mouth of the people and was the breath of God.

And to-day, after eighty years have passed, each time that the Convention comes up before the thought of a man, whatever he may be, historian or philosopher, that man stops and meditates. It is impossible not to give attention to this great procession of shades.

CHAPTER II.

MARAT IN THE LOBBY.

As he had announced to Simonne Evrard, Marat went to the Convention the next day after the meeting in Rue du Paon.

At the Convention there was present a Maratist marquis, Louis de Montaut, the one who later on presented a decimal clock, surmounted by a bust of Marat, to the Convention.

As Marat entered, Chabot had just approached Montaut.

"Ci-devant," he said.

Montaut raised his eyes.

"Why do you call me ci-devant?"

"Because that is what you are."

"I?"

"Since you were a marquis."

"Never."

"Bah!"

"My father was a soldier, my grandfather was a weaver."

"What are you singing about, Montaut?"

"My name is not Montaut?"

"What is it then?"

"I call myself Maribon."

"Indeed," said Chabot, "it is all the same to me."

And he added between his teeth,—

"He won't be a marquis."

Marat stopped in the passageway at the left and looked at Montaut and Chabot.

Every time that Marat entered, it created a commotion, but at a distance from him. All around him it was silent. Marat paid no attention to it. He scorned the "croaking in the marsh."

In the obscurity of the lower row of seats, Conpé de l'Oise, Prunelle, Villars, a bishop who later became a member of the French Academy, Boutroue, Petit, Plaichard, Bonet, Thibaudeau, Valdruche, pointed him out one to another.

"See, Marat!" "Is he ill?"

"Yes, for he is in his dressing-gown."

"In his dressing-gown?"

"By Heavens, yes!"

"He dares to do anything."

"He dares to come to the Convention in this way!"

"Since he came here one day crowned with laurels, he may as well come in his dressing-gown!"

"Face of copper, teeth of verdigris."

"His dressing-gown looks new."

"What is it made of?"

"Of rep."

"Striped."

"Look at his lapels."

"They are fur."

"Tiger skin."

"No, ermine."

"Imitation."

"And he has on stockings."

"That is strange."

"And buckles on his shoes."

"Of silver!"

"The sabots of Camboulas will not forgive him that."

On the other benches they pretended not to see Marat. The people talked of other things. Santhonax addressed Dussaulx.

"Dussaulx, you know—"

"What?"

"The ci-devant Count de Brienne?"

"Who was at la Force with the ci-devant duke de Villeroy?"

"Yes."

"I knew both of them. Well?"

"They were so much frightened that they saluted all the redcaps of all the turnkeys, and one day they refused to play a game of piquet because they were given a pack of cards with kings and queens."

"Well?"

"They were guillotined yesterday."

"Both of them?"

"Both of them."

"On the whole, how did they behave in prison?"

"Like cowards."

"And how were they on the scaffold?"

"Fearless."

And Dussaulx uttered this exclamation,—

"It is easier to die than to live."

Barère was in the midst of reading a report concerning la Vendée. Nine hundred men of Morbihan had set out with cannon to the relief of Nantes. Redon was threatened by the peasants. Paimbœuf was attacked. A fleet was cruising about Maindrin to prevent invasion. From Ingrande to Maure, the entire left bank of the Loire was bristling with Royalist batteries. Ten thousand peasants had possession of Pornic. They were crying, "Long live the English!" A letter from Santerre to the Convention, which Barère read, ended thus: "Seven thousand peasants have attacked Vannes. We repulsed them and they left four cannon in our hands—"

"And how many prisoners?" interrupted a voice.

Barère continued,—"Postscript of the letter: 'We have no prisoners, because we no longer take any.'"

Marat, always immovable, was not listening; he seemed to be absorbed by his own stern thoughts. In his hand he held a paper which he crumpled between his fingers, and if any one had unfolded this paper he could have read these lines in Momoro's handwriting and which were probably a reply to some question asked by Marat.

"Nothing can be done against the sovereign power of the delegated commissioners, above all, against the delegates of the Committee of Public Welfare. It was in vain that Génisseux said, in the session of May sixth: 'Each commissioner is more than a king,' it was of no use. They have power over life and death. Massade, at Angers; Trullard, at Saint-Amand; Nyon, near General Marcé's; Parrein, with the army of the Sables; Millier, with the army of the Niort;—each is all-powerful. The club of the Jacobins has gone so far as to name Parrein, brigadier-general. Circumstance pardons everything. A delegate from the Committee of Public Welfare holds in check a commander-in-chief."

Marat finished crumpling the paper, put it in his pocket, and went slowly towards Montaut and Chabot who were still talking and had not seen him enter.

Chabot was saying,—

"Maribon or Montaut, listen to this: I come from the Committee of Public Welfare."

"And what are they doing there?"

"They are sending a noble to watch a priest."

"Ah!"

"A noble like yourself—"

"I am not a noble," said Montaut.

"To a priest—"

"Like yourself."

"I am not a priest," said Chabot.

Both burst out laughing.

"Give the particulars of the story," continued Montaut.

"Here they are. A priest called Cimourdain has been delegated with full powers to a viscount named Gauvain; this viscount has command of the investigating column of the coast army. The question is to prevent the noble from cheating, and the priest from treason."

"That is very simple," replied Montaut; "all that is necessary is to introduce death into the matter."

"I come for that," said Marat.

They raised their heads.

"Good-morning, Marat," said Chabot, "you come but seldom to our sessions."

"My physician has ordered baths for me," replied Marat.

"You must beware of baths," replied Chabot. "Seneca lied in a bath."

Marat smiled.

"Chabot, there is no Nero here."

"You are here," said a harsh voice.

It was Danton who passed by on his way up to his seat.

Marat did not turn around.

He bent his head down between the two faces of Montaut and Chabot.

"Listen, I have come for a serious matter, one of us three must propose to-day the draft of a decree to the Convention."

"Not I," said Montaut, "they would not listen to me, I am a marquis."

"They would not listen to me," said Chabot, "I am a Capuchin."

"And they would not listen to me," said Marat, "I am Marat."

There was a silence between them.

It was not easy to question Marat when he was absorbed in thought. However Montaut ventured to ask,—

"Marat, what is the decree you wish for?"

"A decree for punishing with death any military leader who lets a rebel prisoner escape."

Cabot interrupted him.

"This decree already exists; it was voted the last of April."

"Then it is as good as a dead letter," said Marat. "All through la Vendée they are letting prisoners go, and giving them protection with impunity."

"Marat, that is because the decree is not in force."

"Chabot, it must be given new life."

"Without doubt."

"And to do that, it is necessary to speak to the Convention."

"The end will be reached," added Montaut, "if the Committee of Public Welfare have the decree posted up in all the communes of la Vendée and make two or three good examples."

"Of the great leaders," continued Chabot. "Of the generals."

Marat growled: "To be sure, that will do."

"Marat," continued Chabot, "go yourself and say so to the Committee of Public Welfare."

Marat looked at him full in the face, which was not agreeable even for Chabot.

"Chabot," he said, "the Committee of Public Welfare is at Robespierre's house; I do not go to Robespierre's house."

"I will go myself," said Montaut.

"Good," said Marat.

The following day an order from the Committee of Public Welfare was sent in every direction, commanding notices to be put up in the towns and villages of Vendée, and the strict execution of the decree of death to any one conniving in the escape of brigands and rebel prisoners.

This decree was but a first step; the Convention was to go still farther. Some months later, the eleventh Brumaire, year II. (November, 1793), with regard to Laval which had opened its doors to the Vendéan fugitives, it decreed that any town which should give asylum to the rebels should be demolished and destroyed.

In their turn the princes of Europe, in the Duke of Brunswick's manifesto, inspired by the refugees, and framed by the Marquis de Linnon, intendant of the Duke of Orleans, declared that all Frenchmen taken armed should be shot, and that if a hair fell from the king's head, Paris should be razed.

Cruelty against barbarism.

PART THIRD.— IN VENDEE.

BOOK FIRST.—LA VENDEE.

CHAPTER I.

THE FORESTS.

At that time there were seven terrible forests in Brittany. The Véndèan war was a priestly revolt. The forests were an auxiliary to this revolt. The spirits of darkness give one another aid.

The seven Black Forests of Brittany were the forest of Fougères, which bars the way between Dol and Avranches; the forest of Princé, eight leagues in circumference; the forest of Paimpont, full of ravines and brooks, almost inaccessible from the side of Baignon, but easily penetrated from Concornet, a royalist market-town; the forest of Rennes, from which was heard the tocsin of the republican parishes, always numerous near the towns (it was there that Puysaye ruined Focard); the forest of Machecoul, where the wild beast Charette had his den; the forest of la Garnache, which belonged to la Trémoille, Gauvain, and the Rohans; the forest of Broceliande, which belonged to the fairies.

A nobleman in Brittany had the title of "Seigneur of the Seven Forests." It was the Viscount de Fontenay, a Breton prince.

For the Breton prince was entirely distinct from the French prince. The Rohans were Breton princes. Garnier de Saintes, in his report to the Convention, the fifteenth Nivose, year II, thus described the Prince de Talmont: "That Capet of the brigands, Sovereign of the Marne and of Normandy."

The history of the forests of Brittany, from 1792 to 1800, would form a history by itself, and it would mingle like a legend in the great scheme of La Vendée.

History has its truth, so has legend. Legendary truth is of a different nature from historical truth. Legendary truth is invention, the result of which is reality. Still, history and legend have the same end, depicting man eternal in the man of the passing moment.

La Vendée can only be fully explained by supplementing history with legend; history is necessary for the effect as a whole, and legend for the detail.

We may say that La Vendée is worth the trouble. La Vendée is a prodigy.

That war of the Ignorant, so stupid and so splendid, abominable and magnificent, desolated France and made it proud. La Vendée is a scar which is a glory.

At certain times human society has its problems; problems which are resolved into light for the wise, and for the ignorant into obscurity, violence, and barbarity. The philosopher hesitates to bestow blame. He takes account of the trouble that is caused by the problems. The problems do not pass without casting beneath them a shadow like that of clouds.

If you would understand la Vendée, imagine this antagonism: on one side the French Revolution; on the other, the Breton peasant. Opposite these unequalled events, seriously threatening all benefits at once, outburst of angry civilization, outburst of mad progress, boundless and unintelligible improvement, place this savage, serious and strange, this man with a clear eye and long hair, living on milk and chestnuts, limited to his thatched roof, his hedge, and his ditch, distinguishing each neighboring hamlet by the sound of its bell, using water only for drink, wearing a leather jacket ornamented with arabesques in silk, uneducated and wearing embroidered garments, tattooing his clothes as his ancestors the Celts tattooed their faces, respecting a master in his executioner, speaking a dead language, which causes him to dwell in a mental tomb, goading his oxen, whetting his scythe, hoeing his grain, kneading his buckwheat bread, venerating first his plough, then his grandmother, believing in the Blessed Virgin and the White Lady, a devotee before the altar and also before the tall, mysterious stone standing in the midst of the moor, a husbandman in the field, a fisherman on the sea-coast, a poacher in the thicket, loving his kings, his seigneurs, his priests, his lice; thoughtful, often perfectly still for hours together on the great deserted sandy shore, listening gloomily to the sound of the sea. And ask yourself if this blind being could accept this light.

CHAPTER II.
THE MEN.

The peasant is dependent on two things; the field which yields his nourishment, the wood where he hides.

It would be difficult for one to imagine what the forests of Brittany were; they were towns. Nothing could be more silent, more mute and wild than those inextricable tangles of thorns and branches; those widespread thickets were the dwelling-places of silence and repose, no desert could seem more dead and more sepulchral.

If the trees could have been cut away suddenly and with a single stroke, like lightning, a swarm of men would have come abruptly into view.

Round, narrow pits, screened outside with coverings of stones and branches, first placed vertically, then horizontally, spread out underground like tunnels, ending in dark, gloomy chambers; that is what Cambyses found in Egypt, and Westermann found in Brittany; the former were in the desert, the latter in Brittany; in the caves of Egypt there were dead men, in the caves of Brittany there were living beings. One of the wildest clearings in the wood of Misdon, completely perforated with galleries and cells where a mysterious people came and went, was called "la Grande ville." Another clearing not less deserted above ground, and not less inhabited below, was called "la Place royale."

This subterranean life had existed in Brittany, from time immemorial. Man had always fled before man there. Hence these dens of reptiles hollowed out under the trees. They dated back to the Druids, and some of these crypts were as ancient as the cromlechs. The larvæ of legend and the monsters of history, all passed over this black country, Teutatès, Cæsar, Hoël, Néomènes, Geoffrey of England, Alain-gant-de-fer, Pierre Mauclerc, the French house of Blois, the English house of Montfort, kings and dukes, the nine barons of Brittany, the judges of the Grands-Jours, the counts of Nantes quarrelling with the counts of Rennes, highwaymen, banditti, the Free companies, René II., Viscount de Rohan, the governors for the king, the "good Duke de Chaulnes," hanging peasants under Madame de Sévigné's window, in the fifteenth century, the seigneurial butcheries; in the sixteenth and seventeenth centuries, the religious wars; in the eighteenth century, thirty thousand dogs trained to hunt men; under this frightful trampling underfoot the people resolved to disappear. The Troglodytes to escape the Celts, the Celts to escape the Romans, the Britons to escape the Romans, the Huguenots to escape the Catholics, the smugglers to escape the excisemen,—each in turn took refuge first in the forests, then under the ground. The resource of wild beasts. Thus it is that tyranny reduces nations. For two thousand years, despotism in all its forms, conquest, feudalism, fanaticism, the exchequer, all hunted down this wretched, desperate Brittany; a sort of inexorable battue, which only ceased in one form to begin under another. The men went to ground.

Dismay, which is a kind of anger, was all ready in their souls, the caves were all ready in the woods, when the French Republic burst forth. Brittany rose in revolt, finding herself oppressed by this forced deliverance, the customary mistake of slaves.

CHAPTER III.

MEN AND FORESTS IN CONNIVANCE.

The tragic forests of Brittany resumed their old rôle again and became the servants and accomplices of this rebellion, as they had been of all the others.

The subsoil of these forests was a sort of madrepore, pierced and traversed in every direction by a labyrinth of saps, cells, and galleries. Each of these blind cells sheltered five or six men. The difficulty was in getting air there. There are certain strange figures, which explain this powerful organization of the widespread peasant revolt. In Ille-et-Vilaine, in the forest of Pertre, asylum of the Prince of Talmont, not a breath could be heard, not a human footstep was to be found, and yet there were six thousand men there with Focard. In Morbihan, in the forest of Meulac, no one was seen, and yet eight thousand men were there. These two forests, the Pertre and Meulac are not numbered among the great forests of Brittany. If one entered them it was terrible. These deceitful thickets, full of combatants crouching in a sort of underground labyrinth, were like enormous concealed sponges, from which, under pressure of that gigantic foot, the Revolution, gushed forth civil war.

Invisible battalions were lying in wait. These unknown armies meandered beneath the Republican troops, came suddenly out of the ground and then went back again, leaping forth in vast numbers and vanished out of sight, it was everywhere and nowhere; an avalanche, then dust, giants with the gift of diminishing in size; giants for fighting, dwarfs for disappearing. Jaguars with the habits of moles.

Beside the forests there were the woods. Just as below cities there are villages, so below forests there are thickets. The forests were bound together by a maze of woods spreading in every direction. The ancient castles, which were fortresses; hamlets, which were camps; freeholds which were enclosures of ambushes and snares; farms, surrounded with trenches and palisades of trees, — these were the meshes of that net which caught the Republican armies.

This whole was called the Bocage.

There was the wood of Misdon, in the centre of which was a pond, and which belonged to Jean Chouan; there was the wood of Gennes, belonging to Taillefer; there was the wood of la Huisserie, belonging to Gouge-le-Bruant; the wood of la Charnie, belonging to Courtillé-le-Batard, called the apostle Saint Paul, chief of the camp of the Vache-Noire; the wood of Burgault, belonging to that puzzling Monsieur Jacques, destined to a mysterious end in the vault of Juvardeil; there was the wood of Charreau, where Pimousse and Petit-Prince, attacked by the garrison of Châteauneuf, seized the grenadiers in the republican ranks around the waist and carried them away prisoner; the wood of la Heureuserie, scene of the rout of the post of the Longue-Faye; the wood of Aulne, from which the route between Rennes and Laval could be seen; the wood of la Gravelle, which a prince of la Trémoille won in playing bowls; the wood of Lorges on the Côtes-de-Nord, where Charles de Boishardy ruled after Bernard de Villeneuve; the wood of Bagnard near Fontenay, where Lescure challenged Chalbos, who, although one against five, accepted the offer; the wood of la Durondais, formerly disputed by Alain le Redru and Hérispoux, son of Charles the Bald; the wood of Croqueloup, on the boundary of that moor where Coquereau sheared the prisoners; the wood of la Croix-Bataille which lent its aid to the Homeric insults given by Jambe-d'Argent to Morière and by Morière to Jambe-d'Argent; the wood of la Saudraie, which we have seen scoured by a Parisian battalion. There were many others beside.

In several of these forests and woods, there were not only subterranean villages grouped about the leader's burrow, but there were also veritable hamlets of low huts concealed under the trees, and so numerous that sometimes the forest was filled with them. Often their smoke betrayed them. Two of these hamlets in the wood of Misdon have become famous, Lorrière, near Létang, and the group of huts called Rue-de-Bau, on the side of Saint-Ouen-les-Toits.

The women lived in the huts, and the men, in the caves. For this war they made use of the galleries of fairies and the old Celtic mines. They brought food to the men buried in the caves. There were those who were forgotten and died of hunger. Beside, there were some who were not bright enough to know how to open their pits. Usually, the cover made of moss and branches, was so artistically fashioned that although impossible to distinguish it outside in the grass, it was very easily opened and closed from within. These retreats were hollowed out with great care. They threw the earth which they removed from the cave into some neighboring pond. The walls inside and the ground were covered with ferns and moss. They called this habitation "la loge." They thrived in them although they were without daylight, without fire, without bread, and without air.

To rise without precaution among the living, and to exhume themselves unseasonably was a serious matter. They might find themselves among the legs of a marching army. Terrible woods; snares with a double trap. The Blues did not dare to enter; the Whites did not dare to leave.

CHAPTER IV.

THEIR LIFE UNDERGROUND.

The men in these dens became restless. Sometimes at night, in spite of the danger, they would leave them and go forth to dance on the neighboring moor. Or else they prayed, to kill time. "All day long," said Bourdoiseau, "Jean Chouan made us tell our beads."

It was almost impossible when the time came round, to prevent those of the lower Maine from leaving to take part in the Fête de la Gerbe. Some had their own ideas. Denys, called Tranche-Montagne, disguised himself as a woman to go to see the comedy at Laval; then he went back to his cave.

They would suddenly make away with themselves, leaving the dungeon for the grave.

Sometimes they would raise the cover of their hole and listen for distant fighting; they followed the struggle with their ears. The firing of the Republicans was regular, that of the Royalists, intermittent; this was their guide. If the firing of the platoons ceased suddenly, it was a sign that the Royalists were worsted; if the irregular firing continued and seemed to disappear in the distance, it was a sign that they had the advantage. The Whites always pursued; the Blues never, for the country was against them.

These underground warriors were admirably drilled. Nothing was swifter than their communications, nothing more mysterious. They had broken down all the bridges, they had destroyed all the wagons, and yet they found a way to tell each other everything and to warn each other in season. Relays of emissaries were established from forest to forest, from village to village, from farm to farm, from hut to hut, from bush to bush.

This stupid-looking peasant went along carrying messages in his stick, which was hollow.

A former constituent, Boëtidoux, to enable them to go from one end of Brittany to the other, furnished them with Republican passports of the new design, with a blank for their names, of which this traitor had large bundles. It was impossible to detect them. "Secrets entrusted to more than four hundred thousand individuals," said Puysaye, "were religiously kept."

It seemed that this square, enclosed on the south by the boundary of the Sables to Thouars, on the east by the boundary of Thouars to Saumur and by the river of Thoué, on the north by the Loire, and on the west by the ocean, had a common nervous system, so that, not a point of this ground could stir without the whole being set in motion. In a twinkling, they were informed of Noirmoutier at Luçon, and the camp of La Loué knew what was going on in the camp of Croix-Morineau. One would have said that the birds had something to do with it. Hoche wrote, the seventh Messidor, year III: "One would have believed that they had telegraphs."

They had clans, like the Scotch. Each parish had its captain. My father took part in that war, and I am able to say something about it.

CHAPTER V.

THEIR LIFE IN TIME OF WAR.

Many of them had no arms but pikes. They had plenty of good fowling-pieces. Their were no more skilful marksmen than the poachers of the Bocage and the smugglers of Loroux.

They were strange, frightful, fearless warriors. The decree to raise three hundred thousand men caused the tocsin to sound in six hundred villages. The crackling of fire burst from every point at once. Le Poitou and Anjou exploded the same day. We may say that the first peal of thunder was heard before 1792, the eighth of July, a month before the tenth of August, on the moor of Kerbader. Alain Redeler, to-day forgotten, was the forerunner of La Rochejaquelein and Jean Chouan. The royalists compelled all able-bodied men to march, under pain of death. They requisitioned horses, wagons, and provisions. Immediately, Sapinaud had three thousand soldiers; Cathelineau, ten thousand; Stofflet, twenty thousand, and Charette was master of Noirmontier. The Viscount de Scépeaux roused Haut Anjou; the Chevalier de Dieuzie, l'Entre-Vilaine-et-Loire; Tristan-l'Hermite, the Bas-Maine; the barber Gaston, the town of Guémenée; and the Abbé Bornier, all the rest. A little thing was enough to raise these multitudes.

In the tabernacle of a priest who had taken the oaths, a *prête jureur* as he was called, they placed a large black cat which jumped out suddenly during the mass. "It is the devil!" cried the peasants, and the whole canton rose in revolt. A breath of fire came from the confessionals.

For attacking the Blues and for leaping ravines, they had a long stick, fifteen feet in length, the *ferte*, a weapon and an aid to flight. In the thickest of the conflict, when the peasants were attacking the Republican squares, if they met a cross or a chapel on the battlefield, all would fall on their knees, repeating their prayers under fire; as soon as their beads were told, those who were left jumped to their feet and rushed on the enemy. Alas, what giants! They loaded their guns as they ran, that was their talent. They could be made to believe anything; some priests showed them other priests whose necks they had reddened with a drawn cord, and said to them: "These are the guillotined brought back to life." They had their fits of chivalry; they honored Fesque, a republican ensign, who let himself be sabred without dropping his flag. These peasants jested; they called the married priests Republicans: *des sans-calottes devenus sans-culottes.*

At first, they were afraid of the cannons; afterwards they jumped on them with their sticks and took them. To begin with, they took a fine bronze cannon, which they named the Missionary; then another dating back to the Catholic wars and on which were engraved the arms of Richelieu and a figure of the Virgin; they called it Marie-Jeanne. When they lost Fontenay, they lost Marie-Jeanne, around which six hundred peasants fell without flinching; then they recaptured Fontenay in order to recapture Marie-Jeanne, and they brought it back under the flag embroidered with a fleur-de-lis, covering it with flowers, and made the women kiss it as they passed by. But two cannons were very little. Stofflet had taken Marie-Jeanne; Cathelineau, jealous, left Poir-en-Mange, besieged Jallais, and took a third cannon; Forest attacked Saint Florent and took a fourth. Two other captains, Chouppes and Saint-Pol, did better; they represented cannons with trunks of trees and gunners with manikins, and with this artillery, which they laughed about heartily, they drove back the Blues at Marcuil. This was the period of their greatness.

Later, when Chalbos routed La Marsonnière, the peasants left thirty-two cannon, with the arms of England, behind them on the dishonored battlefield. Then England paid the French princes, and they sent "the funds to Monseigneur." Nantiat wrote, the tenth of May, 1794, "because Pitt had been told that it was proper to do so." Mellinet, in a report the thirty-first of March, said: "The cry of the rebels is: 'Long live the English!'"

The peasants lingered behind to plunder. These devotees were robbers. Savages have vices. It was through these that civilization captured them later. Puysaye says, Vol. II., page 187: "I have several times saved the town of Plélan from pillage." And further on, page 434, he abstains from entering Montfort: "I made a circuit to prevent the pillage of the houses of the Jacobins." They plundered Cholet; the sacked Challans. After having missed Granville, they pillaged Ville-Dieu. They called the countrymen who joined the Blues, "the Jacobin crowd," and they made an end of these sooner than any others. They loved carnage like soldiers, and massacre like brigands. To shoot the "Patauds" that is the *bourgeois*, pleased them; they called it "se décarémer or *unrelenting.* At Fontenay, one of their priests, the Curé Barbotin, struck down an old man with his sabre. At Saint-Germain-sur-Ille, one of their captains, a nobleman, shot the attorney of the Commune dead, and took his watch. At Machecoul, they cut down the Republicans regularly, at the rate of thirty a day for five weeks; each chain of thirty was called "the rosary." They placed the chain in front of a ditch and shot the men; as they were shot they fell into the ditch sometimes alive, but they were buried all the same. We have already seen this custom. Joubert, president of the district, had his hands sawed off. They put sharp-edged handcuffs, forged for the purpose, on the prisoners of the Blues. They put them to death in the public square, to the sound of war cries. Charette, who signed: "Fraternity; Chevalier Charette," and who, like Marat, wore a handkerchief on his head, tied above his eyebrows, burned the city of Porni and the inhabitants in their houses.

At this time, Carrier was frightful. Terror answered to terror. The insurgent Breton had almost the same appearance as the insurgent Greek, with his short jacket, gun slung over his shoulder, leggings and wide breeches similar to the Greek fustand; the peasant boy resembled the Greek klephth. Henri de la Rochejaquelein, at the age of twenty-one, set out for this war with a stick and a pair of pistols.

The Vendéan army numbered a hundred and fifty-four divisions. They made regular sieges; they held Bressuire blockaded for three days. One Good Friday, ten thousand peasants, cannonaded the town of the Sables with red hot balls. They succeeded in destroying fourteen republican cantonments, from Montigné to Courbeveilles, in one single day.

On the high wall at Thouars, this superb dialogue was heard between La Rochejaquelein and a peasant boy,—

"Carl!"

"Here I am."

"Let me climb up on your shoulders."

"All right."
"Your gun."
"Take it."

And la Rochejaquelein leaped into the town, and the towers which Dugueselin had beseiged, were taken without ladders.

They preferred a cartridge to a louis-d'or. They wept when they lost sight of their own belfry. To flee seemed easy to them; then their chiefs would exclaim: "Throw away your sabots, but keep your guns!" When ammunition gave out, they told their beads and took powder from the ammunition wagons of the Republicans; later d'Elbée demanded powder from the English. When the enemy drew near, if they had any wounded, they concealed them in the tall wheat or among the virgin ferns, and after the affair was ended came back to get them.

They wore no uniforms. Their clothing was in tatters. Peasants and noblemen were dressed in the first rags they could find. Roger Mouliniers wore a turban and a cloak taken from the wardrobe of the theatre of La Fleche; the Chevalier de Beauvilliers wore an attorney's robe and a woman's hat over a woollen cap. All wore the white scarf and belt; the different ranks were distinguished by knots. Stofflet had a red knot; La Rochejaquelein, a black knot; Wimpfen, a semi-Girondist, who never left Normandy, wore the brassart of the Carabots of Caen. They had women in their ranks; Madame de Lescure, who became Madame de Rochejaquelein later; Thérèse de Mollien, La Rouaire's mistress, who burned the list of the parish chiefs; Madame de La Rochefoucauld beautiful, young, sword in hand, rallying the peasants at the foot of the great towers of the castle of Puy-Rousseau; and Antoinette Adams, called Chevalier Adams, who was so courageous that after her capture when she was shot, they stood out of respect.

This epic time was cruel. The people were mad. Madame de Lescure purposely made her horse walk over the disabled republicans lying on the ground; "dead," said she; perhaps they were only wounded.

Sometimes the men were traitors; the women, never. Mademoiselle Fleury of the Théâtre Français left Rouarie for Marat, but from love. The captains were often as ignorant as the soldiers; Monsieur de Sapinaud did not know how to spell; he wrote "*orions*" for *aurions*, "*couté*" instead of *côté*.

The leaders hated each other; the captains of the Marais cried: "Down with those of the High Country!" Their cavalry was not very numerous, and difficult to bring together. Puysaye wrote: "A man who would cheerfully give me his two sons grows cold if I ask for one of his horses." Fertes, pitchforks, scythes, guns old and new, hunting knives, spits, cudgels tipped and studded with iron, such were their arms; some of them carried crosses made of dead men's bones.

They made their attacks with loud cries, springing forth suddenly on every hand, from the woods, the hills, the underbrush, hollow paths; they formed crescents, killing, exterminating, blasting, and disappearing. When they passed through a Republican town, they cut down the Tree of Liberty, burned it and danced in a circle around the fire. All their pleasures were at night. This was the Vendéan rule, always to be unexpected. They would go fifteen leagues in silence without bending a blade of grass on their way. When evening came after determining between the chiefs and the war council, the place where they were to surprise the Republican posts the next morning, they would load their guns, mumble their prayers, take off their sabots, and file in long columns through the woods, barefooted, over the heather and moss, without a sound, without a word, without a breath. A march of cats in the darkness.

CHAPTER VI.

THE SOUL OF THE EARTH ABSORBED BY MEN.

La Vendée during the revolt numbered no less than five hundred thousand men, women, and children. Half a million of soldiers, these were the figures given by Tuffin de la Rouarie.

The federalists gave their assistance; the Gironde was a party to la Vendée, la Lozère sent thirty thousand men to the Bocage. Eight departments united; five in Brittany, three in Normandy. Evreux, which fraternized with Caen, was represented in the rebellion by Chaumont, its mayor, and Gardembas, one of its leading men. Buzot, Gorsas, and Barbaroux, at Caen; Brissot, at Moulins; Chassann, at Lyons; Rabaut Saint-Etienne, at Nismes: Meillan and Duchâtel, in Brittany,—all these mouths blew the furnace.

There were two Vendées, Great Vendée, which carried on the forest war; and Little Vendée, which carried on the war of the thickets, —that was the slight difference which separated Charette from Jean Chouan, Little Vendée was innocent; Great Vendée was corrupt. Little Vendée was more important. Charette was made marquis, lieutenant-general of the king's armies and was decorated with the great cross of Saint Louis; Jean Chouan remained Jean Chouan. Charette inclined to the bandit, Jean Chouan was more of a knight-errant.

As for those magnanimous chiefs, Bonchamps, Lescure, la Rochejaquelein, they were mistaken. The great Catholic army was a foolish attempt; disaster was inevitable. Can one imagine a tempest of peasants attacking Paris? a coalition of villages besieging the Panthéon? a pack of Christmas carols and orisons barking around the Marseillaise? a crowd of sabots rushing on a legion of intellects? Le Mans and Savenay punished this madness. It was impossible for la Vendée to pass the Loire. She could accomplish anything except this stride. Civil war does not conquer. Crossing the Rhine is the crowning work of Cæsar and the additional glory of Napoleon; crossing the Loire kills la Rochejaquelein.

The true sphere of la Vendée is within her own boundaries, there she is more than invulnerable, she is intangible. The Vendéan at home is a smuggler, a farmer, soldier, shepherd, poacher, sharpshooter, goatherd, bellringer, peasant, spy, assassin, sacristan, wild beast of the woods.

La Rochejaquelein is only Achilles; Jean Chouau is Proteus.

La Vendée miscarried.

Other revolts have been successful; the Swiss insurrection for example. There was this difference between a mountainous revolt like the Swiss, and a forest revolt like the Vendéan, that almost always because of the fatal influence of environment, the one is struggling for an ideal, and the other for prejudices. One soars, the other crawls. One fights for humanity; the other, for solitude. One desires liberty; the other, isolation. One defends the Commune; the other, the parish.—"Communism! Communism!" cried the heroes of Marat.—One has to do with precipices; the other, with quagmires. One is the man of torrents and foamy waters; the other, the man of stagnant puddles where fever lurks. The head of one is among the stars; that of the other, in the thicket. The one is on a summit; the other, in a shadow.

Education arising from mountain tops and low lands is not the same.

The mountain is a citadel; the forest, an ambuscade; one inspires boldness; the other, strategy. Antiquity placed the gods on pinnacles, and satyrs in grooves. The satyr is the savage; half man, half beast. Free countries have their Appenines, their Alps, their Pyrenees an Olympus. Parnassus is a mountain. Mont Blanc was the colossal auxiliary of William Tell; behind and above the great contests of spirits, against the darkness which fills the poems of India, the Himalayas are seen. Greece, Spain, Italy, Helvetia, have the mountain for a type; Cimmeria, Germany, or Brittany have the woods. The forest is barbarous.

The formation of the ground affects many of man's actions. It is more of an accomplice than is realized. In sight of some wild landscapes, one is tempted to exonerate man, and incriminate creation; one feels the silent rebellion of nature; the desert is sometimes injurious to conscience, especially an unenlightened conscience; conscience may be gigantic, as with Jesus and Socrates; it may be dwarfed, as with Atreus and Judas. A small conscience quickly becomes reptile; the shady forest trees, the brambles, the thorns, the marshes under the branches, are a fatal habitation for it; it is mysteriously permeated there by evil persuasions. Optical illusions, inexplicable shadows, terrors of the hour or place, throw men into a sort of fear, half religious, half brutal, which in ordinary times engenders superstition, and in periods of violence, brutality. Hallucinations hold the torch which lights the path of murder. There is a touch of madness in the brigand. Wonderful nature has a double meaning, which dazzles great minds and blinds uncultivated souls. When man is ignorant, when the desert is filled with visions, the darkness of solitude is added to the darkness of intelligence; hence, in man, the possibilities of perdition.

Certain rocks, certain ravines, certain copses, certain wild openings through the trees at evening, impel man to mad and awful deeds. One might almost say that there are evil places.

What tragic deeds that gloomy hill between Baignon and Plélan has witnessed!

Wide horizons lead the soul to broad ideas; circumscribed horizons engender narrow ideas; this sometimes condemns great hearts to become small minded: as, for example, Jean Chouan.

Broad ideas hated by narrow ideas,—this is the very struggle of progress.

Country, Fatherland,—these two words comprise the whole Vendéan war; a quarrel of the local idea with the universal idea; peasants against patriots.

CHAPTER VII.
LA VENDÉE WAS THE END OF BRITTANY.

Brittany is an old rebel. Every time that it had revolted for two thousand years, it had been in the right; the last time it was in the wrong. Still, in reality, against the Revolution as against the monarchy, against the acting representatives as against the governing dukes and peers, against the assignats as against the subsidies, whoever the combatants might be, Nicolas Rapin, François de la Noue, Captain Pluviaut and Lady de la Garnache, or Stofflet, Coquereau, and Lechandelier de Pierreville, under Monsieur de Rohan against the king, and under Monsieur de La Rochejaquelein for the king, Brittany was always waging the same war,—the war of the local mind against the central mind.

These ancient provinces were like a pond: these sluggish waters were averse to running; the winds blowing over them did not give them life, it irritated them. France ended at Finisterre; the field given to man terminated there, and there the march of generations stopped. Halt! cried the ocean to the earth, and barbarism to civilization. Every time that the centre, Paris, gives an impulse, whether it comes from royalty or the Republic, whether it be in the direction of despotism or liberty, it is a novelty and Brittany bristles. Let us be in peace. What do they want of us? The Marais takes its pitchfork, the Bocage takes its carbine. All our attempts, our initiative in legislation and education, our encyclopaedias, our philosophies, our geniuses, our glories, have come to naught before the Houroux; the tocsin in Bazouges threatens the French revolution, the moor of Faou revolts against our stormy public squares, and the bell of Haut-des Prés declares war on the tower of the Louvre.

Terrible blunder.

The Vendéan insurrection was a dismal mistake.

A colossal skirmish, chicanery of Titans, boundless rebellion, destined to leave to history but a single word,—a word notorious and black; committing suicide for the absent, devoted to egoism, spending its time in offering great bravery to cowardice, without calculation, without stratagem, without tactics, without plan, without aim, without a chief, without responsibility; showing to what extent will can be powerless; chivalric and savage; absurdity in rut, building a parapet of shadows against the light; ignorance making a long, stupid, superb resistance to truth, justice, right, reason, and deliverance; the dismay of eight years, the ravage of fourteen departments, the devastation of fields, the destruction of crops, burning villages, ruining towns, pillaging houses, the massacre of women and children, a torch in the cottages, a sword in the hearts of the people, the terror of civilization, the hope of Pitt; such was this war,—an unconscious attempt at parricide.

Taken all in all, by demonstrating the necessity of penetrating in every way the old Breton shadow and of piercing that thicket with all the arrows of light at once, la Vendée has been of service to progress. Catastrophes have a gloomy way of settling matters.

BOOK SECOND.—THE 3 CHILDREN.

CHAPTER I.

PLUS QUAM CIVILIA BELLA.

The summer of 1792 had been very rainy; the summer of 1793 was very hot. In consequence of the civil war, there were, so to speak, no roads in Brittany. People went about there, however, thanks to the beauty of the summer. The best route is dry ground. At the end of a serene July day, about an hour after sunset, a man on horseback, who came from the direction of Avranches, stopped before the little inn called the Croix-Branchard, at the entrance of Pontorson, and the sign of which bore this inscription, that was still legible a few years ago: "Good cider on draught." It had been hot all day, but the wind was beginning to blow. This traveller was wrapped in a wide cloak, which covered the horse's back. He wore a broad-brimmed hat with a tricolored cockade, a bold thing to do in this country of hedges and gunshots, where a cockade was a target. His cloak tied at the neck was thrown back to leave his arms free, and underneath was seen a tricolored belt and two pistols sticking out of the belt. A sabre hung down beyond the cloak. As the horse stopped, the door of the inn opened, and the innkeeper came out with a lantern in his hand. It was just between daylight and darkness; it was light on the road and dark in the house.

The host looked at the cockade.

"Citizen," said he, "do you stop here?"

"No."

"Where are you going then?"

"To Dol."

"In that case, return to Avranches or stay at Pontorson."

"Why?"

"Because they are fighting in Dol."

"Ah!" said the cavalier.

And he added,

"Give some oats to my horse."

The host brought a bucket, emptied a bag of oats into it and unbridled the horse, which began to snort and to eat.

The conversation continued,—

"Citizens, is this a horse of requisition?"

"No."

"Is it yours?"

"Yes. I bought it and paid for it."

"Where do you come from?"

"From Paris."

"Not directly?"

"No."

"I knew it, the roads are closed. But the post-wagon still runs."

"As far as Alençon. I left it there."

"Ah! soon there will be no more posts in France. There are no more horses. A horse worth three hundred francs brings six hundred, and fodder is high. I have been post-master, and now I keep a cook-shop. Out of thirteen hundred and thirteen post-masters, two hundred have resigned. Citizen, have you travelled under the new tariff?"

"Of the first of May,—yes."

"Twenty sous per post in a carriage, twelve sous in a cab, five sous in a wagon. Did you buy this horse at Alençon?"

"Yes."

"You have been riding all day, to-day?"

"Since daybreak."

"And yesterday?"

"And the day before."

"I see that. You came by way of Domfront and Mortain?"

"And Avranches."

"Take my advice and rest yourself, citizen. You must be tired. Your horse is."

"Horses have a right to be tired, but men have not."

The host fixed his eyes again on the traveller. He had a solemn, calm, stern face, framed in gray hair.

The innkeeper glanced along the road, which was deserted as far as he could see, and said,—

"And you are travelling alone like this?"

"I have an escort."

"Where is it?"

"My sabre and my pistols."

The innkeeper went to get a pail of water, and watered the horse, and while the horse was drinking, the host contemplated the traveller, and said to himself, "All the same, he looks like a priest."

The cavalier continued,—

"You say that they are fighting at Dol?"

"Yes. It ought to be beginning this very minute."

"Who are fighting?"

"A ci-devant against a ci-devant."

"What did you say?"

"I say that a ci-devant who is for the Republic is fighting against a ci-devant who is for the king."

"But there is no king now."

"There is the little one. And the strange part of it is that the two ex-nobles are two relatives."

The cavalier listened attentively. The innkeeper went on:

"One is young, the other, old; it is a grand-nephew fighting against his great uncle. The uncle is a Royalist; the nephew, a patriot. The uncle commands the Whites, the nephew commands the Blues. Ah! they will give no quarter, be sure of that. It is war to the death."

"To the death?"

"Yes, citizen. Wait, would you like to see the polite speeches they throw at each other's heads? Here is a notice the old man found a way to have posted up everywhere, on all the houses and all the trees, and which he had stuck up even on my door."

The host held his lantern near a square of paper fastened to one of the leaves of his double-door, and as the notice was in large letters, the cavalier was able to read from his horse,—

"The Marquis de Lantenac has the honor to inform his grand-nephew, Monsieur the Viscount Gauvain, that if Monsieur le Marquis has the good fortune to capture his person, he will have Monsieur le Viscount quietly shot."

"And," continued the innkeeper, here is the reply."

He turned around and threw the light from his lantern on another notice posted opposite the first on the other leaf of the door. The traveller read,—

"Gauvain warns Lantenac that if he takes him he will have him shot."

"Yesterday," said the host; "the first placard was pasted up on my door, and this morning, the second. The reply was not long coming."

The traveller, in an undertone, as if talking to himself, uttered these few words, which the innkeeper heard without taking in their full meaning,—

"Yes, it is more than civil war, it is domestic war. It is necessary, and it is well. The great rejuvenations of peoples are at this price."

And the traveller, raising his hand to his hat and fixing his eyes on the second notice, saluted it.

The host continued,—

"You see, citizen, this is how it is. In the cities and the large towns we are for the Revolution, in the country they are against it; that is to say, in the cities they are French, in the villages they are Breton. It is a war of bourgeois against the peasants. They call us boors, we call them clowns. The nobles and the priests are with them."

"Not all," interrupted the cavalier.

"Beyond a doubt, citizen, for we have here a viscount against a marquis."

And he added in a low voice to himself,—

"And I believe that I am speaking to a priest."

The cavalier continued,—

"And which is winning?"

"The viscount at present. But he has a hard time. The old man is terrible. These people belong to the family of Gauvain, nobles of this country here. It is a family with two branches; there is the large branch, the chief of which is called the Marquis de Lantenac, and the small branch, the chief of which is called the Viscount Gauvain. The two branches are now fighting. Such a thing is not seen among the trees, but it is seen among men. This Marquis de Lantenac is all-powerful in Brittany; among the peasants he is a prince. The day he landed he had eight thousand men in no time; in a week, three hundred parishes were raised. If he had been able to take a corner of the coast, the English would have landed. Fortunately, this Gauvain was there, who is his grand-nephew,—a strange occurrence. He is the Republican commander, and he repulsed his great-uncle. And, then, as luck would have it, this Lantenac, on his arrival, while massacring a lot of prisoners, had caused two women to be shot, one of whom had three children who had been adopted by a battalion from Paris. That made them a terrible battalion. It was called the battalion of Bonnet-Rouge. There are not many of these Parisians left, but they are furious soldiers. They have been incorporated into Commandant Gauvain's division. Nothing withstands them. They are determined to avenge the death of the women, and have the children again. Nobody knows what the old man has done with these little things. That is what enrages the Parisian grenadiers. If these children had not been mixed up in it, I suppose this war would not be what it is. The viscount is a good, brave young man. But the old man is a terrible marquis. The peasants call it the war of Saint Michael against Beelzebub. You know, perhaps that Saint Michael is an angel of this part of the country. He has a mountain in the bay. He is said to have overthrown the devil and to have buried him under another mountain which is near here, and is called Tombelaine."

"Yes," murmured the cavalier, "Tumba Beleni, the tomb of Belus, of Bel, of Belial, of Beelzebub."

"I see that you know about it."

And the host said, aside to himself,—

"He knows Latin, and he is surely a priest."

Then he added: "Well, citizen, for the peasants, it is that war over again. It is evident that to them Saint Michael is the Royalist general, and Beelzebub is the patriot commander; but if there is a devil, it is surely Lantenac, and if there is an angel it is Gauvain. Won't you take something, citizen?"

"I have my gourd and a piece of bread. But you have not told me what is going on in Dol."

"This is it. Gauvain is commanding the exploring column of the coast. Lantenac's aim was to rouse a general insurrection, to strengthen Lower Brittany with Lower Normandy, to open the doors to Pitt, and to increase the great Vendéan army with twenty thousand English and two hundred thousand peasants. Gauvain cut short this plan. He holds the coast, and is driving Lantenac into the interior and the English into the sea. Lantenac was here and he drove him away; he has taken Pont-au-Beau away from him, he has driven him from Avranches, he has driven him from Villedieu, he has prevented him from reaching Granville. He is manœuvring to drive him back into the forest of Fougères and to surround him there. All was going well yesterday. Gauvain was here with his column. Suddenly, there is an alarm. The old man, who is shrewd, makes a point; they learn that he is marching on Dol. If he takes Dol, and if he establishes a battery on Mont-Dol, for he has cannon, there is a point of the coast where the English can land, and all is lost. That is why, as there was not a minute to lose, Gauvain, who is a level-headed man, took counsel with no one but himself; did not ask for orders, nor wait for them, sounded the signal to saddle, put to his artillery, collected his troops, drew his sabre, and that is how, while Lantenac was rushing on Dol, Gauvain was rushing on Lantenac. It is at Dol, that these two Breton heads are going to butt. It will be a proud collision. They are there now."

"How long does it take to go to Dol?"

"For a troop with wagons, at least three hours; but they are there."

The traveller put his hand behind his ear and said,—

"To be sure, it seems to me that I hear the cannon."

The host listened.

"Yes, citizen; and the musketry. The fight has begun. You will have to spend the night here. There is no good in going there."

"I cannot stop. I must continue my journey."

"You are wrong. I don't know your business, but the risk is great, and unless it concerns what you hold dearest in the world——"

"That is just it," replied the cavalier.

"Something like your own son——"

"Very nearly," said the cavalier.

The innkeeper raised his head and said to himself,—

"And yet this citizen seems to me like a priest."

Then, after some thought, he added,—

"After all, a priest may have children."

"Put my horse's bridle back," said the traveller. "How much do I owe you?"

And he paid him.

The host set back the trough and the bucket by the side of the wall, and then came toward the traveller.

"Since you are bound to go on, take my advice. It is clear that you are going to Saint-Malo. Well, don't go through Dol. There are two routes, the road through Dol, and the road along the sea coast. One is as short as the other. The road along by the sea goes through Saint-Georges de Brehaigne Cherrueix, and Hirelle-Vivier. You leave Dol to the south and Cancal to the north. Citizen, at the end of the street, you will find the place where the two roads meet; the one to Dol is to the left, the one to Saint-Georges de Brehaigne is to the right. Listen to me now; if you go through Dol, you will fall in the massacre. That is why you must not take the left; take the right."

"Thank you," said the traveller.

And he spurred on his horse.

It had grown quite dark, he plunged into the night.

The innkeeper lost sight of him.

When the traveller came to the end of the street where the two roads branched off, he heard the innkeepers voice cry out from the distance,

"Go to the right!"

He went to the left.

CHAPTER II.

DOL.

Dol, a Spanish town of France in Brittany, as it is termed in the old charters, is not a town but a street. A grand old gothic street, all bordered on the right and on the left by houses with pillars, standing irregularly and making angles and corners in the street, which is everywhere wide. The rest of the town is nothing but a network of lanes running into this large street from opposite directions, and ending there like brooks in a river. The town, without gates or walls, open, overshadowed by Mont-Dol, could not withstand a siege; but the street could withstand one. These promontories of houses that could still be seen there fifty years ago, and the two-pillared galleries which bordered them, formed a very solid battle-ground, capable of great resistance. There were as many fortresses as there were houses, and it was necessary to take one after another. The old market house was very nearly in the middle of the street.

The innkeeper of the Croix-Branchard had told the truth, a furious conflict filled Dol at the time he was speaking. A nocturnal duel between the Whites who had reached there in the morning, and the Blues who had unexpectedly arrived there in the evening, had suddenly burst forth in the town. The forces were unequal, the Whites numbered six thousand, the Blues fifteen hundred, but their fury was equally divided. Strange to say, the fifteen hundred attacked the six thousand.

On one side, a riotous crowd; on the other, a phalanx. On one side, six thousand peasants with sacred hearts on their leather jackets, white ribbons on their round hats, Christian devices on their brassarts, rosaries hanging from their belts, armed with more pitchforks than sabres, and carbines without bayonets, dragging cannons by means of ropes, poorly equipped, badly disciplined, meanly armed, full of frenzy; on the other side, fifteen hundred soldiers wearing three cornered hats with the tricolored cockade, coats with full skirts and wide lappels, shoulder belts crossed, copper-hilted swords, guns with long bayonets, erect, well-trained, docile, and fierce, knowing how to obey like people who know how to command, volunteers, too, but volunteers for their country, in rags, moreover, and shoeless. For the monarchy, paladin peasants; for the republic, barefooted heroes. And the soul of each of these two troops was its chief: that of the royalists, an old man; of the republicans, a young man. On one side, Lantenac; on the other, Gauvain.

Besides gigantic young figures, such as Danton, Saint-Just, and Robespierre, the Revolution had young figures which were ideal, like Hoche and Marceau. Gauvain was one of these figures.

Gauvain was thirty years old, with Herculean form, a prophetic, serious eye, and the laugh of a child. He did not smoke, he did not drink, he did not swear. He carried a toilet case throughout the war, he took great care of his nails, his teeth, and his hair which was brown and abundant; during halts he himself shook his military cloak, riddled with bullets and white with dust. Although he always rushed recklessly into the midst of the battle, he had never been wounded. His very gentle voice had, when necessary, a sharp tone of command. He set the example of sleeping on the ground, in wind, in rain, in snow, rolled up in his cloak, and his graceful head resting on a stone. He was a soul both heroic and innocent. The sword in his hand transfigured him. He had that effeminate appearance which in battle is terrible.

At the same time, he was a thinker and a philosopher—a young sage; Alcibiades to look at, Socrates to listen to.

This young man had at once become a leader in this great improvisation, the French Revolution.

His division, formed by himself, like the Roman legion, was a sort of complete little army; it was composed of infantry and cavalry; it had scouts, pioneers, sappers, pontooniers; and just as the Roman legion had catapults, this had cannons. Three pieces drawn by horses strengthened the column, and at the same time left it easily handled.

Lantenac also was a warrior and still more formidable. He was both more reflective and more daring. The real old heroes have more coolness than the young men because they are farther from the sunrise, and more audacious because they are nearer death. What have they to lose? so little! Hence, Lantenac's rash movements, which were at the same time so skillful. But in the main, in this obstinate hand-to-hand conflict, Gauvain almost always had the advantage. It was more good fortune than anything else. All good luck, even good luck which is terrible, belongs to youth. Victory is in some respects like a young girl.

Lantenac was incensed against Gauvain; first because Gauvain was opposed to him, then because he was his relative. What right had he to be a Jacobin! this Gauvain! this scamp! his heir, for the marquis had no children; a grand-nephew, almost a grandson! "Ah," said this *quasi* grandfather, "if I get my hand on him, I will kill him like a dog!"

Besides the Republic had reason to be troubled about this Marquis de Lantenac. He had hardly landed when he made them tremble. His name had run through the Vendéan insurrection like a train of powder, and Lantenac became at once the centre. In a revolt of this kind, where all are jealous of each other, and each has his bush or his ravine, the coming of a superior rallies the scattered chiefs, who are equals among themselves. Almost all the captains of the woods joined Lantenac, and from far and near, they obeyed him. One alone had left him; he had been the first to join him,—Gavard. Why? Because he was a man of trust. Gavard had known all the secrets, and adopted all the plans of the old system of civil warfare, that Lantenac came to supplant and replace. One cannot follow in the steps of a man of trust; the shoe of la Rouarie did not fit Lantenac. Gavard had gone to join Bonchamp.

Lantenac, as a soldier, belonged to the school of Fredderick II.; he knew how to combine the greater war with the less. He wished to have neither a "confused mass," like the great catholic and royal army, a multitude destined to be destroyed; nor a scattering in the thickets and copses, good for harrassing, powerless to overthrow. The guerilla does not terminate, or terminates unfortunately; it begins by attacking a Republic, and ends by robbing a stage coach. Lantenac did not intend to carry on this Breton war either wholly in the open field, as La Rochejaquelin had done, or wholly in the forest, like Jean Chouan; neither Vendée nor Chouannerie; he wanted real war; to make use of the peasant, but to support him with the soldier. He wished to have bands of men for strategy, and regiment for tactics. He found these village armies, able to disappear so suddenly, excellent for attack, ambuscade and surprise; but he felt that they were too fluid; they were like water in his hand; he wished to create a solid point in this wavering and scattered war; he wished to add to this wild forest army, regular troops, which would be the pivot of the peasants' manœuvres. A profound and awful thought; if it had succeeded, la Vendée would have been impregnable.

But where could he find regular troops? where find soldiers? where find regiments? where find an army ready made? In England.

This was Lantenac's determination: to land the English. Thus party conscience capitulates; the white cockade concealed from his sight the red coat. Lantenac had but one thought: to get possession of a point of the sea-coast, and to give it up to Pitt. That is why, seeing Dol without defence, he rushed on it, in order, through Dol, to have Mont-Dol; and through Mont-Dol, the coast.

The place was well chosen. The cannon on Mont-Dol would sweep le Fresnois on one side, and Saint-Brelade on the other; would keep the cruisers from Cancale at a distance, and would make the coast from Raz-sur-Couesnon to Saint-Méloir-des-Ondes, open to invasion.

To make this decisive move successful, Lantenac had brought with him a little more than six thousand men, the stoutest among the bands at his disposal, and all his artillery, ten sixteen-pound culverins, one eight-pounder, and a four-pounder. He proposed to establish a strong battery on Mont-Dol, on this principle, that a thousand shots from ten cannons would accomplish more than fifteen hundred shots with five cannons.

Success seemed certain. He had six thousand men. He had nothing to fear in the direction of Avranches but Gauvain and his fifteen hundred men, and in the direction of Dinan, only Léchelle. Léchelle, it is true, had twenty-five thousand men, but he was twenty leagues away. Lantenac was confident of success with regard to Léchelle, on account of the great distance against the great number; and, with regard to Gauvain, on account of the small number against the short distance. We may add that Léchelle was an idiot, and later on he allowed his twenty-five thousand men to be destroyed on the moors of la Croix-Bataille; a defeat which he paid for with suicide.

So Lantenac felt perfectly secure. His entrance into Dol was sudden and severe. The Marquis de Lantenac had a hard reputation; he was known to be merciless. No resistance was attempted. The terrified inhabitants shut themselves up in their houses. The six thousand Vendéans took up their quarters in the town with boorish confusion; it was almost a fair ground, without quartermasters, without definite camp, bivouacking at haphazard, cooking in the open air, scattering about in the churches, leaving their guns for their rosaries. Lantenac hastened with some artillery officers to reconnoitre Mont-Dol, leaving the lieutenancy to Gouge-le-Bruant, whom he had appointed field-sergeant.

This Gouge-le-Bruant has left a faint trace in history. He had two nicknames "Brise-bleu," on account of his slaughtering of patriots, and "l'Imânus," because he had in him something strangely, unutterably horrible. "Imânus," derived from *immanis*, is an old word of Low Norman origin, expressing the superhuman and quasidivine ugliness, in the frightful, in devils, satyrs, and ogres. An ancient manuscript said: "*d'mes daeux iers j' vis l'imanus.*" The old men of the Bocage, to-day have no knowledge of Gouge-le-Bruant, nor of the meaning of Brise-bleu; but they have a confused idea of l'Imânus. L'Imânus is connected with local superstition. They still speak of l'Imânus at Trémorel and Plumaugat, two villages where Gouge-le-Bruant left the print of his ominous foot. In la Vendée, others were savage. Gouge-le-Bruant was barbarous. He was a kind of cacique, tatooed with rude letters and fleurs-de-lis; in his face shone the hideous and almost superhuman glare of a soul unlike any other human being. He was infernally brave in battle, and atrocious afterward. He had a heart full of tortuous intricacies, ready for every kind of devotion, inclined to all sorts of madness. Did he reason? Yes, but as serpents crawl: in circles. He left heroism to come to murder. It was impossible to guess whence arose his resolutions, often magnificent on account of their monstrosity. He was capable of every unexpected horror. He had an epic ferocity.

Hence this misshapen nickname, "l'Imânus."

The Marquis de Lantenac had confidence in his cruelty.

It was a fact that l'Imânus excelled in cruelty; but in strategy and tactics he was less superior, and perhaps the marquis was wrong to make him field-sergeant. However that may be, he left l'Imânus behind him, with orders to take his place and watch everything.

Gouge-le-Bruant, more of a warrior than a soldier, was more fit to slaughter a clan than to guard a city, but yet he stationed main guards.

When evening had come, as the Marquis de Lantenac was on his way back to Dol, after having decided on the situation of the projected battery, he suddenly heard the cannon. He looked. A red smoke was rising from the great street. There was a surprise, an irruption, an attack; they were fighting in the town.

Although it was hard to astonish him, he was stupefied. He was not expecting anything of the kind. Who could be there? Evidently, it was not Gauvain. It would be foolish to attack with one against four. Was it Léchelle? But what a forced march to have made! Léchelle improbable; Gauvain, impossible.

Lantenac spurred on his horse; on his way he met the inhabitants in flight; he questioned them, they were mad with fear. They cried: "The Blues! The Blues!" and when he reached the town, the situation was desperate.

This is what had happened.

CHAPTER III.

SMALL ARMIES AND GREAT BATTLES.

On reaching Dol, the peasants, as we have just seen, were scattered through the town, each working his own pleasure, as it happens when people "obey out of friendship," as the Vendéans expressed it. The sort of obedience which makes heroes but not troopers. They had stowed away their artillery with the baggage under the arches of the old market house, and weary, drinking, eating, telling their beads, they lay down helter-skelter through the great street, which was rather blocked up than guarded. As night came on, most of them fell asleep, with their heads on their sacks, some with their wives beside them; for the peasant women often follow the peasants; in Vendée, pregnant women served as spies. It was a mild July night; the constellations shone brilliantly in the deep blue black of the sky. All this bivouac, which was more like the halt of a caravan than the encampment of an army, was beginning to sleep peacefully. Suddenly, in the glimmering twilight, those who had not yet closed their eyes saw three cannons pointed at the end of the great street.

It was Gauvain. He had surprised the main guards, he was in the town, and he held the head of the street with his column.

A peasant jumped up, cried "*Qui vive?*" and fired off his gun, a cannon shot gave answer. Then a furious discharge of musketry burst forth. The entire drowsy multitude leaped to their feet; a rude awakening. They had gone to sleep under the stars and woke under fire.

The first moment was terrible, there is nothing so tragic as the swarming of a bewildered multitude. They pounced on their arms, they screamed, they ran, many fell. The peasant boys assaulted in this way, did not know what to do and began to shoot each other. The people, astounded, rushed out of their houses, went back, came out again, and wandered about in the confusion, like maniacs. Families called out to each other. A dismal fight with women and children intermingled. Hissing bullets streaked through the darkness. There was firing from every dark corner. Everything was smoke and tumult. The entanglement of the baggage wagons and carts added to it. The horses kicked. The people trampled on the wounded. Shrieks rose from the ground. Some from horror, others from amazement. Soldiers and officers were looking for one another. In the midst of all this, there were some gloomily indifferent. A woman nursing her new-born babe, was sitting by a portion of a wall, against which leaned her husband, whose leg had been broken, and while his blood was flowing, he was calmly loading his carbine and shooting at random, killing those before him in the darkness. Men lying on their bellies shot through the wheels of the wagons. Occasionally, arose an uproarious shouting. The great voice of the cannon drowned everything else. It was frightful.

It was like the felling of trees; they all lay one above another. Gauvain, in ambush, fired with a steady shot and lost few of his men.

However, the intrepid disorder of the peasants ended in an attempt to defend themselves; they retreated under the market-house, a vast, dark redoubt, a forest of stone pillars. There they regained a footing; anything resembling a wood gave them confidence. L'Imânus did his best to make up for the absence of Lantenac. They had cannon, but, much to Gauvain's astonishment, they made no use of it; this was because the artillery officers had gone with the marquis to investigate Mont Dol, and the peasants only understood the culverines and eight-pounders; but they riddled with bullets the Blues who cannonaded them. The peasants answered the grapeshot with musketry. They were now under shelter. They had piled up the drays, the carts, the baggage, all the barrels in the old market, and improvised a high barricade with openings through which they passed their carbines. Their shooting through these holes was deadly. All this was quickly accomplished. In a quarter of an hour, the market had an impenetrable front.

This became serious for Gauvain. This market, suddenly transformed into a citadel, was unlooked for. The peasants were there in a solid mass. Gauvain had been successful in surprising them and failed in routing them. He had dismounted. Holding his sword in his hand, under his crossed arms, he stood in the flare of a torch which lighted up his battery, watching all this darkness attentively.

His tall figure in this bright light made him visible to the men behind the barricade. He was their aim, but he was not aware of it.

The discharge of bullets sent from the barricade fell all around Gauvain, who was absorbed in thought.

But against all these carbines he had the cannon. The cannon ball always gets the advantage. He who has artillery has victory. His battery, if made good use of, assured him the superiority.

Suddenly, there was a flash of lightning from the market so full of darkness, something like a peal of thunder was heard, and a cannon ball went through a house above Gauvain's head.

The barricade answered cannon shot with cannon shot.

What had happened? Something new. The artillery was no longer on one side alone.

A second cannon ball followed the first and buried itself in the wall near Gauvain. A third knocked off his hat.

These balls were of large calibre. They came from a sixteen-pounder.

"They are aiming at you, commandant," cried the artillery-men. And they put out the torch. Gauvain, as if in a dream, picked up his hat.

Some one indeed was aiming at Gauvain; it was Lantenac.

The marquis had just entered the barricade from the opposite side.

L'Imânus ran toward him.

"Monseigueur, we have been surprised."

"By whom?"

"I do not know."

"Is the road open from Dinan?"

"I think so."

"We must begin a retreat."

"It has begun. Many have already escaped."

"We mustn't escape; we must retreat. Why haven't you used the artillery?"

"They lost their heads, and then the officers were not here."

"I will attend to it."

"Monseigneur, I have sent all that I could of the baggage, the women, and everything of no use, towards Fougères. What is to be done with the three little children?"

"Ah! those children?"

"Yes."

They are our hostages. Have them taken to la Tourgue."

Having said this, the marquis went to the barricade. The coming of the chief put a new face on the matter. The barricade was badly constructed for artillery, as there was room for but two cannon; the marquis put in position two sixteen-pounders, for which they made embrasures. As he was leaning over one of the cannons, looking at the battery of the enemy through the embrasure, he noticed Gauvain.

"It is he!" he cried out.

Then he took the sponge and rammer himself, loaded the piece, adjusted the sight, and aimed.

Three times he aimed at Gauvain, and missed him. The third shot only succeeded in knocking off his hat.

"Stupid!" muttered Lantenac. "A little lower and I should have had his head."

Suddenly the torch went out, and he had nothing before him but darkness.

"So be it," he said.

And turning toward the peasant gunner, he cried,—

"Fire away!"

Gauvain, on his side, was no less in earnest. The situation grew more serious. A new phase of the struggle presented itself. The barricade had begun to make use of cannon. Who knew but it might pass from the defensive to the offensive? He had before him, not counting the dead and those who had fled, at least five thousand combatants, and he himself had only twelve hundred able men left. What would become of the Republicans, if the enemy should notice their small number? The *rôles* would be reversed. They were attacking, they would be attacked. If the barricade were to make a sortie all would be lost.

What was to be done? attacking the barricade front was not to be dreamed of; to attempt at main force would be risky; twelve hundred men could not drive out five thousand. To hasten matters was impossible, to wait would be fatal. They must come to an end. But how?

Gauvain belonged to the country, he knew the town; he knew that back of the old market, where the Vendéans were embattled, was a maze of narrow, winding lanes.

He turned to his lieutenant who was that brave Captain Guéchamp, famous later for clearing the forest of Concise, where Jean Chouan was born, and for preventing the taking of Bourgneuf, by barring the rebels from the dyke of the pond of la Chaine.

"Guéchamp," he said, "I leave you in command. Fire with all your might. Riddle the barricade with cannon balls. Keep all those people busy."

"I understand," said Guéchamp.

"Mass the whole column with arms loaded, and hold them ready for attack."

He spoke a few words additional in Guéchamp's ear.

"I understand," said Guéchamp.

Gauvain continued,—

"Are all our drummers on hand?"

"Yes."

"We have nine. Keep two, give me seven."

The seven drummers ranged themselves silently before Gauvain.

Then Gauvain cried,—

"Battalion of Bonnet-Rouge!"

Twelve men, with a sergeant, left the main body of the troops.

"I ask for the whole battalion," said Gauvain.

"Here we are!" replied the sergeant.

"Twelve of you!"

"There are twelve of us left."

"Very good," said Gauvain.

This sergeant was the rough, but kind-hearted, trooper Radoub, who had adopted in the name of the battalion the three children found in the woods of La Saudraie.

Only half a battalion, it will be remembered, had been exterminated at Herbe-en-Pail, and Radoub had the good luck not to form a part of it.

A forage wagon was near; Gauvain pointed it out to the sergeant.

"Sergeant, have your men make ropes of straw and twist them around their guns to prevent any sound if they knock against each other."

In a moment's time the order had been executed, in silence and darkness.

"It is done," said the sergeant.

"Soldiers, take off your shoes," added Gauvain.

"We haven't any," said the sergeant.

That made, with the seven drummers, nineteen men; Gauvain was the twentieth.

He cried,—

"Follow me in single file. The drummers behind me, the battalion next. Sergeant, you will command the battalion."

He took the head of the column, and, while the cannonading continued on both sides, these twenty men, gliding along like ghosts, plunged into the deserted lanes.

They marched some time in this way, winding along by the houses. Everything seemed dead in the town; the citizens were crouching in the cellars. There was not a door which was not barred, not a blind which was not closed. No light anywhere.

The great street was making a furious din in the midst of this silence; the cannonading still continued; the Republician battery and the Royalist barricade were angrily spitting out all their volleys.

After twenty minutes of winding about, Gauvain, who led the way with certainty in the darkness, reached the end of a lane running into the principal street; only it was on the other side of the market.

The position was reversed. On this side there was no intrenchment,—such is the everlasting imprudence of those who build barricades,—the market was open and they could enter under the arches, where some baggage wagons were harnessed ready for departure. Gauvain and his nineteen men had before them the five thousand Vendéans, but they were behind the Vendéans' backs and not in front of them.

Gauvain spoke in a low voice to the sergeant; they removed the straw from their guns; the twelve grenadiers stationed themselves in order of battle behind the corner of the lane, and the seven drummers held their drumsticks in readiness for orders.

The discharge of artillery was intermittent. Suddenly, in an interval between two reports, Gauvain raised his sword, and, in a voice which sounded like a trumpet in the silence, cried out,—

"Two hundred men to the right, two hundred men to the left, the rest in the centre!"

The twelve guns fired, the seven drums beat the charge.

And Gauvain uttered the terrible cry of the Blues,—

"Charge bayonets!"

The effect was wonderful.

This entire mass of peasants felt that they were surprised from the rear, and imagined that there was a new army behind them. At the same time, the column holding the head of the street and commanded by Guéchamp, hearing the drums, moved forward, beating the charge in return, and rushed in double-quick time on the barricade; the peasants saw that they were between two fires.

A panic exaggerates everything; in a panic, a pistol shot makes as much noise as a cannon, and sounds are magnified by the imagination, and the baying of a hound seems like the roar of a lion. We may add that the peasant takes fear as the thatch takes fire, and peasant's fear increases to defeat, as easily as the burning thatch grows to a conflagration. Their flight was beyond description.

In a few moments, the market was empty, the terrified peasant boys scattered, in spite of the officers. L'Imânus killed two or three of the deserters to no purpose; this cry was heard above everything else: "Escape, if you can!" and this army fled through the streets of the town as though it were a sieve, out into the country, with the swiftness of clouds driven by a storm.

Some escaped in the direction of Chateauneuf, some toward Plerguer, and others toward Antrain.

The Marquis de Lantenac saw this defeat. He spiked the cannons with his own hand, then retired, the last, slowly and coolly, saying,

— "The peasants are not to be depended upon, most decidedly. We must have the English."

CHAPTER IV.

IT IS THE SECOND TIME.

The victory was complete. Gauvain turned toward the men of the battalion of Bonnet-Rouge, and said,—
"There are only twelve of you, but you are worth a thousand."

Praise from the chief meant the cross of honor at that time.

Guéchamp, sent out of the town by Gauvain, pursued the fugitives and took many of them.

They lighted the torches and ransacked the town.

All who could not escape surrendered. They lighted up the main streets with fire pots. It was strewn with dead and wounded. The end of a battle is always heartrending. A few groups of desperate men here and there still resisted; they were surrounded and they laid down their arms.

Gauvain had noticed in the lawless confusion of the rout, a bold man, a sort of nimble, hardy faun, who had aided the flight of others but had not fled himself. This peasant made masterly use of his carbine, shooting with the barrel, felling with the stock so well that he had broken it; now he had a pistol in one hand and a sword in the other. No one dared approach him. Suddenly, Gauvain saw him totter and lean against a post in the main street. The man had just been wounded. But he still held his sword and pistol. Gauvain put his sword under his arm and went to him.

"Surrender," he said.

The man looked at him steadily. Blood was flowing from a wound under his clothing, and making a pool at his feet.

"You are my prisoner," added Gauvain

The man remained speechless.

"What is your name?"

The man said,—

"My name is Danse-a-l'Ombre."

"You are a brave fellow," said Gauvain.

And he held out his hand to him.

The man replied: "Long live the king!" and collecting all the strength he had left, raising both arms at once, he fired his pistol at Gauvain's heart, and aimed a blow at his head with his sword.

He did this with the swiftness of a tiger; but some one else was quicker still. It was a man on horseback who had just arrived, and had been there for some moments without attracting any one's attention. When this man saw the Vendéan raise his sword and pistol, he threw himself between him and Gauvain. But for this man, Gauvain would have been killed. The horse received the shot, the man received the blow from the sabre, and both fell. All this was done before there was time to cry out.

The Vendéan had dropped on the pavement.

The sabre had struck the man full in the face; he was on the ground, unconscious. The horse was killed.

Gauvain went to him.

"Who is this man?" he said.

He looked at him. The blood was pouring from the gash and formed a red mask over the wounded man's face. It was impossible to make out his features. One could see that he had gray hair.

"This man has saved my life," continued Gauvain.

"Does any one here know who he is?"

"My commandant," said a soldier, "this man has just entered the town. I saw him when he came. He came by the road Pontorson."

The surgeon of the column came running with his case. The wounded man was still unconscious. The surgeon examined him and said,—

"A mere cut. It is nothing. It will heal. In a week he will be on his feet. It is a fine sword cut."

The wounded man had a cloak, a tricolored belt, pistols, a sword. They laid him on a litter. They took off his clothes. They brought a pail of fresh water, the surgeon washed the wound, his face began to appear. Gauvain watched him with deep attention.

"Has he any papers about him?" asked Gauvain.

The surgeon felt in a side pocket and drew out a portfolio, which he handed to Gauvain.

In the meantime, the wounded man, refreshed by the cold water, came to himself. His eyelids moved slightly. Gauvain opened the portfolio; he found in it a sheet of paper folded twice, he unfolded it and read,—

"Committee of Public Welfare. Citizen Cimourdain,—"

He cried out: "Cimourdain!"

This cry made the wounded man open his eyes.

Gauvain was distracted.

"Cimourdain! It is you! This is the second time you have saved my life."

Cimourdain looked at Gauvain. An unutterable joy lighted up his blood-stained face.

Gauvain fell on his knees before the wounded man, crying,—

"My master!" "Thy father," said Cimourdain.

CHAPTER V.

THE DROP OF COLD WATER.

They had not seen each other for many years, but their hearts had never been separated; they recognized each other as though they had only parted the day before.

A hospital had been improvised at the Hotel de Ville in Dol. They laid Cimourdain on a bed in a little room, next to the large general hall for the wounded. The surgeon, who had sewed up the wound, put an end to the effusions between the two men, saying that Cimourdain must be left to go to sleep. Besides, Gauvain was required by the thousand cares which make the duties and anxieties of victory. Cimourdain remained alone, but he did not sleep; he had two fevers, one from his wound, one from his joy.

He did not sleep, and still it seemed to him that he was not awake. Was it possible? his dream was realized. He was one of those who do not believe in luck and he was lucky. He had found Gauvain again. He had left him a child, and found him a man; he found him great, terrible, fearless. He found him in the midst of triumph, and triumph for the people. Gauvain was the point of support to the Revolution in Vendée and it was he, Cimourdain, who had given this column to the Republic. This victorious man was his pupil. "What he saw radiating from this young form, destined perhaps for the Republican pantheon, was his own thoughts,—Cimourdain's; his disciple, the child of his mind, was from this time forth a hero, and after a little would be a glory; it seemed to Cimourdain that he saw his own soul made into a genius; it was like Chiron seeing Achilles in battle. Mysterious relation between the priest and the centaur, for the priest is only a man to the waist.

All the dangers of this adventure, together with his sleeplessness after his wound, filled Cimourdain with a sort of mysterious intoxication. A young destiny was arising magnificently, and what added to his deep joy was the fact that he had full power over this life; another success like the one he had just seen, and Cimourdain would have to say but a word for the Republican to trust him with an army. Nothing dazzles like the astonishment at seeing everything succeed.

It was the time when each man had his own military dream, each wished to make a general: Danton wished to make a general of Westermann; Marat, of Rossignol; Hebert, of Ronsiu; Robespierre wanted to get rid of them all.

Why not Gauvain? said Cimourdain to himself; and he went on dreaming. The unbounded was before him; he passed from one hypothesis to another; all obstacles vanished; when one has once set his foot on this ladder he does not stop, it is an endless climb, one leaves man to reach the stars. A great general is only a chief of armies; a great captain is at the same time a chief of ideas; Cimourdain imagined Gauvain a great captain. It seemed to him, for dreams move swiftly, that he saw Gauvain on the ocean, repelling the English; on the Rhine, punishing the kings of the North; among the Pyrenees, repulsing the Spanish; in the Alps, making a signal for Rome to rise. There were in Cimourdain two men, a tender man and a gloomy man; both were satisfied; foras the inexorable was his ideal, he had seen Gauvain terrible as well as superb. Cimourdain thought of all that destruction must do before construction could begin, and surely, he thought, this is not the time for emotion. Gauvain will be "at the top" "—*à la hauteur*,"—a phrase of that day. Cimourdain imagined Gauvain crushing the shades of night under his foot, having on a breastplate of light, with a meteoric gleam on his brow, spreading the great ideal wings of Justice, Reason, and Progress, and carrying a sword in his hand; an angel, but of destruction.

At the very height of this dream, which was almost an ecstasy, he heard, through the partly opened door, talking in the great hospital ward, next his room; he recognized Gauvain's voice; that voice, which in spite of years of absence was always sounding in his ear, and the voice of the child was recognizable in the voice of the man. He listened. There was a sound of steps. Some soldiers said,—

"Commander, this is the man who shot at you. While nobody was noticing him, he dragged himself to a cellar. We have found him. Here he is."

Then Cimourdain heard this conversation between Gauvain and the man,—

"Are you wounded?"

"I am well enough to be shot."

" Put this man in a bed. Dress his wounds, care for him, heal him."

"I want to die."

"You will live. You wished to kill me in the name of the king; I pardon you in the name of the Republic."

A shadow passed over Cimourdain's face. He woke as it were with a start, and he murmured with a sort of ominous despondency,—

"He is surely merciful."

CHAPTER VI.

HEALED BREAST, A BLEEDING HEART.

A cut heals quickly; but there was some one elsewhere more seriously wounded than Cimourdain. It was the woman who had been shot at Herbe-en-Pail and had been picked up by the beggar Tellmarch in the great pool of blood.

Michelle Fléchard was in even greater danger than Tellmarch had supposed; there was a wound in her shoulder blade corresponding to the one above her breast; at the same time that the bullet broke her collar bone, another went through her shoulder; but as her lung had not been touched she might recover. Tellmarch was a "philosopher," an expression signifying something of a doctor, a little of a surgeon, a little of a sorcerer. He took care of the wounded woman in his den, on his pallet of seaweed, giving her those mysterious things called "simple remedies," and, thanks to him, she lived.

The collar bone knit together, the wounds in her breast and shoulder closed up; after a few weeks the wounded woman was convalescent.

One morning she was able to go out of the carnichot, leaning on Tellmarch; she sat down under the trees in the sun. Tellmarch knew little about her, breast wounds require perfect quiet, and during the agony preceding her recovery, she had hardly spoken a word. "When she wished to talk, Tellmarch made her keep silent; but her delirium was persistent, and Tellmarch noticed in her eyes the gloomy coming and going of painful thoughts. This morning she was strong, she could almost walk by herself; a cure is a paternity, and Tellmarch looked at her with happiness. This good old man began to smile, He spoke to her.

"Well, we are on our feet, we have no more wounds."

"Except in the heart," she said.

And she added,—

"So you don't know at all where they are?"

"Who?" asked Tellmarch.

"My children."

That "so" expressed a whole world of thoughts; it meant "since you never speak to me about them, since for so many days you have been by my side without opening your mouth about them, since you have made me keep silence every time I wished to break it, since you seem to fear that I should speak about them, it must be because you have nothing to tell me." Often in wandering and delirium of fever she had called her children, and had seen, for delirium takes note, that the old man did not answer her.

It was because Tellmarch really did not know what to say to her. It is not an easy matter to speak to a mother of her lost children. And, then, what did he know? Nothing. He knew that a mother had been shot, that this mother had been found on tho ground by him, that when he had picked her up she was almost a corpse, that this corpse had three children, and that the Marquis de Lantenac, after having the mother shot, had carried away the three children. All his information ended here. What had become of these children? Were they even still living? He knew, for he had made inquiries, that there were two boys, and a little girl hardly weaned. Nothing more. He asked himself a multitude of questions about this unfortunate group, but he could answer none of them. The country people whom he questioned could do no more than shake their heads. Monsieur de Lantenac was a man whom they did not willingly talk about.

People did not like to speak of Lantenac and they did not like to speak to Tellmarch. Peasants have a kind of suspicion peculiar to themselves. They did not love Tellmarch. Tellmarch the Caimand was a disquieting man. Why was he always looking at the sky? What was he doing and what was he thinking about in his long hours of inertness? He was really a strange man. In this country full of war, full of conflagration, full of combustion; where all the men had but one business, devastation; and but one work, carnage; where whoever wished burned a house, cut the throats of a family, massacred a port, plundered a village; where people thought of nothing but laying ambushes for each other, drawing each other into snares, and killing one another; this solitary man, absorbed in nature, as it were, submerged in the vast peace of things, gathering herbs and plants, occupied solely with flowers, birds, and stars, was evidently dangerous. Plainly, he had lost his reason; he did not lie in ambush, he shot nobody. Hence there was a certain dread regarding him.

"This man is mad," said the peasants.

Tellmarch was more than an isolated man, he was a man who was avoided.

No one asked him questions, and no one gave him satisfactory answers. He had consequently not been able to get as much information as he would have wished. The war had spread beyond, they had gone to fight farther away, the Marquis de Lantenac had disappeared from sight, and in Tellmarch's state of mind, war had to put its foot on him before he would notice it.

After these words, "my children," Tellmarch no longer smiled, and the mother was lost in thought. "What was passing in her soul? It was like the depths of an abyss. Suddenly she looked up at Tellmarch and cried out again in almost an angry voice,—

"My childen!"

Tellmarch bowed his head as though he were guilty. He was thinking of the Marquis de Lantenac, who was certainly not thinking of him; and, who, probably, was no longer even aware of his existence. He was calling himself to account for it, saying to himself: "A seigneur, when he is in danger, recognizes you; when he is out of danger, he recognizes you no longer."

And he asked himself: "But, then, why did I save this seigneur?"

And he replied: "Because he is a man."

He thought it over for some time, and added to himself,—

"Am I sure of it?"

And he repeated his bitter remark: "If I had known!"

He was overwhelmed by this adventure, for what he had done puzzled him. It was painful for him to think of it. A good action may, then, be a bad action. He who saves the wolf kills the sheep. He who repairs the vulture's wing is responsible for his claw.

He really felt that he was guilty. This mother's unreasoning anger was justifiable.

However, having saved the mother consoled him for having saved this marquis.

But the children!

The mother was thinking about them, too. Their thoughts were in the same direction, and without speaking to each other, they may have met in the shadows of reverie.

However, her eyes, in whose depths was the darkness of night, fastened on Tellmarch again.

"But it cannot go on like this," she said.

"Hush!" said Tellmarch, putting his finger on his lips. She continued,—

"You did wrong to save me, and I am angry with you for it. I would rather be dead, because I am sure I should see them. I should know where they are. They would not see me, but I should be near them. One when dead may be able to protect."

He took her arm and felt her pulse.

"Calm yourself, you will bring on the fever again."

She asked him almost harshly,—

"When can I go away?"

"Go away?"

"Yes, walk."

"Never, if you are not reasonable; to-morrow, if you are good."

"What do you call being good?"

"Having confidence in God."

"God! Where has he put my children?"

She was like one deranged. Her voice grew very gentle.

"You understand," she said to him, "I cannot stay like this. You have never had children, I have had them. That makes a difference. One cannot judge of a thing when he does not know what it is. You have never had any children, have you?"

"No," replied Tellmarch.

"As for me, I had nothing else. Without my children, what am I? I wish some one would tell me why I am without my children. I feel sure something has happened, but I do not understand. They have killed my husband, they shot me, but, all the same, I do not understand it."

"Come," said Tellmarch, "the fever is coming on again. Don't talk any more."

She looked at him and was silent.

After this day, she talked no more.

Tellmarch was obeyed more than he wished. She spent long hours crouching at the foot of the old tree, in a dull stupor. She pondered and was silent. Silence offers a strange protection to simple souls suddenly plunged into the gloomy depths of grief. She seemed to have given up understanding it. To a certain degree, despair is unintelligible to the despairing.

Tellmarch looked at her with emotion. In the presence of this suffering, this old man had a woman's thoughts. "Oh, yes," he said to himself, "her lips do not speak, but her eyes speak; I see what is the matter with her, one all-absorbing thought. To have been a mother and to be a mother no longer! To have been a nurse, and to be so no more! She cannot be resigned to it. She thinks of the little one she nursed not long since. She thinks about it, and thinks about it, and thinks about it. It surely must be delightful to feel a little rosy mouth drawing your soul out of your body, and from your life making a life for itself!"

For his part he was silent too, feeling before such affliction, the powerlessness of words. The silence of an all-absorbing idea is terrible. And how to make this mother's all-absorbing idea listen to reason? Maternity is illogical; one cannot reason with it. What makes a mother sublime is that she is a sort of animal. The maternal instinct is divinely animal. The mother is no longer a woman, she is a female.

Children are her young.

Hence, there is something in the mother inferior and superior to reason. A mother has a guiding scent. The vast mysterious will of creation is in her and guides her Blindness full of clear-sightedness.

Tellmarch now wanted to make this wretched woman talk; he did not succeed. Once, he said to her,—

"Unfortunately, I am old and unable to walk any longer. I come to the end of my strength before I come to the end of my journey. After a quarter of an hour, my legs refuse to go, and I am obliged to stop; otherwise, I should be able to accompany you. Perhaps in reality it is a good thing that I am not able. I should be more dangerous than useful to you; they tolerate me here; but I am suspected by the Blues as a peasant, and by the peasants as a sorcerer."

He waited for her to reply. She did not even raise her eyes. An all-absorbing idea ends in madness or heroism. But of what heroism was a poor peasant woman capable? Of none. She could be a mother, and that was all. Each day she buried herself more deeply in her thoughts. Tellmarch watched her.

He tried to give her occupation; he brought her thread, needles, and a thimble; and she really began to sew, which pleased the poor caimand; she pondered, but she worked, a sign of health; strength was returning gradually; she mended her linen, her garments, her shoes; but her eye still looked glassy. While she sewed, she hummed unintelligible songs in a low voice. She murmured names, probably those of her children, but not distinctly enough for Tellmarch to understand. She stopped to listen to the birds, as if they had news to give her. She watched the signs of the weather. Her lips moved. She talked to herself in a low voice. She made a bag and filled it with chestnuts. One morning, Tellmarch saw her starting away, looking at random into the depths of the forest.

"Where are you going?" he asked.

She replied,—

"I am going to look for them."

He did not try to detain her.

CHAPTER VII.

THE TWO POLES OF TRUTH.

After a few weeks full of all the vicissitudes of civil war, there was nothing else talked of in the country of Fougères, except two men who were opposed to each other, and who, nevertheless, were doing the same work, that is to say, fighting side by side in the great Revolutionary struggle.

The savage Vendéan duel still continued, but la Vendée was losing ground. In l'Ille-et-Vilaine particularly, thanks to the young commandant who at Dol had so opportunely replied to the daring of six thousand Royalists with the daring of fifteen hundred patriots, the insurrection was, if not extinguished, at least, very much lessened and limited. Several more fortunate strokes had followed this, and, of multiplied successes, a new situation was born.

Things had changed in appearance, but a singular complication had unexpectedly arisen.

In all this part of la Vendée the Republic had the supremacy; this was beyond a doubt; but what Republic? In the triumph which was in prospect, two forms of the Republic were present,—the republic of terror, and the republic of mercy; one wishing to conquer by severity, and the other by gentleness. Which would prevail? These two forms, the conciliatory and the implacable, were represented by two men, each with his own influence and authority; one, a military commander, the other, a civil delegate; which of these two men would carry the day?

One of these two men, the delegate, had formidable support; he had come bringing the menacing watchword of the Commune of Paris to Santerre's battalions. "No mercy, no quarter!" To bring everything under his authority, he had the decree of the Convention carrying "pain of death to any one setting at liberty, or helping to escape a captive rebel chief;" he had full power emanating from the Committee of Public Welfare, and an injunction to obey him, as delegate, signed : Robespierre, Dantox, Marat. The other, the soldier, had in his behalf only this force, pity.

He had nothing to aid him but his arms, which conquered the enemy, and his heart, which gave them mercy. As a conqueror, he believed he had the right to spare the vanquished.

Hence, the latent but deep conflict between these two men. They were in different clouds, both fighting the rebellion, and each having his own thunderbolt, one, victory; the other, terror.

Throughout the Bocage, they talked of nothing but them; and what added to the anxiety of the attention everywhere fixed on them, was the fact that these two men, so absolutely opposed to each other, were, at the same time closely united. These two antagonists were two friends. Never were two hearts bound together by a deeper and more profound sympathy; the cruel one had saved the life of the merciful one, and his face bore a scar in consequence. These two were the incarnation, one of death, the other of life; one was the principle of terror; the other the principle of peace; and they loved each other. Strange problem Let one imagine Orestes compassionate, and Pylades merciless. Let one imagine Ahriman the brother of Ormuzd.

Let us add that the one called "cruel" was at the same time the most brotherly of men; he dressed the wounded, cared for the sick, spent his days and nights in the hospitals, was affected at the sight of barefooted children, had nothing of his own, gave all to the poor. When there was fighting, he was in the midst of it: he marched at the head of the columns, and in the thickest of the battle, armed, for he had a sabre and two pistols in his belt, and unarmed, for he had never been seen to draw his sabre or touch his pistols. He faced the shots, and gave none in return. They said he had been a priest.

One of these men was Gauvain, the other was Cimourdain.

There was friendship between these two men, but hatred between the two principles; it was like one soul cut in two, and divided; Gauvain really had received a half of Cimourdain's soul, but the gentle half. It seemed as if Gauvain had received the white rays, and Cimourdain had kept for himself what might be called the black rays. This caused an intimate discord. It was impossible for this secret war not to burst forth. One morning the battle began.

Cimourdain said to Gauvain,—

"Where are we?"

Gauvain replied,—

"You know as well as I do. I have scattered Lantenac's bands. He has only a few men with him. He is driven back into the forest of Fougères. In a week he will be surrounded."

"And in two weeks?"

"He will be captured."

"And then?"

"Have you seen my notice?"

"Yes. Well?"

"He will be shot."

"Mercy again. He must be guillotined.

"For my part," said Gauvain, "I am for military death."

"And I," replied Cimourdain, "am for revolutionary death."

He looked Gauvain in the face, and said,—

"Why did you release those nuns of the convent of Saint-Marc-le-Blanc?"

"I am not making war on women," replied Gauvain.

"These women hate the people. And for hatred a woman is equal to ten men. Why did you refuse to send all that flock of old fanatic priests taken at Louvigné, to the Revolutionary tribunal?"

"I am not making war on old men."

"An old priest is worse than a young one. Rebellion is more dangerous when preached by white hairs. People have faith in wrinkles.

No false pity, Gauvain. Regicides are liberators. Keep your eye on the tower of the temple."

"The tower of the temple! I would release the dauphin. I am not making war on children."

Cimourdain's eye grew stern.

"Gauvain, know that it is necessary to make war on a woman when her name is Marie Antoinette, on an old man when his name is Pope Pius VI., and on a child, when his name is Louis Capet."

"My master, I am not a politician."

"Try not to be dangerous. Why, when the post of Cossé was attacked, and the rebel Jean Treton, driven back and lost, rushed alone, sword in hand, on the whole column, did you cry, 'Open the ranks — let him pass?'"

"Because one does not set fifteen hundred men to kill a single man."

"Why, at the Cailleterie d'Astillé, when you saw that your soldiers were going to kill the Vendéan, Joseph Bézier, who was wounded and dragging himself along, did you cry : 'Forward, march! I will attend to him!' and shoot your pistol into the air?"

"Because one does not shoot a man who is down."

"And you did wrong. Both are to-day chiefs of bands; Joseph Bézier is Moustache, and Jean Treton is Jambe d'Argent. In saving these two men, you gave two enemies to the Republic."

"Certainly, I should like to make friends for it and not give it enemies."

"Why did you not have your three hundred peasant prisoners shot after the victory of Landéan?"

"Because as Bonchamp had pardoned the Republican prisoners, I wished to have it said that the Republic pardoned the Royalist prisoners."

"But if you take Lantenac will you pardon him?"

"No."

"Why not, since you pardoned three hundred prisoners?"

"The peasants are ignorant; Lantenac knows what he is doing."

"But Lantenac is a relative of yours?"

"France is the great relative."

"Lantenac is an old man."

"Lantenac is a foreigner. Lantenac has no age. Lantenac is summoning the English. Lantenac is invasion. Lantenac is the enemy of the country. The duel between him and me can only end in his death or mine."

"Gauvain, remember your words."

"My promise is given."

There was a silence and both looked at each other.

Gauvain added,—

"This year of '93 in which we are living will be a bloody date."

"Take care!" exclaimed Cimourdain. "Terrible duties are before us. Accuse no one who is not at fault. How long has the malady been the fault of the physician? Yes, that which characterizes this tremendous year is that it is pitiless. Why? Because it is the great revolutionary year. This present year is the incarnation of the Revolution. The Revolution has an enemy, the Old World, and is pitiless to it, just as the surgeon has an enemy, gangrene, and is pitiless to it. The Revolution exterminates royalty in the king, aristocracy in the noble, despotism in the soldier, superstition in the priest, barbarity in the judge; in short, everything tyrannous in everything which tyrannies. The operation is frightful, but the Revolution works with a sure hand. As to the amount of sound flesh that it sacrifices, ask Bœrhave what he thinks about it. What tumor can be removed without involving a loss of blood? What fire can be extinguished without requiring a part of the fire? These terrible necessities are the very condition of success. A surgeon resembles a butcher; a healer may give the effect of an executioner. The Revolution devotes itself to its fatal work. It mutilates, but it saves. What! you ask mercy for the virus! you wish it to show clemency toward what is venomous! It does not listen. It holds what has passed, it will finish it. It makes a deep incision in civilization, out of which will emerge the health of the human race. You suffer? Without doubt. How long will it last? during the operation. Then you will live. The Revolution is amputating the world. Hence this hemorrhage, '93."

"The surgeon is calm," said Gauvain, "and the men I see are violent."

"The Revolution," replied Cimourdain, "needs ferocious workmen to assist it. It rejects every hand that trembles. It has faith only in the inexorable. Danton is terrible, Robespierre is inflexible, Saint-Just is immutable, Marat is implacable. Be on your guard, Gauvain. These names are necessary. They are worth whole armies to us. They will terrify Europe."

"And perhaps also the future," said Gauvain.

He stopped and then added,—

"Besides, my master, you make a mistake; I accuse nobody. In my opinion, the chief characteristic of the Revolution is its irresponsibility. No one is innocent, no one is guilty. Louis XVI. is a sheep thrown among lions; he wants to flee, he wants to escape; he tries to defend himself; he would bite if he could. But not every one can be a lion. This desire of his passes for a crime. This sheep, in anger, shows his teeth. 'The traitor!' say the lions, and they devour him. Having done this, they fight among themselves."

"The sheep is a beast."

"And the lions, what are they?"

This reply made Cimourdain thoughtful. He raised his head and said,—

"These lions are consciences, these lions are ideas, these lions are principles."

"They cause the terror."

"Some day the Revolution will be the justification of the terror."

"Fear lest the terror be the calumny of the Revolution."

And Gauvain added,—

"Liberty, Equality, Fraternity, these are dogmas of peace and harmony. Why make them appear frightful? What is it that we wish for? To subject the people to one common Republic. Well, let us not make them afraid. What is the good of intimidation? People are no more attracted by scare-crows than birds are. It is not necessary to do evil in order to accomplish good. The throne is not overturned to leave the scaffold standing. Death to kings and life to nations! Let us knock off the crowns, let us spare the heads! The Revolution is concord and not fright. Gentle ideas are not subserved by pitiless men. Amnesty is in my opinion the most beautiful word in human speech. I will shed blood only while risking my own. Besides, I only know how to fight, and I am only a soldier. But if one cannot pardon, it is not worth while to conquer. During battle, let us be the enemies of our enemies, and after the victory, their brothers."

"Take care!" repeated Cimourdain, for the third time, "Gauvain, you are more to me than a son. Take care!"

And he added, thoughtfully,—

"In times like ours, pity may be one form of treason."

Hearing these two men talk was like hearing the conversation of the sword and the axe.

CHAPTER VIII.

DOLOROSA.

In the meantime, the mother was looking for her little ones. She went straight ahead. How did she live? Impossible to tell. She herself did not know. She walked days and nights; she begged, she ate grass, she slept on the ground, she slept in the open air, in the thickets, under the stars, sometimes in the rain and the wind.

She roved from village to village, from farm to farm, asking for information. She stopped on the thresholds; her dress was in rags; sometimes she was welcomed, sometimes she was driven away. When she could not go into the houses, she went into the woods. She was not acquainted with the country. No region was familiar to her except Siscoignard and the parish of Azé. She had no definite route; she went back on her steps; started on a road that she had already been over; went on useless paths. Sometimes she followed the road, sometimes the tracks of a wagon, sometimes footpaths in the copses. In this life of chance, she had worn out her wretched clothing; she had walked first in shoes, then barefooted, then with bleeding feet.

She went into the midst of the war, in the midst of the firing, hearing nothing, seeing nothing, avoiding nothing, looking for her children. As everything was in revolt, there were no policemen, no mayors, no authorities. She had to do only with those whom she met. She spoke to them, she asked,—

"Have you seen three little children anywhere?"

The passers-by raised their heads.

"Two boys and a girl," she said.

She continued,—

"René-Jean, Gros-Alain, Georgette? You have not seen them?"

She went on.

"The oldest four years and a half, the little one twenty months old."

She added,—

"Do you know where they are? They have taken them away from me."

The people looked at her, and that was all.

Seeing that they did not understand, she said,—

"They are mine, that is why."

The people went on their way. Then she would stop and say no more, tearing her breast with her nails.

One day, however, a peasant listened to her. The good man began to ponder.

"Wait," he said. "Three children?"

"Yes."

"Two boys?"

"And a girl."

Then he asked again,—

"Are you looking for them?"

"Yes."

"I have heard tell of a seigneur, who took three little children, and had them with him."

"Where is this man," she cried. "Where are they?"

The peasant replied,—

"Go to la Tourgue."

"Shall I find my children there?"

"Probably, you will."

"You said?"

"La Tourgue?"

"What is la Tourgue?"

"It is a place."

"Is it a village? a castle? a farm?"

"I have never been there."

"Is it far?"

"It is not near."

"In what direction?"

"In the direction of Fourgères."

"How do you get there?"

"You are in Ventortes," said the peasant, "you leave Ernée on the left and Coxelles on the right, you pass by Lorchamps and you cross the Leroux."

And the peasant pointed toward the west.

"Right ahead of you all the way, in the direction of the sunset."

Before the peasant had dropped his arm, she had started.

The peasant called out,—

"But, take care. They are fighting over there."

She did not turn around to reply to him, but continued on her way.

CHAPTER IX.

A PROVINCIAL BASTILLE.

I.—La Tourgue.

The traveller of forty years ago, who entered the forest of Fougères from the side of Laignelet, and came out on the side of Parigné, was confronted with a forbidding object on the edge of these dark woods. As he emerged from the thicket, la Tourgue arose abruptly before him.

Not the living la Tourgue, but the dead la Tourgue. La Tourgue rent, ruined, scarred, dismantled. A ruin is to an edifice what a ghost is to a man.

There was no more gloomy sight than la Tourgue. Before one's eyes was a lofty round tower, standing alone in a corner of the wood, like a malefactor. This tower, rising from a perpendicular rock, was almost Roman in appearance, it was so regular and solid, and the idea of power was so mingled with the idea of ruin in this mighty mass. It was slightly Roman, for it was Romanesque: it was begun in the ninth century and finished in the twelfth, after the third Crusade. The impost mouldings of its archways told its age.

If the traveller approached it, climbed up the escarpment, noticed a breach, took his risk in entering, went inside, he found it empty. It was something like the inside of a stone trumpet placed upright on the ground. From top to bottom there were no partitions; there was no roof, no ceiling, no floor; there were arch stones and chimney-pieces, and embrasures for ancient cannon; at different heights, bands of granite corbels, and some cross-beams, marking the stories; the beams were covered with the lime of night birds; the colossal wall was fifteen feet thick at the base, and twelve at the summit; here and there were crevices and holes which had been doorways, through which could be seen dark staircases inside the wall. The passer-by who came in here in the evening would have heard the cries of the brown owl, herons, goat-suckers, and other birds; and would have seen under his feet brambles, stones, and reptiles; and above his head, through a black circle, which was the top of the tower and seemed like the mouth of an enormous well, the stars.

There was a tradition in the country that in the upper stories of this tower there were secret doors, like the doors in the tombs of the kings of Judah, made of a single stone turning on a pivot, opening, then closing and losing itself in the wall; a style of architecture brought back from the Crusades with the pointed arch. When these doors were closed it was impossible to find them, they were so well blended with the other stones in the wall. Such doors may be seen at the present time in the mysterious cities of Anti-Lebanon, escaped from the twelve towns which were buried by the earthquakes in the time of Tiberius.

II.—The Breach.

The breach which formed the entrance to the ruin was the opening to a mine. For a connoisseur familiar with Errard, Sardi and Pagan, this mine had been constructed according to rule. The fire chamber, shaped like a mitre, was proportioned to the power of the keep it had to rip open. It must have held at least two hundredweight of powder. It was reached by a winding passage, which is more advantageous than a straight one; the caving in caused by the mine laid bare, where the stones were torn away, the saucission having the diameter of a hen's egg. The explosion had made a deep hole in the wall, through which the besiegers must have been able to enter. This tower had evidently sustained regular sieges at different times; it was riddled with grapeshot; and the grapeshot did not all belong to the same period; each projectile has its own way of marking a rampart; and all had left their scar on this keep, from the stone cannon balls of the fourteenth century to the iron cannon balls of the eighteenth.

The breach opened into what must have been the ground floor. Opposite the breach in the wall of the tower, opened the door to a crypt cut out in the rock, and extending in the foundations of the tower under the entire hall of the ground floor.

This crypt, three quarters filled up, was cleared out in 1835, under the direction of Monsieur Auguste le Prévost, the Antiquary of Bernay.

III.—The Dungeon.

This crypt was the oubliette.

Every keep has its dungeon. This keep, like many torture chambers of the same period, had two stories. The first story which was reached by the door, was a large arched room on a level with the hall of the ground floor. On the wall of this room were seen two parallel, vertical grooves, extending from one side to the other across the arched ceiling, where they made a deep indentation, giving the impression of two wheel tracks. They were two wheel tracks in reality. These two grooves had been hollowed out by two wheels. Formerly, in feudal times, victims had been quartered in this room, by a less noisy process than with the four horses. They had two wheels there, so strong and so large that they touched the walls and the arched ceiling; an arm and a leg of the prisoner were fastened to each of the wheels, then the wheels were revolved in opposite directions, which tore the man asunder. It required force, and this caused the grooves hollowed out in the stone ground by the wheels. At the present time, a room of this kind may still be seen at Vianden.

Under this room there was another. This was the real dungeon. It was not entered by a door, it was penetrated through a hole; the victim, naked, was let down by a rope under the armpits, into the lower chamber, through a hole in the centre of the pavement of the room above. If he persisted in living, food was thrown to him through this hole. A hole of this kind may still be seen at Bouillon.

Air came through this hole. The lower room, dug out under the hall of the ground floor, was rather a well than a room. There was water at the bottom, and it was filled with an icy draught. This draught, which was death to the prisoner below, kept the prisoner above alive; it made it possible to breathe in the prison. The prisoner above, groping about under his arched ceiling, received no air except through this hole. Moreover, whoever went down there, or fell down there never came out again. The prisoner had to keep away from it in the darkness. One false step might make the prisoner of the upper chamber a prisoner of the lower. This was ever before him. If he clung to life this hole was his danger; if he was weary of it, this hole was his resource. The upper story was the dungeon; the lower story, the tomb. A superposition resembling the society of that time.

This was what our ancestors called a "*cul-de-basse-fosse.*" As such a thing has gone out of existence, the name has no meaning for us. Thanks to the Revolution, we can utter these words with indifference.

Outside the tower, above the breach which forty years ago was the only entrance, was an opening larger than the other loopholes, from which hung an iron grating, broken and loose.

IV.—The Little Castle on the Bridge.

On the opposite side of the breach, a bridge of stone with three arches very little injured, was joined to this tower. The bridge had supported a building, some fragments of which were still remaining. There was nothing left of this building, which showed evidence of a conflagration, but charred timbers, a sort of framework through which the daylight penetrated, and which rose near the tower, like a skeleton beside a ghost.

This ruin is now entirely demolished, and not a trace of it is left. One day and one peasant were enough to undo the work of many centuries and many kings.

La Tourgue is a peasant abbreviation for la Tour-Gauvain, just as la Jupelle is an abbreviation of la Jupellière, and as the name of that humpbacked chief, Pinson-le-Tort, means Pinson-le-Tortu.

La Tourgue, which was in ruins forty years ago, and to-day is only a name, in 1793 was a fortress. It was the old bastille of the Gauvain family, guarding the western entrance to the forest of Fougeres, a forest which is hardly a grove now.

This citadel was built on one of those great blocks of schist which abound between Mayenne and Dinan, and are scattered everywhere through the thickets and moors, as though the giants had been throwing stones at each other's heads.

The tower comprised the whole fortress; under the tower was the rock, at the foot of the rock one of those streams of water which the month of January changes to a torrent, and the month of June dries up entirely.

Simplified to this extent, the fortress in the middle ages was almost impregnable. The bridge weakened it. The Gothic Gauvains had built it without a bridge. It was reached by one of those movable foot bridges, which could be destroyed by a single axe blow. While the Gauvains were viscounts, it pleased them thus, and they were satisfied with it; but when they became marquises, and when they left the cave for the court, they threw three arches across the torrent, and made themselves accessible from the plain, just as they had made themselves accessible to the king. The marquises of the seventeenth century and the marchionesses of the eighteenth, did not care to be impregnable. Imitating Versailles took the place of keeping up the ancestral traditions.

In front of the tower on the western side was a very high table-land, extending to the plains; this table-land almost touched the tower, and was only separated from it by a very deep ravine, through which flowed the watercourse which is a tributary of the Couesnon. The bridge connecting the fortress and the table-land was built high on piers; and on these piers was constructed a building like that at Chenonceaux in the Mansard style, and more habitable than the tower. But manners were still very rude; the seigneurs held to the custom of living in the rooms of the keep, which were like dungeons. As for the building on the bridge, which was a sort of chatelet, it contained a long corridor which served as an entrance and was called the guard hall; above this guard hall, which was a sort of entresol, was the library, above the library, a granary. Long windows with little panes of Bohemian glass, pilasters between the windows, medallions carved in the wall; three stories: on the lower floor were the halberds and muskets; on the next, the books; on the next, bags of oats; all this was rather savage and very princely.

The tower beside it was fierce.

It rose above this coquettish building in all its gloomy haughtiness. From the platform, the bridge could be destroyed.

The two edifices, one rude, the other elegant, clashed rather than complimented each other. The two styles were not harmonious; although it seems as if two semicircles ought to be similar, nothing resembles a Roman semicircle less than a classic archivault. This tower, suited to the forest, was a strange neighbor to this bridge worthy of Versailles. Imagine Alain Barbe-Torte giving his arm to Louis XIV. The combination was terrible. A strange ferocity resulted from the union of these two majesties.

From a military point of view, the bridge, we must insist, almost betrayed the tower. It adorned it and disarmed it; in gaining ornamentation it had lost strength. The bridge placed it on a footing with the table-land. Although still impregnable on the side of the forest, it was now vulnerable on the side of the plain. Once it commanded the table-land, now it was commanded by the table-land. An enemy established there, would quickly become master of the bridge. The library and the granary were to the advantage of the besieger, and against the fortress. A library and a granary are alike in this respect, that books and straw are both combustible. It is all the same to a besieger, making use of fire, whether he burns Homer or a bundle of hay, provided it burns. The French proved this to the Germans when they burned the library at Heidelberg, and the Germans proved it to the French when they burned the library at Strasburg. Adding this bridge to la Tourgue was strategically a mistake; but in the seventeenth century, under Colbert and Louvois, the Gauvain princes, as well as the princes of Rohan and the princes of la Trémoille, believed that they would never be besieged again.

However, the builders of the bridge had taken some precautions. First, they had taken the possibility of fire into account; under the three windows on the side next the water they had hung crosswise, to hooks which could still be seen a half century ago, a strong ladder for escape, as long as the height of the first two stories of the bridge, a height greater than three ordinary stories. Second, they had taken the possibility of assault into account; they had isolated the bridge from the tower by means of a low, heavy iron door; this door was arched; it was locked with a large key, kept in a hiding-place known to the keeper alone, and once closed, this door could defy the battering-ram, and almost withstand cannon balls.

It was necessary to pass through the bridge to reach this door, and to pass through this door to enter the tower. There was no other entrance.

V.—The Iron Door.

The second story of the chatelet on the bridge, raised on the piers, corresponded to the second story of the tower; the iron door had been placed at this height to make it more secure.

The iron door opened from the side of the bridge into the library, and from the side of the tower into a great arched hall with a pillar in the centre. This hall, as has already been said, was in the second story of the keep. It was round, like the tower; long loopholes, looking out on the plains, lighted it. The wall was quite rough and bare, and nothing concealed the stones, which were very symmetrically laid. This hall was reached by a winding staircase made inside the wall, a thing easily done when the walls are fifteen feet thick. In the Middle Ages, a town was taken street by street; a street, house by house; a house, room by room. They besieged a fortress, story by story.

La Tourgue was in this respect very ingeniously arranged, very churlish, and very unapproachable. A spiral staircase, extremely steep and inaccessible, led from one story to another; the doors were slanting and not so high as a man, and it was necessary to bow one's head in order to pass through; but a bowed head meant a head knocked off, and at each door the besieged awaited the besiegers.

Below the round hall with the column were two similar rooms, which formed the first story and the ground floor, and above there were three; above these six rooms placed one upon another, the tower was closed over with a roof of stone, which was the platform, and reached by a narrow watch-tower.

The fifteen feet, the thickness of the wall, which they must have had to cut through in order to place the iron door in the middle, imbedded it in a long coving, so that when the door closed, it was as much on the side of the tower as on the side of the bridge, under a porch six or seven feet deep; when it was open the two porches formed one and made the entrance arch.

Under the porch on the side of the bridge, inside the wall, was a low gate with a St. Gilles's staircase, leading to the corridor on the first floor, under the library; this was still another difficulty for the besieger. The chatelet on the bridge presented nothing but a perpendicular wall on the side next the table-land, and the bridge ended there. A draw-bridge, applied to a low door, put it in communication with the table-land, and this draw-bridge, never lowered except on an inclined plane, on account of the height, gave entrance to the long corridor, called the hall of the guards. Once master of this corridor, the besieger, in order to reach the iron door, was obliged to tear away the St. Giles's staircase leading to the second story.

VI.—The Library.

The library was an oblong hall of the same width and length as the bridge, and having a single door, the iron door. A false swinging door, padded with green cloth, and opening with a push, screened the arched entrance to the tower on the inside. The wall of the library from top to bottom, and from floor to ceiling was covered with cabinets having glass doors, in the beautiful style of carpentry of the seventeenth century.

Six large windows, three on each side, one above each arch, lighted this library. From the top of the plateau outside, one could look through these windows and see the inside. Between the windows, on carved oak terminals, stood six marble busts: Hermolaüs, of Byzantium; Athenæus, the grammarian of Naukratos; Suidas; Casaubon; Clovis, king of France; and his chancellor Anachalus, who, by the way, was no more a chancellor than Clovis was a king.

There were books of every kind in this library. One has become famous. It was an old quarto with prints, bearing the title, "Saint Bartholomew," in large letters; and the sub-title, "Gospel according to Saint Bartholomew, preceded by a dissertation by Panteanus, a Christian philosopher, on the question whether this gospel should be considered apocryphal, and whether Saint Bartholomew be the same as Nathaniel."

This book, thought to be the only copy, rested on a desk in the centre of the library. In the last century, people went to see it out of curiosity.

VII.—The Granary.

The granary which, like the library, had the oblong form of the bridge, was merely the space under the timber-work of the roof. It made a large hall and was filled with straw and hay, and lighted by six garret windows. It's only adornment was a figure of Saint Barnabas, carved on the door, with this verse beneath it,—

Barnabus sanctus falcem jubet ire per herbam.

A wide, lofty tower, with six stories, penetrated by an occasional loophole, having for its only means of entrance and exit an iron door opening on a castle bridge, closed by a drawbridge; behind the tower, the forest; in front of the tower, a plateau covered with heath: under the bridge, between the tower and the plateau, a deep ravine, narrow and full of brambles; a torrent in winter, a brook in spring, a stony ditch in summer; such was the Tour-Gauvain, called la Tourgue.

CHAPTER X.

THE HOSTAGES.

July passed. August came, a blast of heroism and cruelty blew over France; two spectres had just crossed the horizon, Marat with a dagger in his side, Charlotte Corday headless; everything was becoming terrible.

As for la Vendée, beaten in great strategic measures, she took refuge in small ones, more frightful, as we have already said; this war was now an immense skirmish in the woods.

The disasters to the great army called Catholic and Royal were beginning; a decree sent the army of Mayence to la Vendée; eight thousand Vendéans were killed at Ancenis; the Vendéans were repulsed at Nates, driven out of Montaigu, expelled from Thouars, driven from Noirmoutier, thrown headlong from Cholet, Mortagne, and Saumur; they evacuated Parthenay; they abandoned Clisson; they lost ground at Châtillon; they lost a flag at Saint-Hilaire; they were defeated at Pornic, at the Sables, at Fontenay, Doué, the Château d'Eau, the Ponts-de-Cé; they were held in check at Luçon; retreated from Châtaigneraye; were routed at Roche-sur-Yon: but, on the one hand, they were threatening la Rochelle, and, on the other, in the Guernsey waters, an English fleet, commanded by General Craig, carrying several English regiments together with the best officers of the French marine, was only waiting for a signal from the Marquis de Lantenac, to disembark.

This disembarkation might give back victory to the royalist insurrection. But Pitt was a State malefactor; treason is to statesmanship what the dagger is to the panoply; Pitt stabbed our country and betrayed his own; betraying his country was dishonoring it; England under him, and through him, waged a Punic war. She spied, cheated, lied. A poacher and a forger, no means were scorned by her; she even descended to the minutiæ of hatred. She caused a monopoly of tallow, which cost five francs a pound; a letter from Prizant, Pitt's agent in Vendée, was taken from an Englishman at Lille, containing these lines,—

"I beg you not to be sparing of money. We hope that the assassinations will be done with prudence; disguised priests and women are the suitable persons for this undertaking. Send sixty thousand livres to Rouen, and fifty thousand livres to Caen."

This letter was read by Barèr to the Convention the first of August. This treachery was answered by Parrein's cruelties, and later on by Carrier's atrocities. The Republicans of Metz and the Republicans of the South asked permission to march against the rebels. A decree ordered the forming of twenty-four companies of pioneers to burn the hedges and fences of the Bocage. An unprecedented crisis. The war only ceased in one direction to begin again in another. "No mercy! no prisoners!" was the cry of both parties. History was full of a terrible darkness.

In this month of August, la Tourgue was besieged.

One evening, as the stars were beginning to shine, in the quiet of a dog-day twilight, when not a leaf trembled in the forest, not a blade of grass stirred on the moor, through the silence of the approaching darkness, the sound of a horn was heard. The sound of this horn came from the top of the tower.

This horn was answered by a trumpet, which sounded from below.

At the top of the tower there was an armed man; below, in the darkness, there was a camp.

A swarm of black figures could be made out in the dim light around the Tour-Gauvain. This swarm was a bivouac. Fires were beginning to be lighted under the trees in the forest and in the heather on the plateau, piercing the darkness here and there with bright points of light, as if the earth wished to shine with stars as well as the sky. Gloomy stars,—those of war! The bivouac, in the direction of the plateau, reached as far as the plains, and in the direction of the forest, it extended into the thicket. La Tourgue was blockaded.

The extent of the besieger's bivouac indicated a numerous force.

The camp was situated close to the fortress, and on the side of the tower, reached to the rock, and on the side of the bridge, to the edge of the ravine.

There was a second blast from the horn, followed by a second blowing of the trumpet.

This horn questioned, and the trumpet gave answer.

The horn was the tower asking the camp, "Can we speak to you?" And the trumpet replied, "Yes."

At this period, as the Vendéans were not considered warriors by the Convention, and as a decree had forbidden the exchange of flags of truce with "these brigands," they supplied, as best they could, the means of communication which the right of nations authorizes in ordinary warfare, and forbids in civil warfare. So on occasion, there was a certain understanding arranged between the peasant's horn and the soldier's trumpet. The first call was only to attract attention, the second call put the question, "Will you listen?" If after this second call the trumpet was silent, it meant refusal; if the trumpet answered, it meant consent. This signified a few moments' truce.

The trumpet having replied to the second call, the man on the top of the tower spoke, and these were his words,—

"Ye men who hear me, I am Gouge-le-Bruant, called Brisebleu, because I have put an end to so many of your men; and called also l'Imânus, because I shall kill still more than I have killed; I had my finger cut off by a sabre stroke on the barrel of my gun, during the attack at Granville, and you had my father and mother, and my sister Jacqueline eighteen years old, guillotined at Laval;—this is who I am.

"I speak to you in the name of Monseigneur the Marquis Gauvain de Lantenac, Viscount de Fontenay, Prince of Brittany, seigneur of the seven forests, my master.

"Know first, that before Monseigneur le Marquis shut himself up in this tower where you have blockaded him, he distributed the war among six chiefs, his lieutenants; he gave to Delière the country between the road to Brest and the road to Ernée; to Treton, the country between la Roë and Laval; to Jacquet, called Taillefer, the boundary of the Upper Maine; to Gaulier, called Great Peter, Château-Gontier; to Leconte, Craon; Fougères to Monsieur Dubois-Guy; and all la Mayenne to Monsieur de Rochambeau; in order that you might accomplish nothing by taking this fortress, and that even if Monseigneur le Marquis should die, la Vendée of God and the king should not die.

"Know this, that what I tell you is to warn you.

"Monseigneur is here by my side. I am the mouth through which his words pass. Ye men, who besiege us, keep silence.

"This is what it is important for you to hear,—

"Do not forget that the war that you are waging against us is unjust. We are people living in our own country, and we are fighting honestly, and we are simple and pure beneath the will of God, as the grass beneath the dew. The Republic has attacked us; it came to disturb us in our fields, it has burned our houses and our crops, and cannonaded our farms, and our women and children have been obliged to flee barefooted into the woods while the winter birds were still singing.

"You, who are present and hear what I say, have driven us into the forest, and you are surrounding us in this tower; you have killed or scattered those who were united to us; you have cannon; you have joined to your column, the garrisons and posts of Mortain, Barenton, Teilleul, Landivy, d'Evran, Tinteniac and Vitré, and the result is that you are attacking us with four thousand five hundred soldiers, and we have but nineteen men for our defence.

"We have provisions and ammunition.

"You have succeeded in contriving a mine and in blowing up a piece of our rock and a piece of our wall.

"That made a hole at the foot of the tower, and this hole is a breach, through which you can enter, although it is not open to the sky, and the tower, still strong and firm, forms an arch above it.

"Now you are preparing to attack us.

"And we, first, monseigneur le marquis, who is Prince of Brittany and secular Prior of the abbey of Saint-Marie de Lantenac, where daily mass was established by Queen Jeanne; and next, the other defenders of the tower, among whom are Monsieur l'Abbé Turmeau, in war, Grand-Francœur; my comrade Guinoiseau, captain of Camp-Vert; my comrade, Chante-en-Hiver, captain of the camp of l'Avoine; my comrade, la Musette, captain of the camp of the Fourmis; and myself, a peasant, who was born in the market-town of Daon, through which the brook Moriandre flows,—we all of us have one thing to say to you.

"Men who are at the foot of this tower, listen.

"We have in our hands three prisoners, three children. These children were adopted by one of your battalions, and they are yours. We offer to give up these three children to you.

"On one condition.

"That is that you will let us go free.

"If you refuse, listen attentively. You can attack us in only two ways; by means of the breach, from the side of the forest; or by means of the bridge, from the side of the plateau. The building on the bridge is three stories high; in the lower story, I, l'Imânus, I who speak to you, have had six tons of tar and one hundred fagots of dried heath placed there; in the upper story, there is straw; the middle story is full of books and papers; the iron door leading from the bridge to the tower is closed, and monseigneur has the key; and I have made an opening under the door, and through this opening passes a sulphur slow-match, one end of which is in the hogsheads of tar, and the other within my reach, inside the tower; I shall set fire to it whenever it seems good to me. If you refuse to let us out, the three children will be placed in the second story of the bridge, between the story where the sulphur match ends and where the tar is, and the story filled with straw, and the iron door will be fastened on them. If you attack by the bridge you will be the ones to set fire to the building; if you attack by the breach, we shall be the ones; if you attack by the breach and the bridge at the same time, the fire will be set by you and by us; and in any case the children will perish.

"Now, accept or refuse.

"If you accept, we leave.

"If you refuse, the children die.

"I have said my say."

The man who spoke from the top of the tower was silent.

A voice from below cried out,—

"We refuse."

This voice was short and stern. Another voice, less harsh, but firm, added,—

"We give you twenty-four hours to surrender at discretion."

Silence ensued, and the same voice continued,—

"To-morrow at this hour, if you do not surrender, we shall begin the attack."

And the first voice added,—

"And then, no quarter."

To this savage voice, another replied from the top of the tower. Between two battlements a tall shadow bent forward, in which, by the light of the stars, could be made out the formidable face of the Marquis de Lantenac, and this face which looked into the darkness as if trying to find some one, cried,—

"Hold, it is you, priest!"

"Yes, it is I, traitor!" replied the harsh voice from below.

CHAPTER XI.

TERRIBLE AS IN ANCIENT DAYS.

The relentless voice really was Cimourdain's; the younger and less imperious voice was Gauvain's.

The Marquis de Lantenac had not been mistaken in recognizing the Abbé Cimourdain.

In a few weeks, Cimourdain, as we know, had become famous in this country made bloody by civil war; there was no more ominous notoriety than his; people said: "Marat, in Paris; Châlier, in Lyons; Cimourdain, in Vendée. They cursed the Abbé Cimourdain in proportion as they had once revered him; such is the effect of a priest renouncing his robes. Cimourdain was a cause of horror. The stern are unfortunate; whoever sees their deeds condemns them, but if their consciences could be seen they would, perhaps, be forgiven. A Lycurgus, who is not explained seems a Tiberius. The two men, the Marquis de Lantenac and the Abbé Cimourdain were equal in the balance of hatred; the malediction of the Royalists against Cimourdain was counterbalanced by the execration of the Republicans against Lantenac. Each of these two men was a monster in the eyes of the opposite party; to such an extent that it produced this singular fact, that while Prieur de la Marne, at Granville, was putting a price on Lantenac's head, Charette, at Noirmoutier was setting a price on the head of Cimourdain.

We may say that these two men, the marquis and the priest, were to a certain extent the same man. The bronze mask of civil war has two profiles; one turned toward the past, the other turned toward the future; both equally tragic. Lantenac was the first of these profiles, Cimourdain was the second; only Lantenac's bitter sneer was full of darkness and night, while Cimourdain's fatal brow glowed with the light of morning.

In the meantime, the siege of la Tourgue had a respite.

Thanks to the intervention of Gauvain, as we have just seen, a sort of twenty-four hours' truce had been agreed upon.

L'Imânus had indeed been well posted, and in consequence of Cimourdain's requisition Gauvain now had under his command four thousand five hundred men, as many National Guards as troops of the line, and with these he was surrounding Lantenac in la Tourgue; and he had been able to point twelve pieces of cannon at the fortress, a masked battery of six pieces on the edge of the forest toward the tower, and an open battery of six pieces on the plateau toward the bridge. He had been able to spring the mine and make a breach at the foot of the tower.

So, at the expiration of the twenty-four hours' truce, the struggle was going to begin under the following conditions,—

There were four thousand five hundred men on the plateau and in the forest.

In the tower, nineteen.

The names of these nineteen besieged men may be found by history among the lists of outlaws. Possibly, we shall come across them.

Cimourdain would have liked to have Gauvain made adjutant-general to command these four thousand five hundred men, who made almost an army. But Gauvain had refused, saying, "When Lantenac has been taken we will see. I have not yet done anything to deserve it."

Great commands with humble rank were, moreover, customary among the Republicans. Later on, Bonaparte was both colonel of artillery and general-in-chief of the army of Italy.

The Tour-Gauvain had a strange fate; it was attacked by a Gauvain, and it was a Gauvain who defended it. This caused some restraint in the attack, but not in the defence, for Monsieur de Lantenac was one of those men who have no regard for anything, and besides he had lived chiefly at Versailles, and had no superstitious feeling for la Tourgue, which he was hardly acquainted with. He had taken refuge because it was the only place, and that was all; but he had no scruple about destroying it. Gauvain was more respectful.

The weak point of the fortress was the bridge; but the library on the bridge contained the family archives; if the attack were made there, the burning of the bridge was inevitable; it seemed to Gauvain that burning the archives was attacking his ancestors. La Tourgue was the family mansion of the Gauvains; all their fiefs of Brittany centred about this tower, just as all the fiefs of France centred about the tower of the Louvre; the family relics of the Gauvains were there; he himself had been born there; the tortuous fatalities of life had brought him as a man to attack these walls which had protected him as a child. Should he be so irreverent toward this dwelling as to reduce it to ashes? Perhaps Gauvain's own cradle was in some corner of the granary over the library. Some reflections become emotions. Gauvain felt moved before the ancient family mansion. That is why he spared the bridge. He had limited himself to rendering all egress and escape impossible by this way, and out of respect guarded the bridge with a battery, and had chosen the opposite side for attack. Hence the mine and the sap at the foot of the tower.

Cimourdain had allowed him to do this; he reproached himself for it, because his severity frowned on all this Gothic rubbish, and he did not wish to be any more indulgent toward buildings than toward men. To care for a castle was a beginning of clemency. Now, clemency was Gauvain's weak side. Cimourdain, we know, watched him with his gloomy eyes and arrested this inclination. However, he himself, and he admitted it with anger, did not look on la Tourgue again without a secret thrill; he felt moved by that studious hall where the first books were which he had taught Gauvain to read; he had been priest of the neighboring village, Parigné; he, Cimourdain, had lived in the top of the castle on the bridge; in the library was where he used to hold the little Gauvain on his knees while he learned the alphabet; between these four old walls he had seen his dearly beloved pupil, the son of his soul, grow as a man and increase as a mind. This library, this castle, these walls, full of his blessings on the child, should he overthrow them and burn them? He pitied them. Not without remorse.

He had let Gauvain begin the siege on the opposite side. La Tourgue had its savage side, the tower, and its civilized side, the library. Cimourdain had allowed Gauvain to make a breach only on the savage side.

Moreover, this old dwelling, attacked by a Gauvain, defended by a Gauvain, was returning, in the midst of the French Revolution, to its feudal customs. Wars between relatives make up the entire history of the Middle Ages; the Eteocles and Polynices are Gothic as well as Greek, and Hamlet does at Elsinore what Orestes did in Argos.

CHAPTER XII.

A SCHEME FOR ESCAPE.

The whole night was spent on both sides in making preparations.

As soon as the ominous conference just heard, was ended, Gauvain's first care was to call his lieutenant.

Guéchamp, whom it is necessary to know somewhat, was a man of secondary abilities, honest, fearless, ordinary, a better soldier than leader, strictly intelligent to the point where it was his duty to understand no further, never compassionate, inaccessible to corruption of any sort, to venality which corrupts conscience, as well as to pity which corrupts justice. Over his soul and his heart he had these two shades, discipline and order, as a horse has blinders over his two eyes, and he walked straight before him in the space which they left free to him. His gait was unswerving, but his path was narrow.

Moreover, he was a man to be depended upon; stern in command, unflinching in obedience.

Gauvain immediately addressed Guéchamp,—

"Guéchamp, a ladder."

"Commandant, we have none."

"We must have one."

"For climbing?"

"No, for rescue."

Guéchamp reflected and replied,—

"I understand. But for what you want, it must be very high."

"At least three stories."

"Yes, commander, that is very nearly the height."

"And it must exceed this to be sure of success."

"Certainly."

"How does it happen that you are without a ladder?"

"Commander, you did not consider the matter of besieging la Tourge from the plateau; you were satisfied to blockade it from this side; you wanted to attack it, not by the bridge, but by the tower. We have paid no attention to anything but the mine and gave up the escalade. That is why we have no ladders."

"Have one made immediately."

"A ladder three stories high cannot be improvised."

"Fasten together several short ladders."

"It is necessary to have short ones."

"Find them."

"They are not to be found. The peasants destroy the ladders everywhere, just as they break up the wagons and cut away the bridges."

"It is true; they want to paralyze the Republic."

"They want to make it impossible for us either to transport baggage, pass a river, or scale a wall."

"I must have a ladder, nevertheless."

"Now I think about it, commander, there is a large carpenter's shop at Javené, near Fougères. They may have one there."

"There is not a moment to lose."

"When do you wish to have the ladder?"

"To-morrow at this time at the very latest."

"I will send an express to Javené post haste. He will carry the order of requisition. There is cavalry stationed at Javené, which will furnish the escort. The ladder could be here to-morrow, before sunset."

"That is good, that will do," said Gauvain. "Be quick about it. Go."

Ten minutes later, Guéchamp returned and said to Gauvain,—

"Commander, the express has left for Javené."

Gauvain went up on the plateau, and remained a long time looking steadily at the bridge castle, which was just across the ravine. The gable of the châtelet, with no opening except the low entrance closed by raising the drawbridge, faced the escarpment of the ravine. To reach the foot of the piers of the bridge from the plateau, it was necessary to descend along this steep cliff, which was not impossible through the underbrush. But, once in the ditch, the assailants would be exposed to all the projectiles that could be rained down from the three stories. Gauvain came to the conclusion that, in view of the present state of the siege, the real assault must be by the breach in the tower.

He took every precaution to prevent the possibility of escape; he completed the close investment of la Tourgue; he drew the ranks of his battalions close together in such a way that nothing could pass through them. Gauvain and Cimourdain divided the investment of the fortress; Gauvain kept the side toward the forest, and gave the side next the plateau to Cimourdain. It was agreed that while Gauvain, aided by Guéchamp, was carrying on the assault by sapping, Cimourdain, with all the linstocks of the battery ready for use, should guard the bridge and the ravine.

CHAPTER XIII.

WHAT THE MARQUIS DOES.

While everything without was making ready for the attack, everything within was making ready for resistance.

There is a real analogy in calling a tower a "douve" and a tower is sometimes pierced by a mine as a cask is by an auger. A bunghole, as it were, is bored through the wall. This is what happened at la Tourgue.

The powerful blast made by two or three hundredweight of powder had made a breach right through the enormous wall. This breach started at the foot of the tower, went through the thickest part of the wall, and ended in a rude arch in the ground floor of the fortress. In order to make this breach practicable for the assault, the besiegers had enlarged it outside and shaped it with cannon shots.

The ground floor into which this breach opened was a large round hall, quite bare, with a central column holding up the keystone of the arch. This hall, the largest in the keep, was no less than forty feet in diameter. Each story in the tower formed a similar room, but smaller, with little cells in the embrasures of the loopholes. The hall on the ground floor had no loopholes, no air holes, no windows; about as much daylight and fresh air as a tomb.

The door to the oubliettes, made of iron rather than wood, was in the hall of the ground floor. Another door in this hall opened on a staircase leading to the upper rooms. All the staircases were built in the thickness of the wall.

The besiegers had an opportunity to reach this low hall through the breach which they had made. This hall taken, it remained for them to take the tower.

No one had ever been able to breathe in this low hall. No one had ever spent twenty-four hours there without being asphyxiated. Now, owing to the breach, it was possible to live there.

This is why the beleaguered did not close the breach.

Moreover, what would be the advantage? The cannon would open it again.

They fixed an iron cresset into the wall, placed a torch in it, and this lighted the ground floor.

Now, how could they defend themselves there?

To wall up the breach was easy, but of no use. A retirade would be more desirable. A retirade is an intrenchment at right angles, a sort of chevronned barricade, which admits of converging the musketry on the assailants, and, while leaving the breach open outside, obstructs it on the inside. The materials were not lacking; they constructed a retirade, with embrasures through which to pass the barrels of the guns. The angle of the retirade rested on the central column; the two sides touched the wall. Having got this ready, they put fougades in suitable places.

The marquis directed everything. Inspirer, disposer, guide, and master,— appalling soul.

Lantenac belonged to that race of warriors of the eighteenth century who, when eighty years old, saved cities. He resembled the Count d'Alberg who, when he was nearly a centenarian, drove the King of Poland from Riga.

"Courage, friends!" said the marquis; "in the beginning of this century, in 1713, at Bender, Charles XII., shut up in a house, with three hundred Swedes, resisted twenty thousand Turks."

They barricaded the two lower stories, they fortified the rooms, they embattled the alcoves, they strengthened the doors with joists driven down with mallets, forming a sort of flying buttresses; but the spiral staircase which communicated with each story they had to leave open, as it was necessary to have free passage through it; to cut this off from the besieger was to cut it off from the besieged. The defence of strongholds always has some such weak side.

The marquis, indefatigable, as robust as a young man, lifted beams, carried stones, set an example, worked, commanded, helped, fraternized, laughed with this savage clan, but still he was always the seigneur, haughty, easy, elegant, cruel.

He allowed no one to reply to him.

He said: "If one half of you were to revolt, I would have that half shot by the other, and I would defend the place with the rest." Such things make a chief adored.

CHAPTER XIV.
WHAT L'IMÂNUS DOES.

While the marquis was engaged with the breach and the tower, l'Imânus was engaged with the bridge. At the beginning of the siege, the ladder of escape, which hung horizontally outside and underneath the windows of the second story, had been taken away by order of the marquis, and put by l'Imânus in the hall of the library. Perhaps it was this ladder which Gauvain wished to replace. The windows of the entresol of the first story, called "hall of the guards," were protected by a triple row of iron bars fastened in the stonework, and it was impossible to get in or out through them.

There were no bars at the library windows, but they were very high.

L'Imânus had three men, who, like himself, were full of resolution, and capable of anything. These men were Hoisnard, called Branche-d'Or, and the two brothers Pique-en-Bois. L'Imânus took a dark lantern, opened tho iron door, and carefully inspected the three stories of the bridge châtelet. Hoisnard Branche-d'Or was as implacable as l'Imânus, having had a brother killed by the Republicans.

L'Imanus examined the upper story, overflowing with hay and straw, and the lower story into which he had brought some firepots in addition to the hogsheads of tar; he had the pile of heather fagots placed close to the hogsheads of tar, and he made sure that the sulphur match, one end of which was in the bridge and the other in the tower, was in a good condition. He poured out on the floor under the hogsheads and over the fagots a pool of tar, in which he placed the end of the sulphur slowmatch; then in the hall of the library, between the ground floor where the tar was and the granary where the straw was, he had placed the three cribs in which were René-Jean, Gros-Alain, and Georgette, sound asleep. They carried the cribs very gently, in order not to waken the little ones.

They were very simple little country cribs, a sort of very low osier baskets, that stand on the floor, allowing the child to get out alone and without assistance. Near each crib, l'Imânus had placed a porringer of soup with a wooden spoon. The ladder for escape, unfastened from its hooks, had been laid on the floor against the wall; l'Imânus had the three cribs arranged, end to end, along the other wall, opposite the ladder. Then, thinking that a draught of air might be useful, he opened wide all six of the library windows. It was a summer night, hot and sultry.

He sent the brothers Pique-en-Bois to open the windows in the upper and lower stories; he noticed on the eastern façade of the building, a large, old, dried-up ivy, the color of tinder, covering one entire side of the bridge from top to bottom, and framing the windows of the three stories. He thought that this ivy would do no harm. L'Imânus took a last look around; after this the four men went out of the châtelet and went back to the keep. L'Imânus fastened the heavy iron door with a double lock, carefully examined the enormous, formidable fastening, and, with a nod of satisfaction, looked at the sulphur slow-match, which passed through the hole he had made, and was henceforth the only communication between the tower and the bridge.

This match started from the round room, passed under the iron door, entered under the coving, went down the staircase leading to the ground floor of the bridge, meandered over the winding stairs, crept along the floor of the corridor in the entresol, and ended in the pool of tar over the pile of dry fagots. L'Imânus calculated that it would take about a quarter of an hour for this match to set fire to the pool of tar in the library, after it had been lighted in the interior of the tower. Having made all these arrangements, and finished all this inspection, he carried the key of the iron door back to the Marquis de Lantenac, who put it in his pocket.

It was important to watch all the besieger's movements. L'Imânus, with his herdsman's horn in his belt, stationed himself like a vidette in the watch tower of the platform, on the top of the tower. While watching with an eye on the forest, and an eye on the plateau, he had beside him in the embrasure of the watch-tower window, a powder flask, a linen bag filled with musket-balls, and some old newspapers, which he tore up to make into cartridges.

When the sun appeared, its rays illumined, in the forest, eight battalions, their swords by their sides, cartridge boxes on their backs, bayonets in their guns, ready for the assault; on the plateau a battery of cannons, with ammunition wagons, cartridges and boxes of grapeshot; in the fortress, nineteen men loading blunderbusses, muskets, and pistols, and in the three cribs, three sleeping children.

BOOK THIRD.

THE MASSACRE OF SAINT BARTHOLOMEW.

CHAPTER I.

THE MASSACRE OF SAINT BARTHOLOMEW (I).

The children awoke.

The little girl first.

The wakening of children is like the opening of flowers; it seems as if a perfume came from their fresh souls.

Georgette, the one twenty months old, the youngest of the three, who was still nursing in May, raised her little head, sat up, looked at her feet, and began to prattle.

A ray of morning light fell on her crib; it would have been hard to tell which was the rosier, Georgette's foot or the dawn.

The other two were still asleep; men are more dull; Georgette, happy and serene, went on prattling.

René-Jean was dark, Gros-Alain was sandy, Georgette was fair. These shades of hair, in harmony with the age during childhood, may change later on. René-Jean looked like a little Hercules; he was sleeping on his stomach, with his two fists doubled up over his eyes. Both of Gros-Alain's legs were hanging out of his little bed.

All three were in rags; the clothes that the battalion of Bonnet-Rouge had given them were in tatters; they hadn't even a shirt on them; the two boys were almost naked. Georgette was dressed in a rag which had once been a skirt and was now nothing but a bodice. Who took care of these children? It was impossible to tell. No mother. These savage peasants, fighting, and dragging them along with them from forest to forest, gave them their share of soup. That was all. The little ones got on as they could. They had everybody for master, and no one for a father. But children's tatters are full of light. They were charming.

Georgette went on prattling.

What a bird sings, a child prattles. It is the same hymn. An indistinct hymn, lisped, profound. The child, more than the bird, has the mysterious destiny of man before it. Hence, the melancholy feeling of those who listen, mingled with the joy of the little one who sings. The sublimest song to be heard on the earth is the lisping of the human soul on the lips of children. This confused whispering of a thought, which is as yet only an instinct, contains a strange, unconscious appeal to eternal justice; perhaps it is a protestation on the threshold, before entering; a humble but poignant protestation; this ignorance smiling at the Infinite compromises all creation in the fate which is to be given to the feeble, helpless being. Misfortune, if it comes, will be an abuse of confidence.

The murmur of a child is more and less than speech; there are no notes, and yet it is a song; there are no syllables, and yet it is a language; this murmur had its beginning in heaven, and will not have its end on earth; it is before birth, and it will continue hereafter. This babbling is composed of what the child said when he was an angel, and of what he will say when he becomes a man; the cradle has a Yesterday, as much as the tomb has a Tomorrow; this to-morrow and this yesterday blend their double mystery in this unintelligible warbling; and nothing proves God, eternity, the responsibility, the duality of fate, like this awe-inspiring shadow on these rosy souls.

What Georgette was prattling about did not make her sad, for her whole lovely face beamed with a smile. Her mouth smiled, her eyes smiled, the dimples in her cheeks smiled. This smile revealed a mysterious acceptation of the morning. The soul has faith in light. The sky was blue, the weather was warm, it was beautiful. The frail creature, without knowing anything, without understanding anything, softly bathed in reverie where no thought is, felt secure in this nature, in these honest trees, in this sincere verdure, in this pure, peaceful country, in these sounds from nests, from brooks, flies, leaves, above which the vast innocence of the sun shone resplendent.

After Georgette, René-Jean, the oldest, the largest, the one who was four years old, awoke. He rose to his feet, gave a manly jump over the side of his basket, looked at his porringer, thought it quite natural, sat down on the floor and began to eat his soup.

Georgette's prattling had not waken Gros-Alain, but at the sound of the spoon in the porringer, he turned over with a start, and opened his eyes. Gros-Alain was the one three years old. He saw his porringer, it was within reach, he took it and without getting out of bed placed the porringer on his knees, took the spoon in his hand, and like René-Jean began to eat.

Georgette did not hear them, and the undulations of her voice seemed to modulate the rocking of a dream. Her large open eyes were looking up and were divine; whether the ceiling or the heavens are above a child's head, it is always the sky which is reflected in its eyes.

When René-Jean had finished, he scraped the bottom of the porringer with his spoon, sighed, and said with dignity,—

"I have eaten my soup."

This woke Georgette from her reverie.

"Poupoupe," said she.

And seeing that René-Jean had eaten his, and that Gros-Alain was eating, she took the porringer of soup beside her, and began also to eat, carrying her spoon much oftener to her ear than to her mouth.

From time to time, she renounced civilization and ate with her fingers.

Gros-Alain after having scraped the bottom of the porringer as his brother had done, went to join him and ran behind him.

CHAPTER II.

THE MASSACRE OF SAINT BARTHOLOMEW (II).

Suddenly, there was heard from without and below, on the side of the forest, the blast of a trumpet, a sort of flourish, haughty and stern. To this trumpet blast, the sound of a horn replied from the top of the tower.

This time it was the trumpet which called, and the horn which gave answer.

There was a second trumpet call, followed by a second sounding of the horn.

Then from the edge of the forest rose a distant but clear voice, which cried distinctly these words,—

"Brigands! a summons! If at sunset, you have not surrendered at discretion, we attack you."

A voice roared out in reply from the platform of the tower,—

"Attack us, then."

The voice below added,—

"A cannon will be fired, as a last warning, half an hour before the assault."

And the voice from above repeated,—

"Attack us."

These voices did not reach the children's ears, but the trumpet and the horn sounded higher and farther, and Georgette at the first blast of the trumpet raised her head and stopped eating; at the sound of the horn, she put her spoon in her porringer; at the second trumpet blast, she lifted the little forefinger of her right hand, and letting it fall and raising it again alternately, marked the cadences of the flourish which prolonged the second blowing of the horn; when the horn and the trumpet were silent, she remained thoughtful, her finger in the air, and murmured half aloud, "Misic."

We think that she meant "music."

The two oldest, René-Jean and Gros-Alain, had paid no attention to the horn and the trumpet; they were absorbed by something else; a woodlouse was crossing the library.

Gros-Alain noticed it and exclaimed,—

"There's a bug."

René-Jean ran to look at it.

Gros-Alain added,—

"It stings."

"Don't hurt it," said René-Jean.

And both began to watch it moving along.

In the meantime, Georgette finished her soup; she looked at her brothers. René-Jean and Gros-Alain were in the embrasure of a window, bending intently over the woodlouse; their foreheads touched, and their hair mingled; they were holding their breath in wonder, and examining the insect which had stopped and did not move, little pleased with so much admiration.

Georgette, seeing that her brothers were looking at something, wanted to know what it was. It was not an easy matter for her to reach them, but she undertook it; the journey bristled with difficulties; there were things on the floor; overthrown stools, piles of old papers, packing cases, unnailed and empty, chests, heaps of all sorts of things, around which she had to make her way, a perfect archipelago of reefs; Georgette ventured.

She began by getting out of her basket, the first difficulty; then she penetrated the reefs, meandered through the straits, pushed aside a stool, crawled between two trunks, went over a heap of papers, climbing up one side, rolling down the other, sweetly exposing her poor little bare body, and thus reached what a sailor would call the open sea, that is to say quite a wide space of unobstructed floor, where there were no more dangers; then she started forward, crossed this space, which was the whole width of the hall, on all fours, with the agility of a cat, and reached the window; here there was a formidable obstacle; the great ladder lying against the wall just reached to this window, and the end of it passed a little beyond the embrasure; this made a sort of cape to double between Georgette and her brothers; she stopped to meditate; having finished her interior monologue, she made up her mind; she resolutely grasped with her rosy fingers one of the rounds, which were vertical and not horizontal, as the ladder lay on one side; she tried to raise herself on her feet and fell back; she tried again twice, and failed; the third time she succeeded; then standing up straight, supporting herself with the rungs one after another, she began to walk along the ladder; when she reached the end, her support failed; she tumbled over, but seizing in her little hands the end of one of the side pieces, which was enormous, she pulled herself up again, rounded the promontory, looked at René-Jean and Gros-Alain and laughed.

CHAPTER III.

THE MASSACRE OF SAINT BARTHOLOMEW (III).

At this moment, René-Jean, satisfied with his observations concerning the woodlouse, raised his head and said,—

"It is a female."

Georgette's laugh made René-Jean laugh, and René-Jean's laugh made Gros-Alain laugh.

Georgette sat down beside her brothers, and they formed a sort of little club together on the floor.

But the woodlouse had disappeared.

Georgette's laugh had given him a chance to crawl into a hole in the floor.

Other events followed that of the woodlouse.

First some swallows flew by.

Their nests were probably under the edge of the roof. Somewhat disturbed by the children they flew close to the window, describing wide circles in the air, and uttering their gentle springtime call. This made the three children raise their eyes, and the woodlouse was forgotten.

Georgette pointed her finger towards the swallows, and exclaimed,—

"Chickies!"

René-Jean reprimanded her,—

"They are not chickens, they are birds."

"Boords," said Georgette.

And all three looked at the swallows.

Then a bee flew in.

Nothing is so like a soul as a bee. It goes from flower to flower as a soul from star to star, and it gathers honey as a soul gathers light.

This one made a great noise as he came in buzzing at the top of his voice, and he seemed to say: "I have just seen the roses, and now I come to see the children. What is going on here?"

A bee is a housewife, and it scolds while it sings.

As long as the bee remained, the children never took their eyes from it.

The bee explored the whole library, searched the corners, darted about as though it were at home in it's hive, and making music on the wing, roved from bookcase to bookcase, looking at the titles of the books through the glass-windows, as though it were a mind.

His visit over, he went out.

"He has gone home," said René-Jean.

"It is a monster," said Gros-Alain.

"No," replied René-Jean, "It is a fly."

"Fly," said Georgette.

Thereupon, Gros-Alain, who had just found on the floor a string with a knot in one end of it, took the other end of it between his thumb and forefinger, made a sort of little mill with the cord, and watched it turn with deep interest.

As for Georgette, having gotten down on all fours again, and taken up her capricious roving, she had discovered a venerable arm-chair covered with moth-eaten tapestry, from which the hair was escaping through numerous holes. She stopped by this chair. She made the holes larger and pulled out the hair as if her life depended upon it.

Suddenly she raised her finger, which meant: "Listsn!"

The two brothers turned their heads.

An indistinct, distant noise was heard from without; it was probably the attacking camp executing some strategic movement in the forest; horses neighed, drums beat, caissons rolled along, chains clanked, military signals called to each other and gave answer, confusion of savage sounds which as they mingled grew into a sort of harmony; the children listened, delighted.

"The good God is doing that." aaid René-Jean.

CHAPTER IV.

THE MASSACRE OF SAINT BARTHOLOMEW (IV).

The noise ceased.

René-Jean remained thoughtful.

How are ideas formed and scattered in these little brains? What is the mysterious commotion in their memories so dim and as yet so short? In this sweet, pensive mind arose a mixture of the good God, prayer, folded hands, a strange tender smile that used to rest on them, and that they had no longer, and René-Jean murmured, half aloud: "Mamma."

"Mamma," said Gros-Alain.

"M'ma," said Georgette,

And then René-Jean began to jump.

Seeing him jump, Gross-Alain jumped too.

Gros-Alain followed René-Jean's example in all his movements and gestures; Georgette not so much. Three years copies four years; but twenty months keeps its independence.

Georgette remained seated, saying a word now and then. Georgette did not put words together.

She was a thinker; she spoke in apothegms. She was monosyllabic.

Nevertheless, after a time, their example affected her, and she finally tried to do as her brothers were doing, and these three little pairs of bare feet began to dance, to run and totter in the dust on the old, polished oak floor, under the serious eyes of the marble busts, toward which Georgette occasionally cast an anxious glance, murmuring,—

"The mummums!"

In Georgette's language a mummum was anything which looked like a man without really being one. Beings seem like phantoms to young children.

Georgette, swaying rather than walking, followed her brothers, but generally she preferred to go on all fours.

Suddenly, René-Jean, as he was approaching a window, raised his head, then dropped it and ran to hide in the corner of the wall made by the window embrasure.

He had just seen some one looking at him. It was a soldier of the Blues from the encampment on the plateau who, taking advantage of the truce and perhaps infringing on it a little, had ventured to the edge of the ravine where he could look into the library. Seeing René-Jean hide, Gros-Alain ran to hide; he took refuge beside René-Jean, and Georgette hid behind them. They stayed there in silence, perfectly still, and Georgette put her finger on her lips. After a few moments René-Jean ventured to put out his head; the soldier was still there. René-Jean drew his head back quickly; and the three little ones did not dare to breathe. This lasted for some time. At last Georgette grew tired of being afraid, and was bold enough to look out. The soldier had gone. They began to run and play again.

Gros-Alain, besides imitating and admiring René-Jean, had a specialty,—that of making discoveries. His brother and sister saw him suddenly whirl wildly around, dragging after him a little wagon with four wheels, which he had brought to light from some corner.

This doll's carriage had been in the dust for years, forgotten,—a good neighbor to the books of geniuses and the busts of wise men. It was perhaps one of the toys which Gauvain had played with when he was a child.

Gros-Alain had made a whip with the string, and was snapping it; it was very fine. Such are discoverers. When they do not discover America, they discover little carts. It is always thus.

But it must be shared. René-Jean wanted to draw the wagon, and Georgette wanted to get into it.

She tried to sit down in it. René-Jean was the horse. Gros-Alain was the driver.

But the driver did not understand his business, the horse had to teach him.

René-Jean cried to Gros-Alain,—

"Say, 'Go along.'"

"Go 'long!" repeated Gros-Alain.

The wagon upset. Georgette tumbled out. Angels can scream. Georgette screamed.

Then she felt half inclined to cry.

"Young lady," said René-Jean, "you are too big."

"I big," said Georgette.

And her size consoled her for her fall.

The cornice of entablature under the windows was very wide, the dust of the fields blown from the heather on the plateau had collected in heaps there; the rains had made earth of this dust; the wind had brought seeds to it, so that a briar had taken advantage of this bit of earth to take root there. This briar was the perennial variety called fox mulberry. It was August, the mulberry bush was covered with berries, and a branch of the briar came in through the window. This branch hung down almost to the floor.

Gros-Alain, after discovering the string, and discovering the wagon was the one to discover this briar. He went toward it. He picked a berry and ate it. "I'm hungry," said René-Jean.

And Georgette, galloping along on her knees and hands, came following after. The three plundered the branch and ate all the berries. They were daubed and stained, and all red with the crimson juice of the berries; the three little seraphs were changed to three little fauns, which would have shocked Dante and charmed Virgil. They laughed aloud. Occasionally, the briar pricked their fingers. No pleasure without pain. Georgette held out her finger, from which oozed a little drop of blood, to René-Jean and said pointing to the briar, "Pricks." Gros-Alain, who had been scratched too, looked scornfully at the briar and said,— "It is a beast."

"No," replied René-Jean, "it is a stick."

"A naughty stick," added Gros-Alain. Georgette, again felt like crying, but she began to laugh.

CHAPTER V.

THE MASSACRE OF SAINT BARTHOLOMEW (V).

In the meantime, René-Jean, possibly jealous of his younger brother, Gros-Alain's discoveries, had conceived a great plan. For some time, while he was picking the berries and pricking his fingers, his eyes had been frequently turning toward the reading-desk mounted on a pivot and standing by itself like a monument in the middle of the library. On this desk was displayed the famous volume of "Saint Bartholomew."

It was really a magnificent and notable folio. This "Saint Bartholomew" had been published in Cologne by the famous publisher of the Bible in 1682, Blœuw, in Latin, Cæsius. It had been printed on movable wooden types, held in position with a band made of ox-sinew.

It was printed, not on Holland paper, but on that beautiful Arabian paper so much admired by Edrisi, made of silk and cotton, and always retaining its whiteness.

The binding was of gilded leather, and the clasps of silver; the fly leaves were of that parchment which the parchment-makers of Paris swore they would buy in the Halle Saint Mathurin and "nowhere else."

This volume was full of woodcuts and copper engravings, and geographical maps of many countries; it was prefaced with a protestation of printers, paper-makers and booksellers against the edict of 1635, placing a tax on "leather, beer, cloven-footed animals, sea-fish, and paper," and on the reverse page of the frontispiece, there was a dedication addressed to the Gryphes, who are to Lyons what the Elzévirs are to Amsterdam.

All this resulted in a famous volume, almost as rare as the *Apostol* at Moscow.

It was a beautiful book; that was why René-Jean looked at it; perhaps too intently. The volume was open just where there was a large engraving representing Saint Bartholomew carrying his skin over his arm. This engraving could be seen from below. When all the berries had been eaten, René-Jean looked at it with a terrible longing, and Georgette, whose eyes followed her brother's, noticed the engraving and said, "Pickshur."

This word seemed to determine René-Jean. Then, to the great amazement of Gros-Alain, he did an extraordinary thing.

A great oak chair stood in a corner of the library; René-Jean walked to this chair, seized it and dragged it all by himself to the desk. Then when the chair touched the desk, he got up on it and placed his two hands on the book.

Having reached this height, he felt that it was necessary to be, generous; he took the "pickshur" by the upper corner and carefully tore it out; Saint Bartholomew's picture tore crosswise, but that was not René-Jean's fault; he left all the left side, with one eye and a little of the old apocryphal evangelist's halo, in the book, and offered the other half of the saint, and all his skin, to Georgette. Georgette took the saint and said,—

"Mummum."

"Give me one!" cried Gros-Alain.

The first torn page is like the first drop of blood shed. It decides slaughter.

René-Jean turned the leaf; after the saint came the commentator Pantœnus; René-Jean bestowed Pantœnus on Gros-Alain.

In the meantime, Georgette tore her large piece into two small ones, then the two small ones into four; so that history might say, that after having been flayed in Armenia, Saint-Bartholomew was quartered in Brittany.

CHAPTER VI.

THE MASSACRE OF SAINT BARTHOLOMEW (VI).

Having finished the quartering, Georgette held out her hand to René-Jean, saying, "More!"

After the saint and the commentator came stern portraits of the glossarists. The earliest was Gavantus; René-Jean tore Gavantus out and placed him in Georgette's hand.

All Saint Bartholomew's glossarists followed. Giving is a privilege. René-Jean kept nothing for himself. Gros-Alain and Georgette were gazing at him; this was enough; he was satisfied with the admiration of his public.

René-Jean, inexhaustible and magnanimous, offered Fabricio Pignatelli to Gros-Alain, and Father Stilting to Georgette; he offered Alphonse Tostat to Gros-Alain, and *Cornelius a Lapide* to Georgette; Gros-Alain had Henry Hammond, and Georgette had Roberti, besides a view of the town of Douai, where he was born in 1619. Gros-Alain received the protestation of the paper-makers, and Georgette had the dedication to the Gryphes bestowed upon her. Then there were the maps. René-Jean distributed these. He gave Ethiopia to Gros-Alain, and Lycaonia to Georgette. When this was done, he threw the book on the floor.

It was a terrible moment. Gros-Alain and Georgette, with an ecstasy of delight mingled with fear, saw René-Jean frown, brace his legs, contract his hands, and push the massive folio volume off the desk. A majestic old book losing countenance is a tragic sight. The heavy volume, displaced, hung for a moment from the desk, hesitated, balanced itself, then fell down; and, torn, rumpled, lacerated, out of its binding, its clasps broken, flattened itself out lamentably on the floor. Fortunately, it did not fall on the children.

They were bewildered, not crushed. The adventures of conquerors do not always end as well. Like all glorious deeds, it made a great noise and a cloud of dust.

Having thrown down the book, René-Jean dismounted from the chair.

There was a moment of silence and awe; victory has its terrors. The children took hold of each other's hands, and drew away, to contemplate the great dilapidated volume.

But after some consideration, Gros-Alain started towards the book with determination and gave it a kick.

This was enough. There is such a thing as an appetite for destruction. René-Jean gave it a kick, Georgette gave it a kick, which made her tumble down, but in a sitting posture; she took advantage of this to throw herself on Saint Bartholomew; the spell was broken; René-Jean rushed on it, Gros-Alain made a dash for it; joyous, wild, triumphant, pitiless, tearing the engravings, slashing the leaves, pulling out the bookmarks, scratching the binding, ripping off the gilt leather, pulling out the nails, from the silver corners, breaking the parchment, marring the noble text, working with feet, hands, nails, and teeth, rosy, laughing, cruel, these three angels of destruction swooped down on the defenceless evangelist.

They annihilated Armenia, Judea, Benevento, where there are relics of the saint; Nathaniel, who is possibly the same as Bartholomew; Pope Gelasius, who declared the Bartholomew-Nathaniel gospel to be apocryphal, all the heads, all the maps, and the inexorable destruction of the old book absorbed them to such a degree that a mouse passed by without their noticing it.

It was an extermination.

To pull to pieces history, legend, science, miracles, true or false, church Latin, superstitions, fanaticisms, mysteries, to tear up a whole religion from top to bottom, is a work for three giants, as well as three children; the hours passed quickly over this labor, but they came to an end; nothing was left of Saint Bartholomew.

When this was at an end, when the last page was torn out, when the last engraving was destroyed, when nothing was left of the book but fragments of the text and pictures, in a skeleton of a binding, René-Jean jumped to his feet, looked at the floor strewn with all these scattered leaves, and clapped his hands.

Gros-Alain clapped his hands.

Georgette took one of the leaves from the floor, got up, leaned against the window, which came just to her chin, and began to tear the large page into little pieces, and threw them out.

Seeing this, René-Jean and Gros-Alain began to do the same. They picked up the leaves and tore them in pieces, picked up and tore them again and again, throwing the pieces out of the window as Georgette had done; and page by page, reduced to scraps by these destructive little fingers, almost the entire ancient book blew away in the wind. Georgette looked thoughtfully after these swarms of bits of white paper, scattered by all the breezes of the air and said,—

"Butterflies."

And the massacre ended with a vanishing into thin air.

CHAPTER VII.

THE MASSACRE OF SAINT BARTHOLOMEW (VII).

Such was the second putting to death of Saint Bartholomew, who had already been martyred in the year 49 of our Lord Jesus Christ.

Meanwhile, evening was approaching, the heat was increasing, the air was full of drowsiness, Georgette's eyes grew heavy, René-Jean went to his crib, drew out the bag of straw which took the place of a mattress, dragged it to the window, stretched himself out on it, and said: "Let us go to bed."

Gros-Alain put his head on René-Jean, Georgette put her head on Gros-Alain, and the three malefactors went to sleep.

Hot breezes came in through the open windows; the perfume of wild flowers, blown from the ravines and hills, floated in, mingled with the evening zephyrs; space was calm and merciful; everything beamed, everything was at peace, everything loved everything else; the sun caressed creation with light; everywhere was felt that harmony which arises from the colossal sweetness of things; there was something of maternity in the Infinite; creation is a miracle in full bloom, its immensity is perfected by its goodness; it seemed as if some invisible power could be felt taking those mysterious precautions which, in the terrible conflict of life, protect the weak against the strong; at the same time it was beautiful, the splendor breathed forth mansuetude.

The landscape, full of an ineffable drowsiness, had that magnificent wavy appearance which the alternations of light and shade give to prairies and rivers; the smoke rose toward the clouds, as a dream toward a vision; flocks of birds whirled above la Tourgue; swallows looked in at the windows, and seemed to have come to see if the children were sleeping well.

They were gracefully grouped, one on the other, still, half-naked, in loving attitudes; they were adorable and pure, all three together were not nine years old, they had dreams of Paradise, which were reflected on their mouths in vague smiles; God, perhaps, was speaking in their ears; they were those whom every human tongue calls weak and blessed, they were innocents worthy of reverence; everything kept silence, as though the breath from their sweet breasts was of consequence to the universe, and was listened to by all creation; the leaves did not rustle, the grass did not quiver. It seemed as if the wide starry world held its breath, that it might not disturb these three humble, angelic sleepers, and nothing was so sublime as the immense respect of nature toward these little creatures.

The sun was going down, and almost touched the horizon. Suddenly, in the midst of this profound peace, there shot forth a bright light, coming from the forest, then a furious noise. A cannon had just been fired. The echoes seized this noise and turned it into an uproarious din. The rumbling, prolonged from hill to hill, was monstrous. It awoke Georgette.

She raised her head a little, lifted her little finger, listened, and said, —

"Boom!"

The sound died away, and silence returned. Georgette laid her head down on Gros-Alain, and went to sleep again.

BOOK FOURTH.— THE MOTHER.

CHAPTER I.

DEATH PASSES BY.

This same evening, the mother, whom we have seen making her way almost by chance, had been walking all day long. Moreover, it was the story of all her days, to go straight on and never stop. For her sleep of exhaustion in the first corner that she came to was no more rest than what she ate here and there, as birds go picking about, wag food. She ate and slept just enough to keep her from falling down dead.

She had spent the night before in a deserted house; civil war causes such ruins. She had found, in a neglected field, four walls, an open door, a little straw under a portion of the roof, and she slept on this straw and under this roof, feeling the rats run over the straw, and seeing the stars shine through the roof. She had slept some hours, then she awoke in the middle of the night and started on her journey again, in order to travel as far as possible before the full heat of the day. For those travelling on foot in summer, midnight is more agreeable than midday.

She followed to the best of her ability the general route indicated to her by the peasant at Vautortes; she went as nearly as possible toward the west. Any one near her would have heard her say repeatedly, in a low voice, "La Tourgue." Besides the names of her three children, she knew nothing but this word.

As she walked along, she was deep in meditation. She thought of all the adventures which she had been through; she thought of all she had suffered, of all she had received; of the encounters, the indignities, the conditions made, the bargains proposed and undergone, sometimes for a shelter, sometimes for a piece of bread, sometimes merely to get some one to show her the way. A wretched woman is more unfortunate than a wretched man, because she is an instrument of pleasure. Frightful wandering on foot. But nothing made any difference to her so long as she found her children.

Her first encounter to-day had been a village on the way; it was scarcely daybreak, everything was still bathed in the gloom of night, still some doors were already ajar in the principal street of the village, and some curious heads were looking out of the windows. The inhabitants seemed as agitated as a hive which has been disturbed. This was on account of a sound of wheels and chains which had been heard.

In the square in front of the church, an astounded group, with upturned faces, was looking at something coming down the road toward the village from the top of a hill.

It was a wagon with four wheels, drawn by five horses harnessed with chains. On the wagon could be made out a heap which looked like a pile of long joists, in the middle of which was something strange and shapeless; it was covered over with an awning, which had the appearance of a shroud.

Ten men on horseback rode in front of the wagon, and ten others, behind. These men wore three-cornered hats, and rising above their shoulders could be seen points, which were apparently bare swords. All this procession, advancing slowly, stood out in clearly defined black against the horizon. The wagon looked black, the horses looked black, the cavaliers looked black. The pale morning light gleamed behind them.

It entered the village and went towards the square. It began to grow light as the wagon came down the hill, and the procession could be seen distinctly; it seemed like a march of ghosts, for not a word escaped the men.

The riders were military men. They had, indeed, drawn swords. The awning was black.

The wretched, wandering mother entered the village and drew near the gathering of peasants just as the team and the mounted men were coming into the square. In the group of spectators, voices whispered questions and answers, —

"What is that?"
"It is the guillotine passing by."
"Where does it come from?"
"From Fougères."
"Where is it going?"
"I do not know. They say that it is going to a castle toward Parigné."
"Parigné!"
"Let it go wherever it will, provided it doesn't stop here."

This great wagon, with its burden covered with a sort of shroud; these horses; these military men; the noise of these chains; the silence of these riders; the dim light, — all this was ghastly.

The procession crossed the square and left the village; the village was in a hollow between two hills. After a quarter of an hour, the peasants, who had remained as though petrified, saw the gloomy procession come into sight again on the top of the hill toward the west. The large wheels jolted over the road, the horses' chains clanked in the morning wind, the sabres glistened; the sun was rising, there was a turn in the road, they all disappeared.

This was at just the moment when Georgette, in the ball of the library, awoke beside her brothers, who were still asleep, and said good morning to her rosy feet.

CHAPTER II.

DEATH SPEAKS.

The mother watched this dark object pass by, but had not understood it, nor tried to understand, for she had another vision before her eyes, — her children lost in the darkness.

She also went out of the village, a little after the procession which had just filed past, and followed the same road, at some distance behind the second squad of policemen. Suddenly, the word "guillotine" came into her mind.

"Guillotine!" she said to herself; this peasant woman Michelle Fléchard, did not know what it was, but her instinct warned her against it; she shuddered without being able to tell why; it seemed horrible to her to walk behind it, and she turned to the left, went out of the road and entered some woods, which were the forest of Fougères.

After roaming for some time, she noticed a church tower and some roofs; it was one of the villages on the borders of the wood; she entered it. She was hungry.

This village was one of those where the Republicans had established military posts.

She went as far as the square where the town hall was.

In this village, too, there was agitation and anxiety. A crowd was gathered in front of a flight of steps which were the entrance to the town hall. On these steps were seen a man escorted by soldiers, holding in his hand a large, unrolled placard. On this man's right stood a drummer, and on his left, a bill-poster carrying a pot of paste and a brush.

On the balcony above the door stood the mayor, wearing a tricolored scarf with his peasant's dress.

The man with the placard was a public crier.

He had on a shoulder belt from which hung a little bag, which indicated that he went from village to village, and that he had something to cry throughout the country.

He had just unrolled the placard, as Michelle Fléchard drew near, and he began to read it. He said in a loud voice, —

"The French Republic. One and indivisible."

The drum rolled. There was a sort of undulation in the crowd. Some took off their caps; others pulled their hats down over their eyes. At this time, and in this country, a person's opinion could almost be told by the headgear; hats were Royalist, caps were Republican.

The murmur of confused voices ceased, the people listened, the crier read, —

"In virtue of the orders to us given, and the power to us delegated, by the Committee of Public Welfare——"

There was a second rolling of the drum. The crier continued, —

"And in execution of the decree of the National Convention, which outlaws rebels taken armed, and which orders capital punishment to whoever gives them shelter or helps them to escape."

One peasant asked his neighbor in a low voice, —

"What is capital punishment?"

The neighbor replied, "I don't know."

The crier waved the placard, —

"In accordance with Article 17 of the law of the thirtieth of April, giving full power to delegates and sub-delegates against the rebels, are outlawed—"

He paused and added, —

"The individuals designated by the name and surnames which follow—"

The crowd was all attention.

The voice of the crier thundered, —

"Lantenac, brigand."

"That is monseigneur," murmured a peasant.

And this was whispered through the crowd, "That is monseigneur."

The crier added, —

"Lantenac, ci-devant marquis, brigand."

"L'Imânus, brigand."

Two peasants looked at each other askance.

"That is Gouge-le-Bruant."

"Yes, it is Brise-Bleu." The crier went on reading the list, —

"Grand-Francœur, brigand."

The crowd murmured, —

"He is a priest."

"Yes, monsieur the Abbé Turmeau."

"Yes, he is a curé somewhere near the wood of la Chapelle."

"And a brigand," said a man in a cap.

The crier read, —

"Boisnouveau, brigand. The two brothers Pique-en-Bois, brigands. Houzard, brigand——"

"That is Monsieur de Quelen," said a peasant.

"Panier, brigand——"

"That is Monsieur Sepher."

"Place-Nette, brigand——"

"That is Monsieur Jamois."

The crier continued his reading without paying attention to these comments.

"Guinoiseau, brigand. Chatenay, called Robi, brigand——"

A peasant whispered: "Guinoiseau is the same as le Blond, Chatenay is Saint-Ouen."

"Hoisnard, brigand," added the crier.

And in the crowd was heard,—

"He is from Ruillé."

"Yes, that is Branche d'Or."

"He had his brother killed at the attack at Pontorson."

"Yes, Hoisnard-Malonnière."

"A fine young man, nineteen years old."

"Attention," said the crier, " Here is the end of the list,—"

"Belle-Vigne, brigand. La Mussette, brigand. Sabretout, brigand. Brin-d'Amour, brigand——"

A boy nudged a girl's elbow. The girl smiled.

The crier went on,—

"Chante-en-hiver, brigand. Le Chat, brigand——"

A peasant said: "That is Moulard."

"Tabouze, brigand——"

A peasant said: "That is Gauffre."

"There are two of the Gauffres," added a woman.

"Both good fellows," growled a rustic.

The crier shook the placard and the drum beat a ban. The crier began to read again,—

"The above named, in whatever place they may be taken, will be immediately put to death after their identity has been established."

There was a stir in the crowd.

The crier added,—

"Whoever gives them shelter, or helps them to escape will be taken before a court-martial and put to death. Signed—"

There was a profound silence.

"Signed: The Delegate of the Committee of Public Welfare, Cimourdain."

"A priest," said a peasant.

"The former curé of Parigné," said another.

A citizen added,—

"Turmeau and Cimourdain. A White priest, and a Blue priest."

"Both black," said another citizen.

The mayor standing on the balcony, raised his hat and cried,—

"Long live the Republic!"

The beating of the drum announced that the crier had finished. Indeed, he made a sign with his hand.

"Attention," he said. "Here are the four last lines of the notice of the government. They are signed by the chief of the reconnoitring column of the coasts of the north commanded by Gauvain."

"Listen!" cried the voices of the crowd.

And the crier read,—

"Under pain of death—"

All were silent.

"It is forbidden, in fulfilment of the above order, to aid and assist the nineteen rebels above named, who are at the present time invested and surrounded in la Tourgue."

"Hey?" said a voice.

It was a woman's voice. It was the voice of the mother.

CHAPTER III.

MURMURINGS OF THE PEASANTS.

Michelle Fléchard was in the midst of the crowd.

She had not listened, but one can hear what one does not listen to. She had heard this word, la Tourgue. She raised her head.

"Hey!" she repeated, "la Tourgue?"

The people stared at her. She looked as though she were demented. She was in rags. Voices murmured,—

"She looks like a brigand."

A peasant woman carrying some buckwheat cakes in a basket approached her, and said in an undertone,—

"Hold your tongue."

Michelle Fléchard looked at the woman in amazement.

Again she failed to understand. This name la Tourgue had passed by like a flash of lightning, and then it grew dark again. Had she no right to ask questions? What was the matter with them, that they looked at her so?

In the meantime, the drum had beaten a last ban, the bill-poster had pasted up the placard, the mayor had gone into the town hall, the crier had departed for some other village, and the crowd had scattered.

A group remained in front of the placard. Michelle Fléchard joined this group.

They were commenting on the names of those men who were outlawed.

There were peasants and citizens in the group; that is to say, Whites and Blues.

A peasant said,—

"No matter, they do not count everybody. Nineteen is only nineteen. They do not count Riou, they do not count Benjamin Moulins, they do not count Goupil, of the parish of Andouillé."

"Nor Lorieul, of Montjean," said another.

Others added,— "Nor Brice-Denys."

"Nor François Dudonet."

"Yes, the one from Laval."

"Nor Huet, from Launey-Villiers."

"Nor Gregis."

"Nor Pilon."

"Nor Filleul."

"Nor Ménicent."

"Nor Guéharrée."

"Nor the three brothers Logerais."

"Nor Monsieur Lechandelier de Pierreville."

"Fools!" said a stern old man with white hair. "They have them all, if they take Lantenac."

"They haven't taken him yet," muttered one of the young fellows.

The old man replied,—

"If Lantenac is taken, the soul is taken. If Lantenac is dead, la Vendée is killed."

"Who is this Lantenac, then?" asked a citizen.

A citizen replied: "He is a ci-devant."

And another added: "He is one of those who shoot women."

Michelle Fléchard heard that, and said: "That is true."

The people turned round.

And she added: "Because they shot me."

These words had a strange effect; it was as though one thought dead was found alive. They began to examine her, somewhat askance.

She was really distressing to look at; trembling at everything, scared, shivering, having a wildly anxious look, and so frightened that she was frightful. In a woman's despair there is a strange helplessness which is terrible. It is like seeing a being suspended at the extremity of fate. But the peasants looked at it more roughly. One of them growled: "She may be a spy."

"Hold your tongue, and go away," said the good woman who had already spoken to her, in a low voice.

Michelle Fléchard replied,—

"I am not doing any harm. I am looking for my children."

The good woman looked at those who were looking at Michelle Fléchard, tapped her forehead, winked, and said,—

"She is half-witted."

Then she took her aside, and gave her a buckwheat biscuit.

Michelle Fléchard, without thanking her, bit eagerly into the biscuit.

"Yes," said the peasants, "she eats like a pig, she is half-witted."

And the rest of the group scattered. They all went away one after another.

When Michelle Fléchard had finished eating, she said to the peasant woman: "It is good; I have had something to eat. Now, for la Tourgue!"

"See how she clings to that!" exclaimed the peasant woman.

"I must go to la Tourgue. Tell me the way to la Tourgue."

"Never," said the peasant woman. "You want to be killed, do you? Besides, I don't know. Ah, so you are really mad? Listen, my poor woman, you look tired. Will you rest in my house?"

"I cannot rest," said the mother.

"Her feet are all raw," muttered the peasant woman.

Michelle Fléchard added,—

"As I tell you, they have taken my children from me. A little girl and two little boys. I come from the carnichot in the forest. You can ask Tellmarch the Caimand about me. And then the man I met in the field down there. It was the Caimand who made me well. It seems that I had something broken. All these are things that have happened. Besides, there was the sergeant Radoub. You can ask him. He will tell you. For he it was who found us in a wood. Three. I tell you three children. And the oldest is called René-Jean. I can prove all this. The other is called Gros-Alain, and the other is called Georgette. My husband is dead. They killed him. He was a farmer in Siscoignard. You look like a good woman. Show me my way. I am not mad; I am a mother. I have lost my children. I am looking for them. I do not know exactly where I have come from. Last night I slept on some straw in a barn. La Tourgue is where I am going. I am not a thief. You see that I am telling the truth. You ought to help me find my children. I do not belong to this country. I have been shot, but I do not know where."

The peasant woman shook her head, and said,—

"Listen, traveller. In times of revolution one must not say things that will not be understood. You may be arrested for it."

"But la Tourgue!" cried the mother. "Madame, for the love of the child Jesus, and the holy, good Virgin in Paradise, I beseech you, madame, I beg you, I implore you, tell me how to go to reach la Tourgue!"

The peasant woman grew angry.

"I do not know! and, if I knew, I would not tell you! It is a bad place there. It is not best to go there."

"Nevertheless, I am going there," said the mother.

And she started on.

The peasant woman saw her going away, and grumbled,—

"She ought to have something to eat."

She ran after Michelle Fléchard, and put a buckwheat biscuit in her hand.

"There's something for your supper."

Michelle Fléchard took the buckwheat bread, did not reply, did not turn her head, and went on her way.

She went out of the village. As she came to the last houses she met three little ragged and barefooted children passing by. She went to them, and said,—

"These are two girls and a boy."

And when she saw how they eyed her bread, she gave it to them.

The children seized it, but were afraid of her.

She plunged into the forest.

CHAPTER IV.

A MISTAKE.

In the meantime, the following had been taking place that same morning before daybreak, in the gloomy depths of the forest, on the section of road leading from Javené to Lécousse.

All the roads in le Bocage are sunken, but the highway from Javené to Parigné, through Lécousse, is one of the most completely embanked. Moreover, it is winding. It is a ravine rather than a road. It starts from Vitré, and once had the distinction of jolting Madame de Sevigné's coach. It is walled in, as it were, by hedges on right and left. No better place for an ambuscade.

This very morning, an hour before Michelle Fléchard, from another part of the forest, reached the village where she had seen the sepulchral vision of the cart escorted by mounted men, the thickets through which the Javené highway runs, after crossing the bridge over the Couesnou, were full of invisible men. All were hidden by interlacing branches.

These men were all peasants, dressed in the *grigo*, that sheepskin jacket worn by the Breton kings in the sixth century, and the peasants in the eighteenth. These men were armed; some with guns, others with axes. Those who had the axes had just made, in a clearing, a sort of funeral pyre of dry sticks and logs, all ready for the fire. Those who had guns were grouped on both sides of the road, in expectant attitudes. Any one who could have peered through the foliage would have seen everywhere fingers on triggers, and muzzles of carbines pointed through the embrasures made by the interlacing boughs. These men were lying in wait. All their guns were focussed on the road, which began to gleam white in the morning dawn.

In the twilight, muffled voices were conversing. "Are you sure of this?"

"Surely; that is what they say."

"Will it pass by here?"

"They say it's in these parts."

"It must not leave."

"We must burn it."

"Here are three villages met for that,"

"Yes, but the escort?"

"The escort must be killed."

"But is it coming this way?"

"That's what they say."

"It'll come from Vitré, then?"

"Why not?"

"Why, they said it was coming from Fougéres."

"Whether from Fougéres or Vitré, it comes from the devil."

"That's so."

"And must go back to him."

"Yes."

"Was it going to Parigné?"

"So it seems."

"It won't get there."

"No."

"No, no, no."

"Attention."

Indeed, prudence was now becoming imperative, for day was breaking. Suddenly, the men in ambush held their breath. A noise of wheels and horses was heard. They peered through the branches and could indistinctly see a long wagon, an escort on horseback, something on the wagon; it was coming toward them. "There it is!" said the one who appeared to be the chief.

"Yes," said one of the men on the watch, "with the escort."

"How many men in the escort?"

"Twelve."

"They said there were twenty."

"Twelve or twenty, let us kill them all."

"Wait till they are in full range."

Soon after, at a turn in the road, the wagon and escort appeared. "Long live the king!" cried the chief peasant.

A hundred guns fired at once. When the smoke disappeared, the escort had disappeared too. Seven of the horsemen had fallen, five had fled. The peasants ran to the wagon. "Hold on," cried the chief;" it is not the guillotine. It is a ladder."

The wagon, indeed, had for its sole burden a long ladder. The two horses had fallen, wounded; the driver had been killed, but not purposely. "It's all the same," said the chief, "a ladder with an escort is suspicious. It was going toward Parigné. It was for scaling la Tourgue, most certainly."

"Let us burn the ladder," cried the peasants. As for the funereal wagon, which they were looking for, It took another road and was already two leagues away, in the village where Michelle Fléchard saw it passing along at sunrise.

CHAPTER V.

VOX OF DESSERTO.

After leaving the three children to whom she gave her bread, Michelle Fléchard began to rove at random through the wood.

Since no one would show her the way, she must find it for herself. Every few moments she would sit down, then she would get up, and then sit down again. She felt that dismal weariness, which first affects the muscles and then passes to the bones, a slavish weariness. She was a slave in reality,—a slave to her lost children. She must find them; every lost instant might be their distraction; whoever has such a duty has no rights; she was forbidden to pause, even for breath. But she was very weary. In such a state of exhaustion, the possibility of one step more is a question. Could it be done? She had been walking since morning. She had seen no village, not even a house. At first she took the right path, then the wrong one, and finally she lost her way entirely among the branches, one just like another. Was she approaching the end? Was she touching the limit of her Passion? She was in the Via Dolorosa, and felt the agony of the "last station." Was she going to fall down on the road and die there? At one particular moment, it seemed impossible for her to go any farther; the sun was sinking, the forest was dark, paths were covered up in the grass, and she did not know what to do. She had nothing left but God. She began to call, no one replied.

She looked about her, she saw an opening among the branches, she went toward it, and suddenly found herself out of the woods.

Before her was a narrow vale like a trench, at the bottom of which, over the stones, ran a clear streamlet of water. Then, for the first time she became aware how very thirsty she was. She went to the brook, knelt down, and drank.

She took advantage of being on her knees to repeat her prayers.

When she arose, she tried to get her bearings.

She crossed the brook.

Beyond the little vale there stretched away as far as the eye could reach, a wide plateau covered with low underbrush, which sloped up from the brook and filled the whole horizon. The forest was a solitude, the plateau was a desert. In the forest behind each bush, there was a chance of meeting some one; on the plateau, as far as one could see, there was nothing. A few birds, which seemed to be escaping from something, flew into the heather.

Then, before this immense deserted plain, feeling her knees give way, as though she had become insane, the desperate mother flung this strange cry into the solitude; "Is there any one here?"

And she waited for the reply.

There was an answer.

A heavy, deep voice burst forth; this voice came from the edge of the horizon; it was reverberated from echo to echo; it resembled a peal of thunder or a cannon; and it seemed as if this voice replied to the mother's question and said: "Yes."

Then all was silent.

The mother rose, with new life; there was some one there. It seemed to her that now she had some one to speak to; she had just relieved her thirst and prayed; her strength returned, she began to ascend the slope in the direction from which she had heard that enormous distant voice.

Suddenly, she saw rising from the extreme edge of the horizon, a tall tower. The tower stood alone in this wild landscape; a ray from the setting sun lighted it up. She was more than a league away from it. Behind this tower, a wide expanse of verdure lost itself in the haze; this was the forest of Fougères.

This tower appeared to her to be on the very point of the horizon from which had come that roaring voice that seemed to her like a call. Had this tower made the noise?

Michelle Fléchard reached the top of the pleateau; she had nothing more before her except the plain. She walked toward the tower.

CHAPTER VI.

THE SITUATION.

The moment had come.
The inexorable held the merciless.
Cimourdain had Lantenac in his grasp.

The old Royalist rebel was taken in his ancestral seat; it was evident that he could not escape; and Cimourdain intended to have the marquis beheaded at his own home, on the spot, on his own territory, and in a certain sense in his own house, in order that the feudal dwelling should see the head of the feudal master fall, and that it might be a memorable example.

This is why he had sent to Fougères for the guillotine. It has just been seen on the way.

To kill Lantenac was to kill la Vendée; to kill la Vendée was to save France. Cimourdain did not hesitate. This man was familiar with the cruelty of duty.

The marquis seemed to be lost; in regard to this, Cimourdain felt easy, but in another respect he was anxious. The struggle would certainly be a frightful one; Gauvain would direct it, and would perhaps desire to take part in it; there was something of the soldier in this young chief; he was a man to throw himself into this hand-to hand encounter; supposing he should be killed? Gauvain! his child! the sole affection that he had on earth! Gauvain had been fortunate thus far, but good fortune becomes weary. Cimourdain trembled. His destiny was strange in this respect, that he was between two Gauvains, one of whom he wished to die, the other to live.

The cannon shot which had disturbed Georgette in her basket and called the mother out of the depths of solitude had done more than that. Whether it was by chance or from the intention of the gunner, the ball, which, however was only a ball of warning, had struck, broken, and half torn away the iron bars which masked and closed the great loophole in the first story of the tower. The besieged had not had time to repair this injury.

The besieged were boastful. They had very little ammunition. Their situation, we insist, was even more critical than the besiegers supposed. If they had had enough powder they would have blown up la Tourgue, with themselves and the enemy in it; this was their dream; but all their reserves were exhausted. They had hardly thirty shots apiece. They had plenty of guns, blunderbusses and pistols, and but few cartridges. They had loaded all their arms, in order to be able to keep up a continuous fire; but how long would this fire last? It would be necessary to use it lavishly and to husband it at the same time. Here was the difficulty.

Fortunately,—ominous good fortune,—the contest would be principally man to man, and with side-arms, with sabre and dagger. There would be more hand-to-hand fighting than shooting. They would cut each other to pieces; this was what they hoped for.

The interior of the tower seemed impregnable. In the lower hall where the breach penetrated was the retirade, that barricade scientifically constructed by Lantenac, which obstructed the entrance. Behind the retirade, a long table was covered with loaded arms,—blunderbusses, carbines, and muskets, and with sabres, axes, and daggers As they had no powder to blow up the tower, they were unable to make use of the crypt of the oubliette communicating with the lower hall, and the marquis had ordered the door to this vault to be closed.

Above the lower hall was the round room of the first story, which could only be reached by a very narrow Saint-Gilles's staircase; this room, furnished like the lower hall with a table covered with arms all ready for use, was lighted by the large loophole, the grating of which had just been smashed by a cannon ball; above this room the spiral staircase led to the round room in the second story, where the iron door opened into the bridge-châtelet.

This room in the second story was called both the "room with the iron door" and the "room of mirrors," on account of the number of little mirrors hung up on old rusty nails against the bare stone, a strange mixture of elegance and barbarism. As upper rooms cannot be defended to advantage, this room of mirrors was what Manesson-Mallet, the authority on fortified places, calls "the last post where the besieged can capitulate."

As we have already said, it was important to prevent the besiegers from reaching this room.

This round room in the second story was lighted by loop-holes; but a torch was burning there. This torch, placed in an iron cresset like the one in the lower hall, had been lighted by l'Imânus, who had placed the end of the sulphur slow-match close beside it. Terrible foresight.

At the end of the lower hall, on a long table made of boards, there was food, as in a Homeric cavern: large plates of rice; of "fur," which is a porridge of buckwheat; of "godnivelle," a hash of veal; rolls of "houichepote," a paste made of flower and fruit cooked in water; and jugs of cider. Any one who wished could eat and drink.

The firing of the cannon put them all on guard. They had only half an hour more before them. L'Imânus, from the top of the tower, was watching the approach of the besiegers. Lantenac had commanded them not to fire, and to let them draw near. He had said,—

"There are four thousand, five hundred of them. It is useless to kill them outside. Don't kill until they are inside. Once inside, we shall be equal."

And he added, with a laugh, "Equality, Fraternity." It was agreed that when the enemy began to advance, L'Imânus should sound a note of warning from his horn.

All, in silence, stationed behind the retirade or on the stairs, waited, with one hand on their muskets, the other on their rosaries.

To sum up, this was the situation:

For the assailants, a breach to penetrate; a barricade to storm; three halls, one above another, to take by main force, one by one; two winding staircases to carry, step by step, under a shower of fire. For the besieged—death.

CHAPTER VII.

PRELIMINARIES.

Gauvain on his side, was arranging the attack. He gave his last instructions to Cimourdain, who, it will be remembered, without taking part in the action was to guard the plateau; and to Guéchamp, who was to wait with the main part of the army in the camp of the forest. It was understood that neither the masked battery in the woods nor the open battery on the plateau should fire, unless there was a sortie or an attempt to escape. Gauvain reserved for himself the command of the attacking column. This was what troubled Cimourdain.

The sun had just set.

A tower on an open field is like a ship on the open sea. It must be attacked in the same way. It is rather a boarding than an assault. No cannon. Nothing useless. What is the good of cannonading walls fifteen feet thick? A port-hole, some storming it, others passing it, axes, knives, pistols, fists, and teeth. This is what takes place.

Gauvain felt that there was no other means of carrying la Tourgue. An attack where the combatants see the whites of each other's eyes is most deadly. He was familiar with the formidable interior of the tower, having lived there as a child. He was deep in thought.

In the meantime, a few steps from him his lieutenant, Guéchamp, with a spyglass in his hand, was scrutinizing the horizon toward Parigné. Suddenly Guechamp exclaimed,—

"Ah! at last!"

This exclamation roused Gauvain from his reverie.

"What is it, Guéchamp?"

"Commander, there is the ladder."

"The escape ladder?"

"Yes."

"What? Hasn't it come yet?"

"No, commander. I was anxious about it. The express which I sent to Javené has returned."

"I know it."

"He announced that, in the carpenter's shop at Javené, he had found a ladder of the required length, that he had it requisitioned, that he had the ladder put on a wagon, that he obtained an escort of twelve horsemen, and that he had seen the wagon, the escort, and the ladder start for Parigné. After which he returned post haste."

"And gave us this report, and he added that as the wagon was drawn by strong horses, and started about two o'clock in the morning, it would be here before sunset. I know all that. Well?"

"Well, commander, the sun has just set and the wagon with the ladder has not yet come."

"Is it possible? Nevertheless, we must begin the attack. The hour has come. If we delay, the besieged will think we are retreating."

"Commander, you can begin the attack."

"But we must have the escape ladder."

"Of course."

"But it is not here."

"It is here."

"How is that?"

"That is why I said, 'Ah! at last!' The wagon had not come; I took my spyglass and examined the road from Parigné to la Tourgue, and, commander, I am satisfied. The wagon is yonder with the escort; it is coming down the slope. You can see it."

Gauvain took his spyglass and looked.

"To be sure. Here it is. There is not enough daylight left to make it all out. But I see the escort; that is plain enough. But the escort seems to me to be larger than you told me, Guéchamp."

"It seems so to me, too."

"They are about a quarter of a league away."

"Commander, the escape ladder will be here in a quarter of an hour."

"We can begin the attack."

It was really a wagon which was coming, but it was not the one they thought.

Gauvain, turning around, saw behind him Sergeant Radoub, erect, his eyes downcast, in attitude of military salute.

"What is it, Sergeant Radoub?"

"Citizen commander, we, the men of the battalion of Bonnet-Rouge, have a favor to ask of you."

"What is it?"

"To have us killed."

"Ah!" said Gauvain.

"Will you do us this kindness?"

"But—that depends on circumstances," said Gauvain.

"You see, commander, since the affair at Dol you have been careful of us. There are still twelve of us."

"Well?"

"This humiliates us."

"You are the reserve."

"We would rather be the advance-guard."

"But I need you to decide the final success of an action. I hold you in reserve."

"Too much so."

"No matter. You are in the column, you march with it."

"In the rear. Paris has the right to march ahead."

"I will think about it. Sergeant Radoub."

"Think about it to-day, commander. There is going to be an engagement. There will be a rough tripping-up, on one side or the other. It will be lively. La Tourgue will burn the fingers of those who touch it. We ask the privilege of being in the fight."

The sergeant stopped short, twisted his moustache, and added in a different tone,—

"And then you see, commander, our babies are in that tower. Our children are there, the children of the battalion, our three children. The terrible face of Gribouille-mon-cul-to-baise, of Brise-bleu, of l'Imanus, that Gouge-le-Bruand, that Bouge-le-Gruand, that Fouge-le-Truand, that thunderbolt of God, man of the devil, threatens our children. Our children, our little ones, commander. When the tower quakes and tumbles, we do not want any harm to come to them. Do you understand this, master? we do not want any harm to happen to them. Just now, I took advantage of the truce to go up on the plateau, and I saw them through a window; yes, they are really there, you can see them from the edge of the ravine and I saw them, and they were afraid of me, the darlings. Commander, if a single hair falls from the heads of those little cherubs, I swear a thousand times by all that is holy that I, Sergeant Radoub, that I will do something desperate. And this is what all the battalion say: 'We want the children saved, or we want to be all killed. This is our right, yes, to be all killed.' And now, good luck and reverence."

Gauvain held out his hand to Radoub, and said,—

"You are a brave man. You shall be in the attacking column. I will divide you. I will put six of you with the vanguard, that the troops may be sure to advance, and I will put six of you in the rearguard, to keep them from retreating."

"Shall I still command the twelve?"

"Certainly."

"Thank you, commander. For I belong to the vanguard." Radoub saluted his commander and went back to the ranks.

Gauvain took out his watch, spoke a few words in Guéchamp's ear, and the attacking column began to form.

CHAPTER VIII.

THE SUMMONS AND THE REPLY.

In the meantime, Cimourdain, who had not yet taken up his position on the plateau and was still at Gauvain's side, stepped to a trumpeter.

"Blow the trumpet," he said to him.

The trumpet sounded, the horn replied.

A blast from the trumpet and an answering blast from the horn rang out again.

"What is it?" asked Gauvain of Guechamp. "What does Cimourdain want?"

Cimourdain had approached the tower with a white handkerchief in his hand.

He spoke.

"Men who are in the tower, do you know me?"

The voice of l'Imânus replied from the top of the tower,—

"Yes."

Then the two voices began to converse, and this was heard,—

"I am the envoy of the Republic."

"You are the former curé of Parigné."

"I am the delegate of the Committee of Public Welfare."

"You are a priest."

"I am the representative of the Law."

"You are a renegade."

"I am the messenger of the Revolution."

"You are an apostate."

"I am Cimourdain."

"You are the devil."

"Do you know me?"

"We hate you."

"Would you be satisfied to have me in your power?"

"There are eighteen of us here who would give our heads in exchange for yours."

"Well, I have come to give myself up to you."

From the top of the tower was heard a burst of savage laughter, and this exclamation,—

"Come on."

There was deep silence in the camp as they awaited the result.

Cimourdain added,—

"On one condition."

"What is it?"

"Listen."

"Speak."

"You hate me?"

"Yes."

"As for me, I love you. I am your brother."

The voice from the top of the tower replied,—

"Yes, Cain."

Cimourdain replied with a singular inflection, both loud and gentle,—

"Insult me, but listen, I have come to parley with you. Yes, you are my brothers. You are poor misguided men. I am your friend. I am light speaking to ignorance. Light always comprises brotherly love. Besides, have we not all the same mother, our native land? Well, listen to me. You will know later, or your children will know, or your children's children, that all that is taking place at this moment is done in fulfilment of the laws above, and that God has caused this Revolution. While waiting for the time when all minds, even yours, will understand this, and, all fanaticism, even yours will vanish, will any one pity your darkness? I have come to you to offer you my life; I do more, I extend my hand to you. I ask you the favor of destroying my life to save your own. I have full power, and what I say I am able to perform. It is a critical moment; I am making a last effort. Yes, he who speaks to you is a citizen, and in this citizen, yes, there is a priest. The citizen is fighting against you, but the priest implores you. Listen to me. Many of you have wives and children. I take the defence of your children and your wives. I take their defence against you. Oh, my brothers——"

"Go on, preach away!" sneered l'Imânus.

Cimourdain continued,—

"My brothers, do not let the accursed hour come. There will be bloodshed here. Many of us who are here before you will not see to-morrow's sun; yes, many of us will perish, and you, all of you, will die. Have mercy on yourselves. Why shed all this blood when it is useless? Why kill so many men when two would suffice?"

"Two?" said l'Imânus.

"Yes. Two."

"Who?"

"Lantenac and myself."

And Cimourdain raised his voice,—

"Two men are enough; Lantenac, for us, myself for you. This is what I offer you, and it will be the saving of all your lives: give us Lantenac and take me. Lantenac will be guillotined, and you will have me to dispose of as you like."

"Priest," howled l'Imânus, "if we had you we would burn you over a slow fire."

"I am willing," said Cimourdain.

And he added,—

"You, condemned, who are in this tower can all be alive and free; in an hour I bring you safety. Do you accept it?"

L'Imânus thundered,—

"You are not only a villain; you are mad. Ah, indeed, why do you come to disturb us? who asked you to come to speak to us? we, give up monseigneur! what do you mean?"

"His head, and I offer you—"

"Your hide. For we would skin you like a dog. Curé Cimourdain. Well, no, your hide is not worth his head; get you gone."

"The struggle will be terrible; once more, for the last time, reflect."

Night fell during the exchange of these ominous words, which were heard inside the tower as well as without. The Marquis de Lantenac kept silent and let them alone. Leaders indulge in such portentous deeds of selfishness. This is one of the rights of responsibility. L'Imânus shouted to those beyond Cimourdain, exclaiming,—

"Men who attack us, we have told you our propositions; they have been made, and we have nothing to change about them. Accept them; if not, woe be unto you! do you consent? we will give up the three children here, to you, and you shall let us all go free and unharmed."

"All of you, yes," replied Cimourdain, "except one."

"Which one?"

"Lantenac."

"Monseigneur! give up monseigneur! never!"

"We must have Lantenac."

"Never!"

"We cannot negotiate, except on this condition."

"Then begin."

Silence ensued.

L'Imânus, after sounding the signal with his horn, went down again; the marquis took the sword in his hand; the nineteen men besieged gathered in silence in the lower hall, behind the retirade, and knelt down; they heard the measured tread of the attacking column advancing towards the tower in the darkness; the sound drew nearer; suddenly, they felt that they were close upon them, at the very mouth of the breach. Then all kneeling down held their guns and their blunderbusses through the cracks in the retirade, and one of them, Grand-Francœur, the priest Turneau, rose, and, a drawn sword in his right hand, a crucifix in his left, said in a solemn voice,—

"In the name of the Father, and of the Son, and of the Holy Ghost."

All fired at once, and the struggle began.

CHAPTER IX.

TITANS AGAINST GIANTS.

It was indeed frightful.

This hand-to-hand struggle surpassed all that could have been imagined.

To find anything equal to it, one must go back to the great combats of Æschylus or to the carnage of old feudal times; or to those "attacks with short arms," which lasted till the seventeenth century, when fortified places were penetrated by means of "fausse-brayes;" tragic assaults in which, says the old sergeant of the province of Alentijo, "when the mines have done their work, the besiegers will advance carrying planks covered with sheets of tins, armed with round shields and mantlets, and provided with plenty of grenades, causing the defenders to abandon the retrenchments or retirades, and, having taken possession, they will vigorously repulse the besieged."

The place of attack was horrible; it was one of those breaches called technically "vaulted breaches;" that is to say, as will be remembered, an opening going through the wall from one side to the other, and not a rupture open to the sky. The powder had worked like a gimlet. The effect of the explosion had been so violent that the tower had been rent more than forty feet above the mine, but it was only a crack, and the practicable opening, serving as a breach and penetrating into the lower hall, resembled a spear-thrust which pierces, rather than an axe-blow which cleaves.

It was a puncture in the side of the tower, a long, deep fracture, something like a horizontal wall under ground, a passage winding and rising like an intestine through a wall fifteen feet thick, a peculiar, shapeless cylinder full of obstacles, snares, explosions, where a man would hit his forehead against the rocks, and would stumble over the rubbish and lose his sight in the darkness.

The assailants had before them this dark porch, like the mouth of an abyss with all the stones of the jagged wall for upper and lower jaws; the jaws of a shark have not more teeth than this terrible rent. It was necessary to enter and to come out by this hole.

Within, there was a rain of fire, outside rose the retirade. *Outside,* that is to say, in the lower hall on the ground floor.

Only in the encounter of sappers in covered galleries when the countermine cuts the mine, or in the carnage on the gun decks of vessels which grapple each other in naval battles, is such ferocity displayed. To fight at the bottom of a ditch is horrible to the last degree. It is frightful to have a battle under a roof.

At the moment when the first swarm of besiegers entered, the whole retirade was covered with lightning, and it was something like a thunderstorm bursting underground. The thunderbolts of the assailants replied to the thunderbolts of the ambuscade. Report answered report; Gauvain's voice shouted,—

"Break them in!"

Then Lantenac's cry: "Hold firm against the enemy!"

Then the cry of l'Imânus: "On, men of the Main!" Then the clashing of sword against sword, and blow on blow, terrible discharges, all devastating. The torch fastened against the wall lighted dimly all this horror. It was impossible to distinguish anything; it was in a reddish blackness; whoever entered there was suddenly deaf and blind,—deafened by the noise, blinded by the smoke. Disabled men were lying in the midst of the rubbish. Corpses were trodden down, the wounded were trampled upon, broken limbs were crushed, while howls of anguish arose; men had their feet bitten by the dying; now and then, there were moments of silence more hideous than the din.

They seized each other by the throat, groans were heard, then the gnashing of teeth, the death-rattle, imprecations; and the thundering began again. A stream of blood began to flow from the tower through the breach, and ran out into the darkness. This dismal pool steamed outside in the grass.

It seemed as if the tower itself were bleeding, as if a giant were wounded.

Wonderful to say, those outside heard hardly any sound. The night was very dark, and all around the fortress, on the plain and in the forest, there was a sort of funereal stillness. Inside, it was like hell; outside, it was like the grave. This conflict of men killing each other in the darkness, these volleys of musketry, this din, this madness, all this tumult died away under the walls and arches; the noise lacked air, and suffocation was added to slaughter. Outside the tower, there was scarcely a sound. The little children slept through it all.

The fury increased, the retirade held its own. Nothing is more difficult to storm than this kind of a barricade, with a re-entering angle. If the besieged had numbers against them, their position was in their favor. The attacking column lost a great many men. Stretched out in a long line outside, at the foot of the tower, it plunged slowly into the opening made by the breach and contracted, like an adder going into its hole.

Gauvain, with the imprudence of a young general, was in the lower hall, in the thickest of the fight, in the midst of all the firing. We may add that he had the confidence of a man who had never been wounded. As he turned round to give an order, a blaze of musketry lighted up a face close beside him.

"Cimourdain!" he exclaimed, "what are you doing here?"

It really was Cimourdain. Cimourdain replied,—

"I come to be near you."

"But you will be killed!"

"Well, what are you doing here yourself?"

"But I am needed here. You are not."

"Since you are here, I must be here also."

"No, my master."

"Yes, my child."

Cimourdain stayed near Gauvain.

The dead were heaped up on the floors of the lower hall.

Although the retirade was not yet forced, the greater number would evidently conquer at last. The assailants were exposed to the enemy's fire, and the besieged were protected. Ten besiegers fell to one besieged, but the besiegers were replaced. The besiegers increased and the besieged decreased.

The nineteen besieged were all behind the retirade, the attack being there. There were dead and wounded among them; fifteen at the outside were still fighting. One of the fiercest among them, Chante-en-Hiver, had been frightfully wounded. He was a thickset Breton, with curly hair, of the small, lively type. He had one of his eyes put out and his jawbone broken. He could still walk. He dragged himself up the winding staircase and went into the room on the first story, hoping to be able to say his prayers there and die.

He leaned back against the wall near the loophole to try to get a little air.

Below, the massacre before the retirade was growing more and more horrible. In an interval between two volleys, Cimourdain raised his voice.

"Besieged!" he cried, "why shed blood any longer? You are taken. Surrender. Remember that we are four thousand five hundred against nineteen, that is to say, more than two hundred to one. Surrender."

"Let us put an end to this sentimentality," replied the Marquis de Lantenac.

And twenty bullets answered Cimourdain.

The retirade did not reach as high as the arched roof; this allowed the besieged to shoot over it, but it also allowed the besiegers to scale it.

"Attack the retirade!" cried Gauvain. "Is there any one willing to scale the retirade?"

"I am," said Sergeant Radoub.

CHAPTER X.

RADOUB.

Then the assailants were dumfounded at what took place. Radoub had entered through the breach at the head of the attacking column, with six others, and, out of these six men of the Prussian battalion, four had already fallen. After he had cried: "I am!" he was seen not to advance but to retreat, and bending down, stooping, crawling almost between the legs of the combatants, he reached the opening of the breach and went out. Was this flight? would such a man flee? what could it mean?

When outside the breach, Radoub, still blinded by the smoke, rubbed his eyes as if to put aside the horror and the darkness, and by the light of the stars looked at the wall of the tower. He gave a nod of satisfaction, as if to say, "I was not mistaken."

Radoub had noticed that the deep cleft made by the explosion of the mine, reached above the breach to the loophole in the first story, the iron grating of which had been broken through and displaced by a cannon ball. The network of broken bars was hanging, half torn away, and a man would be able to creep through.

A man could creep through, but could he climb up there? By the cleft, yes, on condition that he was like a cat.

This was just what Radoub was. He belonged to that race which Pindar calls "agile athletes." An old soldier may be a young man; Radoub, who had been a French Guard, was not forty years old. He was a nimble Hercules.

Radoub laid his musket on the ground, removed his shoulder belt, took off his coat and vest, and kept only his two pistols, which he put in the belt of his trousers, and his bare sword, which he took between his teeth. The handles of the two pistols protruded above his belt.

Thus freed from all encumbrances, and followed in the darkness by the eyes of all those in the attacking column who had not yet entered the breach, he began to mount the stones in the cleft of the wall, like the steps of a staircase. Being without shoes was an advantage to him; nothing clings like a bare foot; he curled his toes into the holes between the stones. He pulled himself up by main force, he braced himself with his knees. The ascent was rough. It was something like climbing over the teeth of a saw. "It is fortunate," he thought, "that there is no one in the room of the first story, for they would not let me climb in this way."

He had no less than forty feet to climb thus. As he mounted, hindered somewhat by the protruding handles of his pistols, the cleft grew narrower and the ascent became more and more difficult; at the same time, the risk of falling increased with the depth of the precipice.

At last he came to the edge of the loophole; he removed the twisted and broken grating so that he had room enough to pass through; by a powerful effort he raised himself up, placed his knee on the cornice of the window-sill, seized the end of a bar on the right, in one hand, and with the other a bar on the left, and rose to his waist in front of the embrasure of the loophole, his sword between his teeth, hanging by his two hands above the abyss.

He had but one more effort to make to enter the hall in the first story.

But a face appeared in the loophole.

Radoub suddenly saw before him in the dim light something frightful. An eye destroyed, a shattered jaw, a face covered with blood. This one-eyed mask looked at him.

This mask had two hands; these two hands came out of the darkness and approached Radoub; one, with a single grasp, snatched the two pistols from his belt, the other removed his sword from between his teeth.

Radoub was disarmed. His knee was slipping on the inclined plane of the cornice, his two hands grasping the ends of the iron bars could hardly hold him, and he had beneath him forty feet of precipice.

This face and these hands belonged to Chante-en-hiver. Chante-en-hiver, suffocated by the smoke pouring up from below, had succeeded in entering the embrasure of the loophole, and here the outside air had revived him, the coolness of the night had stanched his blood, and he had regained a little strength; suddenly, he saw Radoub's form rise up outside in front of the opening, then as Radoub, clinging to the bars with both hands, had only the choice of falling or being disarmed, Chante-en-hiver, calm and frightful, took the pistols out of his belt and his sword from between his teeth.

An extraordinary duel began. A duel between the unarmed and the wounded.

Without doubt, the dying man had the advantage. One bullet would be enough to hurl Radoub into the yawning gulf, under his feet.

Fortunately for Radoub, Chante-en-hiver, having both pistols in one hand, could shoot neither of them and was forced to make use of the sword. He thrust the point of it into Radoub's shoulder. This thrust wounded Radoub and saved him.

Radoub, without arms, but having all his strength scorned his wound, which did not reach to the bone, sprang forward, let go the bars, and leaped into the embrasure.

Then he found himself face to face with Chante-en-hiver who had thrown the sword behind him, and now held the two pistols in his two hands.

Chante-en-hiver, on his knees, aimed at Radoub who was almost close up to the muzzle: but his weakened arm trembled and he did not immediately shoot.

Radoub took advantage of this respite to burst out laughing.

"Tell me, ugly mug," he cried, "do you think I am going to be afraid of your à-la-mode beef jaws? Sapristi, how they have battered your pretty face!"

Chante-en-hiver was still aiming at him.

Radoub continued,—

"It's not a thing to talk about, but the grapeshot crimped your mouth very prettily. My poor boy, Bellona has smashed your physiognomy. Go ahead, go ahead, spit out your little pistol shot, my good fellow."

The pistol went off and the bullet passed so near Radoub's head that it tore off half of his ear. Chante-en-hiver raised his other arm with the second pistol, but Radoub did not give him time to aim.

"I have had enough of you taking my ears off," he cried. "You have wounded me twice, now it is my turn."
And he rushed at Chante-en-hiver, knocked his arm up making the pistol go off aimlessly, and seized hold of his dislocated jaw. Chante-en-hiver shrieked and fainted away.

Rodoub stepped over him and left him in the embrasure.

"Now that I have let you know my ultimatum," said he, "don't move again. Stay there, you rascally sneak. You may rest assured that I am not going to amuse myself now with slaughtering you. Crawl about on the floor at you ease, fellow-citizen of my old shoes. Die; you can still do that. You will soon know what nonsense your curé has been telling you. Depart into the great regions of mystery, peasant."

And he sprang into the hall of the first story.

"You can't see a thing here," he growled.

Chante-en-hiver writhed convulsively and shrieked with agony. Radoub turned around.

"Silence! do me the kindness of keeping quiet, unworthy citizen. I will have nothing more to do with you. I scorn to put an end to you. Let me have peace."

And he ran his hand through his hair in perplexity, as he looked at Chante-en-hiver.

"Ah, now what am I going to do? all this is very good, but here I am without arms. I had two shots to fire. You wasted them for me, you beast! and made such a smoke about it that it would blind a dog!"

And hitting his torn ear,—

"Ow!" he said. And he added,—

"It was very forward of you to confiscate one of my ears; but indeed, I would rather lose that than anything else, for it was only an ornament. You scratched my shoulder too, but that is nothing. Die, clown, I forgive you."

He listened, the tumult in the lower hall was frightful. The fight was more furious than ever.

"They are getting on well down there. Never mind, they are howling 'Long live the king.' They are dying nobly,"

His feet hit against his sword on the floor. He picked it up, and said to Chante-en-hiver who no longer stirred and was perhaps dead,—

"You see, woodsman, this is what I wanted, my sword or 'zut,' it is the same. I will take it out of friendship. But I must have my pistols. Devil take you, savage! Now what shall I do? I am no good here."

He groped along through the hall, trying to see and to get his bearings. Suddenly in the darkness, behind the central column, he made out a long table, and on this table something which shone indistinctly. He felt of it. They were blunderbusses, pistols, carbines, a row of firearms laid in order and seeming to be waiting for hands to lay hold of them; it was the reserve of weapons prepared by the besieged for the second phase of the assault; a perfect arsenal.

"A refreshment table!" exclaimed Radoub, and he pounced on them wildly.

Then he became terrible.

The door leading to the staircase communicating with the upper and lower stories was seen to be wide open beside the table loaded with arms. Radoub dropped his sword, seized a pistol in each hand and fired them together at random through the door into the stairway, then he seized a blunderbuss and discharged that, then he seized a musketoon loaded to the muzzle with buckshot, and discharged that. The musketoon, pouring forth fifteen bullets, seemed like a volley of grapeshot. Then Radoub, getting his breath, cried into the stairway in a thundering voice,—

"Long live Paris."

And seizing another musketoon larger than the first, he aimed it under the archway of the Saint-Gilles's staircase and waited.

The confusion in the lower hall was indescribable. Unexpected surpises like this demoralize resistance. Two of the bullets of Radoub's triple discharges had hit; one had killed the elder of the two brothers, Pique-en-bois, the other had killed Houzard, who was Monsieur de Quélen.

"They are upstairs!" cried the marquis.

This cry brought about the instant abandonment of the retirade; a flock of birds could not be scattered more quickly, and they each tried to rush first into the stairway. The marquis encouraged this flight.

"Be quick," he said. "It is courageous to escape now, let us all go up to the second story! there we will begin again."

He was the last to leave the retirade.

This bravery saved him.

Radoub, in ambush on the first landing of the staircase, his finger on the trigger of the blunderbuss was on the watch for the rout. Those who first appreared around the corner received the discharge full in the face, and fell as if struck by lightning. If the marquis had been one of them he would have been killed.

Before Radoub had time to seize a new weapon, the rest passed by, the marquis last, and slower than the others. They believed the room on the first floor to be filled with the enemy; they did not stop there, but went on to the second story to the hall of mirrors. There was the iron door, the sulphur slow match was there, and there it would be necessary to capitulate or die.

Gauvain, as surprised as they were by the gunshots from the stairway and not being able to explain the assistance which had come to him, without trying to understand had taken advantage of it, had leaped with his men over the retirade, and drove the besieged at the point of the sword up to the first story.

There he found Radoub.

Radoub saluted him and said,—

"One minute, commander. It was I who did this. I remembered Dol. I did as you did. I put the enemy between two fires."

"A good pupil," said Gauvain, with a smile.

After being in the dark for some time one's eyes become accustomed to it, like those of night birds; Gauvain noticed that Radoub was covered with blood.

"But you are wounded, comrade."

"Never mind that, commander. What difference does it make, an ear more or less? I have a sword-cut too, but that is of no consequence. In breaking a pane of glass one always gets cut somewhat. But it is only a little of my blood."

They came to a sort of halt in the halt of the first story, taken by Radoub. A lantern was brought. Cimourdain rejoined Gauvain. They stopped to consider. It was indeed time to reflect. The besiegers were not in the secret of the besieged. They were ignorant of their lack of ammunition. They did not know that the defenders of the place were short of powder; the second story was the last post of resistance; the besiegers knew that the staircase might be mined.

One thing was certain, that the enemy could not escape. Those who were not dead were as good as under lock and key. Lantenac was in a trap.

With this certainty, they could take a little time to try to find out the best possible course to pursue. They already had many dead. It was necessary to try not to lose too many men in this last assault. There would probably be a tough outburst at first to quell.

The combat was interrupted. The besiegers, masters of the ground floor and of the next story were waiting for the general's order to go on. Gauvain and Cimourdain were holding counsel. Radoub listened in silence to their deliberation.

He ventured again to salute his general timidly,—

"Commander?"

"What is it, Radoub?"

"Have I the right to a slight reward?"

"Certainly. Ask what you like."

"I should like to be the first to go up."

It was impossible to refuse him. Besides, he would have done it without permission.

CHAPTER XI.

THE DESPERATE.

While they were taking counsel in the first story, they were building a barricade in the second. Success is madness, defeat is rage. The two stories were about to clash in desperate encounter. To touch victory is intoxicating. Below there was hope, which would be the greatest of all human forces if it were not for despair.

Above, there was despair.

A calm, cold, ominous despair.

On reaching this hall of refuge, beyond which there was nothing left for them, the first care of the besieged was to bar the entrance. It would be of no use to fasten the door. It would be better to block up the stairway. In a case like this, an obstacle through which it is possible to see and to fight is of more value than a fastened door.

The torch placed by l'Imânus in a cresset on the wall, near the sulphur slow match, gave them light.

In this hall on the second floor there was one of those large, heavy oak chests in which clothing and linen were kept before the invention of furniture with drawers. They dragged this chest, and stood it on end in the doorway of the staircase. It fitted in firmly and obstructed the entrance. It left only a narrow space open near the arch, large enough to let a man through, excellent for killing the assailants, one by one. It was doubtful if men would risk themselves there.

Having blocked up the entrance, they took a respite.

They counted their number.

Of the nineteen only seven were left, including l'Imânus. All were wounded except l'Imânus and the marquis.

The five who were wounded, but very active,—for in the heat of battle, all wounds not mortal allow men to come and go,—were Chatenay, called Robi, Guinoiseau, Hoisnard, Branche-d' Or, Brin-d'Amour and Grand-Francœur. All the rest were dead.

They had no ammunition. The cartridge boxes were exhausted. They counted the cartridges. How many shots for the seven had they? Four.

They had reached the moment when there was nothing left but to fall. They were driven to the very precipice, yawning and awful; it would have been difficult to be nearer the edge.

In the meantime, the attack was beginning; but slowly and all the more sure. The sound of the besiegers' gunstocks was heard as they hit against the staircase, step by step.

No means of escape. Through the library? There were six cannons on the plateau pointed at it, with matches lighted. Through the rooms above? what would be the use? They only lead to the plateau. Then their only means of escape would be to throw themselves from the top to the bottom of the tower.

The seven survivors of this epic band saw themselves inexorably imprisoned and held by this thick wall, which protected them and betrayed them. They were not yet taken; but they were already prisoners.

The marquis addressed them,—

"My friends, it is all over."

And after a silence he added,—

"Grand-Francœur, be the Abbé Turmeau once more."

All knelt down, with their rosaries in their hands. The knocking of the assailants' muskets came nearer. Grand-Francœur, covered with blood from the bullet which had grazed his skull and torn off the skin covered with hair, raised his crucifix in his right hand. The marquis, a skeptic at heart, placed one knee on the ground.

"Let each one," said Grand-Francœur, "confess his faults aloud. Monseigneur, speak."

The marquis replied.—

"I have killed."

"I have killed," said Hoisnard.

"I have killed," said Guinoiseau.

"I have killed," said Brin-d'Amour.

"I have killed," said Chatenay.

"I have killed," said l'Imânus.

And Grand-Francœur added,—

"In the name of the Most Holy Trinity, I absolve you. May your soul depart in peace."

"Amen!" replied all the others.

The marquis arose.

"Now," said he, "let us die."

"And let us kill," said l'Imânus.

The blows from the muskets began to shake the chest which barred the door.

"Think on God," said the priest. "Earth no longer exists for us."

"Yes," added the marquis, "we are in the tomb."

All bowed their heads and beat their breasts. The marquis and the priest alone remained standing. Their eyes were fixed on the floor, the priest was praying, the peasants were praying, the marquis was deep in thought; the chest, as though it were struck by hammers, gave forth a lugubrious, hollow sound.

At this moment, a quick, strong voice rang out behind them, crying,—

"I told you the truth, monseigneur."

The heads of all turned around in amazement.

A hole had just opened in the wall.

A stone perfectly jointed with the others, but not cemented, and turning on a pivot above and below, had just revolved on itself like a turnstile, and in turning had opened the wall. The stone having turned on its axis, made a double opening and offered two passages, one to the right, the other to the left, narrow, but large enough to allow a man to pass through. Outside this unexpected door could be seen the first steps of a spiral staircase.

The face of a man appeared in the opening.

The marquis recognized Halmalo.

CHAPTER XII.

A DELIVERER.

"Is it you, Halmalo?"

"It is, monseigneur. You see now that turning stones do exist, and that it is possible to escape through here. I have come in time. But be quick. In ten minutes you will be in the midst of the forest."

"God is great," said the priest.

"Save yourself, monseigneur," cried they all.

"All of you first," said the marquis.

"You first, monseigneur," said the Abbé Turmeau.

"I shall be the last."

And the marquis added in a stern voice,—

"No struggle for generosity. We have no time to be magnanimous. You are wounded. I command you to live and to flee. Be quick and take advantage of this means of escape. Thank you, Halmalo."

"Monsieur le marquis," said the Abbé Turmeau. "Are we going to be separated?"

"Without doubt, below. We can only escape each for himself."

"Monseigneur, will you appoint a rendezvous?"

"Yes. A clearing in the forest, the Pierre-Gauvain. Do you know the place?"

"We all know it."

"I will be there to-morrow at noon. Let all who can walk be found there."

"We will be there."

"And we will begin the war over again," said the marquis.

In the meanwhile, Halmalo pressing against the turning stone had just noticed that it no longer moved. The opening could not be closed.

"Monseigneur," he said, "let us hurry, the stone resists now. I was able to open the passage, but I shall not be able to close it."

Indeed, after long disuse the stone was, as it were, stiffened on its hinges. It would be impossible to stir it henceforth.

"Monseigneur," added Halmalo, "I hoped to close the passage, and that when the Blues entered, they would find no one here, and failing to understand it would believe that you had all vanished into smoke. But here, the stone will not move. The enemy will see the place open, and will be able to pursue us. But do not lose a moment. Quick! all down the stairs."

L'Imânus placed his hand on Halmalo's shoulder,—

"Comrade, how long will it take to go through this passage and reach a place of safety in the forest?"

"No one is seriously wounded?" asked Halmalo.

They replied,—

"No one."

"In that case, a quarter of an hour will be enough."

"So," replied l'Imânus, "if the enemy should enter here in a quarter of an hour?"

"They could pursue us, but they would not reach us."

"But," said the marquis, "they will be here in five minutes, that old chest will not hinder them long. A few blows with the butt-ends of their muskets will finish it A quarter of an hour! who will keep them back for an quarter of an hour?"

"I will," said l'Imânus.

"You, Gouge-le-Bruant?"

"I, monseigneur. Listen. Out of six, five of you are wounded. As for me, I haven't a scratch."

"Neither have I," said the marquis.

"You are the chief, monseigneur; I am the soldier. The chief and the soldier are two different men."

"I know it, we have each a different duty."

"No, monseigneur, you and I have the same duty; that is to save you."

L'Imânus turned toward his comrades.

"Comrades, the enemy must be held in check and their pursuit retarded as long as possible. Listen! I have all my strength, I have not lost a drop of blood; as I am not wounded, I shall hold out longer than any of the rest of you. Go, all of you; leave me your guns, I shall make good use of them. I shall undertake to keep back the enemy a good half hour. How many loaded pistols are there?"

"Four."

"Put them on the floor."

They did as he desired.

"That is right; I will remain. They will find some one to speak to. Now, quick, go all of you."

Critical situations make short thanks. They hardly took time to press his hand.

"I shall see you soon," said the marquis.

"No, monseigneur, I hope not. Not soon; I am going to die."

Once after another they all entered the narrow staircase, the wounded going first. As they were descending, the marquis took the pencil from his note-book in his pocket, and wrote some words on the stone which could no longer be turned, and which left the passage open. "Come, monseigneur, there is no one left but you," said Halmalo. And Halmalo started to go down. The marquis followed him. L'Imânus was left alone.

CHAPTER XIII.

THE EXECUTIONER.

The four pistols had been placed on the flags, for this hall had no floor; l'Imânus picked up two of them, one in each hand.

He went cautiously toward the entrance to the staircase, which was obstructed and screened by the chest.

The assailants evidently feared some surprise. One of those final explosions which are the catastrophe of the conqueror as well as the conquered. The last attack was as slow and cautious as the first had been impetuous.

They had not been able, they had not wished perhaps, to break through the chest with violence; they had demolished the bottom by beating it in with their muskets, and had made holes in the cover with their bayonets, and through these holes they tried to see into the hall before venturing to enter it.

The light from the lanterns with which they illuminated the staircase came through these holes.

L'Imânus noticed an eye looking through one of these holes. He quickly aimed the barrel of one of his pistols at this hole and pulled the trigger. The shot went off, and l'Imânus was rejoiced to hear a horrible cry. The bullet had put out the eye and gone through the head of the soldier who was looking through the hole, and the man had just tumbled backwards down the stairs.

The assailants had broken through the lower part of the cover in two quite large places and had made two kinds of loopholes in it; l'Imânus took advantage of one of these holes to pass his arm through, and to fire his second pistol at random into the throng of besiegers. The ball probably rebounded, for several cries were heard, as if three or four had been killed or wounded, and a great tumult among the men followed in the stairway, as they lost their footing and fell back.

L'Imânus threw down the two pistols which he had discharged, and took the two others; then, with the two pistols in his two hands he looked through the holes in the chest.

He ascertained the first effect produced.

The assailants had gone back down the stairs. The dying were writhing on the steps; on account of the winding he could only see three or four stairs.

L'Imânus waited.

"So much time gained," he thought.

Just then he saw a man on his belly, crawling up the stairs, and at the same moment the head of a soldier lower down, appeared behind the central pillar of the spiral.

L'Imânus aimed at this head and fired. There was a cry, a soldier fell, and l'Imânus changed from his left hand to his right, the last loaded pistol remaining.

At the same time he felt a frightful pain, and it was his turn to shriek. A sword had entered his bowels. A hand, the hand of a man who was crawling, had just passed through the second loophole in the lower part of the chest, and this hand had plunged a sword into l'Imânus's belly.

The wound was frightful. His bowels were cut from one side to the other.

L'Imânus did not fall. He ground his teeth and said,—

"That is good!"

Then tottering and dragging himself along, he went back to the torch burning beside the iron door; he laid down his pistol and took the torch, and holding with his left hand his bowels, which were gushing out, he lowered the torch with his right, and lighted the sulphur match.

The fire caught, the match blazed. L'Imânus left the torch still burning on the floor, took his pistol again, and having fallen on the flags, but lifting himself up again, blew the match with the little breath he had left.

The flame ran along, passed under the iron door, and reached the castle bridge.

Then seeing his accursed success, more satisfied, perhaps, with his crime than with his valor, this man who had just been a hero and was now nothing but an assassin, and was about to die, smiled.

"They will remember me," he murmured; "in these little ones, I avenge our little one, the king in the Temple."

CHAPTER XIV.

L'IMANUS ALSO ESCAPES.

At this very instant a great noise was heard, the chest violently pushed, gave way, letting a man pass who rushed into the hall, sword in hand.

"It is I, Radoub, if you want to know it. I am tired of waiting; I am running a risk. No matter, I have just ripped open one. Now I will attack you all. How many are there of you?"

It was Radoub, indeed, and he was alone. After the slaughter just made by l'Imânus in the stairway, Gauvain, fearing a masked fougade, had recalled his men and consulted Cimourdain.

In this darkness through which the torch almost extinguished, faintly gleamed, Radoub, sword in hand on the threshold, repeated his question.

"I am alone. How many are you?"

Hearing nothing, he went forward. One of those jets of light occasionally given forth by a dying fire, and which might be called sobs of light, flashed from the torch and lighted up the whole hall.

Radoub caught sight of one of those little mirrors fastened to the wall, went towards it, looked at his bloodstained face and hanging ear, and said,—

"What a hideous mutilation."

Then he turned round, astounded to see the hall empty.

"There is nobody here," he exclaimed. " The effective force is zero."

He noticed the turned stone, the opening in the staircase.

"Ah! I see. The key to the fields. Come on, men, all of you! Comrades, come on! they are all gone. They have vanished, melted away, slunk away, decamped. This jug of an old tower was cracked. Here is the hole through which they escaped, the rascals! how can one expect to get the better of Pitt and Cobourg with such trickery as this! the devil himself came to their aid! There is no one here at all!"

Just then a pistol was fired, a bullet grazed his elbow and was flattened against the wall.

"But there is some one here, after all. Who was so kind as to be so polite to me?"

"I was," said a voice.

Radoub looked around and made out something in the dim light which proved to be l'Imânus.

"Ah!" he exclaimed. "I have one of them. The others have escaped, but you will not escape."

"Do you think so? " replied l'Imânus.

Radoub took a step and stopped.

"Hallo, you man on the floor, who are you?"

"I am one who is down and who laughs at those who are on their feet."

"What is that in your right hand?"

"A pistol."

"And in your left hand?"

"My bowels."

"I take you prisoner."

"I defy you to do so."

And l'Imânus, bending over the burning match, blew his last breath on the fire and died.

A few moments later, Gauvain and Cimourdain, and all the others entered the hall. All saw the opening. They explored the recesses, they examined the stairway. It led into the ravine. They assured themselves that the enemy had escaped. They shook l'Imânus. He was dead. Gauvain, with a lantern in his hand, examined the stone, which had given escape to the besieged; he had heard of this turning stone, but he, too, considered the legend as a fable. As he was looking at the stone he noticed something written with a pencil; he held the lantern near and read this,—

"*Au revoir, monsieur le vicomte.*—Lantenac."

Guéchamp had rejoined Gauvain. Pursuit was evidently useless. Their escape was complete; the whole country was in favor of the fugitive; the thicket, the ravine, the copse, the natives; they were, doubtless, already far away; there was no way to find them; and the whole forest of Fougères was an immense hiding-place.

What was to be done? all would have to be begun over again. Gauvain and Guéchamp expressed their disappointment and their conjectures.

Cimourdain listened in solemn silence.

"By the way, Guéchamp," said Gauvain, "where is the ladder?"

"Commander, it has not come."

"But still we saw a wagon escorted by mounted men."

Guechamp replied,—

"It did not bring the ladder."

"What did it bring, then?"

"The guillotine," said Cimourdain.

CHAPTER XV.

NEVER PUT A WATCH AND A KEY IN THE SAME POCKET.

The Marquis de Lantenac was not so far away as they thought.

He was, nevertheless, perfectly safe, and beyond their reach.

He had followed Halmalo.

The stairway down which he had gone with Halmalo, after the other fugitives, ended very near the ravine and the arches of the bridge, by a narrow arched passageway. This passageway terminated in a deep natural fissure in the ground, opening into the ravine on one side, and on the other into the forest.

This fissure, entirely concealed from sight, wound under impenetrable vegetation. It would be impossible to capture a man there. A fugitive, having once reached this fissure had only to crawl away like an adder, and was safe from pursuit. The entrance to the secret passage from the stairway was so obstructed by brambles that those who had made this subterranean passage considered it useless to close it in any other way.

The marquis had nothing to do now but to go on. There was no need of troubling himself about a disguise. Since his arrival in Brittany, he had not taken off his peasant's costume, considering himself thus more of a great seigneur.

He merely took off his sword, the belt of which he unfastened and threw down.

When Halmalo and the marquis emerged from the passage into the fissure, the five others, Guinoiseau, Hoisnard Branche-d'Or, Brin-d' Amour, Chatenay, and the Abbé Turmeau had disappeared.

"They were not long in getting away," said Halmalo.

"Follow their example," said the marquis.

"Does monseigneur wish me to leave him?"

"Certainly. I have already told you so. One can only escape alone. One can pass when two cannot. Together, we should attract attention. You would be the cause of their capturing me, and I should be the cause of their capturing you."

"Does monseigneur know the country?"

"Yes."

"Will monseigneur go to the rendezvous at the Pierre-Gauvain?"

"To-morrow, at noon."

"I shall be there. We shall be there."

Halmalo interrupted himself.

"Ah! monseigneur, when I think that we were together on the open sea, that we were alone, that I wanted to kill you, that you were my seigneur, that you could have told me so, and that you did not tell me! what a man you are!"

The marquis went on to say,—

"England; there is no other resource. The English must be in France in two weeks."

"I shall have many accounts to give to monseigneur. I have fulfilled his commissions."

"We will talk about that to-morrow."

"Good-bye till to-morrow, monseigneur."

"By the way, are you hungry?"

"Possibly, monseigneur. I was in such haste to reach you that I do not know that I have eaten anything today."

The marquis took a cake of chocolate from his pocket, broke it in two, gave one half to Halmalo, and began to eat the other.

"Monseigneur," said Halmalo, "to your right is the ravine, to your left, the forest."

"Very good. Leave me. Go your way."

Halmalo obeyed. He plunged into the darkness. A sound of brambles crackling was heard, then nothing more. After a few seconds it would have been impossible to retrace his footsteps. This land of the Bocage, rough and inextricable, was the fugitive's aid. People did not disappear there; they vanished. It was this facility for swift passing out of sight which made our armies hesitate before this ever-retreating Vendée, and before its combatants—such formidable fugitives.

The marquis remained motionless. He was one of those men who tried to have no feelings; but he could not restrain the emotion of breathing free air after having breathed so much blood and carnage. To feel himself perfectly safe after having been completely lost; after seeing the tomb so near, to take possession of absolute security; to escape from death and come back to life, all this, even for a man like Lantenac, was a shock; and although he had passed through similar experience before, he could not restrain his imperturbable soul from violent emotion for some minutes. He acknowledged to himself, that he was happy. He quickly subdued this feeling which almost resembled joy.

He took out his watch and made it strike. What time was it?

To his great astonishment, it was only ten o'clock.

When one has gone through one of these sudden changes of fortune in human life, when everything has been questioned, one is always amazed to find that minutes so full are no longer than others.

The warning cannon had been fired a little before sunset, and La Tourgue had been approached by the attacking column a half-hour later, between seven and eight o'clock just at nightfall. So, this colossal struggle, begun at eight o'clock, was over at ten. This whole *epopée* had lasted one hundred and twenty minutes. Sometimes the rapidity of lightning is mingled with catastrophes. Events are so surprisingly short.

If we stop to reflect, it is the contrary which is really astonishing; a resistance of two hours with so small a number against a number so large was extraordinary, and surely it was not short or soon over, this battle of nineteen against four thousand.

But it was time to be on his way. Halmalo must be far distant, and the marquis decided that there was no need of staying there any longer. He put his watch back into his vest, not into the same pocket, for he had just noticed that it was in contact with the key of the iron door, which l'Imânus had brought to him, and that the crystal of his watch was liable to be broken against this key, and he prepared to reach the forest in his turn. As he was about to turn to the left, it seemed to him as if he saw a dim light.

He turned around and through the thicket, clearly defined against a red background, and suddenly made visible in its least details, he saw a great blaze in the ravine. Only a few strides separated him from the ravine. He went towards it, then changed his mind, finding that it was of no use to expose himself to this bright light; whatever it might be it did not concern him, after all; he took the direction which Halmalo had shown him, and went a few steps toward the forest.

Suddenly, deeply buried and hidden under the brambles as he was, he heard a terrible cry above his head; this cry seemed to come from the very edge of the plateau above the ravine. The marquis raised his eyes, and stopped.

BOOK FIFTH—IN DÆMONE DEUS.

CHAPTER I.

FOUND BUT LOST.

When Michelle Fléchard caught sight of the tower reddened by the setting sun, she was more than a league away from it. Although she could hardly walk a step, she never hesitated to traverse this league. Women are weak, but mothers are strong. She had walked.

The sun had set: twilight came, then thick darkness; as she walked along she heard from the distance eight o'clock, then nine, ring out from a belfry which could not be seen. This belfry was probably that of Parigné. Now and then she stopped to listen to certain strange sounds like dull blows, which were possibly some of the mysterious noises of the night.

She went on straight ahead, breaking away the furze bushes and the sharp heath under her bleeding feet. She was guided by a feeble light coming from the distant keep making it stand out, and giving a mysterious radiance to this tower. This light became brighter as the sound of blows grew more distinct, then it went out.

The vast plateau where Michelle Fléchard was passing along was nothing but grass and heather, without a house or a tree; it rose imperceptibly, and as far as one could see, rested its long, straight, hard line against the dark, starry horizon. What kept her up in this ascent was the fact that the tower was continually before her eyes.

She saw it slowly increase in size.

The muffled reports and the pale gleams of light coming from the tower, as we have just said, were intermittent; they would cease, then begin again, offering a strange, cruel enigma to the wretched mother in distress.

Suddenly they ceased; both sound and light, all disappeared; there was a moment of perfect silence, a sort of melancholy peace ensued.

At this very moment, Michelle Fléchard reached the edge of the plateau. She saw at her feet a ravine, the bottom of which was lost in the thick darkness of the night; at some distance on the top of the plateau an entanglement of wheels, taluses, and embrasures, which was a battery of cannons, and in front of her, dimly illumined by the lighted matches of the battery, an enormous edifice which seemed built with shadows blacker than all the other shadows which surrounded her.

This edifice was composed of a bridge, the arches of which plunged into the ravine, and of a sort of castle rising above the bridge, and the castle and the bridge were joined to a lofty, dark, round object, which was the tower towards which the mother had walked from so great a distance.

The lights were seen to come and go through the windows of the tower, and from the noise proceeding from it one would have guessed that it was filled with a crowd of men, and the shadows of some of them were cast above, even on the platform.

Near the battery there was an encampment, the mounted sentries of which Michelle Fléchard had noticed; but in the darkness among the brambles, she had not been seen by them.

She had come to the edge of the plateau, so near the bridge that it seemed to her as if she could almost touch it with her hand. The depth of the ravine separated her from it. In the darkness she could make out the three stories of the castle on the bridge.

All measure of time had been blotted out of her mind, and she remained long absorbed and dumb before this yawning chasm and this shadowy building.

What was it? what was going on there? was it la Tourgue? she was dizzy with a strange expectation, so that she could hardly tell whether she was just arriving or going away. She asked herself why she was there.

She looked, she listened.

Suddenly, she could no longer see anything. A cloud of smoke rose between her and what she was looking at. A keen smarting sensation made her shut her eyes. She had hardly closed her eyelids when they grew red and became luminous. She opened them again.

It was no longer night before her, it was light as day; but a kind of funereal daylight, the daylight which comes from a fire. The beginning of a conflagration was before her eyes.

The black smoke had grown scarlet and in it there was a great flame; this flame appeared, then disappeared, with the ferocious twisting peculiar to lightning and snakes.

This flame came out like a tongue from something resembling a mouth, and which was a window full of fire. This window grated with iron bars already red hot, was one of those in the lower story of the castle built on the bridge. This window was the only feature of the whole building which could be seen. The smoke covered everything, even the plateau, and only the edge of the ravine, black against the red flame, could be made out.

Michelle Fléchard looked on in astonishment. Smoke is a cloud; a cloud is a dream; she no longer knew what she saw. Ought she to go away? ought she to remain? she felt almost beyond reality.

A breath of wind passed by and broke through the curtain of smoke, and through the rent the tragic bastille, suddenly disclosed, rose visible in its entirety,—keep, bridge, châtelet; dazzling, terrible, magnificently gilded by the fire, illuminated by it from top to bottom. Michelle Fléchard, in the ominous distinctness of the fire, could see it all.

The lower story of the castle built on the bridge was burning.

Above it, the two other stories could be seen, still untouched, but as if borne in a basket of flames. From the edge of the plateau, where Michelle Fléchard was, the interior could be dimly seen through the rifts between the fire and the smoke. All the windows were open. Through the windows in the second story, which were very large, Michelle Fléchard could see, against the walls, the bookcases, which seemed to her to be filled with books, and, in front of one of the windows, on the floor, in the dim light, a little confused group; something which looked indistinct and huddled together, like a nest or a brood, and which looked as if it moved now and then.

She looked at it.

What was this little group of shadows?

Occasionally, it came into her mind that it resembled living forms; she was feverish, she had eaten nothing since morning, she had walked without resting, she was worn out, she felt as though she were in a sort of hallucination which she instinctively mistrusted; still, her eyes becoming more and more fixed, could not leave that dark heap of objects, probably inanimate, and apparently motionless, lying there on the floor of that hall above the fire.

Suddenly, the fire, as if it had a will power, sent forth from below, one of its jets, towards the great dead ivy covering the same front at which Michelle Fléchard was looking. It seemed as if the flame had just discovered this network of dry branches; a spark seized it eagerly, and began to mount along the shoots with the frightful swiftness of a train of powder. In a twinkling, the flame reached the second story. Then, from above, it lighted up the interior of the first. A sudden blaze brought into relief three little beings fast asleep.

It was a charming little heap,—arms and legs intertwined, eyelids closed, a smile on their fair faces.

The mother recognized her children.

She uttered a frightful cry.

This cry of inexpressible anguish is only given to mothers. Nothing is more fierce, and nothing more touching. When a woman utters it, one would think it was a she-wolf; when a she-wolf gives it, it sounds like a woman.

This cry of Michelle Fléchard's was a howl. Hecuba bayed, says Homer.

It was this cry which the Marquis de Lantenac had just heard.

We have seen that he stopped.

The marquis was between the outlet of the passage through which Halmalo had helped him to escape and the ravine. Through the brambles intertwined above him, he saw the bridge in flames, la Tourgue red from the reflection, and, through the opening between two branches, he saw above his head, on the other side, on the edge of the platform, opposite the burning castle and in the full light of the fire, a haggard, pitiful figure, a woman bending over the ravine.

This figure was no longer Michelle Fléchard; it was Medusa, The wretched are terrible. The peasant woman was transformed into one of the Eumenides. This country woman, vulgar, ignorant, unreasoning, had suddenly asumed the epic proportions of despair. Great sorrows have a gigantic power of enlarging the soul; this mother represented maternity; everything which sums up humanity is superhuman; she rose then, on the edge of this ravine, before this conflagration, before this crime, like a power from the grave; her cry was like that of a wild beast, and her gestures like those of a goddess; her face, from which proceeded imprecations, seemed like a masque of flame. Nothing could be more sovereign than the lightning of her eyes bathed in tears; her eyes flashed lightning on the fire.

The marquis listened. This fell on his ear; he heard something strangely inarticulate and heartrending, more like sobs than words.

"Ah! my God! my children! those are my children! help! fire! fire! fire! but you are bandits! is there no one there? but my children will be burned! Ah! how terrible! Georgette! my children! Gros-Alain, René-Jean! but what does it mean? who put my children there? they are asleep. I am mad! it is impossible! Help!"

Meanwhile, there was a great confusion in la Tourgue and on the plateau. The whole camp ran around the fire, which had just burst out. The besiegers, after being concerned with the firing, were now concerned with the fire, Gauvain, Cimourdain, Guéchamp, gave orders. What was to be done? there were but a few buckets of water to be drawn from the shallow brook in the ravine. Their distress increased. The whole edge of the plateau was covered with frightened faces looking on.

It was a frightful sight.

They looked on, and could do nothing.

The flames, by means of the ivy which had taken fire, Had reached the upper story. There it had found the granary full of straw and had seized upon it. The whole granary was now burning.

The flames danced; the joyfulness of flames is a doleful thing. It seemed as if some malicious breath were fanning the fire in this funereal pile. It might have been thought that the grim l'Imânus was wholly there, changed to a whirlwind of sparks, living in the murderous life of the conflagration, and as if this monster of a soul had turned to fire.

The story where the library was had not yet been reached, the height of its ceiling, and the thickness of its walls retarded the time when it would take fire, but the fatal moment was drawing near; the fire in the first story licked it, and the flames in the third story caressed it. The awful kiss of death touched it. Below, a cellar of lava, above, an arch of embers; if a hole should break through the ceiling, the children would be buried in the live coals. René-Jean, Gros-Alain, and Georgette were not yet awake, they were sleeping the deep, quiet sleep of childhood; and through the folds of flame and smoke, which alternately covered and disclosed the windows, they could be seen in this grotto of fire, behind this meteoric blaze, peaceful, graceful, motionless, like three confiding child Jesuses, asleep in a hell; and a tiger would have wept to see these roses in this furnace and these cradles in this tomb.

Meanwhile, the mother was wringing her hands.

"Fire! fire! I say. Are they all deaf that they do not come? They are burning my children! Come, you men over yonder. I have walked days and days, and and this is how I find them. Fire! help the angels! Indeed they are angels! What have those innocent little creatures done? the men shot me, and now they are burning them! Who does such things? Help! save my children! Don't you hear me? One would take pity on a dog! My children! they are asleep! Ah! Georgette! I see her dear little stomach! René-Jean! Gros-Alain! Those are their names. You see that I am their mother. It is abominable that such a thing as this should happen. I have walked days and nights, as I told a woman this morning. Help! help! fire! You are monsters! It is horrible! the oldest is not five years old, the little one less than two. I see their little bare legs. They are asleep, good, holy Virgin! the hand of Heaven gave them to me. and the hand of hell is taking them from me. And I have walked so far! My children that I fed from my breast! And I thought I was unfortunate not to find them! Have pity on me! I want my children, I must have my children! And yet they are in the fire! See how my poor feet are all covered with blood. Help! It is not possible that there are men on the earth who would leave these poor little ones to die like this! Help! murder! The like of this was never seen before. Ah, yon brigands! What is this frightful house? You stole them away from me to kill them! Jesus have pity! I want my children. Oh, I do not know what I can do! I cannot let them die! help! help! help! Oh, if they should die like this I should hate God!"

During the mother's awful supplication, voices were heard on the plateau and in the ravine.

"A ladder!"

"There is no ladder!"

"Water!"
"There is no water!"
"Up there in the tower, in the second story, there is a door."
"It is of iron."
"Burst it open!"
"It cannot be done!"
And the mother redoubled her desperate appeals,—
"Fire! help! Hurry! Oh, kill me! My children, my children! Ah! the horrible fire! Take them out of it, or throw me in, too!"
In the intervals between her cries was heard the calm crackling of the fire.
The marquis felt in his pocket and touched the key to the iron door. Then bending down under the archway through which he had made his escape, he went back into the passage from which he had just come out.

CHAPTER II.

FROM THE STONE DOOR TO THE IRON DOOR.

A whole army in despair over an impossible rescue; four thousand men unable to help three children; such was the situation.

They had no ladder; the ladder sent from Javené had not arrived; the conflagration increased like the opening of a crater; to try to put it out with water from the brook in the ravine, which was almost dry, was ridiculous; it would be like throwing a glass of water on a volcano.

Cimourdain, Guéchamp, and Radoub had gone down into the ravine; Gauvain had gone back into the hall in the second story of la Tourgue, where were the turning stone, the secret way of escape, and the iron door of the library. It was there that l'Imânus had lighted the sulphur match; it was there that the fire had started.

Gauvain had taken twenty sappers with him. The only resource was to break open the iron door. It was fatally closed.

They began by using axes. The axes broke. A sapper said,—

"Steel is like glass against this iron."

The door was made of double sheets of wrought iron, bolted together, each three fingers in thickness.

They took iron bars and tried to pry open the door. The iron bars broke.

"Like matches," said the sapper.

Gauvain, dubious, murmured,—

"Nothing but a cannon-ball could open this door. We should have to bring a cannon up here."

"But how?" said the sapper.

There was a moment of despair. All these powerless arms hung motionless. Dumb, conquered, dismayed, these men were considering the horrible immovable door.

A red reflection passed underneath. The fire was increasing behind it.

The frightful corpse of l'Imânus was there, ominously victorious.

A few minutes more, perhaps, and everything would give way.

What was to be done? there was no more hope.

Gauvain in exasperation cried, with his eye fixed on the turning stone in the wall and on the exit left open by the fugitives,—

"And yet here is where the Marquis de Lantenac made his escape!"

"And where he returns," said a voice.

And a white head appeared in the stone framework of the secret door.

It was the marquis.

Gauvain had not seen him so near for many years. He drew back.

All who were there remained in the same position, petrified.

The marquis had a large key in his hand. He cast a haughty look at the sappers in front of him, walked to the iron door, bent under the arch and put the key into the key-hole. The lock grated, the door opened, a gulf of flame met their eyes, the marquis entered it.

He went into it with a firm step, holding his head high.

All followed him with their eyes, shuddering.

The marquis had taken but a few steps in the burning hall, when the floor, undermined by the fire and shaken by his footsteps, fell in behind him, leaving a precipice between him and the door. The marquis never turned his head but went straight on. He disappeared in the smoke.

Nothing more was seen of him.

Had he been able to go farther? Had a new pit of fire opened under him? Had he only succeeded in being lost himself? They could not tell. They had nothing before them but a wall of smoke and flames. The marquis was beyond it, dead or alive.

CHAPTER III.

THE CHILDREN AWAKEN.

In the meantime, the children had at last opened their eyes.

The fire, which had not yet reached the library, threw a rosy glow on the ceiling. The children were not familiar with this kind of a dawn. They looked at it. Georgette contemplated it.

All the splendors of the fire were displayed there; the black hydra and the scarlet dragon appeared in the shapeless smoke, superbly dark and vermilion. Long tongues of flame blew off and lighted up the darkness, and it seemed like a battle of comets running one after another.

A fire is prodigal; the live coals are full of jewels, which are scattered to the winds; it is not without reason that charcoal is identical with the diamond.

In the wall of the third story, cracks opened, through which the embers poured down into the ravine cascades of precious stones; the heaps of straw and oats burning in the granary began to stream through the windows in avalanches of gold dust, the oats became amethysts, and the straws, carbuncles.

"Pretty," said Georgette.

All three had risen.

"Ah!" cried the mother; "they are waking up!"

René-Jean got up, then Gros-Alain got up, then Georgette got up.

René-Jean stretched out his arms, went towards the window and said,—

"I'm warm."

"I warm," repeated Georgette.

The mother called to them.

"My children: René! Alain! Georgette!"

The children looked around them. They tried to find out what it all meant. When men are terrified, children are only curious. It is difficult to frighten those who are easily astonished; ignorance causes fearlessness. Children have so little claim on hell, that if they should see it they would admire it.

The mother repeated,—

"René! Alain! Georgette!"

René-Jean turned his head; this voice attracted his attention; children have short memories, but their power of recollection is quick; to them the past is but yesterday.

René-Jean saw his mother, found it quite natural, and, surrounded as he was by strange objects, feeling a vague need of support, he cried,—

"Mamma!"

"Mamma!" said Gros-Alain.

"Mamma!" said Georgette.

And she held out her little arms.

And the mother shrieked, "My children!"

All three came to the window; fortunately, the fire was not on that side.

"I am too warm," said René-Jean.

He added,— "It burns."

And he looked at his mother.

"Come, mamma."

"Tum, mamma," repeated Georgette.

The mother with disordered hair, all scratched, and bleeding, had let herself roll through the brambles into the ravine. Cimourdain was there with Guéchamp, as helpless below as Gauvain was above. The soldiers, in despair at being of no use, swarmed around them. The heat was intolerable but no one felt it. They considered the escarpment of the bridge, the height of the arches, the elevation of the stories, the inaccessible windows, and the necessity for prompt action. Three stories to climb; no means of accomplishing it.

Radoub, wounded, with a sword-cut in his shoulder, and one ear torn off, dripping with sweat and blood, came running up; he saw Michelle Fléchard.

"Hold on," said he, "you are the woman who was shot! so you have come back to life again?"

"My children," said the mother.

"You are right," replied Radoub; "we have no time to spend with ghosts."

He began to scale the bridge, a futile attempt; he buried his nails in the stone, he climbed up a little way; but the courses were smooth, not a break, not a relief, the wall was as correctly pointed as though it had been new, and Radoub fell back.

The dreadful fire continued; in the window frame, now all red, could be seen the three fair heads. Then Radoub shook his fist towards heaven, as if looking for some one, and said,—

"Is this thy dealing, good God."

The mother on her knees clasped the piers of the bridge, crying, "Mercy!"

Heavy cracking was heard above the snapping of the fire. The panes of glass in the bookcases in the library cracked, and fell with a crash. It was evident that the woodwork was yielding. No human power could avail. A moment more and all would be destroyed. They were waiting for the fatal moment. The little voices were heard calling: "Mamma! Mamma!" The people were in a paroxysm of despair. Suddenly, at the window next the one where the children were, against the crimson background of the flames, appeared a tall form.

Every head was raised, every eye became fixed. A man was up there, a man was in the library, a man was in the furnace. This form stood out black against the flames, but it had white hair. They recognized the Marquis de Lantenac.

He disappeared, then he appeared again.

The terrible old man rose before the window with an enormous ladder. It was the escape ladder which had been placed in the library, and which he had gone to look for, and had dragged from the side of the wall to the window. He seized it by one end, and with the masterly agility of an athlete he slid it out of the window, supporting it on a jutting of the wall, and let it down to the bottom of the ravine. Radoub, below, wild with delight, held out his hands, took the ladder, held it firmly in his arms, and cried: "Long live the Republic!"

The marquis replied: "Long live the King!"

And Radoub growled: "You may cry anything you like, and say all the foolish things you will, you are from the good God, all the same."

The ladder was fixed in place; communication was established between the burning hall and the ground; twenty men ran forward, with Radoub at their head, and in a twinkling they placed themselves in a row on the rounds, like masons carrying stones. It made it a living ladder over the ladder of wood. Radoub at the top of the ladder touched the window. He was facing the fire.

The little array, scattered in the heather and on the slopes, pressed forward, distracted by every emotion at once, rushed over the plateau into the ravine, on the platform of the tower.

The marquis disappeared again, then re-appeared, bringing one of the children.

There was a tremendous clapping of hands.

The marquis happened to have seized the oldest. It was Gros-Alain.

Gros-Alain cried: "I'm afraid."

The marquis gave Gros-Alain to Radoub, who passed him down behind him to a soldier, who passed him to another, and, while Gros-Alain, very much frightened and crying, was being taken thus from arm to arm to the bottom of the ladder, the marquis, after a moment's absence, came back to the window with René-Jean struggling and crying. The little fellow struck Radoub just as the marquis passed him on to the sergeant.

The marquis went back into the hall full of flames. Georgette was left alone. He went to her. She smiled. This man of stone felt something moist come into his eyes. He asked: "What is your name?" "'Orgette," she said.

He took her in his arms; she was still smiling, and just as he gave her to Radoub this conscience so lofty and yet so dark was dazzled by her innocence, and the old man gave the child a kiss.

"It is the little girl!" said the soldiers; and Greorgette in her turn passed down from hand to hand to the ground, amidst cries of adoration.

They clapped their hands, they stamped their feet; the old grenadiers sobbed, and she smiled at them. The mother was at the foot of the ladder, panting for breath, beside herself, intoxicated with all this surprise, suddenly exalted from hell into paradise; excess of joy bruises the heart in its way. She held out her arras, she received first Gros-Alam, then René-Jean, then Georgette, she covered them with kisses, then she burst out laughing and fell down in a faint.

A great cry arose: "All are saved!"

Indeed, all were saved, except the old man.

But no one gave him a thought; perhaps, he did not even think of himself.

He remained at the edge of the window for some moments, in thought, as if he wished to give the gulf of flame time to decide upon its action. Then, slowly, deliberately, proudly, he stepped out through the window, and, without turning round, straight, erect, leaning back against the rounds, with the fire behind him, facing the precipice, he began to descend the ladder in silence, with the majesty of a phantom.

Those who were on the ladder hastened down; all present shuddered. This man coming from above filled them all with a holy horror, as though he had been a vision. But he plunged solemnly into the darkness before him; while they drew back, he was approaching them; the marble pallor of his face was without a change; his ghostly eyes had not a gleam of light; at each step that he took towards these men, whose frightened eyes were fixed on him in the darkness, he seemed taller, the ladder trembled and creaked under his solemn step, and he seemed like the statue of a commander going down into the tomb.

When the marquis was at the bottom, when he had reached the last round and had placed his foot on the ground, a hand was laid on his collar. He turned around.

"I arrest you," said Cimourdain.

"I sanction it," said Lantenac.

BOOK SIXTH—THE BATTLE AFTER THE VICTORY.

CHAPTER I.

LANTENAC TAKEN.

The marquis had really descended into the tomb. They led him away. The crypt dungeon in the ground floor of la Tourgue was immediately re-opened under Cimourdain's stern eye; a lamp, a jug of water, some hard tack, were placed in it, a bundle of straw was thrown into it, and, in less than a quarter of an hour after the moment when the priest's hand had seized the marquis, the door of the dungeon was closed on Lantenac. Having done this, Cimourdain went to find Gauvain; just then the distant church of Parigné sounded eleven o'clock in the evening; Cimourdain said to Gauvain,— "I am going to convoke a court-martial; you will not take part in it. You are a Gauvain, and Lantenac is a Gauvain. You are too nearly related to be a judge; and I blame Egalité for having judged Capet. The court martial will be composed of these judges: an officer, Captain Guéchamp; a sub-officer, Sergeant Radoub; and myself, who will preside. Nothing of all this will concern you. We shall conform to the decree of the Convention; we shall limit ourselves to establishing the identity of the former Marquis de Lantenac. To-morrow, the court-martial; the day after, the guillotine. La Vendée is dead."

Gauvain made no answer, and Cimourdain, preoccupied with the final duty which remained for him to perform, left him. Cimourdain had hours to appoint and places to select. Like Lequinio at Granville, like Talien at Bordeaux, like Châlier at Lyons, and like Saint-Just at Strasbourg, he was in the habit of being present in person at executions, as it was considered a good example; the judge came to see the executioner do his work; a custom borrowed by the terror of '93 from the parliaments of France and the Inquisition of Spain. Gauvain, too, was preoccupied. A cold wind was blowing in the forest. Gauvain, leaving Guéchamp to give the necessary orders, went to his tent in the meadow on the border of the wood, at the foot of la Tourgue, and got his hooded cloak and wrapped himself up in it. This cloak was edged with the simple braid which, according to the Republican fashion for sober ornaments, designated the commander-in-chief. He began to walk about in this bloody meadow, where the assault had begun. He was alone there. The fire was still burning, although of no consequence now; Radoub was with the children and their mother, almost as maternal as she; the châtelet on the bridge was nearly burned to the ground, the sappers were attending to the fire, men were digging ditches, burying the dead, caring for the wounded; the retirade had been destroyed, the corpses removed from the rooms and stairways, the place made clean after the carnage, the terrible filth of victory swept away, the soldiers, with military quickness, did what might be called the house-work after the battle. Gauvain saw nothing of all this. So deep in thought was he that he scarcely glanced at the post near the breach, doubled by Cimourdain's orders. He could see this breach in the darkness about two hundred feet from the corner of the meadow where he had, as it were, taken refuge. He saw the black opening. It was there that the attack had begun, three hours before; it was through this that Gauvain had entered the tower; there on the ground-floor was where the retirade had been; the door leading to the dungeon where the marquis was confined was on this ground floor. The men posted at the breach guarded the dungeon. While he was straining his eyes to make out this breach, these words, like a knell, came back confusedly to his ear: "To-morrow, the court-martial; the day after, the guillotine."

The fire, which had been isolated, and on which the sappers threw all the water they could obtain, did not die out without a struggle, and occasional flames still leaped forth; now and then the cracking of the ceilings and the crash of one story falling on another was heard; then eddies of sparks whirled through the air as though a torch had been shaken, a bright light illuminated the farthest horizon, and the shadow of le Tourgue, grown suddenly gigantic, stretched out as far as the forest. Gauvain walked slowly back and forth in this shadow, in front of the breach of assault. Occasionally, he crossed his hands behind his head, covered with the hood of his war-cloak. He was lost in thought.

CHAPTER II.

FREEDOM OR DEATH—WHICH?

His thoughts were fathomless.

An unexpected change of opinion had just taken place in him.

The Marquis de Lantenac had been transfigured.

Gauvain had been a witness of this transfiguration.

He would never have believed that such things could result from any complication of events. Never, even in his dreams, had he imagined that anything of the kind could happen.

The unforeseen, that strange, haughty power which plays with man, had seized Gauvain and held him fast.

Gauvain had before him an impossibility become a reality, visible, palpable, inevitable, inexorable.

What did he, Gauvain, think of this?

It was not a matter to be evaded; it must be decided.

A question was asked him; he could not escape from it.

Asked by whom?

By events.

And not alone by events.

For when events, which are changeable, ask us a question, justice, which is immutable, calls upon us to reply.

Behind the cloud, which casts a shadow over us, there is a star, giving us a ray of light.

We can no more escape from the light than from the shadow.

Gauvain went through an examination.

He was in the presence of some one.

Before a formidable judge.

His own conscience.

Gauvain felt everything wavering within him. His firmest resolutions, his most carefully made promises, his most irrevocable decisions, everything was swaying in the depths of his will.

There are earthquakes in the soul.

The more he reflected on what he had just seen, the more he was disturbed.

Gauvain, a Republican, believed himself to be, and really was just.

A superior justice had just been revealed to him.

Above Revolutionary justice, there is human justice.

What was taking place was not to be evaded; the fact was solemn; Gauvin was a part of this fact; he was in it, and could not get out of it; and, although Cimourdain had said to him, "this no longer concerns you," he felt something as a tree does when it is pulled up by the roots.

Every man has his base; if this base is shaken it causes a profound disturbance; Gauvain felt this disturbance.

He pressed his head between his hands, as if to press out the truth; to get at the exact bearings of such a situation was not an easy matter, nothing could be more difficult; he had formidable figures before him, of which he must get the sum total; to do the addition of destiny, how bewildering! he undertook it; he tried to give an account of himself; he endeavored to collect his ideas, to discipline the struggling forces which he felt within him, and to recapitulate the facts.

He laid them out before his mind.

Who has never taken a similar account of himself, and questioned himself, in extreme circumstances, on the course to pursue, whether to advance or retreat?

Gauvin had just seen a miraculous spectacle.

A celestial battle had taken place at the same time as the terrestrial.

The battle of good against evil.

A terrific soul had just been vanquished.

Gauvain had just seen a miracle performed in the case of a man full of all that is bad:—violence, error, blindness, unhealthy obstinacy, pride, selfishness.

The victory of humanity over man.

Humanity had conquered the inhuman.

And by what means? in what way? how had it overcome the giant of anger and hatred? What arms had it used? what engine of war? The cradle.

Gauvain had just been dazzled. In the midst of civil war, in the midst of the conflagration of all enmity and all vengeance, in the darkest and maddest moment of the tumult; just as the crime was giving forth all its fire and hatred, all its blackness; at that instant in conflict when everything becomes a projectile, when the struggle is so shrouded in darkness, that justice, honesty, and truth are lost sight of;—suddenly the Unknown, the mysterious monitor of souls, poured forth resplendently, above all human light and darkness, the great light eternal.

Above the dismal encounter, between the false and the relative, out of the depths, the face of truth had suddenly appeared.

All at once, the strength of the weak had intervened.

Three poor beings, almost newborn, unconscious, deserted, orphaned, alone, lisping, smiling, were seen face to face with civil war, retaliation, the frightful logic of reprisals, murder, carnage, fratricide, rage, malice, all the Gorgons, and yet triumphant. He had seen the failure and defeat of an infamous fire, set to commit a crime; he had seen atrocious intentions baffled and frustrated; he had seen the ancient feudal ferocity, the old inexorable disdain, the pretended experience of the necessities of war, the reason of State, all the arrogant determinations of a cruel old age, vanish before the blue eyes of those who had scarcely begun to live; and it was very natural, for one who has not yet lived can have done no harm; it was justice, it was truth, it was purity and the mighty angels of heaven are in little children.

A useful spectacle; advice; a lesson; the frantic participants in a merciless war had suddenly seen, in the face of all the crimes, of all the outrages, of all the fanaticism, of the murderer, of vengeance stirring the funeral pile, of death coming with a torch in his hand, above the enormous legion of sins, arise this all-conquering power, innocence.

And innocence had been victorious.

And one could say: "No, civil war does not exist; barbarity does not exist; hatred does not exist; crime does not exist; darkness does not exist: this aurora, childhood, is sufficient to scatter all these spectres.

Never, in any struggle, had Satan been more visible nor God.

This battle had had a human conscience for its arena.

The conscience of Lantenac.

Now, it was beginning over again, more furious and still more decisive, perhaps, in another conscience.

The conscience of Gauvain.

What a battle-field is man!

We are slaves to these gods, to these monsters, to these giants,—our thoughts.

Often, these terrible combatants trample our souls under foot.

Gauvain meditated.

The Marquis de Lantenac, surrounded, blockaded, condemned outlawed; held fast, like the wild beast in the circus, like a snail in pincers; shut up in his home, now become his prison; enclosed on all sides by a wall of iron and of fire,—had succeeded in getting away; he had performed a miracle of escape. He had made that masterstroke, the most difficult of all in such a war, flight. He had taken possession of the forest, to intrench himself there; of the country, to fight in it; of the darkness, to disappear in it. He had again become the terrible one, coming and going; the sinister wanderer; the captain of the invisible; the chief of underground men; the master of the woods. Gauvain had the victory; Lantenac had liberty. Lantenac, henceforth, had security, a boundless course before him, an inexhaustible choice of places of refuge. He was intangible, lost to sight, unapproachable. The lion had been taken in a snare, and had escaped from it.

Well, he had returned to it.

The Marquis de Lantenac had voluntarily, spontaneously, of his own free will, left the forest, darkness, security, liberty, to return undauntedly into the most frightful danger. Once, Gauvain had seen him, when he rushed into the fire at the risk of being swallowed up by it; a second time, when he came down the ladder to give himself up to his enemies—that ladder, a means of safety for others, for him a means of destruction.

And why had he done this?

To save three children.

And now, what was going to be done with him?

He would be guillotined.

Were these three children his own? No. Did they belong to his family? No. To his rank? No. For three poor little ones, foundlings, unknown, in rags, barefooted, this nobleman, this prince, this old man, saved, delivered, a conqueror,—for escape is a triumph,—had risked everything, compromised everything, put all things into doubt; and, while he was delivering the children, he proudly surrendered his life,—his life till then so terrible, now so majestic, he offered it up.

And what were they going to do with it?

Accept it.

The Marquis de Lantenac had the choice between the life of others and his own; in this superb option, he had chosen death.

And they were going to grant it to him.

They were going to kill him.

What a reward for heroism!

To respond to an act of generosity with an act of cruelty!

To give this stab to the Revolution!

What a belittling of the Republic!

While a man of prejudices and slavish ideas, suddenly transformed, was returning to humanity, they, the men of freedom and enfranchisment, clung to civil war, to the routine of blood, to fratricide.

And the lofty divine law of pardon, of abnegation, of redemption, of sacrifice, existed for the combatants of error, and did not exist for the soldiers of truth!

What! not engage in this struggle of magnanimity! Be resigned to this defeat; the stronger to become the weaker, the victors to become murderers, and to have it said that on the side of the monarchy there were those who saved children, and on the side of the Republic those who killed old men!

He would see this great soldier, this powerful octogenarian, this unarmed warrior, stolen rather than taken, captured while doing a good deed, bound ith his own permission, with the sweat of a splendid self-sacrifice still on his brow, mount the steps of the scaffold as one mounts the degrees of an apotheosis! And they would put this head, around which would soar in supplication the three souls of the little angels he had saved, under the chopping knife. And before this punishment so infamous for the executioners, a smile would be seen on the face of this man, and on the face of the Republic, a blush!

And this would take place in the presence of Grauvain, the chief!

And, although able to prevent it, he would refrain from doing so! And he could content himself with this haughty dismissal,—"this no longer concerns you! And he was not to perceive that in a deed so monstrous, between the one who accomplishes it and the one who allows it to be done; the one who allows it to be done is the worst, because he is a coward!

But the death of this man, had he not promised it? he, Gauvain, the merciful man, had he not declared that Lantenac was an exception, and that he would give Lantenac up to Cimourdain?

This head, it was his debt. Well, he was paying. That was all.

But was it the same life?

Thus far, Gauvain had only seen in Lantenac the barbarous warrior, the fanatic support of royalty and feudalism, the slaughterer of prisoners, the assassin set loose by war, the deadly man. He had not feared this man; this proscriber, he would proscribe him; this implacable one would find him implacable. Nothing could be more simple, the way was marked out, and dismally easy to follow, everything had been foreseen, they would kill him who killed others, they were in the straight line of horror. This line had been unexpectedly broken, an unforseen turning revealed a new horizon, a metamorphosis had taken place. An unknown Lantenac entered on the scene. A hero came forth from the monster; more than a hero,—a man. More than a soul,—a heart. It was no longer a murderer that Gauvain had before him, but a saviour. Gauvain was overcome by a flood of celestial light. Lantenac had just struck him with a thunderbolt of kindness.

And Lantenac transformed would not transform Gauvain! What! this blow of light would have no counterblow. The man of the past would go ahead, and the man of the future remain behind! The man of cruelty and superstition would spread sudden wings, and would soar above and see crawling under him, in the mire and in the darkness, the man of ideals! Gauvain would remain in the old cruel rut, while Lantenac would rise.

Still another thing.

The family!

This blood that he was going to shed,—for to allow it to be shed was the same as shedding it himself. Was it not his own blood, Gauvain's? his grandfather was dead, but his great-uncle was alive; and this great-uncle was the Marquis de Lantenac. Would not the brother who was in the grave rise to prevent the other from entering it? would he not order his grandson henceforth to respect that crown of white hair, sister to his own halo? had there not passed between Gauvain and Lantenac the indignant glance of a spectre?

Was the aim of the Revolution then to pervert man's nature? had it been brought about to destroy the family, to stifle humanity? far from it. It was to affirm these supreme realities, and not to deny them that '89 had arisen. Overthrowing the bastilles was delivering humanity; abolishing feudalism was founding the family. The author being the starting-point of authority, and authority being included in the author, there can be no other authority than fraternity; hence the legitimacy of the queen bee who creates her people, and, being mother, is queen; hence the absurdity of the man king who, as he is not the father, cannot be the master; hence the suppression; hence the Republic. What is all this? it is the family, it is humanity, it is the Revolution. The Revolution is the accession of the people, and at bottom the people is man.

The question was whether, when Lantenac had just returned to humanity, Gauvain would return to the family.

The question was whether the uncle and the nephew would be united in the superior light, or whether the nephew would respond to the uncle's progress by taking a backward step.

The question, in this pathetic debate between Gauvain and his conscience stood thus, and seemed to solve itself: to save Lantenac.

Yes, but France?

Here the face of the perplexing problem suddenly changed.

What! France at bay I France betrayed, opened, dismantled! She was without a moat, Germany had crossed the Rhine; she was without a wall, Italy had passed the Alps, and Spain, the Pyrenees. She had the great gulf, the ocean, left. She had that in her favor. She could depend on that, and, a giantess, supported by the mighty sea, could fight against the whole earth. An impregnable situation after all.

Well, no, this situation would fail her. This ocean was no longer hers. In this ocean there was England. England, it is true, did not know how to cross it. Well, a man was going to throw a bridge across to her, a man was going to hold out his hand to her, a man was going to say to Pitt, to Craig, to Cornwallis, to Dundas, to the pirates:

"Come!" A man was going to cry: "England, take France!"

And this man was the Marquis de Lantenac!

They held this man. After three months of chasing, of pursuit, of desperation, they had finally captured him. The hand of the Revolution had just been laid on the wretch; the clenched hand of '93 had taken the royalist murderer by the collar; through one of the effects of that mysterious premeditation from on high which mingles with human affairs, this parricide was now awaiting punishment in his own family-dungeon; the feudal man was in the feudal oubliette; the stones of his own castle rose against him and closed over him, and he who wished to betray his own country was betrayed by his own house.

God had evidently planned all this; the hour of justice had come, the Revolution had taken this public enemy prisoner; he could no longer wage war, he could no longer fight, he could no longer do any harm; in this Vendée where there were so many arms, he was the only man with brains; to put an end to him was to put an end to the civil war; they had possession of him; tragic but fortunate catastrophe; after so much massacre and carnage, he was there, the man who had killed others, and whose turn it was to die.

And if he should find some one to save him!

Cimourdain, that is to say '93, held Lantenac, that is to say the monarchy, and if he should find some one to snatch its prey from this claw of bronze! Lantenac, the man in whom concentrated that sheaf of scourges called the past, the Marquis de Lantenac was in the tomb, the heavy, eternal door was closed on him, and if some one should come from outside to slide the bolt! this social malefactor was dead, and with him the revolt, the fratricidal contest, the beastly war, and if some one should bring him back to life!

Oh! how this death's head would laugh!

How this spectre would say, "Very good, here I am alive; idiots!"

How he would set himself to his hideous work again! How Lantenac would plunge again, implacable and full of delight, into the gulf of hatred and of war! The very next day how the people would again see houses burning, prisoners massacred, the wounded finished, women shot!

And, after all, did not Gauvain exaggerate this deed which fascinated him so?
Three children were lost; Lantenac had saved them.
But who was the cause of their being lost?
Was it not Lantenac?
Who had put those cradles into the fire?
Was it not l'Imânus?
Who was l'Imânus?
The lieutenant of the marquis.
The general is the one responsible.
So the incendiary and the assassin was Lantenac.
What had he done that was so admirable?
He had not carried out his purpose—nothing more.

After havng planned the crime he had retreated from it. It had seemed to him too horrible. The mother's cry had awakened in him those inmost depths of human pity, a sort of storehouse of universal life, which exists in all souls, even the most hardened. At this cry he had retraced his steps. From the night into which he had plunged, he had gone back towards the daylight. After having done the crime, he undid it. All his merit lay in this, that he had not been a monster at the very last.

And for so little give him back everything! give him back space, the fields, the flames, the air, daylight; give him back the forest, which he would use to protect his bandits; give him back liberty, which he would use for servitude; give him back life, which he would use for death!

As for trying to come to an understanding with him, as for any desire to treat with this proud soul, as for proposing to give him his liberty conditionally, as for asking him to consent, provided his life was saved, to abstain henceforth from all hostility and all revolt,— what a mistake such an offer would be, what an advantage they would give him, what scorn they would strike against, as he would buffet the question with his reply, as he would say: "Keep your shame for yourselves! Kill me!"

There was really nothing to be done with this man but to kill him or to set him free. There was no way of access to this man. He was always ready to take flight or to sacrifice himself; he was his own eagle and his own precipice. A strange soul.

Kill him? What an anxiety! Set him free? What a responsibility!

If Lantenac should be saved, the war with la Vendée would have to be begun all over again, as with a hydra, as long as its head is not cut off. In a twinkling, and with the swiftness of a meteor, the flame, extinguished by the disappearance of this man, would blaze forth again. Lantenac would not rest until he had realized that execrable plan of placing, like the cover of a tomb, the monarchy over the Republic, and England over France. To save Lantenac was to sacrifice France; Lantenac's life meant the death of a multitude of innocent beings, men, women, and children, taken in the toils of domestic war; it meant the landing of the English, the retreat of the Revolution, towns plundered, the people slaughtered, Brittany bleeding, the prey given back to the lion's claws. And Gauvain, in the midst of all sorts of uncertain glimmerings and contradictory lights, saw dimly outlined in his thoughts this problem rising before him: setting the tiger at liberty.

And then the question came back again under its first aspect; the stone of Sisyphus, which is nothing but the quarrel of man with himself, fell down again: Was Lantenac this tiger?

Perhaps he had been, but was he any longer? Gauvain went through those winding mazes of the mind coiling about itself, which make thought resemble an adder. Really, even after examination, could he deny Lantenac's devotion, his stoic abnegation, his superb disinterestedness; What! In the presence of all the open mouths of civil war to testify to humanity! What! in the conflict of inferior truths to bring in truth superior! what! to prove that above royalties, above revolutions, above earthly questions, there is the immense emotion of the human soul? the protection due to the weak from the strong; safety due to those who are lost, from those who are safe; paternity due to all children, from all old men! To prove these magnificent things, and prove them by the gift of his life! What! to be a general, and renounce strategy, battle, revenge! What! to be a royalist, to take the scales, to place on one side the king of France, a monarchy of fifteen centuries, the reestablishing of old laws, the restoration of ancient society, and on the other, three little insignificant peasants, and to find the king, the throne, the sceptre, and the fifteen centuries of monarchy tip the beam, against this weight of three innocent children! What! all that go for nothing! What! one who had done that remain a tiger and deserve to be treated like a wild beast!

No! no! no! it was not a monster of a man who had just illuminated civil war with the light of a divine action! The sword-bearer had been metamorphosed into an angel of light. Infernal Satan had returned as the celestial Lucifer. Lantenac had been redeemed from all his barbarities by an act of sacrifice; in losing himself materially, he had saved himself morally; he had become innocent; he had signed his own pardon. Does not the right to pardon one's self exist? Henceforth, he would be worthy of worship.

Lantenac had just been extraordinary, it was now Gauvain's turn.

Gauvain was called upon to respond to him.

The struggling of good and evil passions at this moment were turning the world into chaos; Lantenac, ruling over this chaos, had just freed humanity from it; it was now for Gauvain to free the family from it.

What was he going to do?

Would Gauvain disappoint trust in God?

No. And he stammered in his inmost heart: "We must save Lantenac."

Well, that is good. Go on, help the English. Be a deserter. Pass over to the enemy. Save Lantenac and betray France.

And he shuddered.

Thy solution is no solution at all, oh dreamer! Gauvain saw in the darkness the ominous smile of the sphinx.

This situation was a sort of terrible meeting of roads, where struggling truths come to an end and confront each other, and where man's three highest ideas, humanity, the family, the fatherland, look each other steadily in the face.

Each of these voices in turn began to speak, and each in turn spoke the truth. How to choose? Each in turn seemed to find the union of wisdom and justice, and said: "Do this." Was this what he ought to do? Yes. No. Reason said one thing, sentiment said another; the two counsels were contrary. Reasoning is only reason; sentiment is often conscience; one comes from man, the other from above.

That is why sentiment has less clearness and more power.

But what strength in stern reason!

Gauvain hesitated.

Fierce perplexities.

Two abysses opened in front of Gauvain. To destroy the marquis? or to save him? It would be necessary to plunge into one or the other.

Which of these two abysses was duty?

CHAPTER III.

THE GENERAL'S CLOAK.

It was indeed a question of duty.
Duty rose forbidding, before Cimourdain; terrible before Gauvain.
Plain, before one; complex, varied, tortuous, before the other.
The hour of midnight struck, then one o'clock in the morning.
Without being aware of it, Gauvain had imperceptibly approached the entrance of the breach.
The fire now only threw a diffused reflection and was dying out.

The plateau, on the other side of the tower, was lighted with the reflection, and became visible occasionally, and then was eclipsed as the smoke covered the fire. This blaze, flaring up suddenly and then cut off by sudden darkness, robbed objects of their proportions, and gave the sentinels in the camp the appearance of ghosts. Gauvain, as he meditated, vaguely watched them flames and smoke come and go. This appearance and disappearance of light before his eyes was strangely analogous to the appearance and disappearance of truth in his mind.

Suddenly, between two clouds of smoke, a flame from the dying bed of coals vividly lighted up the top of the plateau and brought out the crimson form of a wagon. Gauvain looked at this wagon; it was surrounded by horsemen wearing military caps. It seemed to him that it was the wagon which Guéchamp's spyglass had brought into sight on the horizon, some hours before, just as the sun was setting. Some men were on the wagon, and seemed busy unloading it. What they were taking from the wagon seemed heavy, and occasionally gave out a sound like iron; it would have been difficult to tell what it was; it looked like framework; two of them got down and placed a box upon the ground, which, to judge from its shape, contained some triangular object.

The flame died out, everything disappeared in the darkness; Gauvain, with his eyes still fastened on the spot, wondered what there was over there in the darkness.

The lanterns were lighted, there was coming and going off the plateau; but the forms moving about were confused, and, moreover, Gauvain, below, and on the other side of the ravine, could not see what was on the very edge of the plateau.

Voices were talking, but he could not tell what they said. Now and then, blows sounded on wood. He heard too, a strange metallic grating, like the sound of the whetting of a scythe.

Two o'clock struck.

Gauvain went slowly towards the breach, like one who would willingly take two steps forward and three back. Recognizing, in the dim light, the cloak and braided hood of the commander, the sentinels presented arms at his approach. Gauvain went into the hall on the ground floor, now transformed into a guardroom. A lantern was hanging from the arch. It gave just light enough to enable one to cross the hall without stepping on the men belonging to the post, who were lying on the straw on the floor, and for the most part asleep.

They had lain down there; a few hours before, they had been fighting there; the grapeshot, scattered under them in grains of iron and lead, which had not been entirely swept away, disturbed their rest somewhat; but they were weary, and sank to sleep again. This hall had been the place of horror; here had been the attack; here they had roared, howled, gnashed their teeth, given blows, killed, expired; many of them had fallen dead on the pavement where they were now lying asleep; this straw which served them for beds had drunk up the blood of their comrades; now, it was over, the blood was stanched, the sabres were dried, the dead were dead; they were sleeping peacefully. Such is war. And then to-morrow everybody will sleep the same sleep.

As Gauvain entered, some of these drowsy men rose, among others, the officer commanding the post. Gauvain pointed to the door of the dungeon,—

"Open for me," he said.
The bolts were drawn, the door opened.
Gaavain went into the dungeon.
The door closed behind him.

BOOK SEVENTH.—FEUDALISM AND REVOLUTION.

CHAPTER I.

THE ANCESTOR.

A lamp stood on the flagstones of the crypt, beside the square air-hole of the oubliette. The jug filled with water, the soldier's bread, and a bundle of straw were also on the floor. As the crypt was hewn out of the rock, the prisoner who had a fancy for setting his straw on fire would have his trouble for his pains; no risk of fire for the prison; certain asphyxiation for the prisoner. When the door turned on its hinges, the marquis was walking about his dungeon; a mechanical going to and fro, peculiar to all caged wild beasts. At the noise made by opening and then closing the door, he raised his head, and the lamp on the floor between Gauvain and the marquis shone full on these two men, now face to face. They looked at each other, and this look was such that it made them both motionless. The marquis burst out laughing, and exclaimed,— "Good-morning, sir. It is many years since I have had the good fortune to meet you. You are very kind to come to see me. I thank you. I ask nothing better than to have a little talk. It was beginning to be tedious. Your friends are losing time, establishing identity, court-martial, all these formalities take a long time. I should be quicker about it. I am at home here. Have the goodness to come in. Well, what do you think of all that is going on? It is original, isn't it? Once there was a king and a queen; the king was the king; the queen was France. They cut off the king's head, and married the queen to Robespierre; this gentleman and this lady had a daughter whom they named the guillotine, and it seems that I am to make her acquaintance to-morrow morning. I shall be charmed to do so,—as I am to see you. Have you come for that? Have you risen in rank? Shall you be the executioner? If it is merely a visit of friendship, I am touched by it. Monsieur le Vicomte, perhaps you no longer know what a nobleman is. Well, here is one; that is, myself. Look at him. It is strange. He believes in God, he believes in tradition, he believes in the family, he believes in his forefathers, he believes in the example of his father, in fidelity, in loyalty, in the duty towards his prince, in respect for old laws, in virtue, in justice; and he would have you shot with pleasure. I beg of you, have the kindness to sit down. On the floor, it is true; for there are no easy-chairs in this drawing-room; but he who lives in the mire can sit on the floor. I do not say this to offend you, for what we call mire, you call the nation. Doubtless, you will not compel me to cry 'Liberty! Equality! Fraternity!' This was once a room in my own house; formerly, the seigneurs put peasants here; now, the peasants put seigneurs here. This nonsense is called a Revolution. It seems that I am to have my head cut off in thirty-six hours. I see no inconvenience in that. But, if they were polite, they would have sent me my snuff-box, which is up in the room of mirrors, where you played when a child, and where I used to trot you on my knee. Sir, I am going to tell you one thing; you are called Gauvain, and, strange to say, you have noble blood in your veins, by Heaven! the same blood as mine, and that blood which makes me a man of honor, makes you a blackguard. Such are circumstances. You will tell me that it is not your fault. Nor mine. By Heaven! one may be a malefactor without being aware of it. It is in the air one breathes; in times like ours, one is not responsible for his acts; the Revolution makes a rascal of everybody; and our great criminals are great innocents. What blockheads! Beginning with yourself. Allow me to admire you. Yes, I admire a boy like you, who, a man of rank, of good position in the State, having noble blood to shed for noble causes, viscount of this Tour-Gauvain, prince of Brittany, a duke by right, and a peer by inheritance, which is nearly all that can be desired here below, by a man of good sense,—amuses himself, being what he is, by being what you are, so that he seems to his enemies like a villain, and to his friends like an idiot. By the way, give my regards to monsieur the Abbé Cimourdain."

The marquis spoke easily, calmly, without emphasizing any of his words, in his social tone of voice, his eye clear and quiet, both hands in his pockets. He stopped speaking, drew a long breath, and went on,—

"I will not conceal from you the fact that I did what I could to kill you. Just as you see me, I have myself personally aimed a cannon at you. A discourteous proceeding, I admit; but it would be depending on a bad maxim to imagine that an enemy in war should try to be agreeable to you. For we are at war, my nephew. Everything is fire and blood. Nevertheless, it is true that the king has been killed. Fine times!"

He stopped again, then went on,—

"To think that none of these things would have happened if Voltaire had been hanged and Rousseau had been sent to the galleys! Ah! People of intelligence, what a shame! Ah, what do you reproach this monarchy with? It is true, they sent the Abbé Pucelle to his abbey in Corbigny, giving him the choice of an equipage, and all the time he wished in which to make the journey; and, as for your Monsieur Titon, who, if you please, had been a very dissipated man, and who frequented the houses of loose women before taking part in the miracles of Deacon Pâris,—he, I say, was transferred from the castle of Vincennes to the castle of Ham in Picardy, which is, I confess, a pretty detestable place. There were grievances; I remember very well; I have also protested in my time; I was as stupid as you are!"

The marquis felt in his pocket, as though searching for his snuff-box, and went on,—

"But not so bad. We talked for the sake of talking. There was also a meeting in the way of investigations and petitions; and then came these philosophers, but they burned their works instead of their bodies; and court intriguers got themselves mixed up in it. We had all those boobies,—Turgot, Quesnay, Malesherbes, the physiocrats, etc.,—and the quarrel began again. It was all the fault of these scribblers and poetasters. The Encyclopædia! Diderot! d'Alembert! Ah, those rascally good-for-nothings! The idea of a man of good birth like the King of Prussia getting taken in by them. If I had been he, I should have squelched all paper scratchers. Ah! we Gauvains used to be great lovers of justice in old days! Here, on the wall, you can see the marks left by the quartering- wheels! We did not allow any nonsense. No, no; no scribblers. As long as there are men like Arouët, there will be Marats. As long as there are low fellows who use their pens, there will be knaves who use their daggers; as long as there is ink, there will be blots; as long as the paw of man holds the goose quill, frivolous stupidities will engender cruel stupidities. Books cause crimes. The word 'chimæra' has two meanings: it signifies 'dream' and it signifies 'monster.' How dear we have to pay for trash. What is the meaning of your song about 'rights'? Rights of man! rights of the people! All that is empty enough, stupid enough, imaginary enough, senseless enough! Now, when I say: 'Havaise, sister of Conan II., brought the County of Brittany to Hoël, Count de Nantes, and Cornwall, who left the throne to Alain Fergant, uncle to Bertha, who married Alain le Noir, Seigneur of la Roche-sur-Yon, and had by him Conan le Petit, grandfather of Guy or Gauvain de Thouars, our ancestor,' I make a definite statement, and there is a right for you. But your idiots, your knaves, your miserable wretches, what do they call their rights? Deicide and regicide. Ah! how hideous it all is! Ah, the scoundrels! I am sorry for you, sir; for you are of the proudest blood of Brittany; you and I have for our grandfather Gauvain do Thouars; we have, moreover, among our ancestors that great Duc de Montbazon, who was a peer of France, and honored with the Collar of the Orders, who attacked the suburb of Tours and was wounded at the battle of Arques, and died. Master of the Hounds, in his own house of Couziéres in Touraine, at the age of eighty-six. I might name to you also the Duc de Landunois, son of the Lady of la Garnache, of Claude de Lorraine, Duc de Chevreuse and of Henri de Lenoncourt, and of Françoise de Laval-Boisdauphin. But what is the use? Monsieur has the honor of being an idiot, and he claims the right of being the equal of my groom. Know this: I was an old man when you were still a brat. I have wiped your nose for you, and I could do it still. In growing to the stature of a man, you have succeeded in belittling yourself. Since we last met, we have each gone in our own way: I, in the direction of honesty; you, in the opposite direction. Ah! I do not know how all this will end; but these gentlemen, your friends, are noble beggars! Ah! yes; it is fine; I am in perfect sympathy with all these splendid signs of progress; in the army, the punishment of giving the drunken soldier a pint of cold water for three days running has been abolished; you have your maximum, your convention, your Bishop Gobel, your Monsieur Chaumette and Monsieur Hébert, and you have wiped out all the past at one fell swoop, from the Bastille to the Almanach. You are putting vegetables in place of saints. All right, citizens, be our masters, rule, take your ease, do what you please, do not stand on ceremony. But it will not in the least prevent religion from being religion, or royalty from filling fifteen hundred years of our history, and the old French nobles, even after you have cut off their heads, from standing higher than you.

"As to your quibbles about the historic right of royal families, we shrug our shoulders at it. Chilpéric, in reality, was only a monk named Daniel; Rainfroi set up Chilpéric to annoy Charles Martel. We know these things as well as you do. That is not the point. This is the question: to be a great Kingdom, to be the ancient France, to be this magnificent land of system, according to which first the sacred person of the monarch, absolute lord of the state, is regarded, then the princes, then the crown officers in charge of the army on land and sea, of the artillery, and the direction and superintendence of finances. Then came the judges of the higher and lower courts, followed by the officials engaged in the revenues and receipts of custom, and lastly the police of the kingdom in its three orders. There was something fine and noble in this system. You have destroyed it. You have destroyed provinces, like the miserable ignoramuses that you are, without having an idea of what the provinces were. The genius of France is made up of the very genius of the continent, and each one of the provinces of France represented a virtue of Europe. The ingenuousness of Germany was in Picardy; the generosity of Sweden, in Champaign; the industry of Holland, in Burgundy; the activity of Poland, in Languedoc; the sobriety of Spain, in Gascony; the wisdom of Italy, in Provence; the subtility of Greece, in Normandy; the fidelity of Switzerland, in Dauphiné.

"You knew nothing of all that. You have broken, shattered, smashed, destroyed, and you have been blindly acting like brutes. Ah! you will have no more nobility. Very well, your wishes will be gratified. Mourn for them. You will have no more paladins, no more heroes. Farewell, grandeur of old! Find me an Assas now! You are all afraid for your skins! You will have no more chevaliers like Fontenoy, who saluted before dealing the deathblow. You will have no more combatants like those who fought in silk stockings at the siege of Lérida; you will have no more of those proud tournaments when plumes flashed by like meteors; you are a people which has run its course; you will indure invasion, which is a rape. If Alaric II. returned from the dead he would not find himself confronting Clovis; if Abdérame came back he would not find Charles Martel to face him. If the Saxons came back they would not find Pepin. You will have no more heroes like Agnadel, Rocroy, Lens, Staffarde, Nerwinde, Steinkirk, La Marsaille, Raucoux, Lawfeld, Mahon. You will no longer have a Marignan with François I.; no longer Bouvines, with Philippe-Auguste taking prisoner with one-hand Renaud, Count of Bologna, and with the other, Ferrand, Count of Flanders. You will have Azincourt, but you will have no Sieur de Bacqueville, grand bearer of the oriflamme, wrapping himself in his banner, to meet his death. Go! go! do your work! Be the new men! Become pigmies!"

The marquis was silent for a moment and then continued,—

"But leave us great. Kill the kings, kill the nobles, kill the priests, slaughter, destroy, massacre, trample everything under foot; grind the ancient maxims under your heels, trample on the throne, stamp down the altar, blot out God, dance on the ruins! That is your affair. You are traitors and cowards, incapable of devotion and sacrifice. I have spoken. Now have me guillotined, monsieur le vicomte. I have the honor to be your most humble servant."

And he added,

"Ah! I tell you the truth about yourself! What difference will it make to me? I am dead."

"You are free," said Gauvain.

And Gauvain stepped towards the marquis, took off his commander's cloak, threw it over Lantenac's shoulders and pulled the hood down over his eyes. They were of the same height.

"Well, what is this that you are doing?" said the marquis.

Gauvain raised his voice and cried: "Lieutenant, open the door!"

The door opened. Gauvain said: "Take care to close the door behind me." And he pushed the astonished marquis outside.

The lower hall changed to a guardroom, as will be remembered, was lighted only by a horn lantern making objects dimly visible, and the darkness there was more powerful than the light. In this faint glimmer, those of the soldiers who were not asleep saw walk through their midst towards the entrance a tall man wearing the braided cloak and hood of the commander-in-chief; they gave the military salute, and the man passed on.

The marquis slowly crossed the guardroom, made his way through the breach, hitting his head more than once, and went out.

The sentinel, thinking it was Gauvain, presented arms.

When he was outside, with the grass of the fields under his feet, two hundred paces from the forest, with space, night, liberty, life, before him, he stopped and stood still for a moment like a man who has offered no resistance, who has yielded to surprise, and having taken advantage of an open door, tries to find out whether he has acted well or ill, hesitates before going farther, and listens to a last thought. After a few moments of careful reflection, he raised his right hand, snapped his thumb and middle finger, and said: "*Ma foi!*"

And he went on his way.

The door of the dungeon had closed again. Gauvain was inside.

CHAPTER II.

THE COURT-MARTIAL.

Courts-martial at that time were endowed with very nearly discretional powers. Dumas, at the legislative Assembly, had sketched out a plan for military legislation, revised later on by Talbot, at the Council of the Five Hundred, but a final code for councils of war was not framed till the time of the empire. It is from the empire, by the way, that dates the obligation imposed upon military tribunals to begin taking votes from officers of inferior rank. This law was not in existence at the time of the Revolution.

In 1793, the presiding officer of a military tribunal was practically the whole tribunal himself; he chose the members, classed the orders of rank, regulated the mode of voting; he was master as well as judge.

Cimourdain had selected for the council-room of the court-martial, this same hall on the ground floor where the retirade had been and where the guardroom was now. He intended to make short work of everything, the way from the prison to the tribunal, and the passage from the tribunal to the scaffold.

At noon, in conformance with his orders, the court was in session with the following adjuncts,—three straw-seated chairs, a deal table, two lighted candles, a stool in front of the table.

The chairs were for the judges and the stool for the accused. At each end of the table there was another stool, one for the commissioner-auditor, who was a quartermaster, the other for the clerk, who was a corporal.

On the table was a stick of red sealing-wax, the copper seal of the Republic, two ink-stands, some sheets of white paper, and two printed placards, spread out open, one containing the declaration of outlawing, the other the decree of the Convention.

Behind the middle chair was a group of tricolored flags; in these times of rude simplicity, decorations were quickly made, and it took little time to change a guardroom into a court of justice.

The middle chair, destined for the presiding officer, faced the door of the dungeon.

The soldiers were the public.

Two gendarmes guarded the stool.

Cimourdain was seated on the middle chair, having Captain Guéchamp on his right as first judge, and on his left the Sergeant Radoub, as second judge.

He wore his hat with a tricolored plume, his sabre at his side, his two pistols in his belt. His scar, which was a vivid red, added to his ferocious appearance.

Radoub had at last allowed his wound to be dressed. Around his head he had a handkerchief on which a bloodstain was slowly increasing in size.

At noon before the court had opened, an express, whose horse could be heard pawing the ground outside, stood near the table of the tribunal. Cimourdain was writing. He wrote this,—

"Citizens, members of the Committee of Public Welfare,—

Lantenac is taken. He will be executed to-morrow."

He dated the despatch, signed it, folded it, sealed it, and gave it to the messenger who started away.

Having done this, Cimourdain said in a loud voice,—

"Open the dungeon."

The two gendarmes drew back the bolts, opened the dungeon and went in. Cimourdain raised his head, folded his arms, looked at the door and cried,—

"Bring in the prisoner."

A man appeared between the two gendarmes, under the arch of the open door.

It was Gauvain.

Cimourdain shuddered.

"Gauvain!" he exclaimed.

And he added,—

"I demand the prisoner."

"I am the prisoner," said Gauvain.

"You?"

"I myself."

"But where is Lantenac?"

"He is free."

"Free!"

"Yes."

"Escaped?"

"Escaped."

Cimourdain trembling stammered,—

"To be sure, this castle is his, he knows all the means of exit; perhaps the oubliette communicates with some way out; I ought to have thought that he would find some way to escape; he would need no one's aid for that."

"He was aided," said Gauvain.

"To escape?"

"To escape."

"Who aided him?"

"I did."

"You?"
"Yes."
"You are dreaming!"
"I entered the dungeon; I was alone with the prisoner; I took off my cloak, I threw it over his shoulders, I pulled the hood down over his eyes; he went out in my place, and I remained in his. Here I am."
"You did not do that!"
"I did do it."
"It is impossible."
"It is a fact!"
"Bring Lantenac here!"
"He is no longer here. The soldiers, seeing the commander's cloak, took him for me, and let him pass. It was still night."
"You are mad."
"I am telling you the truth."
There was a silence. Cimourdain stammered,—
"Then you deserve—"
"Death," said Gauvain.
Cimourdain was as pale as a corpse. He was as motionless as a man who has been struck by lightning. It seemed as if he could no longer breathe. Great drops of sweat stood on his forehead.
He steadied his voice and said,—
"Gendarmes, seat the accused."
Gauvain sat down on the stool.
Cimourdain added,—
"Gendarmes, draw your swords."
This was the customary formality when the accused was under sentence of capital punishment.
The gendarmes drew their swords.
Cimourdain's voice had regained its usual tone.
"Accused," he said, rise."
He no longer addressed Gauvain familiarly.

CHAPTER III.

THE VOTES.

Gauvain rose.
"What is your name?" asked Cimourdain.
Gauvain replied, "Gauvain."
Cimourdain questioned him further.
"Who are you?"
"I am commander-in-chief of the reconnoitring column of the Coasts of the North."
"Are you a relative or connection of the man who has escaped?"
"I am his grand-nephew."
"Are you familiar with the decree of the Convention?"
"I see the notice of it on your table."
"What have you to say to this decree?"
"That I countersigned it, that I ordered it to be carried out, and that it was I who had the placard printed, and that my name is at the bottom of it."
"Choose a defender."
"I will defend myself."
"You may speak."
Cimourdain had grown calm again. Only his calmness was less like the composure of a man than the tranquillity of a rock.
Gauvain remained silent for a moment, and, as it were, collecting his thoughts.
Cimourdain spoke again.
"What have you to say in your defence?"
Gauvain slowly raised his head, without looking at anybody, and replied:—
"This: one thing prevented me from seeing any other; a good action, seen too near, concealed a hundred criminal actions from my eyes; on one side an old man, on the other, children, all this came between me and duty. I forgot the villages burned, the fields ravaged, the prisoners massacred, the wounded murdered, the women shot. I forgot France betrayed to England; I liberated the murderer of his country. I am guilty. In speaking thus, I seem to speak against myself; it is a mistake. I am speaking for myself. When the guilty person confesses his fault, he saves the only thing worth the trouble of saving—honor."
"Is this," replied Cimourdain, "all that you have to say for your defence?"
"I will add that being the chief, I owe an example, and that you, for your part, being the judge, owe one too."
"What example do you demand?"
"My death."
"Do you think it just?"
"And necessary."
"Be seated."
The quartermaster, as commissioner-auditor, rose and gave a reading; first of the sentence, which outlawed the *ci-devant* Marquis de Lantenac; secondly, the decree of the Convention inflicting punishment of death on any one aiding the escape of a rebel prisoner. It ended with some lines printed at the bottom of the notice of the decree, forbidding any one "to carry aid and assistance" to the above-named rebel "under pain of death," and signed,—
"The commander-in-chief of the reconnoitring column, Gauvain."
Having finished these readings, the commissioner-auditor sat down again.
Cimourdain folded his arms and said,—
"Accused, pay attention. Audience, listen, look, and be silent. You have the law before you. It will now be put to vote. The sentence will be given according to the simple majority. Each judge will give his opinion in turn, aloud, in presence of the accused, justice having nothing to conceal.
Cimourdain continued,—
"The first judge has the floor. Speak, Captain Guéchamp."
Captain Guechamp appeared to see neither Cimourdain, nor Gauvain. He dropped his eyelids, which concealed his motionless eyes fixed on the notice of the decree, and considering it as one considers an abyss. He said,—
"The law is positive. A judge is more and less than a man; he is less than a man, for he has no heart; he is more than a man, because he has the sword. In the year 414 of Rome, Manlius put his son to death for the crime of having won a victory without his order. Violated discipline demands an expiation. In this case it is the law which has been violated; and the law is still higher than discipline. In consequence of an outburst of pity, the country is again placed in danger. Pity may have the proportions of a crime. Commander Gauvain has caused the escape of the rebel Lantenac. Gauvain is guilty. I vote death."
"Write it down, clerk," said Cimourdain.
The clerk wrote, "Captain Guéchamp: death."
Gauvain raised his voice,—
"Guéchamp," he said, you have voted well, and I thank you."
Cimourdain proceeded,—
"The second judge has the floor. Speak, Sergeant Radoub."
"Radoub rose, turned towards Gauvain and saluted the accused. Then he cried out,—

"If it is so, then, guillotine me, for I give you here, in the sight of God, my most sacred word of honor that I should like to have done, first what the old man did, and then what my commander has done. When I saw that man, eighty years old, throw himself into the fire to save three babies, I said, "Good man, you are brave!" and when I learn that my commander had saved this old man from your beast of a guillotine, by a thousand saints I say, "My commander, you ought to be my general, and you are a true man, and as for me, by thunder! I would give you the cross of Saint Louis, if there were still crosses, and if there were still saints, and if there were still Louis!"

"Ah! are you going to be idiots now? If it was for such things as this that we won the battle of Jemmapes, the battle of Valmy, the battle of Fleurus, and the battle of Wattignies, then it must be admitted. What! Here Commander Gauvain, for four months, has been leading these jackasses of royalists to the beat of the drum, and saving the Republic by his sword, and did a thing at Dol which required a pretty amount of cleverness, and when you have this man here, you try to have him no longer! And instead of making him your general, you want to chop off his head! I say that it is enough to make one throw himself head first over the parapet of the Pont-Neuf, and that if you yourself, Citizen Gauvain, my commander, were my corporal instead of my general, I would tell you that what you said just now was infernal nonsense. The old man did well in saving the children, you did well to save the old man; and if people are to be guillotined for good deeds, then get you gone to all the devils, for I don't know at all what it is about. There is no reason at all for stopping anywhere. All this is not true, is it? I pinch myself to know whether I am awake. I do not understand. So the old man ought to have let the babies burn alive, my commander ought to let the old man's head be cut off. Yes, and then guillotine me. I like the one idea as much as the other. I suppose if the little ones had died, the battalion of Bonnet-Rouge would have been dishonored. Is that what was wanted? Then let us eat each other. I know my politics as well as you. I belonged to the club in the section of the Piques. Sapristi! We are growing brutal at last! I sum it all up according to my way of looking at it. I do not like things which have the inconvenience of making us unable to tell at all where we are. Why the devil do we have each other killed? Why kill our chief? Not that, Lisette. I want my chief! I must have my chief. I love him better to-day than I did yesterday. But to send him to the guillotine, why, you make me laugh! We want none of this: I have listened. You may say whatever you like, but it is not possible."

And Radoub sat down. His wound had opened again. A thread of blood came out from under the bandage and ran down his neck, from the place where his ear had been.

Cimourdain turned towards Radoub,—

"Do you vote that the accused be absolved?"

"I vote," said Radoub, "to have him made general."

"I ask if you vote to have him acquitted."

"I vote to have him made the first in the Republic."

"Sergeant Radoub, do you vote to have the Commandant Gauvain acquitted,—yes or no?"

"I vote to have my head cut off instead of his."

"Acquittal," said Cimourdain. "Write, clerk."

The clerk wrote, "Sergeant Radoub: acquittal."

Then the clerk said,—

"One voice for death. One voice for acquittal."

It was Cimourdain's turn to vote.

He rose. He took off his hat and laid it on the table.

He was no longer pale nor livid. His face was the color of earth.

If all present had been lying in their shrouds, the silence would not have been more profound.

Cimourdain said in a solemn voice, slowly, and with decision,—

"Accused Gauvain, the cause has been heard. In the name of the Republic, the court-martial, by the majority of two to one—"

He stopped, there was a moment of suspense; did he hesitate before death? did he hesitate before life? All held their breath. Cimourdain continued,—

"Condemn you to death."

His face expressed the torture of an awful triumph.

When Jacob compelled the angel whom he had overthrown in the darkness to bless him, he must have worn that terrible smile.

It was only a glimmer, and it passed away. Cimourdain became again like marble, sat down, put his hat on his head, and added,—

"Gauvain, you will be executed to-morrow, at sunrise."

Gauvain rose, saluted him, and said,—

"I thank the court."

"Lead away the condemned," said Cimourdain.

Cimourdain made a sign, the door of the dungeon was opened, Gauvain went in, the dungeon was closed. The two gendarmes remained on guard at each side of the door, with drawn sabres.

They carried away Radoub, who had just fallen unconscious.

CHAPTER IV.

AFTER CIMOURDAIN AS A JUDGE, CIMOURDAIN AS MASTER.

A camp is a wasp's nest. Especially in times of Revolution. The civic sting which is in the soldier acts readily and quickly, and does not hesitate to attack the chief after having driven away the enemy.

The valiant troop which had taken la Tourgue made various complaints; at first against the Commander Gauvain, when they learned of Lantenac's escape. When they saw Gauvain come out of the dungeon which they supposed held Lantenac, it was like an electric shock, and in less than a minute the whole corps was informed. A murmur burst forth from the little army; the first murmur was,—

"They are judging Gauvain. But it is only a sham. Oh, yes, have great faith in ex-nobles and in priests! We have just seen a viscount save a marquis, and we shall see a priest pardon a noble!"

When they learned of Gauvain's sentence, there was a second murmur, "That is too much! our chief, our brave chief, our young commander, a hero! He is a viscount, well it is all the more credit to him for being Republican! What! he, the liberator of Pontorson, of Villedieu, of Pont-àu-Beau! The conqueror of Dol and of La Tourgue! He through whom we are invincible; he who is the sword of the Republic in la Vendée! The man who, for five months, has held the Chouans at bay, and made up for all the folly of Léchelle and the rest! This Cimourdain dares condemn him to death! Why? Because he saved an old man who had saved three children! A priest kill a soldier!"

Thus the victorious but discontented camp grumbled. A sullen anger surrounded Cimourdain. Four thousand men against one: it seems as if this must be strength; not at all. These four thousand men were a multitude, and Cimourdain was a will.

They knew that Cimourdain frowned easily, and nothing more was needed to hold the army in respect. In these times of severity, it was enough for the shadow of the Committee of Public Welfare to be behind a man to make this man feared, and to make an imprecation end in a whisper, and the whisper end in silence. After as well as before these murmurs, Cimourdain remained the arbiter of Gauvain's fate, and the fate of all. They knew there was nothing to ask of him, and that he would obey nothing but his conscience, a superhuman voice heard by himself alone.

Everything depended on him; what he had done as judge-martial, alone, he could undo as civil delegate. He alone was able to pardon him. He had full power; by a sign he could set Gauvain free; he was the master of life and of death; he was commander of the guillotine. At this tragic time, he was the man above all others.

They could only wait.

Night came on.

CHAPTER V.

THE DUNGEON.

The hall of justice had become the guardroom again; the watch was doubled, as the day before; two sentinels guarded the door of the closed dungeon.

About midnight a man holding a lantern in his hand, crossed the guardroom, made himself known, and had the dungeon opened. It was Cimourdain.

He went in and the door remained ajar behind him.

The dungeon was dark and silent. Cimourdain took a step into the darkness, set the lantern on the floor, and stood still. He heard the regular breathing of a man asleep. Cimourdain listened thoughtfully to this peaceful sound.

Gauvain was on the bundle of straw on the floor of the dungeon. It was his breath which was heard. He was sound asleep.

Cimourdain went forward with the least possible noise, came close to Gauvain and began to look at him; a mother looking at her sleeping babe would have no more tender and unspeakable fondness in her face. This sight was perhaps too much for Cimourdain; Cimourdain pressed both hands over his eyes, as children do some times, and remained motionless for a moment. Then he knelt down and raised Gauvain's hand gently to his lips.

Gauvain stirred. He opened his eyes, with the vague surprise of one suddenly awakened. The lantern feebly lighted the dungeon. He recognized Cimourdain.

"Ah!" he said, "it is you, my master."

And he added,—

"I was dreaming that death kissed my hand."

Cimourdain shuddered, as we sometimes do at the abrupt invasion of a surge of thoughts; sometimes this tide is so high and so stormy that it seems as if it would drown the soul. Nothing escaped from the depths of Cimourdain's heart. He could only say —

"Gauvain!"

And they looked at each other; Cimourdain with his eyes full of those flames which burn tears, Gauvain with his gentlest smile.

Gauvain rose on his elbow, and said—

"This scar which I see on your face is from the sabre cut that you received for me. Yesterday, again; you were in the struggle beside me and on account of me. If Providence had not placed you near my cradle, where should I be to-day? In darkness. If I have any idea of duty, it has come from you. I was born bound. Prejudices are ligatures; you removed these bands from me, you have given me liberty of growth, and of what was only a mummy you made a child once more. You gave a consciousness to the abortion that would otherwise have been. Had it not been for you, I should have grown up a dwarf. I exist through you. I was only a seigneur, you made me a citizen. I was only a citizen, you made me an intellect; you made me fit, as a man, for this earthly life, and, as a soul, for the life celestial. You gave me the key of truth, that I might enter the reality of human life, and the key of light, that I might go beyond. Oh! my master, I thank you. You have created me."

Cimourdain sat down on the straw beside Gauvain, and said to him,—

"I have come to take supper with you."

Gauvain broke up the black bread and offered it to him. Cimourdain took a piece of it; then Gauvain passed him the jug of water.

"Drink first," said Cimourdain.

Gauvain drank and passed the jug to Cimourdain, who drank after him. Gauvain only took one swallow.

Cimourdain took a long draught.

At this supper, Gauvain ate and Cimourdain drank, a sign of calmness in one and of feverishness in the other.

A strange, terrible serenity was in this dungeon. The two men talked.

Gauvain said,—

"Great things are being planned. What the Revolution is doing at this moment is mysterious. Behind its visible work there is a work invisible. One conceals the other. The visible work is cruel, the invisible work is sublime. At this moment I can see everything very clearly. It is strangely beautiful. It was necessary to make use of the materials of the past. Hence this extraordinary '93. Under a scaffolding of barbarism, a temple of civilization is building."

"Yes," replied Cimourdain. "Out of things temporal will arise the definitive. The definitive, that is to say right and duty, in parallel lines, proportional and progressive taxes, obligatory military service, levelling without deviation, and above all and through all, that straight line, law. The Republic of the Absolute."

"I prefer," said Gauvain, "the Republic of the Ideal." He hesitated, then continued,—

"Oh, my master, in all that you have just said, where do you place devotion, sacrifice, abnegation, the magnanimous intertwining of benevolence, love? Putting everything in equilibrium is good; making everything harmonious is better. Above the scales is the lyre. Your republic doses, measures, and rules man; mine carries him up into the clear sky; that is the difference between a theorem and an eagle."

"You will be lost in the clouds."

"And you in mathematics."

"Harmony is a dream."

"There are unknown quantities in Algebra."

"I would have man made according to Euclid."

"And I," said Gauvain, "I would rather have him made according to Homer."

Cimourdain's stern smile rested on Gauvain, as if to hold back his soul.

"Poetry. Place no trust in poets."

"Yes, I know that saying. Put no trust in breezes, sunbeams, put no trust in perfumes, put no trust in flowers, put no trust in constellations."

"None of them will give you anything to eat."

"How do you know. Ideas too, are food. To think is to eat."

"No abstractions. The Republic is two and two make four. When I have given to each what belongs to him——"

"It will remain for you to give to each what does not belong to him."

"What do you mean by that?"

"I mean the vast reciprocal concession that each owes to all, and all owe to each, and which is the whole social law."

"There is nothing beyond strict law."

"There is everything."

"I see nothing but justice."

"For my part, I see higher."

"What is there above justice?"

"Equity."

Occasionally, they stopped, as if to catch glimpses of light.

Cimourdain resumed,—

"I challenge you to explain."

"I will do so. You would have military service obligatory; against whom? Against other men. But I would not have any military service at all. I want peace. You would have the wretched assisted, but I would have misery suppressed. You would have proportional taxes. I would have no taxes at all. I want the common expenses reduced to their simplest form, and paid by the overplus of society."

"What do you mean by that?"

"This: first, to suppress every form of parasite; that represented by the priest, that represented by the judge, that represented by the soldier. Then make some use of your waste riches; you throw manure into the sewers, throw it on the fields. Three-quarters of the soil is waste land; clear up France. Put an end to useless pastures, divide the communal lands. Let every man have a piece of ground, and every piece of ground have a man. It would multiply the products of society a hundredfold. France, at the present time, only gives her peasants meat four days in the year; if well cultivated, she ought to feed three hundred millions of men,—all Europe. Utilize nature, that great auxiliary so much scorned. Make all the winds, all the waterfalls, all the magnetic effluvia work for you. The globe has a network of subterranean veins; in this network there is a prodigious circulation of water, oil, and fire; pierce the veins of the globe, and let this water gush forth for your fountains, this oil for your lamps, this fire for your hearths. Reflect on the motion of the waves, the flux and reflux, the ebb and flow of the tides. What is the ocean? An enormous force wasted. How stupid the earth is not to make use of the ocean."

"You are lost in a dream."

"That is to say, in actual facts."

Gauvain went on,—

"And woman—what use do you make of her?"

Cimourdain replied,—

"Let her be what she is, the servant of man."

"Yes. On one condition."

"What?"

"That man shall be the servant of woman."

"Is that your belief?" exclaimed Cimourdain. "Man a servant! Never. Man is master. I admit but one royalty, that of the fireside. Man is king at home."

"Yes. On one condition."

"What is that?"

"That woman be queen there."

"That is to say that you want for man and for woman——"

"Equality."

"Equality! Are you dreaming? The two beings are different."

"I said equality. I did not say identity."

There was a pause again, like a sort of truce between these two minds exchanging flashes of thought. Cimourdain broke the silence.

"And the child? To whom would you give it?"

"First to the father who begets it, then to the mother who bears it, then to the master to teach it, then to the city to make a man of it, then to the country, which is the mother supreme, then to humanity, which is the great ancestor."

"You say nothing of God."

"Each of these steps,—father, mother, master, city, country, humanity,—is a round in the ladder which leads up to God."

Cimourdain was silent. Gauvain went on,—

"When one is at the top of the ladder, one has reached God. God opens the door; there is nothing to do but to go in."

Cimourdain made the gesture of a person who is calling some one back.

"Gauvain, come back to earth. We want to realize possibilities."

"Begin by not making them impossible."

"The possible can always be realized."

"Not always. If Utopia is maltreated it is killed. Nothing is more defenceless than the egg."

"But it is necessary to seize Utopia, place it under the yoke of reality, and frame it, in fact. Abstract ideas must be transformed to concrete ideas; what it loses in beauty it will gain in utility; it will be less but better. Right must enter into law; and when right has become law, it is absolute. This is what I call the possible."

"The possible is more than that."

"Ah! you are dreaming again."

"The possible is a mysterious bird always hovering above man."

"It must be caught."

"Alive."

Gauvain continued,—

"My motto is: Always forward. If God had wished man to go backward, he would have put an eye in the back of his head. Let us always look towards the sunrise, development, birth. Whatever falls encourages whatever is trying to rise. The shattering of the old tree is a call to the young tree. Each century will do its work; to-day, civic; to-morrow, humane. To-day the question of right, to-morrow the question of wage. Wage and right are the same word in reality. Man does not live to receive no wage; God, in giving life, contracts a debt: right is innate wage; wage is acquired right."

Gauvain spoke with the assurance of a prophet. Cimourdain listened. The rôles were exchanged, and now it seemed as if the pupil had become the master.

Cimourdain murmured,—

"You go too fast."

"Perhaps it is because I am somewhat pressed for time," said Gauvain, with a smile.

And he added,—

"O my master, this is the difference between our two Utopias. You want the barracks obligatory, while I want a school. You dream of a man as a soldier, I dream of him as a citizen. You want him to be terrible, I would have him thoughtful. You would found a republic of swords, I would found——"

He hesitated,—

"I would found a republic of intellects."

Cimourdain looked at the pavement of the dungeon and said,—

"And till then what would you have?"

"What now exists."

"Then you absolve the present moment?"

"Yes."

"Why?"

"Because it is a tempest. A tempest always knows what it is about. For one oak struck by lightning, how many forests purified! Civilization had a pestilence, this great gale is sweeping it away. It does not discriminate enough, perhaps. Can it do otherwise? It has such a rough cleansing to perform. Before the horror of miasma, I understand the fury of the blast."

Gauvain continued,—

"Moreover, what is the tempest to me, if I have the compass? and what difference can events make to me, if I have my conscience?"

And he added in a low voice, which was solemn as well,—

"There is one who must always be allowed to do his will."

"Who?" asked Cimourdain.

Gauvain pointed above his head. Cimourdain followed the direction of his finger, and through the ceiling of the dungeon it seemed to him as if he saw the starry heavens.

They were again silent.

Cimourdain took up the discourse.

"Society greater than nature! I tell you it is not possible, it is a dream."

"It is its aim. Otherwise, what is the good of society? Remain in nature; be savages. Otaheite is a paradise. Only, in that paradise they do not think. Much better an intelligent hell than a stupid paradise. But no, let us have no hell. Let us have human society. Greater than nature. Yes. If you add nothing to nature, why leave nature? then, be content with work like the ant, and with honey like the bee. Remain the stupid workman rather than sovereign intelligence. If you add something to nature, you will necessarily be greater than she is. To add is to increase, and to increase is to enlarge. Society is nature made sublime. I would have everything which beehives lack, everything which ant-hills lack, monuments, arts, poetry, heroes, geniuses; to carry everlasting burdens is not the law of man. No, no, no; no more pariahs, no more slaves, no more convicts, no more condemned! I would have each attribute of man a symbol of civilization, and a pattern of progress; I want liberty in the mind, equality in the heart, fraternity in the soul. No! no more bondage! man was made, not to drag chains, but to spread his wings. No more of man as a reptile. I would have the larva transformed to a lepidopter; I would have the earthworm changed to a living flower, and fly away. I would have——"

He stopped. His eye grew bright. His lips moved, he ceased speaking. The door had been left open. Noises from outside penetrated into the dungeon. Sounds of distant trumpets were heard. It was probably the réveillé; then gun stocks striking the ground as the sentinels were relieved; then, quite near the tower, as far as could be judged in the darkness, a sound, as if they were moving boards and planks, with dull, intermittent thuds, like the blows of a hammer. Cimourdain listened, and grew pale. Gauvain did not hear it. His reverie grew more and more profound. It seemed as if he no longer breathed, he was so absorbed in what he saw in the visions that haunted his brain. His frame underwent gentle tremors. The dawn-like brightness in his eyes increased. Some time passed thus. Cimourdain asked,— "What are you thinking about?"

"The future," said Gauvain. And he relapsed into thought again. Cimourdain rose from the bed of straw where they were sitting together. Gauvain did not notice him. Cimourdain, with his eyes fixed with infinite affection on the young dreamer, stepped slowly backwards to the door, and went out. The dungeon was closed.

CHAPTER VI.

NEVERTHELESS, THE SUN RISES.

Daylight did not delay appearing on the horizon. Just as day dawned, a strange, motionless, amazing object, which the birds of heaven were not familiar with, came into sight on the plateau of la Torgue, above the forest of Fougères.

It had been placed there in the night; it was set up, rather than built. From a distance, its straightened lines stood out against the horizon, having the appearance of a Hebrew letter or one of those Egyptian hieroglyphics which formed a part of the alphabet of the ancient enigma.

At first sight, the idea that this object awakened was the idea of uselessness. It stood there among the blossoming heather. One asked what purpose it could serve. Then one felt a shudder come over.

It was a sort of trestle-work, with four posts for legs. At the end of the trestle rose two high joists, upright and straight, joined together at the top by a crossbeam, from which was suspended a triangle which looked black against the blue morning sky. At the other end of the Framework there was a ladder. Between the two joists below, under the triangle, could be seen a sort of panel composed of two movable sections which, when fitted together, showed a round hole about the size of a man's neck. The upper section of the panel slipped into a groove in such a way that it could be raised or lowered. For the time being, the two semicircles which, when united, formed the collar, were apart. At the foot of the two posts was seen a plank, which moved on hinges and looked like a balance. Beside this plank, there was a long basket, and between the two posts, in front, and at the end of the trestle, a square basket.

It was painted red.

Everything was of wood, except the triangle, which was of iron. One felt that this had been built by men, it was so ugly, mean, petty; and that it was worthy of being set up there by genii, it was so formidable.

This misshapen structure was the guillotine.

In front, a few feet away, in the ravine, there was another monster, la Tourgue. A monster of stone offering a counterpart to the monster of wood, and, we may add, when man has touched wood and stone, the wood and stone are no longer merely wood and stone, but become a part of man.

An edifice is a dogma, a machine is an idea.

La Tourgue was that fatal result of the past which is called the Bastille in Paris, the Tower of London in England, the Spielberg in Germany, the Escurial in Spain, the Kremlin in Moscow, the castle of Saint-Angelo in Rome.

Fifteen hundred years were condensed in la Tourgue, the Middle Ages, vassalage, serfdom, feudalism; in the guillotine, one year, '93; and these twelve months counterbalanced these fifteen centuries.

La Tourgue was the monarchy; the guillotine was the Revolution.

Tragic comparison.

On one side, debt; on the other, maturity. On one side, the inextricable Gothic complication, the serf, the seigneur, the slave, the master, the commonalty, the nobility, the complex code with its ramification of customs, judge and priest in coalition, innumerable bonds, the treasury, the salt taxes, the mortmain, the capitations, the exceptions, the prerogatives, the prejudices, the fanaticisms, the royal privilege of bankruptcy, the sceptre, the throne, the regal will, divine right; on the other side, this simple thing,—a chopping-knife.

On one side, a knot; on the other, an axe.

La Tourgue had long stood alone in this wilderness. It stood there filled with enormous tragedy; with his machicolations, out of which had been poured boiling oil, burning pitch, and melted lead; with its oubliettes, paved with bones; with its quartering room; its funereal form had dominated this forest; it had had fifteen centuries of cruel repose in this shady spot; it had been the sole power, the sole object of awe, and the sole terror in this land; it had reigned; it had been the unique example of barbarism: suddenly, there arose before it and against it something,—more than something,—some one as horrible as itself—the Guillotine.

Stone sometimes seem to have strange eyes. A statue observes, a tower watches, the façade of a building contemplates.

La Tourgue seemed to examine the guillotine.

It seemed to query it?

"What is that?"

That object seemed to have come up out of the earth.

And, in reality, it had come up out of the earth.

In the fatal earth had germinated the ill-favored tree. Out of this earth, watered with so much sweat, with so many tears, with so much blood;—out of this earth, where so many trenches had been dug, so many tombs, so many caves, so many ambushes;—out of this earth, where had rotted all kinds of dead, deprived of life by all kinds of tyranny;—out of this earth, placed over so many abysses, and where had been buried so many dreadful crimes, seeds of horror;—out of this deep earth had arisen, on a notable day, this strange avenger, this cruel swordbearer, and '93 had said to the old world: "Here I am!"

And the guillotine had the right to say to the keep: "I am thy daughter."

And at the same time the keep—for these fatal objects live with a mysterious vitality—felt that it was killed by her. La Tourgue, in the face of this terrible apparition, felt strangely frightened. It seemed as if it were afraid. The huge mass of granite was majestical and infamous; this plank, with its triangle, was worse. The declining omnipotence felt all the horror of the new omnipotence.

Criminal history surveyed justiciary history. The violence of the past was compared with the violence of the present: the ancient fortress, the ancient prison, the ancient seigneurie, where victims had shrieked as they were torn limb from limb; the building of war and of murder, now useless, disabled, profaned, dismantled, laid bare, a heap of stone, worth no more than a heap of ashes, hideous, magnificent, and dead, full of the dizziness of centuries of horror,—watched the terrible living hour of the present pass by.

Yesterday frowned on to-day, the old cruelty verified and submitted to the new power, that which was a mere nothingness opened its ghastly eyes before this terror, and the phantom regarded the spectre.

Nature is pitiless; she will not consent to withdraw her flowers, her music, her perfumes and her sunbeams from before the face of human abomination; she overwhelms man with the contrast between divine beauty and the ugliness of society; she spares him neither the wing of a butterfly, nor the song of a bird; in the midst of murder, in the midst of vengeance, in the midst of barbarity he must submit to the sight of holy things; he cannot get away from the vast reproach of the universal sweetness and the implacable serenity of the blue sky. The deformity of human laws must be exposed in their nakedness, in the midst of the dazzling beauty of the eternal. Man breaks and crushes, man destroys, man kills; the summer is summer still, the lily is the lily still, the stars of heaven are the stars of heaven still.

Never had the fresh sky of early dawn been more charming than on this morning. A mild breeze stirred the heather, the mists hovered gently over the trees, the forest of Fougères, permeated with the breath of the brooks, was steaming in the dawn like a great censer filled with incense; the blue firmament, the whiteness of the clouds, the clear transparency of the waters, the verdure, that harmonious scale of color from aquamarine to emerald, the groups of brotherly trees, the carpet of grass, the far-stretching plains,—all possessed that purity which is the eternal counsel of nature to man.

In the midst of all this was exposed the frightful shame of human beings; in the midst of all this appeared the fortress and the scaffold, war and punishment, the two figures of the bloodthirsty eld and the bloody present; the night-owl of the past, and the bat of the twilight of the future.

In the presence of creation, blooming, balmy, loving and lovely, the splendid heavens deluged La Tourgue and the guillotine with the light of morning, and seemed to say to man: "See my work, and behold what you are doing."

Such are the terrible uses that the sun makes of his rays.

This spectacle had spectators.

The four thousand men belonging to the little reconnoitring army were ranged in order of battle on the plain. They surrounded the guillotine on three sides, in such a way as to form around it, in a geometrical figure, the shape of a letter E; the battery placed in the centre of the upright line made the notch of the E. The red machine was enclosed in these three battle fronts, a sort of wall of soldiers, reaching on two sides to the very edge of the escarpment of the plateau, the fourth side, the open side, was the ravine itself, and faced la Tourgue.

This made a long square, in the midst of which was the scaffold. As the day approached, the shadow of the guillotine decreased on the grass.

The artillery-men were at their guns, the matches lighted.

A gentle blue smoke was rising from the ravine; it came from the dying fire of the burning bridge.

This smoke covered without concealing la Tourgue, the high platform of which dominated the whole horizon. Between this platform and the guillotine there was only the ravine. They could talk across it.

The table of the tribunal and the chair draped with tricolored flags had been brought to this platform. The day was drawing behind la Tourgue, and making the mass of the fortress stand out black, and above it in the chair of the tribunal, and under the drapery of flags, the form of a man sitting motionless, with folded arms.

This man was Cimourdain. As on the day before, he wore his civil delegate's dress, the hat with tricolored cockade on his head, his sabre by his side, and his pistols in his belt.

He was silent. All were silent. The soldiers stood with their guns grounded, their eyes downcast. Their elbows touched, but they did not speak. They were thinking confusedly about this war,—so many battles, the fusillades of the hedges so bravely faced, the swarms of furious peasants driven before their breath, the citadels taken, the battles won, the victories, and it seemed to them now that all this glory turned to shame. A gloomy expectation oppressed the hearts of all.

On the platform of the guillotine they saw the executioner, walking back and forth. The increasing brightness of the morning majestically filled the sky.

Suddenly there was heard that muffled sound made by drums covered with crape. The funereal rumbling came nearer; the ranks opened, and a procession entered the square, and went towards the scaffold.

At first the black drums; then a company of grenadiers, with arms lowered; then a platoon of gendarmes, with drawn swords; then the condemned,— Gauvain.

Gauvain walked free. Neither his feet nor his hands were bound. He was in undress uniform; he carried his sword.

Behind him came another platoon of gendarmes.

Gauvain still wore that expression of thoughtful joy on his face which had lighted it up when he said to Cimourdain, "I am thinking of the future." Nothing could be more ineffably sublime than this lasting smile.

On reaching the melancholy spot, he first looked towards the top of the tower. He disdained the guillotine.

He knew that Cimourdain would consider it his duty to be present at the execution. His eyes sought him on the platform. He found him there.

Cimourdain was pale and cold. Those near him could not hear him breathe.

When he saw Gauvain, he did not stir.

Meanwhile, Gauvain was approaching the scaffold.

As he walked along, he looked at Cimourdain, and Cimourdain looked at him. It seemed as if Cimourdain strengthened himself with that look.

Gauvain reached the foot of the scaffold. He mounted it. The officer commanding the grenadiers followed him. He unfastnened his sword and gave it to the officer, he took off his cravat and gave it to the executioner.

He was like a vision. Never had he looked so beautiful. His brown hair floated in the wind; it was not the custom to cut off the hair at that time. His white neck was like a woman's, his heroic, sovereign eye was like an archangel's. He was on the scaffold, deep in thought. This place, too, is a summit. Gauvain stood there, superbly calm. The sun wrapped him about as with a halo of glory.

It was necessary, nevertheless, to bind the criminal. The executioner came with a rope in his hand.

At this moment, when the soldiers saw their young captain so evidently destined to the knife, they could contain themselves no longer; the hearts of these warriors burst. That enormous thing, the sob of an army, was heard. A shout arose,—

"Mercy! mercy!"

Some fell on their knees; others threw down their guns and raised their arms towards the platform where Cimourdain was.

A grenadier mounted the steps to the guillotine, crying, "Will you receive a substitute? Take me." All repeated frantically, "Mercy! mercy!" and if this had been heard by lions, they would have been moved or frightened, for soldiers' tears are terrible.

The executioner stopped, not knowing what to do.

Then a short, low voice, which could be heard by all, it was so gruesome, cried from the top of the tower,—

"Enforce the law!"

They recognized that inexorable tone. Cimourdain had spoken. A shudder passed over the army.

The executioner hesitated no longer. He approached, holding his cord.

"Wait," said Gauvain.

He turned towards Cimourdain, with his right hand, which was still free, waved a farewell to him, and then let it be bound.

After it was bound, he said to the executioner,—

"Pardon. One moment more."

And he cried,—

"Long live the Republic!"

They laid him on the plank. That lovely proud head was placed in the infamous collar. The executioner laid back his hair gently, he pressed the spring, the triangle became detached and slipped down slowly at first, then quickly; a hideous sound was heard—

At the same instant another sound was heard. A pistol shot responded to the blow of the axe. Cimourdain had just seized one of the pistols which he had in his belt, and, as Gauvain's head rolled into the basket, Cimourdain sent a bullet through his heart. The blood poured from his mouth; he fell down dead.

And these two souls, tragic sisters, departed together, the darkness of one mingling with the light of the other.

THE END